Entwined Publishing books by Maren Jenner

Sweet Nothings
The Cupcake Standard
The Jellybean Dilemma
The Red-Hot Stakes

Wrighting the Wrongs
The Wrong Brother
The Wrong Idea

I0564014

Wrighting the Wrongs

THE WRONG IDEA

MAREN JENNER

ENTWINED PUBLISHING

The Wrong Idea
ISBN # 978-1-80250-725-6
©Copyright Maren Jenner 2025
Cover Art by Kelly Martin ©Copyright April 2025
Interior text design by Entwined Publishing
Published by Entice, an Entwined Publishing imprint

Published in 2025 by Entwined Publishing, United Kingdom.

Entwined Publishing is a division of Totally Entwined Group Limited.

THE WRONG IDEA

Dedication

This book goes out to all those who don't feel seen, even by those you love. May you find someone to embrace every part of you and find the courage to stand up to those who hurt you. I see you. You are worth it.

Acknowledgements

First of all, I'd like to thank Entwined Publishing for helping this story reach its full potential and allowing me to continue my dream of becoming a published author. I'd also like to thank Rebecca for her editing help. I couldn't have done this without my beta readers, specifically Lindsay, and my friend Damian who is always there to cheer me on. But the biggest thank-you goes to my CP Christine who is always available to hear my ideas or read another revision. To all my friends and family who supported me on this journey, who believed in me, who never let me give up — thank you and I love you. Lastly, a big thanks to you, my readers, because this wouldn't be possible without you. A full list of trigger warnings for this and all my books is available on my website at marenjennerbooks.com.

Chapter One

Sebastian

Months of research have culminated in this moment. I position the blank paper on the desk in front of me, aligning my pencil parallel to the sleek edge of the sheet. Fixing my eyes on the empty page, I focus on the problem in my mind.

Excitement fills me as my brain begins piecing the information together. The equation forms in halting bits, and I let my hand hover over the pencil, ready to snatch it up the moment the formula coalesces. A few more seconds and —

A knock sounds on my office door...my *open* office door. I swear I closed it. My frustration turns to full-blown annoyance when I see Professor Harrison's daughter, Calliope, in my doorway. I'm his TA, and my path crosses hers much more often than I'd like, especially when I'm working here on campus in the botany department.

"Yes?" I growl with more heat than usual as the remnants of my equation slip away. *She couldn't have waited one more minute?*

But no, Calliope will not be ignored. It goes beyond her electric purple hair, her brilliant blue eyes, and the shiny stud in her left nostril. She garners attention wherever she goes, with her magnetic smile and infectious laugh. People are drawn to her as if she is the tempting light on a murky night and they are all moths.

Being pulled in, even when they don't want to be.

"Well?"

Still she hesitates, rubbing her index finger over her thumbnail as a flash of uncertainty crosses her face. Then I blink and her usual confidence is restored. She saunters in, one hand behind her back as she shoots me an impish smirk.

"Here."

When she tosses a package on my desk, my blank page floats to one side in the sudden draft of air, and I grit my teeth. Then my pencil rolls off my desk, landing in the trash can with a plunk. All I can think about is the immaculate graphite tip I'd just perfected snapping off.

She's only been here two seconds and already my office is in chaos. I draw in a deep breath through my nose. "What is this?" I try to sound civil, looking at the rectangle wrapped in shiny blue paper complete with a silver bow on top.

It's obviously a gift of some sort, though why Calliope would ever give me a present is beyond my reasoning. We aren't anywhere close to being friends — we hardly tolerate one another.

"Dad said I should get you something. You know, for saving my life." A bitter edge lines her tone, and her lips pucker slightly, as if the words leave a sour taste in her mouth.

Images assault me, flashes from that night. I'd only gone to the party to support my best friend, Leah, but I'd stayed because Calliope was there. She may be in college, but she's only nineteen and shouldn't have been at a party like that in the first place. As her father's TA, I felt responsible, like I needed to look out for her.

Chaos broke out after Calliope strutted into the kitchen, shirtless and slurring her words. Her date confessed to giving her Rohypnol, and I'd called nine-one-one as she passed out. It was terrifying. She'd looked so pale and fragile lying on the tile.

I followed the ambulance to the hospital, not wanting her to wake alone. The handful of times I've been rushed to the ER due to my hypoglycemia still haunt me, and I only made it through it because of my family. Professor Harrison met me there moments before the doctor came out to tell us Calliope was stable and waking up.

Her father had me come back with him, so she could thank me personally. But when she opened those brilliant eyes, even bluer against her paper-white skin, she saw her dad first, and hatred blazed to life when her gaze landed on me.

"You called my dad?"

I cut off the acidic memory, rubbing my temple as I try to shut out the accusing words that echo in my mind.

"It's chocolate."

I blink, looking up again. I'd forgotten she was still here.

She nods to the package and repeats, "It's chocolate. I mean, everyone likes chocolate, right?"

The sharp smell of astringent lingers in my nostrils from the memory, and the very idea of throwing my blood sugar out of balance has my stomach rolling. I nudge the box to the edge of my desk. "Um, thank you." That is what one should say after being given a gift, no matter how impersonal it is.

She doesn't move, as if waiting for more, but I don't have time to babysit. If I concentrate hard enough, I might still be able to salvage that equation. I lean over to find my pencil.

"You're not even going to open it?" Anger flashes in her eyes, and her hands curl into fists.

I'm surprised she doesn't stomp her foot in her typical spoiled-brat behavior. "No." I retrieve the pencil, biting back an exasperated sigh as I sit upright. The tip had snapped off, leaving a jagged edge behind. I open the drawer to take out my sharpener. Again. "You've already told me what it is, and I've thanked you. Now, I have work to do."

A frustrated noise erupts from her, a cross between a snort and a growl. "You're such a jackass, you know that? I come here to thank you, and you ignore the present, then dismiss me like I'm wasting your time."

I stare back, unnerved by her tantrum. "If we're discussing bad decorum, I could point out that you interrupted my train of thought, disrupted my workspace and are now scolding me because *I'm* the one being rude." I push back from my desk and walk to the door.

She merely gapes, her pert little mouth hanging open like a fish.

"As far as displays of gratitude go, your track record is less than stellar, if we're counting how you yelled at me after saving your life." I pause, pushing my glasses up my nose. "How about we both agree to stop wasting time? You can find someone else to bestow your thanks upon, someone who might appreciate your particular manner of showing it."

She glares for a long moment, her face turning an odd shade of red that almost complements her hair. "You...!"

I wait, but when she says nothing more I glance at the open doorway, hoping she will finally take the hint. I don't know how much more blatant I can be.

Her lips purse together. With a toss of her violet hair and murder in her eyes, she finally strides for the door. Pausing at the threshold, she raises her chin to stare at me. I study her, anticipating a snarky comment as the final blow as she departs.

But evidently I'm not worth the effort because she squares her shoulders and marches down the hall without another word. I can't help watching her go, a little tornado of fury rushing away. Amusement twitches my lips until she disappears, then I close the door. Any hint of glee disappears when I repeat the process of trying to summon the equation.

Nothing happens. It doesn't help that every time I move, the ridiculously shiny package catches the light and draws my attention.

Maybe I *should* have opened it. Is she going to tell Professor Harrison I was rude? I try to push the thoughts aside, to concentrate on the formula I need, but a pair of glaring blue eyes swim in my mind when I close my eyelids.

Calliope really does ruin everything.

* * * *

The next morning, I wake with a start, bolting upright and wincing immediately at the ache in my erection from the sudden movement. *How inconvenient.* A quick glance at the clock shows I have twenty minutes before my alarm is scheduled to go off.

Most mornings I lie here, ciphering through one problem or another until the blood flows back to my brain — a much more useful place for it. And I can begin my day without the mess that sort of release brings.

Today is not one of those days.

This is no mere blood flow issue that a simple distraction will solve, and I resign myself to taking care of it. I make sure my box of tissues is positioned within reach, then spit on my palm. Shoving my boxers down, I grit my teeth as I position myself to finish this as quickly as possible.

I'm not physically attracted to many people, so my material for stimulation is limited. Several summers ago, I had an internship at my dad's office and entered into a casual relationship with the secretary. Elaine was older, petite, with an easy smile and a comforting air that made exploring with her a diverting and educational experience.

I settle on a memory of her astride me as I begin to stroke myself and close my eyes. If I try hard enough, I can remember the feel of her thighs gripping me and her heat as she rode me. I grow harder still.

"Sebastian," the feminine voice calls.

To my horror, it's not the secretary. A phantom Calliope bounces on me, her black lacy bra barely covering her taut nipples. I try to yank my hand away, cringing as she whispers my name again, and I force my eyes open.

But I'm already ejaculating.

Hot liquid spills over my fingers, jetting onto my stomach as my body betrays me. *Fuck.* The rare curse popping into my mind only frustrates me further. This is exactly the sort of complication I don't need.

* * * *

Callie
Three weeks later

I step outside into the glorious sunshine and suck in the fresh May air. Spring is in full swing as I walk across Southwestern Michigan University's campus, Smoo to us students, feeling freer than the songbirds singing in the trees. I'm in a celebratory mood since I'm officially done with my second year here. Plus, it was my twentieth birthday earlier this week, and my friends want to take me out tonight. They're even trying to bring some guy named Silas they've been raving about from their English class.

Now I just have to convince Dad to let me go.

His office is in the botany department, on the other side of campus from my last class. Professor Harrison to most, my dad is revered as the expert on all things plants. Parenting, on the other hand, he gets a little overzealous with. I know he loves me, but I wish he'd loosen the reins a bit.

With Dad as a tenured professor, I don't pay for tuition, a perk I can't ignore and one Dad lords over me every chance he gets. My studies must be my topmost priority and, since he's responsible for my free ride, he's decided he has full say in every aspect of my life. Where I live—at home, with him. Where I work—I can't. And how much I'm allowed to do.

This phase of my life is supposed to be about spreading my wings and finding out who I am. Instead, I'm stuck in the nest with my overbearing dad.

I step into the botany building, frowning as my eyes adjust to the dim light. I ease down the hallway, tiptoeing when I see that Sebastian's door is open. The last thing I want to do is talk to my dad's arrogant, know-it-all assistant, especially after our last encounter. A sour taste floods my mouth even thinking about it.

Hurrying past his office, I glimpse him hunched over his desk and breathe a sigh of relief when he doesn't notice me. Dad's office is also open, so I waltz in, greeting him with a smile. He holds up a finger, pointing to the phone cradled between his shoulder and ear. I wander around the small office as he finishes his conversation. I always love looking at the photos in here because they remind me of happier times.

Us in the greenhouse, him standing behind me with his hands cupped under mine as I help him transplant a rose. Our smiles are identical. Another has us with Mom before she died, standing in front of the newest greenhouse as my dad cut the ribbon at the opening ceremony. She looks so proud of him. Always his biggest fan.

A lump forms in my throat as I move away from Mom, grateful when I hear Dad hang up.

"Callie, done with school?" he asks, like I'm twelve.

But I nod. "Yep. Last day, check." I make a flourish with my hand, emphasizing my words.

"Wonderful, and what's next on the agenda?"

I rub the pad of my index finger over my thumbnail then catch myself. "Well, Jess and Lyssa are hoping to take me to dinner. We haven't been out yet for my birthday, and we can celebrate the end of another year, too. If you don't mind. They promised to have me back before curfew."

I don't know any other twenty-year-olds whose curfew is midnight, but fighting that rule is a losing battle, as I've learned. One I no longer have the strength for.

He laces his fingers over his stomach and leans back in his swivel chair. "I suppose you have been on decent behavior since the incident that landed you in the hospital."

I grit my teeth at his favorite bargaining chip of late, as if it were my fault some asshole roofied me. But I keep my tone sweet as I say, "And you know Jess and Lyssa. There might be a few other people coming, but I'm not sure yet. Lyssa mentioned inviting someone from her English class."

His index finger taps his other hand as he thinks. "If you let me know where you end up, and promise there won't be any drinking, you can go."

It takes a lot not to punch my fist in the air. Instead, I beam and nod. "I'll text you as soon as we know where we're going. And no drinking, I promise."

"Very well. Have fun."

"Thanks, Dad. I will!"

I rush away to find Jess, who is hovering outside a greenhouse with her nose pressed to the glass. She just graduated, was accepted into the Master's program and got handpicked by Professor Maia for TA. Most of my friends are in the botany department since this is where I hang out. Luckily, there are some pretty cool people here, and not all of them have a stick up their ass like Sebastian.

I poke Jess in the side, startling her enough that she yelps, then laughs when she sees me.

"Hey!" she says. Her dark skin contrasts with her usual brightly colored top, and I envy the confidence of her closely shaved head. Her signature golden hoops dangle from both ears, catching my eye as I lean in for a quick hug.

Then I turn to the greenhouse to see what's so fascinating. "What are we watching?"

"My bees," she squeals. For her thesis, she did a whole study on one hive, and she's obsessed with her babies, as she calls them. "They're pollinating away. Just look at them."

Lyssa, Jess' girlfriend, groans as she joins us. "Not the bees again." She'll graduate next year, but has been testing several different projects to determine which will be her thesis.

"Hey, you!" Jess gives Lyssa a huge hug and a kiss.

The two make an adorable couple. Jess is all put-together chic, while Lyssa embraces chaos. Her twin braids have pieces of her black hair escaping in wild bits and lumps. Her tawny skin has several darker places where dirt is smudged, one in particular on her right cheek.

Jess wets her thumb, then wipes at the spot, even as she grins. "It's official. I'm dating a senior. How's it feel to only have one year to go?"

Lyssa purses her lips and puffs her cheeks as she blows out a breath. "Scary."

I squeeze her shoulder. "You've got this."

Jess nods, then looks at me. "So, we going out?"

"Yep!"

All three of us squeal and jump around in true giddy fashion before Lyssa fumbles for her phone. "Okay, I'll text Silas."

An hour later, we're sprawled at Jess' apartment as we finish getting ready. After leaving campus, we stopped by my house to grab a few things, then came back here. I found a cute, tight miniskirt with a peasant blouse that shows off my shoulders. As I put the finishing touches on my makeup, I lean back to do a final once-over in the mirror.

It's only five, but I want to make the most of my freedom, so we're going out early. Silas offered to drive, even after he was informed of my curfew. He sounds like a great guy—easy going, laidback. Not every guy is okay with my dad's demands, and it gives me hope for a fun evening.

Anticipation flutters within me, bubbling into my grin. It's been a while since I've had anything to look forward to in the relationship department.

Lyssa's phone chimes, and she gives me a knowing smile. "He's here," she says in a singsong voice.

We hurry outside as excitement pulses through me. A man leans on the side of a sleek black SUV, and I know by his devastating smile that it must be Silas. He matches the girls' description perfectly. Tall—he has a good six inches on my five-foot-seven height. Curly, dark hair and amber eyes that twinkle above his perfect white smile. He is the definition of handsome.

I can't help smiling back, but there's not a hint of a pull or a stomach flip or any sparks as we introduce ourselves and shake hands. Disappointment ripples through me, and I brush it off. We can still have fun.

We eat at a local Mexican restaurant, and I text my dad when we arrive. The food is great. Conversation flows steadily with Silas involved. He's hilarious and chatty, but I'm obviously not his type either, since he keeps eyeing our curvy, dark-haired waitress. I don't mind. It takes some of the pressure off me, so I can relax and enjoy the celebration without trying to impress someone new.

Dancing is a passion of mine, and after dinner we go line dancing. A quick text to my dad to update him on my whereabouts, then I hurry to the middle of the dance floor.

I'm right at home, tearing up the floor for song after song with whoever will stay out with me. Silas has one drink, but switches to root beer afterward. I stick with water, wishing I could celebrate like Jess and Lyssa, who enjoy their whiskey sours with obvious abandon.

At ten, we take a break. Silas tells a story about a blind date that went hilariously wrong, and Lyssa howls with laughter. She darts forward, clutching her stomach with one hand and her full drink in the other.

It sloshes over the side, drenching my arm and I yelp. She immediately sobers, apologizing repeatedly. I dab the wet splotch with the napkins Silas hands me, but the damage is done. I push away from the table and hurry to the bathroom, annoyance swirling with a hint of panic. *If Dad smells alcohol on me...*

I don't think twice, yanking off my shirt and running the sleeve under the tap. Then I grab some paper towels and wipe my arm. I use the hand dryer to speed things along and it takes a while, but I think I smell better. The worry won't leave me, though. It hovers in the back of my mind, taking over my thoughts.

My friends have to keep pulling me back into the conversation or snapping their fingers to get my attention. Eventually, they give up and leave me be. We pay our bill and head out in time to get me home before curfew.

I try to relax in the front seat, letting the others chatter around me as I stare out of the window. We're ten minutes from home when the SUV stutters, then makes a funny noise. Silas steers us into a nearby strip mall parking lot, barely reaching the parking space before the car dies.

"What just happened?" I ask, panic rising in me.

"I...I don't know. It sounds like we ran out of gas, but the gauge shows we still have a quarter tank." He frowns then adds, "I'm sorry, Callie. Let me call one of my brothers. I'm sure someone can run us some gas."

I nod, drumming my fingers on the door. Any other person could calmly text their parent and explain. I mean, running out of gas isn't anything I could control, and we're not far from home. Dad could even come get me.

But I can hear the disappointment now. It isn't my fault, yet he'll blame me. For bringing him out of the house, for interrupting, for missing curfew. Nothing can ever go smoothly for me. Tears prick my eyes, but I blink them away, refusing to cry. It won't help anything.

Silas pokes his head back in. "All taken care of. My brother will be here in no time, so don't worry. We'll get you home."

The minutes pass, each one eating away at me as I continue rubbing my thumbnail. I keep flexing my fingers, pushing them apart, only to realize I'm rubbing again.

At last, headlights flash behind us, and I watch anxiously in the mirror as Silas gets out to greet his brother. The man appears, silhouetted by the lights — a lean, shapely form, taller than Silas by a couple of inches. The low pitch of his voice reaches me, and I'm intrigued. Especially when I see the outline of glasses as he turns his head.

My mouth goes dry. A taller, leaner, glasses-wearing version of Silas? That would be my own personal type of crack. Anticipation coils within me as he steps into the swath of streetlight.

Fuck.

When Sebastian's hazel eyes meet mine in the mirror, his jaw clenches. The remnants of desire still tumble within me, like a dryer turning off as reality crashes in. Sebastian hates me, thinks I'm a spoiled brat who exists only to get attention. And I hate him just as much, the arrogant know-it-all, so deep in my dad's pocket he has Dad's asshole memorized.

This night couldn't get any worse.

Chapter Two

Sebastian

The words swim on the page before me as the letters jumble together, and I squeeze my eyes closed. Pushing up my glasses, I press my thumbs into my eyelids while I brace myself against the wave of dizziness. I sit back, blinking as I sag against my wooden desk chair.

What time is it?

My smart watch doesn't wake when I move my wrist, a sure sign it's dead, and when I pull my phone from my pocket, it too greets me with a blank screen. The biggest flaw in today's technology is that it requires its owner to remember to charge it. *Drat.*

Luckily, my trusty old alarm clock is still plugged into the wall near my bed, so I crane my neck to see it's eleven p.m. I quickly do the math. My meeting with Professor Harrison ended at five, and I came straight home to delve into my notes. This is the first time I've looked up.

I roll my stiff shoulders as my stomach growls and another wave of dizziness hits me. But it's to be expected after almost six hours of research.

As I berate myself for my carelessness, I hurry to plug in my phone and watch, knowing that's what I should have done before I even cracked a book — then my alarms reminding me to eat would have gone off. Next, I take out my glucose test and prick my finger.

The results are predictably low, explaining my dizziness. Hypoglycemia and Type 1 diabetes go hand in hand, which I know all too well. My body can't regulate my insulin output, and if I don't eat regularly, my sugars drop low enough that I could even pass out. Hence the alarms.

Which only work if the technology is charged.

I pop a glucose tab into my mouth, then raid my emergency stash in the bottom desk drawer. Deciding what I want to eat, I give myself the appropriate amount of insulin before I drain an apple juice and scarf a granola bar. I wait a solid ten minutes to retest, relieved to find my numbers climbing. I'm at least able to make my way downstairs and get a solid meal, which I bring back to my desk.

My brain needs a break from botany, though all my research is paying off. My first batch of roses are coming along nicely, grafted and potted and healing well. It's hard for me to leave them each night.

I'm pleased with their progress, but one thing is still missing for my thesis. If only I could perfect my formula.

I'd love to switch to my other book on butterflies, my latest side research, but my eyes still feel tired. Animals fascinate me, and when my input for botany becomes too full, I switch gears to the animal kingdom where I'm constantly surprised by the fortitude and ingenuity of each species. My photographic memory makes it easy for me to retain the facts I learn, though my brothers tease that I'm a walking encyclopedia.

But I never lack for topics of conversation.

Once my food is gone and my water bottle mostly empty, I study my reflection in the dark window. The house is quieter than usual for a Friday night. I know today ended the semester at Southern Michigan University, so I assume everyone is out celebrating.

I live with my three brothers. The oldest, Steven, works at an IT job and graduated a couple of years ago. Shawn, the next oldest and directly above me, is probably out with his girlfriend — who also happens to be my best friend — because they both just graduated. For Leah, that's no surprise, but for Shawn? It's a big deal.

I couldn't be prouder of him. He and I are very close, despite our differences. He's two years older than my twenty-three years, but I graduated high school a year early. While he took a gap year before starting college, I stacked my classes and fast-tracked my way through my Bachelor's degree. Now I'm halfway through my Master's.

Hopefully, he and Leah are having a wonderful time. They are two of my favorite people, though my history with Leah is slightly more complicated. We dated for several months. I knew it would never go anywhere, that I was only a stepping stone for her to become comfortable with the dating world again. And I always thought she and Shawn were meant for each other.

It doesn't make it any easier for me to be alone again. It was nice having her as a constant in my life, but watching her and Shawn together — how they better each other, push each other, sharpen one another... I want that.

Leah loves me, and I love her, but she merely tolerates my idiosyncrasies. That's a normal occurrence for me. I'm aware I annoy people when I go on my tangents about my latest animal facts, so I try to rein it in. Sometimes, though, I can't help it, and I have to share with someone.

That and my diabetes are complicated enough, but it's all compounded by how seldom I'm attracted to others. I also prefer not to be touched until I'm very comfortable with a person. That doesn't make me the most eligible of bachelors.

I'm not at the top of anyone's list.

My phone rings, pulling me from my macabre thoughts, and I frown, wondering who would be calling this late. Everyone knows I'm generally in bed by now.

Seeing my youngest brother's name on the screen has worry gripping my gut. "Hello?"

"Hey, Sebastian," Silas says in his normal casual tone. "I didn't wake you, did I?"

"No, actually." I push my glasses higher on my nose, thankful things seem to be on the non-emergency end of the spectrum.

"Oh, good." He sounds relieved. "Listen, I know it's late, but you're the only one who doesn't have plans tonight and I've got three women in my car. One of them's got a curfew..."

I huff at his ramblings. "Silas, what happened?"

"I ran out of gas."

Somehow, I'm not shocked. The resigned breath I let out fills the line. "Where are you?"

"Thanks, Sebastian! You're the best!"

He quickly explains his location, and I calculate how long it will take me to gather the gas can then meet him. "I'll be there in fifteen minutes."

"Great." And we hang up.

Fourteen minutes later, I pull into the parking lot behind his SUV, positioning my Volvo so the headlights shine on the side with the tank. Silas pops out, rushing around to meet me. He thanks me profusely as I hand over the gas can.

The interior lights of his vehicle are still on, illuminating the passengers and my eyes catch on a familiar violet mane. I stare for a long second as a flare of annoyance burns through me. *It can't be Calliope, can it? But who else has hair that purple?*

I take an extra beat, staring at the side mirror and confirming her identity. Then I resign myself to the fact that the universe has cursed me with the continued crossing of our paths. "Silas..."

He glances over from where he's pouring the gas but doesn't say anything.

"I don't suppose Calliope Harrison is the one with a curfew."

His eyebrows jump up. "Hey! How'd you know?"

"Professor Harrison is a man who values punctuality." I check my partially charged watch, frowning. "You're never going to get her home on time."

Unfortunately, I am quite familiar with not only Calliope's curfew but her tendency to stay out past it. If Professor Harrison finds out my own brother is responsible, that won't look good for me. *Drat.*

Silas lifts a shoulder. "We ran out of gas. It happens."

I shake my head, already striding past him. "I'll take her home."

Her blue eyes meet mine in the side mirror, and by the time I approach, her lips are pressed together so tightly they've almost disappeared. I yank open the passenger door, the coolness in her gaze biting right through my light jacket.

"Come on," I order.

"You both know Sebastian, right?" Calliope says, not batting an eyelash at my annoyance or the limited time we have.

I glance into the back seat, unsurprised to see Jess and Lyssa from the botany department. I nod. "Ladies."

Lyssa gapes. "Wait, *you're* Silas' brother?"

I jut my jaw to one side, returning my attention to Calliope, who peers down her nose at me. In this position, she is nearly eye level, quite a feat for her small frame.

"Look, Calliope —"

"It's Callie," she corrects, acid dripping from every syllable.

"Calliope," I say, stepping closer so our noses are almost touching. I don't miss the way her breath hitches, and satisfaction courses through me. "You're wasting valuable time. If we leave now, you'll be a few minutes late at most, and I can explain to Professor Harrison what happened."

Her eyes narrow. "What do you care?"

"My brother was responsible for getting you home on time. He failed in his duty and —"

She cuts me off with a wry bark of laughter. "Save the chivalrous act, Sebastian. You just want to earn brownie points with my father."

I force myself to step back, allowing her to think whatever she wants.

"Fine." She says a quick goodbye to her friends, then hops down, glaring at me. "You can take me home."

As if she's letting me do her a favor. It takes all my self-control to keep from telling her exactly what I think of her spoiled-brat tendencies, and I mutter to myself as she saunters to my car, waiting for me to open her door.

I force myself not to slam it once she's in, then I hurry around, calling goodbye to Silas. It's only a ten-minute ride to her house, but we'll be cutting it close. Calliope's bare knee bounces, making her already short skirt ride higher on her thigh.

But I keep my eyes on the road. It's a warm night, so I reach over to adjust the temperature, getting a solid whiff of alcohol as I do, and I rear back in surprise. "You've been drinking?"

Her head snaps up, her eyes wide. "No, I haven't!" And it actually sounds like she's telling the truth. She smacks her hand on her thigh. "Fuck." She turns her head toward me. "Your brother had Lyssa laughing so hard, she spilled her drink on me. I tried to rinse it out in the sink..."

I risk a glance at her, the story plausible and her tone earnest. But I also know Calliope. Professor Harrison and I had to come home early from our last conference because of some trouble she got into. Not to mention the party that ended with her getting her stomach pumped. Though that wasn't her fault—the date rape drug was all Vance's doing, and her pale face flashes in my mind.

"I can feel you judging me," she mutters, crossing her arms and glaring.

"Can you blame me?"

She lets out a short, frustrated exhale. "I'm telling the truth, Sebastian. If it weren't for this shirt, you wouldn't smell any alcohol. I didn't touch the stuff tonight. I was good." She cranes her neck, looking into the back seat. "You don't happen to have a breathalyzer back there, do you?"

"No," I scoff. "Why would I have one of those?"

"I don't know. You seem like the type."

I frown, trying to understand her comment, only to be derailed by her assessing gaze. I shift when it doesn't leave me. "What?"

"Give me your shirt."

"*What?*"

She tugs on my jacket sleeve as I lean away from the unwanted touch, but she persists. "Come on. I'm sure you've got a shirt on under there. You can drive home in your jacket, and no one will be the wiser."

I shake her off. "Calliope —"

"Please, Sebastian." The passing street lamps illuminate her big, blue eyes as she begs. "You don't understand. I'm already going to be late. If Dad smells alcohol on me too…" She hangs her head, turning back to the window. "Never mind. Why would you care?"

The defeat in her voice triggers my instinct to help, and I hear my reply before I even register I'm speaking. "There's a shirt in the pocket behind your seat."

What am I doing? She's right. I don't care if she gets in trouble for her own carelessness. But then she beams, reaching around to grab the shirt, and I have to blink in the wake of her smile.

She faces front, not giving me any warning before she whips off her shirt. I force myself to keep my eyes on the road, not turning my head one inch. Except I can still see her in my peripheral vision. It takes her way too long to unfold my shirt, giving me ample opportunity to notice the curve of her perfect breasts in her nearly see-through lavender bra, lighter than her hair by several shades. As we pass under a streetlight, I notice two freckles dotting her ribcage right below the lacy fabric.

This isn't the first time I've seen her in her bra, and thanks to my photographic memory, I have a perfect recall of that other night. That party, before I'd realized she had been drugged, she'd sauntered in with a confident swagger, her shirt dangling from her fingers.

She'd worn black lace that night. I'd made out each darkened areola, each tightened nipple. And until I'd realized she was drugged, I'd reacted.

The same way I'm reacting tonight.

Most people would expect a twenty-three-year-old man in the front seat with a topless woman to get an erection. In fact, I've had women become affronted when I remained unruffled at their attempts at seducing me, be it undressing or touching or otherwise.

The fact that I react to *her* infuriates me beyond measure.

Her. Calliope Harrison, daughter of my boss. Spoiled brat, entitled troublemaker with no regard for rules or order. Chaos causing, violet-haired, flashing blue-eyed nymph with confidence oozing from every pore. That's who I start getting hard-ons for? And at the most inconvenient times.

I adjust my grip on the steering wheel, shifting my hips slightly, and I feel her glaring. Now what? She rolls her eyes so hard I'm surprised she doesn't sprain something. Silence hangs between us, tense enough to at least reroute whatever blood had been rushing to my dick.

Finally, I oblige her. "What?"

"You didn't even look, did you?" She finishes knotting my shirt at her waist.

The action quills any remnants of attraction, and I nearly bite my tongue to keep from scolding her for ruining my shirt. "I'm not that kind of guy," I grind out.

The memory of her invading my indulgence the other morning says otherwise. But that was a fluke and in no way indicative of a new pattern in my behavior.

"Whatever."

Evidently, we're back to muttering.

We have several blocks until we reach our destination, and she faces away from me, staring silently at the scenery passing by. All I can see every time I blink are flashes of her underthings, which I desperately need a distraction from.

So I pull out one of my tried and true conversation techniques — the versatile and unique animal fact. "Did you know that butterflies taste with their feet?" Excitement fills me at all the various ways this conversation could go.

It opens a wide variety of doors, like how the butterflies check plants for poison – both for food and laying their offspring. Or, if we go the taste route, we could talk about how what most people call their tongue is actually their proboscis and is more similar to a straw than anything.

But she only gapes, then turns back to the window in silence.

Disappointment has my shoulders sagging though I keep my expression carefully neutral, playing my own conversation out in my head. Like I've done countless times before. I guess I shouldn't have expected anything different from a spoiled brat like her.

By the time we pull into her driveway, her knee is jiggling again and her finger rubs over her thumbnail. The clock flicks from midnight to twelve-oh-one as we pull into the driveway, and she groans, flopping her head against the seat.

"Dammit." The defeat on her face is such a contrast to the easy grin she usually wears. "I'm so close, but I might as well have stayed out another hour." She looks down at my shirt, shaking her head. "Coming home in someone else's clothes after curfew. It's not even my fault, but why would he believe me?"

She doesn't look my way, and the quiet tone of her voice makes me wonder if she even remembers I'm here.

"Even if I do my best..." She trails off with a sigh and silence reigns for several moments before she says, "Get a grip, Callie." She sits straighter, shoving her seatbelt off and squaring her shoulders. The confident mask returns as she tosses her hair.

Unease sits in my gut as I watch her stride to her front door. I'm not sure if it was the defeat or the few moments she forgot me or the fact that she didn't even say goodbye. Usually I'm worth a parting shot...even in the hospital, she managed to give me the finger.

My gaze lands on her shirt next to me, and I find myself shutting off the car. Before I know it, I'm hurrying up the sidewalk after her. I catch the door and nudge my way inside. Professor Harrison's annoyed features quickly change to confusion as Calliope whirls to face me, her eyes widening.

"Pardon the intrusion," I apologize. "You forgot your shirt." I hand her the garment. Anger flashes across her face, but I ignore it. "I'm sorry, Calliope, I know you didn't want me to come in, but I took the shirt as a sign."

I have no idea what I'm doing. Her bewilderment matches mine, but I allow my instincts to take over as I turn to address my boss. "Professor Harrison, it's my fault Calliope is home after curfew. Well, mine and my brother's. He ran out of gas on the way home, and Calliope begged me to get her home. Which I was happy to do."

When I shoot her my best apologetic look, she takes a shocked step backward. I realize I may be overdoing it, so I try to scale back.

"If I'd gone the way she'd suggested, I'd have gotten here on time. But she didn't want me to get in trouble with you, so she was just going to accept her punishment." I sigh. "On top of that, when my brother's car ran out of gas, he had to dart into a parking lot, and she spilled her soda all over her shirt. I've not only returned her late, but in less than perfect condition."

I hang my head, wondering what the hell has gotten into me. "I'm sorry, sir." *Sticking my neck out for Calliope? Maybe my blood sugar dipped again. Am I safe to drive home?*

Professor Harrison chuckles and shakes his head. "Sebastian, my boy, that sounds like quite a night." He walks over to clap his hand onto my shoulder, ignoring my flinch at the unwanted touch. "Thank you for getting her home safely."

Relief flows through me, especially when he lets go. I nod, meeting his eyes with a tight smile. "Yes, sir." I glance at her, finding her astounded gaze pinned on me. I have no explanation, so I continue the act and think about my roses, about my happy place. Then I give her my best smile. "Good night, Calliope."

Her lips part, and her breath hitches.

"Callie," her father admonishes.

She jerks as if startled, then quickly says, "Oh, um, good night, Sebastian." She pauses, searching my face before adding a quiet, "And thank you."

I blink in surprise at the sincerity of the words, and her heartfelt gratitude settles over me like a kitten's purr. I dip my chin and head out of the door. When I slide into the passenger seat, I sit there for many moments as I ponder what came over me.

But the only explanation I can come up with is that she bewitched me somehow.

Chapter Three

Callie

In the two weeks that follow, my sole interaction with Sebastian is a passing glimpse as I meet my dad at his office. I don't know what happened the night he dropped me off. Not only did he seem like a normal human being with real feelings and a fucking actual smile...he seemed to care about me.

Talk about a glitch in the Matrix.

I can't get that smile out of my head. How his face lit up, his hazel eyes crinkled behind his glasses, and he became—I hate to use the word—handsome. Too bad he's in such a serious relationship with that stick up his ass, or maybe someone else would have a fighting chance.

The worst part of all this is that now I owe him. The last time I brought him a gift replays in my mind, and I have no clue what I can possibly do. My debt looms over my head during my day with Jess and Lyssa and gnaws at me as Dad drives me home. We grab our standard Thursday night fare of Chinese takeout, then eat together at home.

The dinner choice goes back to when Mom was alive. Thursday was my day to hang with Dad at the greenhouse, and we'd pick up dinner on our way home. I remember Mom checking my grubby hands when we returned and how she scolded him when she found dirt under my nails. But there was always a twinkle in her eye.

He became different after she passed. Rigid and unbending. As if she'd softened his hard edges and he forgot what it was like to have fun without her around. I miss her.

Especially this weekend.

Dad's end-of-the-school-year party is legendary, and Mom would take most of the week to prep. Tomorrow, I'll spend the day cooking. Meatballs, pinwheels with layers of ham, cream cheese and tortillas, veggie pizza, plus a charcuterie board to die for. I hand-picked the cheeses myself, and Dad approved.

I can't be bitter about the work because it makes me feel closer to Mom. Plus, it usually earns me brownie points with Dad, putting us on better terms for a week or two.

Right before bed, I'm running over my list, making sure I have everything so I can get started first thing.

Dad pauses on his way to bed. "Oh, Callie?"

I glance up.

"Sebastian won a fairly prestigious award this week. I thought it'd be a nice gesture if we baked him a cake. Like the ones your mother used to make."

My emotions jolt hot and cold through me, as if someone opened both taps, full force. "What?"

Those cakes took hours to create. I could never pull that off on top of everything else. I try to reason with him. "I've already got a full plate, Dad, with the menu we went over. I don't have the ingredients, plus I've never made one before. Not on my own."

And I don't want to. I don't want to make Mom's famous German chocolate cake without her there to guide me through the process. That was her thing, and she should be the one to teach me. That can't happen now. Anything I make will be a farce in the face of her memory.

But my protests might as well be made to a brick wall.

He waves me off. "I'm sure you're perfectly capable of managing your time. Good night, Callie."

As soon as he's out of sight, I slump onto the nearest bar stool and fight to keep from bursting into tears. He is the king of pressure and unrealistic expectations. I stare at the front door, my walkway to freedom, feeling the leash tighten around my neck.

I've learned that cages come in all shapes and sizes, but a cage is still a cage. If it weren't for my free tuition, I'd be out of that door in a second. I am grateful, so grateful for my education because it's my ticket out of here.

But just once...one time in my life...I want something to be mine and mine alone. Today is not that day, and neither is my time this weekend. Resigned, I look over my list, then dig out my mother's cookbook, setting about the impossible task of trying to fit in making her impeccable German cake. From scratch.

By the time Saturday rolls around, I'm exhausted. I barely slept last night, yet I've been awake since six a.m., and I am not—nor have I ever been—an early bird. Though I finished the cake. I slathered the dented dessert with enough frosting that it looks passable. I really hope it tastes all right.

Instead of having a leisurely morning to get myself ready for the party, I have to do all the non-baking items today—pinwheels, the toppings for the veggie pizza, and the charcuterie board. After I've assembled everything, I hurry upstairs to make myself presentable, knowing anything less than my best will result in a lecture on how my appearance reflects on my father.

I'm still not sure how I get away with the violet hair and the nose ring. Dad must have been too deep in the throes of grief when I first dyed my hair and by the time he emerged, he'd decided it wasn't worth the fight. Not that I'm complaining.

I pull on an indigo sundress swirled with teal and green, a perfect mix of vibrant colors that I hope will help my mood. I swipe on some eyeliner and complete the look with bubble-gum-pink lip gloss, then rush back downstairs. Outside, I find all the rented tables already set up, so I begin placing the decorations.

By the time Jess and Lyssa get here, my feet are killing me in my wedge sandals. My friends help me bring out the food and plates as Professor Franklin shows up first and empty-handed. Both are usual occurrences.

"Callie, don't you look festive. You even match the décor!" he says cheerily.

I look around, noting that yes, I did somehow manage to coordinate with the teal and green place settings. My dad will be thrilled. The knowledge weighs on me—just one more way I fit into my father's perfectly orchestrated plans. Another stone on the pile of expectations I carry with me.

Dad emerges from the air-conditioned house, not having lifted a finger as of yet. I stand off to one side, my hands clasped in front of me while I wait for his approval even as I brace myself for the double-edged sword of his words that I know is coming.

He hums, surveying the yard and the table. I allow my guard to drop too soon because he adds, "You must have forgotten the mustard and ketchup I asked for. No matter. I'll get those while you greet our guests." And he disappears inside.

Jess pats my shoulders as I stiffen my jaw to keep it from quivering. I haven't sat down in hours, and he's the host, yet I get to go stand at the front gate.

"I'll save you a seat," she says sympathetically as Lyssa nods.

"Thanks," I murmur before trudging around the house.

Half an hour later, my cheeks hurt and I want nothing more than a hot bath surrounded by no louder noise than bubbles popping as I sink into them. I can't wait to eat after seeing all the dishes everyone brought in. It'll be a hell of a potluck. I count to one hundred and twenty then start to turn, but of course a familiar Volvo drives up.

A tall, lanky, glasses-wearing, arrogant Sebastian unfolds from it before ducking into the back seat to emerge with a crockpot. I force one more smile, reminding myself that I owe him for saving my ass when he dropped me off. Then I hold open the gate for him.

"Calliope," he says, nodding.

"Hi, Sebastian. Come on, and I'll clear you a spot." Then I get a whiff of the contents of his crockpot, and it's hard to keep the disgust off my face. Sauerkraut. I have to tilt my head away, making sure I breathe through my mouth to dampen the stench.

Who was the first person to smell that and think ooh, yummy, I want to eat this?

I run away as soon as humanly possible and sink into the seat next to Jess, uncaring if the guests are done arriving or not. There are balloons tied to the gate for a reason. If they're too stupid to figure that out, they need to switch majors.

Within ten minutes, Dad starts the afternoon with his customary end-of-the-year speech complete with horrid jokes that we all laugh at politely. Everyone claps at the end, and I try not to bristle when I'm not even acknowledged for all my hard work.

My blisters are not so quiet in their protest.

I wait until the line dies down, knowing there will be fewer food options but preferring to spend the least amount of time on my feet. Once I have my plate and am back in my chair, there I stay, content at my little table with Jess, Lyssa, and a few other fun people from the department. We laugh, we joke, and the afternoon flies by. All too soon, Dad signals me that it's time for dessert.

At least I have my second wind and can actually walk to the kitchen. I touch up the smudged exclamation point at the end of "Congratulations!" and take one more admiring look at my masterpiece. Sure, it's dented and a little lopsided, but I can practically feel my mom smiling.

Dad clears a path, directing me to set the cake right in front of an embarrassed-looking Sebastian. As Dad prattles on with yet another speech, his hand repeatedly comes to rest on Sebastian's back. Sebastian's cheeks flush a darker shade of red, and he curls into himself, hunching over the cake. I've seen him flinch before when Dad touches him but this time, Sebastian seems on the verge of panic.

I'm sure it doesn't help that everyone is hovering around, almost drooling over the cake as they close in eagerly. After the cheering and clapping quiet, I wave my hands to take on the attention.

"Jess will be moving the cake over to the dessert table." Her eyes widen, but she steps forward, and I smile in thanks before I add, "So follow her over there and help yourselves."

As the crowd dissipates, I hang back, wanting to make sure Sebastian gets a piece of the dessert I slaved so hard over in his honor. I sit in a nearby chair, careful not to touch him. "You okay?"

His expression still looks pinched, and he drains his glass of water, but he nods.

"Not one for the spotlight, huh?"

A small breath escapes him, almost a snort, and one corner of his lips raises slightly as he shakes his head.

"Well, I've successfully diverted them, *and* I'll even bring you a piece of cake." I grin, standing up. "What'll you have? Corner piece? Middle? All the frosting?"

His mouth pinches again, and his voice is strained as his gaze hits the table. "No, thanks."

"What?" I try to play it off, hoping that maybe it's because he's still uncomfortable. "I can't have heard you right. I made that cake from scratch, just for you, so, what piece can I get you?" My frustration seeps into my tone, but I can't help it.

He shifts in his seat. "Sorry, Calliope." He studies the table, distinctly not meeting my searing gaze. "I'm full."

Tears spring to my eyes, burning in the face of his rejection as it adds to all the heaped-up little digs of this hellish day. "Fine," I bite out. "It's not like I went to any trouble."

All that work and all that effort, only for him to dismiss me like it didn't mean anything? *He can't even try a bite?* I swallow my hurt, reminding myself that this is Sebastian. It just further reinforces the idea that the other night had been a fluke.

Sebastian having a heart? Actually caring about someone? I must have been dreaming.

* * * *

Sebastian

The pain in Calliope's voice only adds to my discomfort, but I'm already overloaded. Being the center of attention and Professor Harrison's extra back slaps combined with the pressing crowd and the noise, all sprung on me without any preparation... I can't take any more. I say a quick goodbye to the professor before I make a hurried exit.

No one in the department knows I'm diabetic, and I like it that way. It's nice having a place where people don't hover while worrying about my eating habits or me fainting. Where they see me for my contributions and not my shortcomings.

But this is the fallout.

I remind myself it's Calliope. She'll get over it, if it actually affected her in the first place. Still, the crack of her voice and the hurt in her deep blue eyes haunt me the whole way home.

The week is uneventful as I continue prepping my roses. Professor Harrison is preparing for an important conference that I'm not attending, so I have minimal duties from him. I keep thinking I'll see Calliope. I'd like to, if only to be one hundred percent sure she is in one piece, but she doesn't appear.

When the professor calls me on Saturday, asking me to bring a set of files from his desk at the office to his house, I think nothing of it. He wants to check some data when he gets home from the conference tomorrow and doesn't want to go out of his way to get to campus. I'm happy to do it.

I amble downstairs, hesitating on the landing when I hear the raised voices of Meg and Silas echoing from the kitchen.

"It had my name on it," Meg yells.

"I don't know what to tell you," Silas shouts back. "I ate a sandwich. I didn't see a name. I'm sorry." He sounds anything but.

I inch my way along the wall, hoping to sneak by without drawing their attention. I'm tying my shoes when Silas storms out.

"Silas, we're not done here!" Meg stands in the doorway with her arms crossed.

"What do you want me to do? Throw it up? You're not getting your sandwich back, Meg. Cut your losses." His eyes narrow, then he rushes over to me. "I'm coming with you."

I frown, looking from him to Meg, but he shoves his feet into the nearest shoes and raises his eyebrows. "Well?"

So I walk outside and get into the car. Silas drops into the passenger seat, shutting his door with more force than necessary as he groans. I watch pointedly until he buckles his seatbelt. Only then do I start the car.

"Why is she always such a bitch?" he asks.

"You ate her food. She has a right to be upset." I'm finished taking sides in this world war. They're both wrong and some day it's all going to combust in their faces. I just hope I'm not a casualty.

"I didn't see her name," he mutters.

"You either didn't look or you ignored it. That's a flimsy excuse. You ate her sandwich, knowing it would upset her, and now you're annoyed you got caught."

He slouches down in his seat, confirming my accusations. The rest of the drive is quiet, and I tell him I'll be right back once I park on campus. A few minutes later, I return with the files, and Silas already looks more like his usual upbeat self.

Eagerly looking around, he asks, "So, where we going?"

"I've got to drop these at Professor Harrison's."

One eyebrow bobs as he gives me a knowing look. "Reconnaissance. All right."

"What?" I pull out of the parking lot, glancing at him in confusion.

"Oh, come on, Sebastian. You know the prof is sending you there to check on his daughter."

I frown, considering the idea and feeling uneasy at being used against my knowledge. Then again, this is all speculation. Though, it is Calliope, and she might need checking on...

Either way, I will drop off the requested files, because I said I would.

"What are you going to do if she's having a party?"

My frown deepens.

"Really, Sebastian? Let the poor girl have some fun. Her dad sounds like a tyrant if you ask me, getting all bent out of shape for running out of gas. It's not like I did it on purpose. She could probably use a break."

"She's underage," I mutter.

He rolls his eyes. "At least think about it before you go pissing all over her carefully laid plans. She's not the idiot you think she is." He laughs when I rear back and sputter. "She's a lot smarter than you give her credit for. I should know. I went out with her."

An odd buzzing starts in the back of head where my spine and cranium meet, as if his words have implanted a hive of bees in my brain. I clench my jaw, annoyed and unsettled as I stop at the curb in front of their house, the exact same spot I parked for Professor Harrison's party last weekend.

When Silas starts to unbuckle, I grab his arm. "You wait here." He's caused enough trouble putting ideas in my head.

I tuck the folders under my arm, relieved to see the house quiet and calm — though it is only five p.m. The day is still young. I walk up the two front steps and gently push the doorbell, enjoying the deep tones that echo through the house. Light footsteps dance closer. The buzzing in my head dissipates as a surge of anticipation in my midsection catches me off guard.

Calliope never does anything small, even opening a door. She flings it wide, her sunny smile stealing my breath, as if I have been placed in a Ziploc bag and the air has been sucked from it. Then the smile drops, her eyes narrowing as the familiar loathing and frustration take over. *Same old Calliope.*

Definitely not broken.

Panic overrides her expression, and she nearly shoves me right off the step. I grab the door jamb, barely managing to hang on as her shoulders sag in relief. Then she glares while I regain my balance.

"What the hell are you doing here, Sebastian? Besides giving me a heart attack."

"Me?" I let go of the door frame as I keep a wary eye on her. "I just rang the doorbell. You're the one trying to push me off your steps."

"I thought you were with my father this weekend."

The pieces click into place, and my suspicions go on red alert. "So, what are you up to that you don't want your father knowing about?"

She blinks, a blank look on her face. "Um…"

"Calliope," I say as sternly as I can.

A squawking of brakes fills the air, and a large box truck pulls into the driveway. A frustrated moan escapes her lips, then defeat juts her lower lip as a smiling man jumps out with a wave.

"Hey, Callie. Where d'ya want the keg?"

She grimaces. "One second, Paul."

"A keg?" I ask. "Are you serious?"

All hint of sheepishness disappears, eaten away by the fury and indignance that sweep in. "This is my house, Sebastian. No one invited you."

I hold up the folders. "Actually, your father did. *He* asked me to drop these off."

She rolls her eyes. "I'm sure that's all he asked you to do. Are you going to add spy to your little resume now, Mr. Wrighting?"

Her cavalier attitude only incenses me more, and I step closer, glowering. "Your prior incidents lead me to believe that extra supervision is warranted."

An image of her pale and fragile as they lifted her onto the gurney at the last party swims before me. The memory shakes me now. Though her drugged state wasn't her fault, she almost died on my watch. I press my lips together, trying to keep my composure.

But she sets her jaw. "You're not my keeper, and I'm not your responsibility."

Silas bounds over to us as she holds out her hand.

"I'll make sure those get put in his office." She taps her foot, waiting for me to pass over the files.

"Did someone say something about a keg?" Silas asks, oblivious to our tension.

I ignore him. "Calliope." I tighten my grip on the folders. "You almost died."

"And I brought you chocolates to thank you for your efforts. Now, give me the folders."

Silas rears back, scoffing. "Chocolates? For Sebastian? But he's —"

"Silas," I cut him off. "Shut up."

He blinks twice, then nods before scurrying toward the truck. I sigh, swiping my hand over the lower half of my face as Calliope watches me intently.

"Look, Sebastian," she begins in a much quieter tone. The pleading note in her voice catches on the soft corner of my heart, and I can't help listening as she continues, "I've been working my butt off. Between finals, helping Dad wrap up the term, then making all that food for Dad's picnic..."

I frown picturing last weekend's setup, the decorations, the food. "Wait, *you* did all that?" When she nods, my frown deepens. I remember her dad's speech, but not a single mention of her efforts. Why hadn't he acknowledged her?

"I need a chance to unwind, and this is how I do it. With friends, music —"

The list has me snapping my focus back to the issue at hand. "Drinking," I interject.

"I'm twenty," she protests. "Only a year away from being legal, and I swear, all my friends are older. I basically hang out with the botany department and upper classmen."

Her eyes find mine, and the hope in them punches me in the gut. Vulnerability lurks in the depths of her gaze, pulling me in as she casts her spell.

And I find myself making an offer. "I stay, and no one leaves without a DD." She starts to groan, but I hold up my finger. "Or I tell Paul to return the keg to its previous home, and I call your father now."

She scrunches her face for a long moment, then bites out, "Fine." Stomping by me, she waves to Paul. "Keg in the kitchen. Silas, can you help him?"

Silas punches the air with a whoop and hurries into the truck. Calliope grabs my wrist, tugging me inside, but I quickly pull away. Her touch settles like lead in my stomach, though the unnerving sensation isn't as strong as other times. Like when her father claps me on the shoulder.

"Sorry," she mutters, then sweeps out her arm. "Dad's study is this way."

Chapter Four

Sebastian

I compose myself as I follow her. Once she's opened the door, I place the folders neatly in the center of his desk.

"I'm going to lock this room during the party, so if you want to borrow one of his books or anything, now's the time." She offers me a tight smile.

I nod, appreciating the offer. While I do have my current read in the car, I doubt it'll last me the night. I select two tomes and find an out-of-the-way place to tuck them in the kitchen. Jess and Lyssa are the next to arrive, and the surprised looks they shoot my way are all too familiar.

Even as a child, parties were not my thing. I remember once, when I was four, I got shoved into the pool at my parents' house. For several brief seconds, I didn't know which way was up. I couldn't breathe, and water spilled into my mouth. I finally emerged, coughing and sputtering.

That's what parties feel like to me — getting shoved underwater without being able to take a breath.

So the fact that I volunteered to attend one, for Calliope Harrison no less, mystifies me. Maybe I *should* check my sugar. I settle in the corner of the dining room with my book. I'll be out of the way here, but also have a perfect vantage point to keep an eye on the room.

A violet head of hair catches my attention as Jess hands Calliope a red plastic cup and Calliope laughs. She looks relaxed. At ease. Nothing like the broken woman I saw at the picnic, or the stressed-out woman preparing to face her father when I dropped her off past curfew. My eyebrows pull together as I contemplate just how tight a ship Professor Harrison runs.

Two chapters later, Silas smacks his palm on the table and grins. "Look, she got DJ Walker. This is going to be some party." And he races off again.

I watch the DJ setting up and stifle a groan. What did I get myself into?

An hour later, the house is full, of both people and noise. I can barely feel my heart beating in my chest over the thump of the bass. The only house lights still on are in the kitchen, so people can see to grab snacks or drinks, and Calliope turned on a lamp behind me so I could keep reading.

The lasers the DJ brought with him permeate the darkness with raucous flashes of color. I stride into the kitchen to give my eyes a break, though, now that I think about it, I am hungry.

Surveying the snacks, I sigh. If I'd known I was going to be staying, I'd have brought some food of my own. I take a few slices of cheese, avoiding the crackers, chips and cookies. For me, the best diet is low carb, since carbs translate to sugar in the blood stream. I take some veggies off the tray along with a spoonful of dip, all while wishing for some nuts or meat. My stomach growls as Calliope sashays in.

Maybe I could ask her.

She starts pouring another drink, her hips wiggling to the beat. She seems freer now, looser with the alcohol flowing through her system. When her glass is full, she turns to grin at me.

"Hey," I start, not wanting to give too much away. "I didn't have much lunch. Do you have anything more substantial I could eat? Like deli meat or nuts?"

She taps her lower lip, pretending to think. "I suppose you have kept your end of the bargain." Setting her cup down, she rummages in the fridge and hands me a container of turkey, then she opens several cupboards before giving me a canister of nuts. "It's your lucky day. We have both."

"Thank you."

Our fingers brush as I take the nuts from her, and I wait, but the lead doesn't fill my stomach. I brush aside the surprise, chalking it up to the fact that it was just a little touch. She looks over my plate and shakes her head.

"What?"

"You're not a dessert man, are you?"

"I'm…sweet enough as it is?" I sound robotic as I try to play it off as a joke. I've never been good at teasing — it always sounds forced from me.

Except she laughs, and it freezes me. It's the most beautiful sound I've ever heard. Infectious and airy, as if someone bottled up starlight then released it. I can only stare at her.

"You? Sweet?" She lets out a derisive snort. "Uh-huh."

I take my plate to the table, ignoring the prick of pain at her jab. She's only seen me as her father's TA, enforcing his rules, so I understand. I like order, I like to be in control, while she embraces the chaos.

No wonder we don't get along.

To my surprise, she follows me to the table, then sits beside me, taking a sip of her drink and swaying with the so-called music. I watch her for a moment, comparing her now to when I last saw her, and I become curious about her reaction. Maybe I don't have all the information.

"The cake at the party seemed very important to you. Why?" I find myself asking before I take a bite of turkey.

Her whole upper body tenses, then she turns to me. Her throat moves as she swallows before saying, "It was my mother's recipe. She used to make it all the time for Dad's year-end party."

Everyone in the department knows Professor Harrison is a widower, that he's Calliope's only parent. But I don't know many of the details.

She sets her cup down, staring at the table. "Dad kind of sprang it on me last second. I'd already finalized the menu. Had my time perfectly allotted to fit everything in." Her gaze flicks to me. "He told me the night before that he wanted to celebrate that grant you received." And she looks down once more. "With Mom's cake."

I have never felt lower in my entire life than I do at this moment. My tongue feels glued to the roof of my mouth, stuck there by guilt and regret.

"I'd never made it before," she continues, running her finger through the condensation on her plastic cup. "Of course, she made everything from scratch, so it was a lot of work." She lifts a shoulder, then leans back in her seat. "But everyone seemed to like it."

"Calliope, I had no idea…" I could have had a small piece. I can eat some sugar as long as I compensate with insulin, especially if I move afterward and drink plenty of water. I hadn't even had any other dessert. "I'm sorry."

Her eyes find mine and the sorrow in them guts me. "He never even said thank you." Her voice cracks on the last word, and a muscle ticks in her cheek.

I can't fathom that. To have her go through all that trouble, all that work, and not even acknowledge her efforts? How invisible she must feel. No wonder she has purple hair and a nose ring. How else is she going to be seen?

Jess calls her name, and Calliope swipes at her eyes. All traces of anything but happiness disappear as she stands up. I study her, pondering how long she's been wearing that mask.

And what else is hiding underneath.

After she leaves, the lasers are too distracting, so I turn off the lamp and pull my chair into the corner of the kitchen. But I still can't focus on the words. Instead, I keep hearing Callie telling me about her mom. All I can see is her in this very kitchen, working hard to make all that food, especially that cake. *Just how badly have I misjudged her?*

At eleven-thirty, I turn the last page of my last book, fighting yet another yawn. My brain has been overloaded to the point that I had to step outside for a quick walk earlier, leaving a slightly drunk but still coherent Silas in charge. Calliope wobbles on the dance floor, more than tipsy, though not dangerously so.

I've noticed Jess has been drinking water for the last hour while Lyssa drapes herself more and more over her girlfriend. I make eye contact with Jess, pointedly looking at my watch. She checks her phone, then nods in agreement.

We each take half the room, meeting at the DJ and telling him that at midnight, the music dies. He doesn't protest. People trickle out, and I check them at the door, fulfilling my end of the deal of ensuring they have a designated driver. By the time the DJ packs his equipment, only Jess, Lyssa, Silas, and I remain with Calliope, who is dancing by herself in the middle of the living room to music only she hears.

Jess has to drag Lyssa to the door, and she apologizes for not staying to clean, but I wave her off. Silas hums a tune as he grabs a trash bag, then begins the task of collecting the empty cups littering every surface. The DJ departs with a cheerful wave, and I'm thankful Callie paid him early on.

She sings off key as she weaves to the kitchen. I follow behind her, right there when her toe catches the threshold. She stumbles, unable to right herself, but I grab her waist and keep her from falling. I drop my hands as soon as she stops swaying, only then realizing that the lead never came.

"Sebastian," she slurs, staring up at me. "You're tall."

I can't help chuckling at the understatement. I'm six foot four, the tallest of my brothers. "Maybe you're just short."

"Five foot seven is not short." She stops talking to glance around. "Where'd everybody go?"

"They left. It's time for bed."

"Oh." Her face falls. "Back to reality."

A pang hits my chest at her obvious disappointment, but I shove it aside. "Water first." I snag a bottle, propping her against the counter and helping her open it.

She tips it up for a sip, though some of the water sloshes onto her chin. "You're kind of nice when you don't hate me."

The words stab my chest, echoing my earlier thoughts about misjudging her. "I don't hate you, Calliope."

"Ish Callie." But it lacks her usual zest, and she sags against the counter. "Sebastian?"

"Yeah?"

"How am I going to get upstairs?"

"Don't worry. I'll take care of it." I reach out one arm, and she falls against my chest. I tense, like I do anytime someone I'm not close to touches me. But the lead doesn't come. Again.

Curious.

After I screw the top on her water, I bend, scooping her easily into my arms bridal style, then grab her water. She's light, like carrying a doll. Silas shakes his head as we go by, but I ignore him. I seize the opportunity to really look at the woman I'm holding.

Her features are delicate, but I know from experience how fierce she can be. I don't know many people who can pull off purple hair, yet it somehow only adds to Calliope's ethereal beauty. I'm not one for facial piercings either, but the stud in her nose enhances the dainty feature. And her lips…

They look soft. Kissable. I try to remember the last time I felt this pull, like I wanted to kiss someone.

My mind flits again back to my affair with Dad's secretary. After Elaine moved away, I focused once more on my work. Even the few kisses I'd shared with Leah had been more obligatory than out of desire, and I have to admit I'd been attracted to Leah's brain, but never to her body.

But here? Now? Looking at Calliope, a faint stirring echoes within me, as if waking from a deep slumber.

I lay her on the bed, taking off her canvas sneakers and covering her with the blankets, then I frown. Desire means being out of control, and the last person I can afford to lose control with is my boss's daughter. I brush a piece of hair out of her face, set her bottle of water on her nightstand and walk from the room.

I've never given in to temptation before, and I don't intend to start now.

* * * *

Callie

I'm not sure which is harder, prying my eyelids open or trying to swallow. My eyes are crusted, and I feel like I slept with a mouth full of cotton balls. The bottle of water on the nightstand next to me practically glows with a heavenly light as I lunge for it. I can almost hear the angels singing and, as long as they keep it down, my head should be fine.

I chug half the bottle, replaying the end of the night. Or trying to. It gets a little fuzzy. I remember people leaving, me dancing on the floor, the room spinning and...

Sebastian?

I replay the glimpses, doubting my blurry memory. *He put me to bed? Sebastian, who flinches at the slightest touch, carried me upstairs, laid me in my bed and pulled the covers up?* I frown, lifting the covers. Yep, fully dressed, not that I can imagine anything else from him.

His face dances in my mind, his brow furrowed in concern. I try to remember. Then the memories flood in, and I nearly smack myself, stopping just in time from making my dull headache worse. I told him about the cake. About Mom. The scene unfolds, but the most astonishing part is the way he reacted.

I can clearly picture the guilty expression, how he'd even started to reach for me. Can hear his heartfelt apology. Maybe the stick isn't as far up his ass as I'd originally thought.

"Calliope Marie Harrison!" my father bellows, and I almost pee my pants.

A quick glance at the clock shows that it isn't even eleven a.m. He shouldn't be home for hours. He shouldn't have even checked out yet!

Unless…

I shake my head, flinging the covers aside as I grit my teeth. I can't believe I trusted Sebastian not to tell my dad. He's Professor Harrison's TA first and foremost, so why would he stick his neck out for someone like me? The furious footsteps across the living room send me racing to the doorway.

"Coming," I yell.

Reality is here, in my face and harsher than ever. Good thing I got my fun in last night. I rush downstairs, expecting the mess of the party to be yet another tally mark against me. But the house is clean…pristine even, and I frown.

Dad bellows again, this time from the kitchen, so I jog in to find him with his hands on his hips standing over three trash bags piled around the garbage can. Jess and Lyssa must have stayed to clean up.

He points an accusing finger. "What is all this?"

"Oh, um, hi, Dad." I drag my top teeth over my lower lip. "I didn't think you'd be home until later."

"That makes it okay to throw a party in my absence?"

"No." I sigh. "At least the house isn't trashed?"

He rubs his temple. "I don't understand why you can't follow the rules. They aren't that difficult and…" I brace for lecture mode, but evidently he decides it isn't worth it. "You're grounded for a month."

It takes a massive effort not to roll my eyes. "Dad, I'm twenty years old." A muscle in his jaw jumps, and I immediately regret saying anything.

"Who pays your phone bill? Who owns the car you drive? Who works at a university enabling you to have free tuition?"

Who doesn't think I can handle a job, making me focus solely on my studies? Who made it so I don't have access to Mom's money until I turn twenty-five? But the retorts are only in my mind as I respectfully answer, "You do." I remove all emotion from my face despite the frustration churning within me.

"If you'd like to continue having these privileges, you will follow my rules and abide by my decisions. Is that clear?"

"Yes, sir." Two more years until I graduate, I remind myself. He'll have to let me get a job then.

He assesses me for a long moment before he turns his attention to the coffee maker. "Get this trash out of here."

Resigned, I fill my hands with trash bags, the only remnants from an otherwise flawless night. Annoyed thoughts stomp through my head, but I'm unable to voice any of them without risking an even greater punishment.

"Oh, and Callie?" He waits until I look at him to continue. "You'll be accompanying me to my conference next Sunday. You've proven you're not capable of being left on your own for an entire week."

Indignation and resentment swirl within me, tangling with a wave of hurt. But I only dip my chin in silent acknowledgment. *The next time I see Sebastian...* I clench my jaw, steeling myself as I spin on my heel and stalk outside.

The following day, Dad drags me to work with him. As if I'm so irresponsible that I'm going to throw a massive party during the middle of the day on the heels of him grounding me. But I dutifully follow him into the office, acting like I'm happy to be there, even when he sticks me in the filing room with a mile-high stack of papers he's been meaning to get to.

I found out more about the conference, and I'm slightly mollified that Jess is going to be there. She's attending as Maia's TA, but not lecturing. I'm hoping Dad will let us room together.

The monotony of my task stretches on, and I'm surprised the papers don't burst into flames from my inner fuming. Two hours later, I barely manage to keep from swearing as I get yet another paper cut. *Of all the ridiculous tortures. Whatever happened to the punishment fitting the crime?* I sigh, sticking my finger in my mouth as I plop onto the floor.

Dad loves me. I know he's only doing what he thinks is best. He only knows how to do tough love, to keep a tight hold, and I can't blame him. He already lost Mom. I know he just doesn't want to lose me too.

My mind flits to Mom, and the all-too-familiar ache pierces my chest. Her lungs had been weak all her life, and she was extra careful to protect herself. I went to a private school with a low class count because friends equaled germs to her. At twenty years old, I've never even been to a sleepover.

Despite her precautions, she ended up with pneumonia. It took her from us, and we haven't been the same since. She came from money, a good portion of which is now mine. However, it's locked in a trust that I don't have access to until I'm twenty-five — the magic age when I become *responsible*.

I snort at the absurd idea. Grabbing the stack of papers once more, I kneel to open the drawer containing the Rs. Another hour passes before I take a bathroom break, biting back a stream of curses as I pass Dad's office where the sun streams in.

Dad drags me with him for three days straight, and I don't even get the satisfaction of telling Sebastian off. I don't see him, not once. All I see are papers, papers, and more papers — I even find myself reciting the alphabet in my sleep.

Thursday when I go in, the pile is higher still. I wonder if someone is pulling out random pieces of paper that were already filed, to give me something to do. I set my jaw and hop to it. I've only been working for an hour when Sebastian saunters in.

He has dirt under his fingernails, a sure sign he's been working in the greenhouse. Maybe even grafting. Longing pulls at me to get out of this damn office, to play with plants like I used to with Dad when I was younger. But I push it aside, quickly reaching for my anger since he's the reason I'm here in the first place.

He frowns when he sees me glaring. "Calliope, what are y — ?"

"Sebastian," my dad calls. "Down here."

They disappear into his office, and I push aside the hurt, reminding myself that he was just being a good little yes-man. My fingers ache as I shuffle through the Ts, but it doesn't matter. I'm here for the foreseeable future all because I dared to be a normal college kid and throw a party.

Dad's door cracks open, and Sebastian appears in the hallway. He meets my eyes again, then turns back around. "Actually, sir, I thought perhaps..." His voice lowers to a quiet rumble that I can't discern.

Then Dad says my name. "Callie?"

"Yes, sir. If it's not too much trouble."

I don't know whether to fume or hold my breath before Dad fills my doorway. I stare at him, the paper halfway into the correct slot in the file.

"Callie, Sebastian needs an extra pair of hands in the greenhouse. Are you interested?"

I leap to my feet so fast I send papers flying, but I can't bring myself to care. The filing will be here when I get back. I open my mouth to blurt out a hearty yes, then my eyes catch on Sebastian, and I hesitate. This is the man who said he'd keep quiet about the party, but told Dad anyway. The whole reason I'm grounded.

The sunshine streaming behind Dad brightens at that moment, and I give in, nodding. I can handle working with this liar to get out of this miserable room. Anything is better than this windowless cell.

"All right, then." He glances at Sebastian. "She's all yours."

Sebastian's nostrils flare. I'm puzzled at the odd reaction, but I ignore it, silently striding out into the hallway, down the corridor and into the bright sunny day. The moment I step into the sun, I stop. Closing my eyes, I tilt my head up and back, then suck in a huge breath.

I'm free.

Sebastian clears his throat, reminding me of the contingencies to my freedom, and I resist the urge to snarl. He walks by me to hold the greenhouse door open, his hazel eyes assessing me as I pass. Once we're both inside, he asks quietly, "Are you upset with me, Calliope?"

I snort, walking over to study his roses. "No, Sebastian, why would I be upset with you?" Sarcasm drips from my tone, and I glance over my shoulder, making sure he registers it.

Confusion contorts his face. "I don't know. The last time I saw you was the night of your party." He shoves his hands into his khaki pockets. "I haven't seen you since."

"You didn't have to see me to call my dad and tell him about the party," I bite out.

"What?"

My fury takes over, and I march over to him, toe to toe as I poke my finger into his surprisingly firm chest. "My dad was right there the next morning. He wasn't supposed to be home until that afternoon, and I would have had plenty of time to get rid of all the evidence. I thought we had a deal, Sebastian."

He studies me for a long moment. "I gave you my word, Calliope, and that is not something I do lightly. The only time I spoke to your father that weekend was on Saturday when he asked me to drop the files off at your house." He holds out his phone, offering it to me. "Here. See for yourself."

I blink. The earnestness of his response tells me he's not lying—so does my gut—and I shake my head.

"Silas and I were the last ones there. Did we not do a satisfactory job cleaning up?"

"Dad found the trash bags," I start, then his words sink in. "*You* cleaned up?"

He nods. "After I helped you to bed, Silas and I worked together. I'm sorry about the garbage, but we didn't see an outdoor bin."

My lips part as my gut sinks. He wouldn't have stayed to clean if he'd planned on tattling on me. He wouldn't have put me to bed. I knew it didn't add up, but I wanted to blame someone. My throat grows thick at how wrong I was. "Sebastian, I—" My voice cracks. "I'm sorry."

"Okay," he says simply, then he walks past me to his roses. "These are the ones that need to be repotted. You can help if you want to, or if you just want to be out of that dark—"

"No," I interrupt. "I want to help." He looks over in surprise, and I give him a shy smile. "Actually, I saw the dirt under your fingernails when you came in, and it made me jealous. Dad used to bring me here when I was little. He'd let me have my own pot, my own plant. He'd tell me it was my job to keep it alive."

I graze a finger over one of the light green leaves. "They need more nitrogen."

"How...?"

"Just because I'm not studying botany doesn't mean I don't know a thing or two."

Sebastian walks over to me, admiration in his gaze. "It's been corrected. This morning."

"Good."

We stare at each other for a long moment, then Sebastian steps away. He shows me where all the supplies are, tells me to ask if I need anything, then he walks to the other end of the greenhouse where he studies the papers on his desk. I watch him go, appreciating the way he moves with purpose in every motion.

Then I roll up my sleeves and dig my hands into the soil, feeling as if I've come home.

Chapter Five

Sebastian

She believed me, just like that. No further explanation, no swiping through my phone to double check. I can understand her doubt, especially since I'm the most logical candidate to have alerted her father, but I thoroughly expected to have to fight for her to realize my innocence.

I shove my glasses further up on my nose as I watch her. She doesn't even flinch before plunging her hands into the dirt, and I know it will stick under her nails like it does mine, which are considerably shorter than hers. I have a feeling that what I'm learning about Calliope Harrison is merely scratching the surface.

But I have other things on my mind, like the equation my entire thesis hinges upon. I can't seem to get it right. I'm on the verge of a breakthrough, yet it hovers just out of reach.

I know from experience that mindless tasks are best for this sort of thing, so I give my notes one more cursory glance. A useless endeavor because they are imprinted in my brain, but it doesn't hurt. Then I pick up my shears and walk across the room to the overgrown forsythia my aunt gave me. It's time for a pruning.

"Sebastian!"

By the volume Calliope uses, I infer this isn't the first time she has tried to get my attention, and I lower my shears. "I'm sorry. Did you need something?"

She studies me with a bemused expression. "I'm finished with the repotting."

"Already?"

Laughter trickles from her lips. "It's been two hours."

"Oh." I set the shears down on the closest surface, flexing my hands. No wonder my fingers hurt. "I hadn't realized..." I walk over to the newly potted roses, inspecting each one as my smile grows. "Well done, Calliope. These look fantastic." I dip my finger into the soil, pleased to find exactly the right amount of moisture. "Thank you. This is a great help."

She ducks her head, tucking her hair behind her ear, and her cheeks flush. It makes me think that the lack of accolades from the party wasn't a fluke, that she is rarely thanked for her work. It sends an unexpected surge of protectiveness through me. I want to keep her out here, away from those who take her for granted or hide her away in dark rooms.

Wiping my finger on the nearest rag, I quickly swipe the dirt from beneath my nail. Then I look around, trying to decide if I can invent more work for her.

But she wanders toward my desk. "What were you thinking so hard about?"

Her interest takes me by surprise. "I'm trying to iron out an equation. I should be able to predict the amount of pollen a plant will produce using leaf mass area and growth rate, but I haven't quite perfected it."

I've carefully cultivated the roses, selecting exactly what genes I want for maximum pollen output. If people could grow flowers that produce more pollen with the same amount of space, the bees and butterflies would have more food. But my whole thesis rests on being able to predict the outcome, and I'm stuck.

She hums. "That could be handy. What do you have so far?"

I blink several times, unable to comprehend her question. Most people would be running away by now, or, at the very least, their eyes would be glazed over as they feigned interest. "You want to know more?"

"Yes," she says eagerly. "Please."

Stunned, I walk over to the desk and sit in my chair, then I grab my notes, splaying the pages before me. I hesitantly explain what I've come up with, and she asks intelligent questions, her interest never waning. Once I've finished, she looks over all the sheets, and her eyes widen. She leans down next to me, her shoulder grazing mine in the process, and we both freeze.

But I don't flinch.

She notices, turning to look at me, her face closer than we've ever been. "You didn't pull away."

I can't answer, can't form words, can only shake my head an infinitesimal amount. Panicked tendrils squeeze my chest at her proximity, but it's not accompanied by that lead that sours my stomach. Unexpected longing wells up, that she'll keep touching me. That she'll lean in, even closer. Only a few inches separate her face from mine, and it's too much but not enough.

The control I prize above all else threatens to slip from my fingers, but I grip it tighter, determined to be its master.

"What does that mean?" she whispers.

"I don't know," I rasp out, unable to focus on anything but the way her lips are parted.

"Sebastian?" Empathy pools in her pretty eyes. "Should I move?"

At my minuscule nod, she shifts away, and it's like the oxygen is turned back on to my brain. I gasp in a breath as she frowns. I try to wave her off, try to act like I'm in full command of myself. "You were saying?"

Carefully leaning in, avoiding any contact, she taps her finger on my latest equation. "Don't you need to square the variable?"

The pieces in my head completely untangle as the last knot falls away, and I gape at her perfect little finger. At the black line beneath her nail, underlining the missing variable that I couldn't see.

Elated, I beam at her. "Calliope, you did it."

My movement has us too close again. Her still leaning down as she stares at me with those cerulean eyes and that perfect mouth. The uncontainable joy I'm feeling surges through me, demanding an outlet, and I barely resist kissing her.

I clear my throat and look away, studying the page again. "Wait till I tell your dad." He'll have to recognize her then.

She ices over completely, freezing me out and stepping away. "No."

Beyond confused at the change in her demeanor, I ask, "What? Why not?"

"You are not to mention a word of me helping with your equation to my dad. Or to anyone in the department." She shakes her head violently. "I've worked too hard, come too far. I'm not a botanist, Sebastian. That's not up for discussion, is that understood?"

Her fingers are clenched into fists, and her chest heaves with an anger I don't comprehend, but I nod.

"Good. I'm going back inside. I'll…" Her words falter. "I'll talk to you later."

She rushes out as I stare after her. Maybe there's an instruction manual somewhere, a book that I can read on how to avoid scenarios like this in the future. I wish it were that simple.

* * * *

The rest of the week flies by before an odd request from Professor Harrison comes in on Saturday morning. I tell him I'll let him know, and immediately go looking for Shawn. I find him shooting basketball on the cement out front with Silas. Not my first choice for advice, but I'm short on time, so I explain my situation to both of them.

Silas grabs the ball when Shawn misses the shot, asking, "He said what?" They both gape.

"Yeah, he wants me to 'keep an eye' on Calliope."

Shawn snorts, facing the basket as Silas shoots. "She's an adult. What's there to keep an eye on?"

A month ago, I might have argued in the professor's favor, but now, I have to wonder how much *watching* Calliope actually needs. "What do I do?"

"Well," says Silas, "if Dad told one of his legal assistants they needed to keep an eye on me, I'd want to know." He winks. "For all the right reasons, of course."

Shawn chuckles. "Of course." He grabs the ball from under the basket, then bounces it as he walks back and eyes me. "I thought you couldn't stand this woman."

Silas smirks. "He hates her the way you 'hated' Leah."

Understanding dawns on Shawn's face even as my cheeks get hot, and I protest, "It's not like that."

Shawn picks up the ball, studying me seriously. "Tell me straight, Seb. What's going on?"

This is why I came to him, because he knows me. He'll know exactly how complicated this situation is when I explain the attraction I'm feeling. But that requires admitting it. Out loud.

"Um…"

He tosses the ball to Silas. "Come on. Let's go get some lunch."

I share a look with Shawn, many years of silent communication giving us the ability to talk without words. Then I turn back and arch an eyebrow at Silas. "Well? Are you coming with us?"

His grin is huge as he scampers to catch up.

Shawn slings an arm over his shoulder, shooting me a wicked glance. "So, this hate between Seb and Callie…is that anything like what's going on with you and Meg?"

Silas shoves him away as Shawn and I burst into laughter. Silas elbows me next, but I don't feel any pain. Just the sense of knowing I have the support of my brothers and the camaraderie that comes with that.

* * * *

The next day, I put my plan into action. Shawn and Silas helped me start to come to terms with what I'm feeling, and the best place to begin is with friendship. I can't help smiling at the irony, since I'd given him that very advice when he was at a loss for how to proceed with Leah.

After arriving at the office, I bide my time until lunch. I caught a glimpse of Calliope filing away again, and I hate seeing her cooped up. The way she tilted her head back the moment we stepped outside is ingrained in my mind, and I hope I can kill two birds with one stone with my idea.

"Professor Harrison?" I ask, leaning in his open door. "I was going to walk to Eat at Joe's for lunch. Would you like anything? It's so nice that I can't handle being inside another minute."

He chuckles. "I completely understand. It's a beautiful day, and sure, bring me back one of their bacon cheeseburgers, would you?"

I jot down the details in my phone to make sure I have them right, then I pause. "Um, would Calliope want anything? She could join me if she liked."

His eyebrows shoot up, like he forgot she was here. "Oh, maybe. Why don't you ask her? She might enjoy getting out of the office."

Still I linger. "I thought I'd eat there, so we might be a little while. If it's okay with you, sir."

"As long as she's with you, that'd be fine."

"All right, I'll see what she would like to do."

I rush into the windowless office. Calliope looks at me expectantly. Her V-neck shirt hangs loose as she bends forward over the files and gives me an ample view of her chest.

But I clear my throat and look at the wall instead. "I'm going to walk to Eat at Joe's for lunch and bring your dad back a burger. Would you like to come?"

"Oh, um…" She stands, brushing her hands over her shorts.

"He said you could walk with me, and I thought maybe you'd enjoy going outside for a while. It's a beautiful day."

A furrow creases her brow. "Really?"

I'm not sure if she's questioning my invitation or her father's permission, so I settle for, "If you want."

A wide smile slides over her face. "Yes. Definitely yes."

I can't help returning it. "Okay, then."

It only takes two steps outside before she does it again. Tilting her head back, she closes her eyes and basks in the sunshine. I can't look away.

"Thank you," she says as we fall into step.

I don't answer immediately, knowing this is my chance to tell her the real reason I invited her. "I have an ulterior motive," I confess.

"Oh?"

"I hear you're attending our conference this week."

Her lips go tight, and her finger flicks over her thumbnail before she nods.

"Is…is this all because of that party?" I ask, unable to believe a simple gathering where there was no fallout, no police involvement, and no mess or destruction could garner such a punishment.

She sighs. "Yep."

"You didn't go rob a bank or break someone out of jail?"

Satisfaction hits me when her lips twitch, then she breaks into a real smile. "No, it was just the party."

"Huh." I shove my hands into my pockets. "I don't remember anything getting broken. Did I miss a puddle of beer on his favorite chair or something?"

"Sebastian..." She pauses. "What's this all about?"

It's my turn to sigh. "Your dad asked me to keep an eye on you this week."

Any softness in her gaze disappears as a hard, angry glint takes over.

"I'm sorry. I thought you should know."

We walk the remaining block to the restaurant in silence, and I hold the door open for her.

She pauses at the threshold, staring at me. "What'd you say?"

"Nothing. I was waiting until I talked to you."

Her eyes widen, then a pensive look crosses her face before she strides inside. I let my breath out with a whoosh and follow her. She doesn't speak again until after we order our drinks.

"Why?"

"I thought—" My idea sounds stupid now that it's on my lips, but she's still waiting. "I thought maybe we could be friends."

Her forehead furrows deep. "But you don't like me."

"I..." Admitting I made a mistake is never easy, but as Shawn and Silas assured me, it needs to be done. "I think I had the wrong idea about you." Her lips part, astonishment in her gasp, and I hurry to continue. "I'd only heard about you from your father, and we left that one conference early so he could 'deal with you'."

Anger flashes over her face.

"His words, not mine." I lace my fingers together in my lap. "Any time after that, I saw you through his lens. Then came the party where Vance…"

Her gaze drops to the table, and her cheeks lose their rosy glow. "I'm sorry I yelled at you in the hospital, Sebastian. You really did save my life. I was just embarrassed and hurt, and my dad was there looking all disappointed. I knew I'd never live it down, so I took it out on you." Her eyes find mine. "Thank you."

It's the first sincere thanks I've had from her regarding that incident, and my mouth goes dry. I swallow twice before I can speak. "You're welcome. And I'm sorry for judging you."

One corner of her mouth ticks up. "I judged you, too. Arrogant know-it-all."

"Well, you're not wrong."

Her burst of laughter takes us both by surprise. "Now you're making jokes. I'm *sure* the world is ending."

The waitress comes to take our order, smiling at the two of us. I order Professor Harrison's burger to go, then get my usual turkey burger with a side salad.

Calliope orders a chicken wrap with waffle fries, and after the waitress is gone, she tilts her head. "So, now that you've told me about my dad's plans, what do you want to do about it?"

Callie

I can't believe I'm sitting here across from Sebastian Wrighting with an offer of friendship on the table. I *can* believe my dad would ask him to keep an eye on me. That's par for the course.

But I never expected his TA to jump the fence and land on my side. I'm still reeling.

Usually I try to sway my dad's TAs from the get-go. I've even dated a few, but I've never seen someone as in awe of my father as Sebastian. Still, he didn't tell Dad about the party, and he's kept quiet about me helping him with that equation. Plus, he told me up front about Dad's request.

Before responding to Dad.

I wait for his reply, trying to keep from squirming in my seat as my mind races to what his answer will be. How does he want to handle this? Our food comes, lengthening his reprieve before answering. We thank the waitress, and I dig into my wrap. *Delicious.*

"Nothing specific. I thought maybe we could spend time together." He drizzles the side of dressing onto his salad, so neatly. "I know your father will be busy giving and attending lectures, so I doubt he'll want an account of every minute."

He digs into his salad as I digest how inaccurate that statement is. My dad needs to know where I am at all times. Regardless of how busy he is. I mean, I have alarms and everything.

"I also thought if I said no he'd just ask someone else." He frowns as if concerned at that thought.

He's right on that account, and to be concerned. I chew on a fry, trying to picture the coming week. "So, your free time would be spent with me?"

"It doesn't have to be every minute, but if you wanted company and a solid alibi, we could make that work." Sebastian glances at his burger, then looks down at his lap. "I'm going to use the facilities. I'll be right back."

I mull over the idea of purposely spending time with him. I'm rooming with Jess, so I'll have her for company. But she also has TA duties, and I know she's excited about attending the lectures. I did have fun with Sebastian in the greenhouse, but we'd talked for all of two seconds. And the night he monitored my party wasn't as bad as I'd thought it would be.

When he returns, I ask, "Do you do anything besides play with plants and read? I want to know what I'm committing to here." His rumbly chuckle has me stuffing a fry in my mouth to distract myself from the jolt shooting right to my core.

"I enjoy being outside and am an avid hiker. There's plenty to do on Mackinac Island, and the weather is supposed to be beautiful. I'm sure we can find some way to pass the time other than reading." He frowns, studying me. "What else do you do besides party?"

It's my turn to laugh. We really don't know a thing about each other. "I read, too. Not as much as you do, but..." We share a grin. "I also enjoy dancing." He nods encouragingly as he continues eating, and I find myself talking about the one thing I never talk about.

My mom.

She used to dance. I was enamored by the way she moved, liquid, light as air. Her basement studio is now mine, and while she never made it big time, she had hopes for me. I took any class I could get my hands on, loved every moment of it, until I hit my preteen years.

Every child goes through an awkward phase, and when I started growing out instead of up, my "career" was on the line. Mom fought for me, told me I was beautiful, that it was likely a phase, that I'd grow into myself. But I listened to my instructor. I counted every calorie and worked out even harder.

When I did grow into myself and realized Mom was right, I took a step back. This wasn't the dancing I fell in love with. This was a mindset, a rigid lifestyle that I would never be rid of if I committed to it.

So I quit.

Mom supported me fully, and we danced together to trends or videos. Right until she went into the hospital.

It took me years to go back into that studio. All I could see was Mom falling to her knees, wheezing for air she couldn't find. But eventually I danced again. It became my sanctuary, my connection to her.

"And every time I learn a new dance, I feel close to her."

"That's...that's beautiful, Calliope."

"Thanks, Sebastian." I have to clear my throat to be able to talk over the lump that's formed. "As for this week, I think I'd like to try. On one condition," I add sternly. "You're my friend when we're together. Not Dad's TA, not my babysitter, and — most important — not a spy."

His eyes soften as he pushes his glasses up his nose. "Deal." And he stretches out his hand to voluntarily shake mine.

The ease of the gesture surprises me, but it further solidifies the knowledge that I made the right choice. He doesn't flinch at my touch and his lips stay tilted up. A far cry from a month ago.

I can feel his warm fingers long after he's pulled away, and I can't help wondering what else I don't know about Sebastian Wrighting.

Chapter Six

Callie

The Sunday of our departure is gorgeous — blue skies and sunshine. Not a cloud in sight. I inhale deeply as I lean over the railing of the ferry, waiting for our voyage to get underway. I grip the metal bar tighter as a gust of wind sends us rocking and waves splash the dock.

Jess frowns at her watch. "Lyssa's going to miss the ferry."

A ping of annoyance zips through me, but I push it aside and try to keep my voice light. "I can't believe she's actually coming."

"I know!" She beams, and guilt hits me.

This is supposed to be for grad students only, and Jess was going to be my sole roomie. I'd been looking forward to some one-on-one time with my bestie. I'd planned to hide in our room as a way to escape my dad in the evenings, but now, I'll be the third wheel, sharing a room with them.

I can't begrudge them, though. Lyssa is thrilled to be coming, and Jess is thrilled at the prospect of spending more time with her girlfriend. The two of them rarely have any alone time with their tiny apartments and their roommates, and it's not like I don't like Lyssa. She's great.

"I'll, um, try to figure out a way to give you two some privacy." Jess' smile grows impossibly wider, and I glare. "Just keep it on your own bed, all right?"

She laughs. "Deal."

A screeching voice hollers from the dock, "Wait for meeeee!"

Jess laughs even harder, and I join in at the sight of Lyssa barreling down the ramp with her braids flying behind her. Her suitcase wobbles and bounces along as she runs like we're pushing away from the dock when in fact she has plenty of time. She makes it with no problem, stumbling her way toward us and collapsing against the railing.

"You still had four minutes," Jess points out.

"What?" Lyssa cries. She looks at her watch that shows it's five after one, then her mouth drops open and she glares at Jess. "You!"

"You're always late. I didn't want you to *actually* miss the ferry."

I quietly back away, not wanting to get in the middle of their lovers' spat. When I turn around and walk down the aisle, I notice Sebastian sitting on his own near the end of one bench. A book hides the lower half of his face and no one pays him any attention.

Just the way he likes it.

Fuck, he's handsome. I study him as I get closer, loving the way his silky brown hair lies so nicely and those hazel eyes framed by his black glasses. And his hands holding that thick tome. I'm a sucker for hands anyway, but his…long, nimble fingers, a little rough from all his work with plants. Even still, no dirt lingers under his nails. I bet those fingers would feel amazing if he shoved them inside—

The thought catches me so off guard I stumble over myself and can't catch my balance with the extra rocking of the boat. It sends me flailing right into the object of my naughty imagination.

I careen into Sebastian and his book tumbles to the floor. A surprised *oof* leaves him, but those strong hands catch me. I brace myself on his firm chest and end up sitting on top of his muscular thighs.

I'm in Sebastian's lap.

Shock fills me as I wait for him to get mad or throw me off.

Instead, one side of his mouth tips up. "If you wanted my attention, you could have just asked."

"I—I'm sorry," I stammer, my fingers splaying over his pecs of their own accord. Does he work out? Or is it all from lifting potting soil and caring for his roses? I shift my weight as desire courses through me.

His eyes darken, and his fingers grip my waist harder for a brief second, then the stormy look I've been expecting creeps into his gaze. His mouth tightens as his muscles grow rigid under my fingers, under my thighs. He doesn't like being touched, and here I am, sprawled over him like a sack of potatoes.

I bolt to my feet, only for another wave to throw me off balance. He keeps his hand at my waist, spreading his fingers over my entire abdomen, so close to where I want him. I risk a glance back, and I wish I hadn't. I could have gone my entire life without seeing that glower, the barriers so firmly between us as he clenches his jaw and arches an eyebrow.

Even though he hates every moment of this, he's not letting go until he knows I'm okay.

The realization has my knees wobbling, and I shove his hand aside before I make a bigger fool of myself. "Um, thanks." The ferry horn sounds, signaling that we'll be leaving and should take our seats. "Bye." I scramble away, needing to be anywhere but there.

I skid into an empty spot next to Lyssa and Jess near the front of the boat, and they both frown, silently asking what's wrong. I shake my head. No way am I getting into the tangled mess of want inside me right now, especially with a man who can't stand the thought of even laying a hand on me.

Stupid body, always wanting what it can't have. I sink lower in my seat, clenching my thighs as I stare out at Lake Michigan. I'd better make sure there's no more accidental touching this week or our brand-new attempt at friendship will be doomed from the start.

* * * *

Sebastian

I adjust my book, smooth out the crumpled page and focus on the same paragraph I've been staring at since Calliope departed. Her purple hair hovers above the tome, drawing my attention. Again.

I can still feel her on my lap, her warm thighs on mine, her rounded buttocks cradled between my legs. Her hem drove me crazy. It pressed into my leg, teasing me through the fabric of my pants because I didn't know if it was the edge of her skirt or the seam of her panties. If I'd been wearing shorts, how much of that creamy skin would I have been touching?

Her skirt rode up, and I couldn't look away from her milky thighs. Her fingers seared into my chest as I felt her heart pounding where I cradled her back. Of course my body reacted. She was there, in my arms, staring with parted lips begging me to thrust my tongue, my cock —

I'd had to reel in those thoughts, cutting them off abruptly. Then before I could say anything more, she scrambled away. And almost fell again.

But in the split second that I caught her, when my hand sprawled over her abdomen…it took everything in me not to haul her right back onto my lap. How would that have looked? I ask her to be friends, then turn around and maul her.

No wonder she couldn't wait to get away.

Focus eludes me for the rest of the short voyage, though I keep my book in front of my nose for pretense purposes. It cuts down on unnecessary conversation and gives me something to stare at besides Calliope. Except my eyes seek her out every chance they get.

I wait for her and her friends to saunter past before I lower the tome, then I let out a massive breath. This week is supposed to be about botany. Me presenting tomorrow, hearing lectures about new techniques and findings, catching up with colleagues. How am I supposed to do any of that when my thoughts are consumed by a woman with purple hair and blue eyes and a smile that steals my breath?

It's a question I have no answer to, even after I disembark. Professor Harrison catches my attention as he waits for a carriage to take him to the hotel, and he gives me a pointed look before he glances at his daughter then back to me. I dip my chin in return, acknowledging my promise.

I will keep an eye on her, even if it's for selfish reasons. Even if it distracts me to no end. After all, I gave my word.

Large wagons with bench seats await us. Each is pulled by three draft horses, saving us the trek up the hill with all our luggage. I wait for Calliope to choose a seat with Jess and Lyssa near the front, then I find a place in the back, giving my most imperious look to anyone who tries to squeeze in next to me. I end up with plenty of space for the ride.

Mackinac Island fascinates me to no end, and I drink in the quaint scenery as we lurch forward. No motorized vehicles are allowed on the island, with the exception of emergency services, of course. The main street is filled with shops, pedestrians, bicyclists, and horse-drawn carriages of various sizes.

I'll have to research draft horses next, once I finish flamingos. The massive strength of the majestic animal intrigues me, but I'd love to study them in particular context with the island. They are the muscle on which this town was built.

I also have a guidebook for the island, the book I'd been attempting to read on the ferry. I can't wait to explore some of the historical sites. The old cemeteries, divided by religion. There is even a fort, now a tourist trap, but it had been an actual stronghold during the War of 1812.

And to top it all off, we're staying in the Grand Hotel, the history of which is overwhelming. Movies have been filmed here, stars have vacationed here, and many conferences hosting myriad great minds have been held on these perfectly manicured grounds. All of it surrounded by the glorious Lake Michigan.

Once I have my bags, I go through the check-in process. My room is three-thirty-eight and supposedly overlooks the gardens, a welcome view.

"Texting every hour? Dad!"

Calliope's raised voice catches my attention as I walk toward the elevators, and I pause. Professor Harrison looks less than pleased with his daughter's outburst. I can't help making my way over.

"It's an island. What kind of trouble can I get into?" she continues, slightly quieter.

I clear my throat. "Sorry to interrupt. I wanted to clarify about spending time with Calliope. If —"

"Oh, she doesn't need to check in when you two are together." His hand clamps on my shoulder, and I immediately tense, but as usual, he doesn't notice. "I trust you."

Calliope flinches. I can't blame her, the implication that he trusts me but not his own daughter is a harsh blow. I'm at a loss for what to say, so I stand there, looking between them.

"Well," Professor Harrison says cheerily, "now that that's settled, I'm going to go find my room. Don't forget to —"

"Text you," Calliope finishes. "Yeah, Dad. Got it."

We both watch him disappear into an elevator. I'm still shocked that he would embarrass his daughter so publicly. "Calli —"

"Don't," she says, staring straight ahead. "Just..." Her shoulders sag, and she glances my way. "Please, I want to get to my room and forget about this."

I nod, sweeping my hand out for her to lead the way. We walk onto an elevator, and I push the button for the third floor, then raise an eyebrow, waiting for her to tell me her floor.

"Oh. I'm on three, also."

We stand in awkward silence until the ding sounds, and the doors open. Again, I let her go first, but that only makes things more uncomfortable when I follow on her heels.

She glances back with an annoyed glare. "Sebastian, I don't need an escort."

I sigh. "My room is three-thirty-eight."

"Oh." Her lips twitch, and she pauses until I'm walking beside her. "I'm three-thirty-six. I guess we're neighbors."

When I grin, she starts laughing, and I'm relieved to see her looking less burdened once more. We stop at our rooms.

"Calliope?"

She glances over, pausing in the open doorway.

I lift a shoulder. "You can tell your dad you're hanging out with me anytime we're both in our rooms. He'll never know the difference, and it's not really a lie since we'll be in such close proximity."

An odd mix of gratitude and frustration floods her gaze, and she dips her chin. "Thanks, Sebastian. I'll be sure to give you a heads-up." She starts to go in, but I stop her again.

"Um, you might need my number for that. Unless you want to yell through the wall."

Her tinkly laugh fills the hallway, and we exchange numbers, then she disappears into her room. I stare at her door after it closes, her friends greeting her carrying through the thin walls. Despite ending on a lighter note, a heaviness settles on my shoulders as I push into my own room.

I'm frustrated because here I am, in the lap of what was considered one of the most opulent destinations in our area, and I can't even begin to enjoy it. Instead of marveling at the fleur-de-lis wallpaper, all I can see is the hurt in Calliope's eyes. Instead of soaking in the draped canopies over the beds, all I can hear is Professor Harrison implying his daughter isn't worthy of his trust.

I toss my roller bag onto the luggage rack and stalk angrily toward the double glass doors, then throw them open. The view is beautiful, my balcony overlooking the immaculate gardens. Any other day I would be salivating over the right angle of the hedges, the riotous colors of the blooms in careful placement so pleasing to the eye.

But I can't.

A sigh escapes me as I sag against the door frame. I'm not a hasty judge of character. I don't make snap judgments in the heat of the moment, based on a whim or a feeling. It takes time for me to decide what I think about a person. Careful consideration over a compilation of evidence after meeting them at least several times. It isn't something I take lightly, and I'm rarely wrong because of the studious way I approach it. Yet here I am, wrong—not once, but twice.

Professor Harrison may be a decent teacher and botanist, but as a father he is rapidly losing favor in my opinion of him. The more I see of his daughter, the more I see our similarities when before I saw only our differences. She hides behind a wall of confidence, masked with purple hair and a nose ring. But all she really wants is to be seen for who she is.

Just like me.

I'm more than a diabetic, more than a socially awkward introvert. And she is more than the professor's daughter.

Movement on the balcony next to mine catches my eye, and the object of my thoughts emerges. Her cheeks are damp. The sunlight reflects off a single tear gliding near her chin, then she swipes a hand over her face, and it's gone.

I move out of sight, so I don't bother her, even as a wave of protectiveness sweeps over me, similar to that day in the greenhouse but stronger. Its ferocity catches me off guard. I have to clench my jaw to keep from growling, curl my fingers into fists to keep from reaching for her. She isn't mine to protect, I remind myself.

Besides, she is fierce in her own right and quite independent. Jess calls to her from the room, and she heads back inside without noticing my presence. She has friends — she doesn't need me.

I set about unpacking. My need for routine is only satisfied when my clothes are stored in the dresser drawers and my toiletry bag rests on the bathroom counter. I plug in my chargers, so they are ready when I go to bed, then my phone dings with my alarm, reminding me to eat.

The need to walk fills me. The room has no refrigerator or microwave, so I'll need to get some easy to prep snacks, and I decide to explore my options closer to town. Calliope's laughter echoes through the walls as I leave, ringing in my ears even after I've left the hotel. I don't know if I've ever been this…obsessed before. Not for a person.

Feeling quite unsettled, I pull my phone from my pocket and call Leah before I can think twice. She answers on the third ring.

"Hey, Leah, can I talk to you for a moment?"

"Oh, um, hey." A pause drags out, and she doesn't answer my question.

"Unless you're busy."

"No, it's okay." The sound of pages rustling fills the air and she sighs then asks, "What's up?"

I take her at her word, trusting that she would tell me if I was interrupting. Then I explain in halting bits about how Calliope is affecting me. I start with what really happened when she dropped off the chocolates to the day in the greenhouse, then at the party and finally today. "I talked to Shawn and Silas before I left, but…I need help, Leah. What do I do?"

Silence meets me. Not even breathing. Worry creeps along my spine, so I pull the phone back to make sure I didn't lose my connection. The seconds are still ticking away, showing we're still on call. "Leah?"

"I'm sorry, Sebastian," she bursts out. "That was a lot. Give me a minute." Then a muffled smack sounds and her voice sounds funny, as if she's not speaking into the phone. "You knew about this?"

Shawn's deeper voice echoes to me, and I grin, picturing the two of them. I'm still grinning when Shawn comes on the line. "What the hell, Seb? Throwing me under the bus like that?"

"Sorry." I chuckle. "I wasn't trying to get you into trouble. I just…I need some advice. I'm not sure how to proceed here. We're trying the friendship route, but I can't seem to stop thinking about her."

"Well, this isn't your first rodeo."

"What?" Leah exclaims, and Shawn shushes her.

"I know. But…that wasn't really a normal relationship either." I've never experienced the normal dating ritual. My previous relationship was more about exploring. More of a tryst. "What do people talk about on dates?"

"Oh, Sebastian," Leah says, my name almost a sigh. "Common interests, things you've done. Day to day activities. At the beginning, get to know each other, make sure you're a good fit."

"So…we can talk about plants?" I remember how well we coexisted in the greenhouse, how at ease she seemed.

"Well," Leah hesitates. "Some. But, don't, um, let it take over completely."

Chagrin hits me, and I know what she's referencing. "I understand."

"Make sure to let her talk too, okay, Seb?" Shawn adds.

I know how carried away I can get on a topic I'm passionate about, and I nod even though they can't see me. I stifle my sigh, wishing this weren't so complicated. Wishing I could just be myself and find someone I didn't have to hide from. "Thanks, guys." My stomach rumbles. "I'm about to have dinner, so I'll say goodbye now. But I appreciate the advice."

"Okay, Sebastian. Call us if you need anything. Love you!" Leah exclaims, light and giddy.

"Good luck," Shawn calls.

I hang up, the weight on my shoulders even heavier. The smell of bread hits me, and I inhale, looking up to find a small mom and pop sub shop. I haven't had my carb meal yet today, so I decide to try it out.

When I push open the door, the jangle of bells sounds cheerily, and I'm at ease as soon as I walk inside. It reminds me of Eat at Joe's. The décor, the tables, even the waitress looks like my favorite from Joe's, Sally. I study the menu, a chicken avocado sub catching my eye.

I order, heavy on the veggies, then eat my sub in the restaurant. Next, I wander until I find a little corner store where I stock up on protein bars and shakes as well as a few other things. Their options are limited and their prices are high, but I'd rather be prepared. I want to be well-fueled for my presentation tomorrow, and I don't have time for the kind of fancy breakfast served at the hotel.

The weight doesn't leave me as I walk back, despite the beautiful scenery. I need a distraction, and I welcome the text from Professor Harrison inviting me to a mixer with other professors and their TAs.

He may not be the best father, but I can still let him mentor me in the botany field. And his connections are stellar. I'm here to learn, after all, not to activate my love life. I need to make sure my priorities stay in order.

After a mediocre evening with tedious small talk, I welcome the relief of retreating to my room. Alone. Sleep comes quickly, and I wake refreshed and ready for my big day.

I go about my normal routine, ignoring thoughts of Calliope when she tries to steal in. After I've showered and dressed, I'm arranging my notecards when my alarm goes off, reminding me to eat. I hurry to shut it off, then a text comes in. From Calliope.

Good luck today. I'll be there, cheering you on.

Stunned, I reread the message, once, twice. I hastily type out a response, wanting to confirm because I can't believe she texted me of her own volition. Maybe her father put her up to it.

You will?

The immediate response swooshes in.

Yes! That's what friends do, silly.

I find myself smiling like an idiot at my screen. Friends, that's what we are now. I turn that idea over in my head, finding how much I like it, then another text appears.

So if you need someone to ask a particular question or just a friendly face, you can count on me.

My throat grows thick. Her offer is kind and unexpected, an olive branch to solidify this new agreement between us. And I appreciate it more than I can say.

Thank you.

The words feel inadequate, but it's the best I can manage. I set the phone down, feeling lighter already, and I don't stop smiling as I try to remember what I was doing. My eyes catch on the notecards. That's right, I was organizing them. I go back to making sure they're in the correct order, feeling confident I'm all set for my big moment.

Chapter Seven

Callie

I clap eagerly as Sebastian wraps up his lecture, smiling at the response from the crowd. I mean, there aren't any cheers or whistles, but it's a good reaction for a bunch of botanists. The crowd flocks to him as he leaves the podium.

But my smile falls when I glimpse his face. He is quite pale, and his lips are pressed together. *Is that sweat on his forehead?* My concern grows as the people surround him, and I wonder if he's having a panic attack. I elbow my way through, not caring about anything other than reaching him.

"Sebastian!" I call when I get close. He turns unfocused eyes on me, and I slip my arm through his. "Come on. You promised me lunch."

The man he was talking to glares, but I smile sweetly. "Sorry, sir. His contact information is in the pamphlet. I'm famished and can't wait another minute." Then I guide Sebastian to the hall.

Once we're in the elevator, he sags against the wall, looking worse than ever.

"Are you okay? You're not sick, are you?"

"No," he mutters, almost sounding angry. "I forgot to eat this morning." He reaches in his pocket, producing something that looks like a mint to pop into his mouth.

"A mint isn't going to solve that."

"I have food in my room, Calliope. I'll be fine once I eat."

"Good!" I retort, my tone just as short. "I'm still walking with you because you look like you're on the verge of passing out."

"I don't need a babysitter."

"Welcome to the club. Now you know how I feel every day of my life, but it hasn't stopped you from butting in at every turn. And, oh yeah, if you hadn't, I'd be dead now. So, I'm going to return the favor, no matter how much of an asshole you pretend to be. I owe you."

We glare at each other for a long moment, then the elevator dings and the doors slide open. He blinks and holds his glasses up to swipe his hand over his face. "I'm sorry."

"It's okay. Come on, let's get you some food." In his room, I find a six-pack of apple juice and hand him one, which he downs.

Then he grimaces. "I need to use the facilities."

"Okay, but if I hear a big thud I'm coming in after you."

His chuckle has me smiling, even though I'm serious. I'll break down the door if I have to. Or find someone to do it. Thankfully, he emerges a minute later, and I offer him a protein bar and some nuts.

He unwraps the bar, then takes his time chewing before he asks, "What did you mean by you owe me?"

I lift a shoulder. "You saved my life. Not exactly something a box of chocolates will repay." I shift my weight, leaning against the wall. "Not only that, you came in the night I was late for curfew, and you didn't have to. You didn't tell my dad about my party. Plus, you got me out of filing. I'm in your debt."

A furrow appears in his brow. "I didn't do those things so you could repay me, Calliope. You owe me nothing."

I blink several times, unable to comprehend. "But...we weren't even friends!" To do something and not expect a favor in return — the concept is too foreign.

He sighs, setting his food down, then he stands and walks over to lean on the wall next to me. "I appreciate you being there for me today. I'm sorry I was a jerk to you. You didn't deserve it. But I want to make one thing clear — you owe me nothing. There is no debt, no back payment for services rendered. That's not how I operate." He leans closer, waiting until I meet his hazel eyes. "Okay?"

I nod, beyond taken aback.

Then he returns to his bed and takes another bite of the bar. "Thanks again for this."

My voice still hasn't returned. My world feels like someone put it through a wringer and all at once it popped out 3D again. I don't know how to process this information.

"I'm..." He sighs, leaning forward to rest his elbows on his knees. "I'm hypoglycemic. If I forget to eat, it can be dangerous. I have alarms set, and I got distracted this morning as I was getting ready."

"By what?" I can't imagine what could be more important than eating, especially with his condition.

His cheeks turn pink. "You."

My knees nearly buckle. "Me?" Guilt hits me. *I did this to him?*

But he smiles. "I was so blown away by your support, I got thrown off."

"I'm so sorry."

"No!" He frowns. "I don't want you to be sorry. I wasn't telling you to make you feel bad. I…" He stops, pressing his lips together. "I'm not good at this. I appreciate you, Calliope. Your support just now. Your support at my speech. I haven't told anyone in the office about my condition because I don't want them to hover or worry, but I know you'll understand. So I'm trusting you with this."

"Oh." The gravity of what he's gifting me with hits, and I stumble back to sit in the nearest chair. Someone is trusting *me* with information? "Are you sure?" The voice coming out of my lips isn't mine. This sounds broken and tremulous while I'm usually confident and sure and cocky.

Sebastian smiles, chewing and swallowing before he answers. "Yes. I'm quite sure. I know I can rely on you."

The room swims before me, blurred by tears. I've never had anyone so blatantly trust me before, and I feel like I could explode with happiness. "I won't let you down," I say, my words thick.

"I know."

I scramble to my feet, needing to leave before I make a bigger fool of myself. "Are you all set? Need anything else?"

"I'm fine, Calliope. You've already helped plenty." And he pops the last bite into his mouth, then smiles. A real smile that has my knees wobbling.

I hurry out of the door with a quick "Okay, bye" and try not to collapse in the hallway. When was the last time someone truly trusted me? I have Jess and Lyssa, but they also have each other to lean on. More often than not, I'm relegated to the third wheel.

My phone dings, saving me from further introspection. It's a summons from my father. He wants me to come for a cocktail hour—no, I'm not included in the drinking—then join him and several of his professor friends for dinner at the Grand. I reread the text, sighing at the way it's worded. A demand, not a request.

He wants to show me off, or, more accurately, he wants to play the part of the doting father and me to be the dutiful daughter. I glance at the time. Three hours, enough to get ready, but barely…not for his standards.

I feel the beginnings of a headache already.

Luckily I came prepared, knowing my dad might want to parade me around, so at exactly four-fifty-seven p.m. I push the elevator button for the lobby and practice my fake smile in the mirrored walls as I descend.

The navy blue dress I chose has cap sleeves and a square neckline. The hem goes well past my knees. My pumps are sleek, not too high and close-toed, and I kept my makeup tame. Though my hair is still purple and I left the stud in my nose because I'm not changing everything for him.

My phone dings in my clutch right before the elevator stops. I glance at it, ignoring it when I see it's

Dad asking where I am. The doors slide open, and he's waiting, arms folded, with the glare I know all too well.

I give him my sweetest smile. "Hi, Dad, sorry I'm cutting it close. Wanted to make sure I looked presentable for you."

His glare softens, and inwardly I punch my fist in the air. *One point for Callie.* I savor it all the more because it will likely be one of the few I score this evening. He offers his arm, not even paying me a compliment on my outfit. I guess it's better than complaining about it, so I slip my hand onto his arm and follow him to the lounge area where his colleagues gather.

I get a virgin daiquiri, then perch on a cushioned chair near Dad as he slips seamlessly into the conversation. I know better than to speak until someone acknowledges me. Not one other student is in this circle, so I sip my drink as they all catch up.

My stomach rumbles. In all the hubbub, I never ate lunch. The realization makes me think of Sebastian, and I wonder how he's doing. I know better than to pull out my phone, though. The lecture I'd get afterward on my rudeness wouldn't be worth it.

I get asked a few mundane questions about my plans for the summer, but they lead nowhere since Dad is occupied in other conversations. Because I have no plans that don't include him. That aren't approved by him. I take another sip of my drink, allowing the icy cold to spread through my limbs and coat my body. If only to make it through this beyond boring gathering.

We finally move to the dining room and are seated at a long table covered with a white linen cloth. Umpteen pieces of silverware surround each plate and pats of butter rest in white dishes, each square stamped with the Grand Hotel's logo. I gape at the ornateness of it all.

A waiter in a full tux with gloves and a bow tie brings out a basket of rolls, so I help myself. Grabbing a pat of butter, I take a moment of satisfaction in mutilating the emblem as I smear it on my roll.

"So, Callie, what are your career aspirations?" Professor Gray always has a sneer in his voice and the worst timing. "Are you going to follow in your father's illustrious footsteps? Become a botanist?"

I fight a sigh as I set down my roll. "I'm actually studying genetics." And I stop, knowing that's as far as I'll get before Dad takes over. I pick up my roll again when he begins to speak.

"Not that Callie wouldn't make a brilliant botanist. She used to help me all the time in the greenhouse. I remember one day when..."

I tune him out. Even if I do love plants and digging in the dirt, I would never make that my career. If I gave the slightest hint of interest in that field, he'd be scheduling all my classes, getting me in with teachers he knows, making sure my paper topics were acceptable to his standards... I'd lose my only avenue of autonomy.

As it is, genetics isn't that far removed, and I can translate it to my love of plants. But I try to keep that quiet, off his radar, so to speak.

My dad is a great botanist, or was before Mom passed away. He had groundbreaking theories that shaped how scientists today view plant reproduction, but he hasn't found anything new since. Hasn't even tried. I still go to his lectures, but each one is the same as the previous, down to the tired old jokes he works in. For some reason, everyone still acts like he walks on water.

I tune back in as my dad fields questions about my future, and my salad suddenly tastes like dirt, so I push my plate away. Everyone looks at Dad as if he's a saint for taking such good care of me when all I feel is the weight of my heavy future choking me.

As soon as dessert is served, I use my headache to excuse myself. Dad's eyes narrow, and I nod, knowing I need to text him the moment I get to my room.

One more tightening of the collar on my too-short leash.

The pounding in my head has intensified to the point that I can hardly think. I might have to take one of my migraine meds if it gets much worse, or I'll have no hope of sleeping tonight.

I lean against the cool metal wall in the elevator, thankful for the quiet, and I wish the ride could go on forever. That I could keep ascending, never coming back to this dreary place of unrealistic expectations. I trudge to my room, but yelling sounds from inside.

Jess and Lyssa do this occasionally. I suppose it's normal since every couple fights, but they do it at such a high volume, and I can't deal with it. Not now. I'm wincing even through the door. Sebastian's room number catches my eye, and jealousy hits me because I just want to sleep. He's probably in there, reading a book, all quiet and snug.

I knock before I can stop myself.

A moment later, he opens the door, and I gape at his casual outfit. Bare feet, plaid pants, white T-shirt that shows off surprising muscle definition. I have the sudden urge to throw myself at him, to curl up in his lap and have him hold me until I feel better. I push it aside, attributing it to the growing pain in my head.

"Calliope?" His brow furrows in concern then his eyes widen. "You look very nice. Are you going to dinner?"

Tears spring to my eyes. In two short seconds, the man I thought was the biggest, most arrogant asshole noticed my outfit and complimented me. More than my father ever thought of doing. I shake my head, sniffing to hold back the tears, but before I can say anything, a particularly loud shout comes from my room.

He frowns. "It's even louder out here."

I nod, pressing my fingers to my temple, which is now pulsing too. "It is, and I have a terrible headache. I can't handle the noise. Are...?" I trail off, staring at the dark quiet of his room and completely second-guessing myself. I know how private he is. The last thing I want to do is intrude.

But he steps aside, holding the door wide open. "Would you like to come in?"

A fresh wave of tears threatens, but I suck in a breath instead and nod. "Thank you."

I hurry in and sink onto the bed that hasn't been used to take off my heels, then I flop onto my back with a long sigh. I quickly pull out my phone, texting my dad that I made it. I'm close enough. More shouting comes through the wall, but it's muffled to a level I can tune out.

"Can I get you anything?"

Sebastian's quiet concern makes my throat thick. "You're a lot sweeter than I thought, you know that?"

One corner of his mouth tips up. "Don't go spreading that around. You'll ruin my reputation."

I try to laugh, but the stabbing pain in my head turns the noise into a groan, and I curl onto my side.

"Calliope, what can I do?"

"I need sleep." It's the best thing for this. Hopefully, a good night's sleep will nip it in the bud, so I don't get a full-blown migraine. "My medicine would help, but quiet, dark and sleep are the best cure."

"Okay." Then he strides away.

I hear the door to the hallway open, then latch behind him as I let my eyes drift closed, unable to keep them open. A haze envelopes me, and soon several voices permeate it. Jess and Lyssa guiding me into comfier clothes, prodding me to take my medicine, calling to Sebastian that the coast is clear.

A moment later, I catch a whiff of coffee and mint before firm arms scoop me up, then I'm repositioned so my head rests on a pillow. The covers are tucked around my shoulders as the comforting voices blend together in muted tones before I drift completely off to sleep.

The next time I wake up, it's still dark. I fumble for my phone, but touch a bottle of water instead and gratefully take a long drink. When I do find my phone, it's completely charged, and the time says it's almost noon. I frown, looking again at the dark room.

My headache has dulled considerably, more of a quiet pain in the back of my skull. Much more manageable. I can't believe I slept this long, but that medicine knocks me out.

Pushing out of bed, I walk over to the windows, my lips parting when I find an extra set of blankets rigged over the curtain edges to keep out any hint of light. *Sebastian.* I told him before I crashed out that I needed my medicine, but I also needed sleep, quiet and darkness. Well, he certainly provided.

I click on the bedside lamp, thrilled when the dull light doesn't send a stabbing knife through my head. I know I'm on the upswing now. A note in Sebastian's careful handwriting tells me to keep hydrated, that my medicine is here if I need it — along with the time of my last dose — and to help myself to any of his food or drinks.

I smile at his thoroughness, then take stock of how I'm doing. My limbs still feel heavy and my head is also weighted, sure signs I'm not one hundred percent. I walk over and peek out into the dreary day. I push open the curtains anyway, wanting the little bit of light.

My stomach rumbles, reminding me how little I ate yesterday. I'm weighing my options when the door opens, but it's not Sebastian.

Jess grins at me. "Hey! You're awake." She comes in, a to-go bag in her hand.

"What are you doing here?"

"I was worried about you. So was Sebastian." She bobs her eyebrows. "He was thrilled when I offered to check on you and made sure I brought you this. In case you're hungry."

Taking the bag, I see a small container and plastic ware inside. I lift the lid to find a steaming cup of chicken noodle soup. "This smells amazing." I look up at her with a smile. "Thank you."

"No problem. I'm between lectures, and he had another one your dad wanted him to attend." She pauses, assessing me as I sit on the bed. "He seemed really concerned about you, gave me his key and everything."

I lift a spoonful of broth, blowing on it before sipping the hot liquid. "Oh, that hits the spot."

But she's staring at me, as if waiting for an explanation.

"I don't know what to tell you that you don't already know. We're friends, and friends worry about each other?"

She smirks. "Yeah, sure. That's all this is. I happen to know that man is exactly your type."

My cheeks warm, and I hurry to eat more soup, trying to wrap my head around Sebastian and his thoughtfulness. "He keeps surprising me," I admit.

"Good." She pats my leg and grins again. "Someone needs to. It looks like you're in good hands here, so I'll leave you to it." She pauses before going into the hallway. "Just remember, girl, our room is there if you need it."

"Thanks, Jess." I lift the soup. "For everything."

After she leaves, I finish the soup, warmed from more than the hot liquid. It's been a long time since anyone took care of me.

The soup makes me feel even more like myself. I notice that my bag and toiletries are in here as well and get choked up that my friends made sure I had all my things. I take a quick shower, wishing I knew when Sebastian will be back.

Once I'm clean, I eat some nuts next and read until my eyelids are too heavy, allowing myself to drift off once more. When I wake again, I feel normal. And thirsty. I help myself to an orange soda, pour myself a glass over ice from the ice bucket, then settle back on the bed. After checking my phone to make sure I haven't missed anything, I send messages to Jess and Lyssa, letting them know I'm doing better.

I debate texting Sebastian, but decide I don't want to bug him. Setting my phone on my lap, I take another drink of my pop only for my phone to buzz. I jerk, spilling soda all down my chin, neck and chest.

I sit there for a moment, annoyed with myself, but at least it all got on me and not the bed. Since my shirt is already wet, I wipe the dripping can with the hem, then set the pop on the night stand and hop to my feet to go change. I whip off the wet shirt, dabbing my chest before I toss it aside to wash later.

For now, though, I need something else to wear. At least my bra isn't too wet. I dig through my suitcase, wanting another comfy shirt.

The hallway door unlatches and in walks Sebastian. I freeze. Our eyes lock as he steps in, letting the door swing shut behind him. I swallow at the way his lips part, at how his eyes darken, at his breath hitching.

I affect him?

I'm upright before I know it, unable to help myself. I've never been shy, and I can't help craving Sebastian's reaction. The way he is always so controlled grates on me. How he didn't even glance at me when I changed in the car. How he barely noticed when I sat on his lap.

I want his attention.

He clears his throat, not stepping further into the room. "I take it you're feeling better."

"Yes. Thank you for, um…" I gesture to the unmade bed I slept in. "For getting my friends, my meds. For the food. For making the room extra dark." My words come out in a breathless rush as I stare at him, waiting for…I don't know what.

"You're welcome." His gaze drops, lingering on my chest, and heat bursts to life within me. "I thought they brought over your clothes."

"Oh, they did. I spilled soda on myself. Was in the middle of changing when you…" Pure longing washes over his face, stealing my breath, and I wrap my arm around my waist, clamping my hand onto my opposite wrist to hold me in place.

"Will you please put a shirt on?" he asks in a strangled voice as he looks away.

The rejection hits me right in the stomach. The idea that Sebastian could ever want someone like me is ridiculous. Of course he reacted, but it was because he was caught off guard by a pair of tits in his bedroom. I fumble through my suitcase as humiliated tears sting my eyes.

I'll never be good enough for anyone.

Each movement is sharp as I yank a T-shirt over my head, then thrust my arms through the holes and tug the hem down to cover my stomach. But I don't stop there. I begin packing. I don't belong here, intruding on Sebastian's space when I'm so obviously not wanted.

"Calliope?" He crouches next to me. Not touching, but hovering with that furrowed concern evident in his brow. "What happened? Did…did I do something?"

"No, Sebastian," I bite out. "It's not you. It's obviously me. I need to go before I waste any more of your precious time."

But he rests a hand on my arm, voluntarily touching me for the first time. I still my movements as I stare at his fingers on my skin. Heat blooms in me, a star exploding in my chest at the gesture.

"I didn't ask you to leave."

"Not with words," I whisper.

His frown deepens, and he stands, then crosses his arms. "Just why do you think I asked you to put on a shirt?"

My cheeks flame as I look at my suitcase. "Please don't make me say it."

He grips my wrist, tugging lightly until I get to my feet. His hazel eyes study me, his throat bobs, and his fingers send sparks up my arm. "You think I can't stand you, even still."

Hearing the words aloud is a knife to my gut, and I realize how much I want them not to be true. "You've been more than kind, and a great friend, Sebastian. It's not your fault you don't find me — "

"Attractive?" The word bursts from him, full of incredulity. He shakes his head. "I promise it's not that. Quite the opposite, in fact."

Hope peeks around the jaded corner of my heart before I can scold her. His hand circles my wrist, and his thumb rests against my pulse, which beats wildly.

"Calliope, I hate not being in control. I'm not a person to give in to baser needs very often, but you..." His thumb brushes over that sensitive place on the inner part of my wrist. "I never know what to expect from you. Or how I'll react. I haven't been in control since the day I first laid eyes on you, this little purple-haired tornado who demanded attention."

I gape, feeling as if the slightest puff of wind will knock me over.

He lets go, stepping back and taking a deep breath. "This is overwhelming for me on many levels. Though, I'd like it if you would stay, and not just for me." He grins, stealing what little breath I have left. "Jess and Lyssa have definitely made up, and I'm sure they would appreciate the privacy."

"You...want me to stay?"

He nods, a hint of pink tinging his cheeks.

I can't help teasing. "As long as I keep my shirt on, right?"

He chuckles, hiding a murmur of words. I can't be sure, but they sound an awful lot like "for now", and that sliver of hope rises within me.

Chapter Eight

Sebastian

I can't believe I told her the stark truth like that, just laid myself out to be vulnerable and exposed. But she'd looked so upset and in her head. I had to do something. Silence hung between us as we walked down the hill to the little sub shop I suggested. She wanted to get out of the hotel, get some fresh air, so I mentioned that I knew a place.

Now neither of us has spoken in five minutes.

Animal facts race around my mind, pummeling my self-control as I try to hold them in. I remember Leah's advice, and I don't want to overwhelm Calliope, not on the heels of my confession. Not with her having a rough day already. But that's all I can think of, so I stay quiet.

Finally a different topic comes to mind, and I blurt out my question, "Do you get headaches often?" I immediately wonder if that was too forward or personal and I chide myself, but it's already hanging between us.

She lifts a shoulder. "They happen. Headaches more frequently, but once in a while they become migraines, and I'm out for a full day or two."

I frown, trying to imagine a level of pain so intense it becomes that debilitating. "That sounds terrible."

Her sunny smile makes an appearance, shining right at me. "Which is why I'm so grateful for everything you did. Today could have been much worse."

I can't help smiling back, my lips tilting up without me telling them to. I like seeing her happy. It satisfies this need inside my chest that I've never felt before and creates a fullness that makes me...content. "Good. I'm glad it wasn't worse. I didn't like seeing you in pain." Again, the moment the words are out, I wish I could take them back.

But her expression softens. "I know what you mean," is all she says.

Warmth spreads through me as I remember her herding me to my room after my speech and how grumpy I was with her. But she took care of me despite it. Is she saying it wasn't completely because she thought she owed me?

I hope so.

The delicious smell from the sub shop wafts toward us, and I watch her chest rise as she inhales. A flash of her pulses in my mind, shirtless, standing before me with those too blue eyes and that turbulent storm of emotions swirling within them. But I shove it away, then open the door.

I get the same thing I had yesterday, ordering while she peruses the menu. She gets a chicken wrap and a side of fries, and I pay for both of us. I excuse myself to take my insulin, then come back in time for our food. We carry our trays to a booth, sliding in across from one another.

"So," she says, "how many more lectures are you planning to attend this week?"

My schedule for this conference is fairly light. I came along more for the scenery and at Professor Harrison's request, even before I knew he wanted me to babysit. Though now I'm doubly glad I came. "I'll attend your father's lecture tomorrow morning, but Wednesday is free. I'll have to review the rest of the week because there were several lectures I wanted to sit in on."

She nods, finishing chewing before she speaks. "You mentioned hiking. Would you want to hang out tomorrow after Dad's lecture? Do some exploring?"

Disbelief courses through me. Between our awkward silence on the walk and my blurting out personal questions, I wouldn't have been surprised if she wanted to spend the rest of the conference in her room, away from me. But here she is, requesting to do one of my favorite activities.

I nod eagerly. "I'd love to."

It gives us something to talk about, keeping me away from my boring animal facts as we plan our sightseeing for the next day. The air between us is more comfortable on the return, but it changes again when we enter the hotel room.

I hesitate after we get inside. My social battery is running low and I need a moment to recharge.

"You okay?" she asks, setting down her purse.

I sigh. *How truthful should I be? At what point will my honesty send her running for the hills?* "I'm a little worn out and, um, I'm hoping you don't mind if I read for a while." I lift a shoulder. "Being with people, even those

I'm comfortable with, and having to talk or respond is like being in the 'on' position, and I can only do that for so long."

A slight frown crinkles her forehead, and I realize how my words sounded. A hint of panic hits me, that she might leave, and to my astonishment, I don't want that either.

"Not that I need to be completely alone." The words tumble from me, rolling off my tongue before I can assess what I'm saying. "You're welcome to stay...if you don't mind being ignored for a while."

An understanding smile tips her lips and her eyes dance as she walks over to pick up a book of her own. "It's perfect, actually. I left off at a good part, and I need to see what happens."

"You...you don't mind just reading with me?"

She shakes her head, her smile never dimming. "I'm gonna text Dad that I'm in for the night, and go change into my comfies, then we can read away."

I'm still dumbfounded when she returns from the bathroom in a hooded sweatshirt and sweatpants that hug her ankles. I follow her lead, slipping into the bathroom to change into my plaid pants and T-shirt. When I emerge, she's curled up in the extra bed, and I can't help the chuckle that escapes me.

She lowers her book, tilting her head. "What?"

"It's just..." I gesture between us. "If I had ever been asked to describe a night in a hotel room with Calliope Harrison, this is not what I would have pictured."

Her eyebrows shoot up. "And what would you have said?"

"Honestly?" At her nod, I tell her the truth. "Well, I would have imagined you to prefer lingerie." Her lips twitch, and I smirk, then continue, "And you wouldn't have been reading. More like, blaring outrageous music and begging me to dance with you."

She tips her head back and laughs. "Don't worry, I'm saving all my seduction techniques for later." At my raised eyebrows and instant panic, she laughs again. "I'm kidding, Sebastian. I have no plans to seduce you, so you're safe from all my schemes."

A hint of disappointment pricks me at her declaration. I try to push the unwanted feeling aside, but my mind breaks free of my hold, running rampant with the word *seduce.* The image of her now, carefree and at ease, relaxed in the bed next to me, overlays with the future. With her, wearing less, tugging at my wrist, wanting me to dance. A jolt of pure desire shoots straight to my groin, and I clear my throat, discomfited with the reaction she elicits from me.

But I have the perfect thing to calm me down.

I prop the pillows against the headboard exactly the way I like — one lengthwise, one vertical, then a third lengthwise in front. After I settle on the bed, I bring my knees up and rest my book against my thighs. Soon I'm engrossed with the rich history of Mackinac Island, and my book comes to an end before I'm ready.

Setting the completed tome on the bed, I stare at the wall, absorbing the information before I retrieve my other book. About flamingos.

"Look at you go," Calliope murmurs sleepily, tilting her head to look at me. "A two-book night, huh?"

I laugh with a sheepish shrug. "I guess so."

She yawns and stretches. "I don't think I'll make it much longer, but I do want to finish my chapter."

I hesitate once I've settled back into bed, unused to having to worry about disturbing someone else. "Do you want me to be done? Turn out the lights?"

"No, you're fine."

Taking her at her word, I delve into my book, but I glance over at my new roommate every so often. She must be tired because soon enough the book is sliding out of her hands, and her head lolls to one side. I can't help smiling at the picture she paints.

I tuck my bookmark into place, then cross over to take care of her book. I peek, shaking my head when I find she's two pages shy of the chapter's end. *So close.* I murmur that she needs to scoot down, and she readily obeys as I lift the covers.

But I don't move after she's settled in. I stand there for a long moment, letting my eyes trace the curve of her cheek and nose, the plump fullness of her lips. She's here in my room, trusting me with her safety and well-being.

I know her father keeps close tabs on her, know she probably finds it easier since she doesn't have to text him when she's with me. Jess and Lyssa had promised to cover for her when she had her headache, in case her phone showed she wasn't quite in her own room. But we're so close, I doubt he could tell the difference.

I can always tell him the truth and say she fell asleep reading. Hopefully, it doesn't come to that. The need for sleep weighs on me, so I brush my teeth then climb into bed and turn out the light, knowing Calliope will sleep better with it off. I always do.

* * * *

The next morning, I've almost finished my routine. Dressed, showered, and insulin administered, I've just polished off one of the protein drinks. I can't wait to brush my teeth to get the taste out of my mouth. It reminds me of chalk. Not that I've eaten chalk, but if I had to name a flavor, that would be it.

Emerging from the bathroom, I hear a moan. Calliope is still sleeping, so I rush over, hoping she's not having a nightmare. Then my name escapes her lips in a longing tone, freezing me on the spot.

My cock hardens instantly at the pure lust in her voice, and she moans again. I stare at her in horror, unable to let this continue. We're supposed to go to her father's lecture together, and I can't show up in front of my colleagues with the echoes of her moans in my head or be hiding an erection in my pants.

I touch her shoulder, saying her name gently, then with more force. She bolts upright, looking around with wide eyes, and I try to reassure her with a smile. "I didn't want you to miss the lecture," I say.

She glances at the phone. "Oh, shit." She looks me over. "Are you, um, done in the bathroom?"

"It's all yours."

Tearing from the bed, she grabs her clothes and flies into the bathroom. The door slams shut behind her as the water starts going. I lie back on the bed with a groan because my imagination starts up, picturing her behind that door. Will she touch herself? Was the dream invigorating enough that she needs to relieve the ache?

I can't take this torture, so I grab my book on flamingos, then stomp onto the balcony where I read in peace. Whenever an image of Calliope swims before me, I shove it aside and focus on the page.

"Flamingos, huh?" she says, startling me. I look up to find her looking damp and beyond appealing, but she just smiles. "Ready when you are."

Words stick in my throat because, at the moment, I feel anything but.

* * * *

Sitting together in the lecture hall, I'm wholly unprepared for Calliope next to me. Professor Harrison drones on with his familiar speech that I've memorized, but I can't focus on anything but Calliope's shorts, riding up her thigh. All that creamy skin exposed...would she feel as silky as she looks?

I realize I'm staring. When I move to distract myself, my program drifts off my lap to the floor. I bend to retrieve it, and I graze my knuckles against her thigh on the way back up. Her sharp intake of breath has my muscles locking, unsure if it was a good thing, or if she's upset with me for the accidental liberty. But a moment later, she shifts in her seat, moving her hips until her thigh touches mine.

And she stays that way.

I'm still rigid from shock, and I notice her sidelong look of trepidation. I want to reassure her I'm all right, so I lean down as I press my leg to hers. Then I quietly say Professor Harrison's joke at the same time he does, "What did one hungry plant say to the other?"

Her lips twitch, and she whispers the punch line with me. "I could use a light snack."

We sit like that in perfect harmony as the minutes tick by until he's finished. Once he opens the floor, the questions flood in. The questions are the reason I attend, because they are always different.

When a booming voice asks a question behind us, Calliope turns, her breasts brushing my arm. She freezes at the same time I do, assessing me. My whole body shifts to red alert, knowing I'm approaching my limit of self-control. I quickly lean away, needing the space as panic nudges me.

It blares at the edges of my vision. I can't lose my carefully crafted control, not here, surrounded by colleagues and professionals. Calliope moves until she no longer touches me, though disappointment wafts off her. After a long moment, she meets my unwavering gaze, registering how close I am to becoming unhinged.

Her eyes widen, then she reaches over to rest her hand on my arm. I watch her draw an exaggerated breath, feel her tapping her finger as she counts the beats. *One, two, three, four.* She doesn't move, holding her breath. *One, two.* Her chest deflates with an exhale, and she purses her lips slightly. *One, two, three, four.*

I find myself mimicking her, using the steady tap of her fingers to measure each breath until the panic dissipates and my mind is clear. I marvel at the simplicity of the strategy, smiling when I fully recover. "Thank you."

But my whisper is lost in the thunderous applause breaking out around us. The lecture is over. Calliope moves completely away from my space, and I feel bereft without any part of me touching her. A foreign notion, indeed.

As we step out into the beautiful day, I adjust my backpack and breathe the fresh air. The sun is shining, the sky blue, and the temperature in the mid-seventies. Perfect for a hike. I'm so busy soaking it in that Calliope's quiet question startles me.

"So, what'd I miss yesterday? I assume you went to a lecture or two while I was sleeping off my headache."

I deliberate how much detail she wants. I start in hesitating bits, telling her about one I attended on fertilization and plant nutrition, but her eager smile stays in place, so I relax. Her eyes never get the glazed look I keep anticipating, even when I go into my own thoughts about the new techniques.

When I'm finished, we walk in silence for a few steps before she asks, "What's up with you not thinking I'm interested in your work?" She frowns. "Or in anything you do, for that matter. What gives?"

I focus on the sidewalk as I try to decipher the best way to answer the question. "Growing up, people would assume I played basketball because of my height. Sports never interested me, so I switched the subject to things I actually enjoyed – plants, animals." I pause and shrug. "And I got picked on. A lot. My brother Shawn always defended me, but eventually I learned what was socially acceptable. Most people would be bored to tears hearing my thoughts on a lecture."

"What about your family?" she says indignantly. "What about that girl that comes to visit you at work, the one I met at Dean's party? They don't care about your interests?"

I blink at her exuberance, surprised she cares so much. "You mean Leah? She listens better than most, but I know it's just to placate me. My brothers, well... Silas has the attention span of a gnat unless you have curves and dark hair."

She laughs, making me grin as well.

"Steven is several years older than me, and we've never been particularly close." My smile falters as I admit, "I don't think he understands me at all."

"I'm sorry," she whispers.

"It is what it is." I hurry to add, "They all love me and have supported me through plenty of tough times. We're family. If it makes me happy, they encourage me in the ways they know how, and that's good enough."

A pinched look crosses her face, and I'm pricked with guilt. Even if my family doesn't understand me, they support me, but Calliope...she doesn't have anything like that. I open my mouth to say something, but she changes the subject.

"So, this Leah...is she family?"

I shake my head as a quiet laugh escapes me. "Not blood-related. We dated for several months, but we've always been better friends. Although she understands me the best out of all of my family."

I smile, thinking fondly of my friend, until I realize Calliope is staring at me with a tight expression. The sub shop isn't far, so I stride ahead to open the door, hoping I didn't say something I shouldn't have. She gives me another assessing look, but doesn't say anything more before walking over to peruse the menu.

My order hasn't changed, so I put it in then wait for her. She gets a three-meat sub with a side salad. I briefly imagine what that would be like, trying a new meal every day, but it's easier to stick with one thing. Not only do I know I enjoy it, I also know exactly how much insulin I need.

I excuse myself to go to the bathroom where I give myself a quick injection for the meal, then return in time to get my food. We sit in the same corner booth, with the window facing the street. Per the rules of conversation, it's my turn to find a topic.

"So, tell me more about dancing. What types have you done?"

Her face lights up as if I asked the perfect question. I sit back and enjoy my food as she tells me about her various dances and which she prefers.

She tilts her head. "You know, I've taught dance too. And I bet you're the type who would rather not dance."

I fight the urge to wrinkle my nose. "How'd you know?"

She just laughs. "I've met quite a few people in my classes. It comes with the territory." Leaning forward, she whispers conspiratorially, "It's not that bad once you get started. It's not as chaotic as you'd think."

My mouth drops open at the way she reads my thoughts. I've always felt out of place dancing, that the floor and the movements were pure chaos, unable to be controlled. My face feels warm, and I shift in my seat, uncomfortable with how deep in my head she is.

Again, she reads me, leaning back into her own space. "So, your second book last night…flamingos?"

Even more uncomfortable, I set my sub down and nod. I don't want to be over-exuberant, don't want to ruin this.

"Oh, neat. What's the most fascinating thing you've learned about them?"

I peek at her, surprised to find her expression as interested as her tone. The fact that immediately sprang to mind tumbles out of my mouth. "Did you know they're not really pink?"

She leans forward again, eyes bright and shining with eagerness as she shakes her head—the very definition of interested.

"A flamingo's main diet is shrimp and algae. The same pigment that colors carrots or tomatoes is found in the algae, plus the shrimp also eat the algae." The words tumble out as I let myself relax as she keeps listening. "So, the flamingos get a double dose of it. Their body metabolizes the pigment, and it stains their feathers in the process."

"I had no idea. What else?"

"They actually aren't even all pink. Depending on their location, their hue differs. For example, in the Caribbean, they're often bright red or even orange. When they molt, their feathers come in grayish or white." I pause, making sure I still have her attention as I decide what other facts I want to tell. "They're also monogamous, and only lay about one egg a year."

As she finishes chewing, she frowns and tilts her head. "Why do they stand on one leg?"

"To conserve body heat."

"Really? That's...not nearly as fantastic as I thought it'd be."

We both grin before we finish our food. Hope wells within me, that maybe I can be myself and not have to hide my interests or awkward parts. She hasn't kicked me out so far, and seems genuinely interested in all my facts.

"Where do you want to go first?" I ask.

"I love Arch Rock. Ooh and Skull Cave!" She raises her eyebrows. "Have you been here before?"

I shake my head.

"Well, you're in for a treat." She pulls up the map on her phone and screenshots it, an intelligent foresight in case we don't have service out there.

Friendly silence hangs between us as we meander along the main thoroughfare of the quaint town. The air is filled with sounds unlike any city I've been to — bustling people, the steady clip-clop as a horse-drawn carriage passes, or bikes dodging through the crowd. All the storefronts are absolutely pristine, complete with covered porches and awnings.

I stop to look in the window of one of the many fudge shops, fascinated by an employee scooping the liquid fudge with a wide silver paddle on a marble counter. "Did you know that those tables weigh seven hundred and fifty pounds?" I can't help saying, transfixed by the man's rhythm.

"I had no idea." We watch for another minute, then, as we resume our strolling, she asks, "How do you remember all this?"

"I have a photographic memory."

"Ah." She gives me a sidelong glance. "So, you're saying we should never play Trivial Pursuit."

I can't help smirking in the face of her teasing. "Not if you want to win."

Chapter Nine

Callie

As we leave the main thoroughfare, the shops become scarcer. The sound of waves lapping the shore grows stronger as we round a bend along the outer edge of the island, giving us a beautiful view of Lake Michigan. I grin at the ferry skimming its surface. The water is a deep blue, the sky like a robin's egg, and there isn't a cloud in the sky. What a perfect day.

The walk is less than a mile. The lake hovers to our right while the bluffs on our left grow ever taller. Finally, the arch comes into view. It's high above the lake, a huge limestone archway carved out of the bluff. I pull out my phone to snap pictures.

Sebastian shields his eyes with his hand as he looks at it. "Wow, that is impressive. Did you know that it's almost fifteen stories tall and over fifty feet wide?"

"What else?" I remember reading a blurb about it the last time I was here, but that was eight years ago.

The year before Mom passed away. I hold up my hand before he answers. "Do you want to go to the top?" A steep staircase allows tourists to climb the bluff rather than scaling the rocks.

"Sure."

"Tell me while we climb." We share a quick smile before heading toward the staircase. I take the lead, and he begins speaking.

"The arch is made of a type of limestone called breccia, which is rare in this area. It took thousands of years to form." He continues to talk about the importance the Native Americans placed on the landmark, as well as the legends surrounding how the arch came into existence.

By the time we reach the top, my calves ache and my thighs burn. I grab my water bottle from my bag to take a refreshing swig between gulps of air while Sebastian is barely huffing.

"I guess you were serious when you said you enjoy hiking." When he just grins, I smile back. "Thanks for telling me about the arch. It took my mind off the stairs."

His "You're welcome" is so quiet the breeze nearly carries it away.

A sidewalk with railings on both sides juts out near the bluff, and we meander along it. We take our time wandering around the lookout area, snapping more pictures. I soak in the sun, the rhythm of the waves, the gentle breeze.

After a while, I glance at Sebastian, surprised to find we've passed the last several minutes in completely comfortable silence, and not for the first time today. It's rare to find a person I'm okay being quiet with. Being still is not my first choice, but certain people allow me to relax enough that I can take a minute. My mom made me feel like that, and so does Jess.

Feeling a bit off balance at this new discovery, I ask, "Ready to walk more?"

He nods. We follow the trail and the signs inland to another rock formation called Skull Cave. When we get to it, I lean against the railing. The gray limestone is cut out at the bottom, leaving a gaping hole.

The dark opening seems foreboding, and I repress a shudder. "I always like visiting this place, but it kind of gives me the creeps."

"Well, it is a Native American burial ground." When I gape, he chuckles. "A fur trader hid here during a Native American uprising and his account of staying in the cave is truly frightening."

I wrinkle my nose. "No thanks."

"You don't enjoy being scared for entertainment?" There's no judgment in his tone, only curiosity.

I adamantly shake my head. "There are enough lighthearted stories, books and movies out there that I can never read them all. Why waste my time being scared on purpose?"

His assessing stare weighs on me. As if he's seeing another of my facets and doesn't quite know what to do with it.

"An interesting perspective."

Our explorations take several hours. My stomach growls as we walk back to the main part of town. I'm more than ready for dinner. "Want to eat before we go back to the hotel?"

"Sure. I could go for another sub."

I gently touch his arm, so he looks at me as I stop walking. "Is that your favorite food or something?"

His cheeks flush, and he dips his chin. "No."

"Then why do we need to eat subs again?" I'm curious, genuinely wanting to know his reasoning.

"Um..." He sighs, shifting his weight. "I have a difficult time trying new things. Once I find a place or meal I like, I tend to stick with it."

His words fill a gap in my understanding of him. A big piece clunks into place as I comprehend the restrictions he places on himself, and I know the weight of those short tethers. Maybe I can free him of them or stretch them. At least a little.

"What's your favorite meal?"

He scrunches his brow. "Where?"

I shake my head, not allowing him to dodge the question like that. "If you had a personal chef and could ask them to cook you anything, right at this very moment, what would it be?"

A moment of hesitation hangs between us before he speaks. "Steak. A big, juicy, melt-in-your-mouth steak with onions and mushrooms. And a green veggie. I could demolish a plate of asparagus or green beans."

I pull out my phone to search for the nearest place to eat steak. The Pink Pony looks adorable and is near the top of the list of recommendations, so I string together a plan on the spot. "Come to dinner with me tonight. My treat, my choice. And I'll take you to the butterfly house tomorrow."

"Why would I want to go to the butterfly house?"

Taken aback, I blink. "You spouted butterfly facts when you took me home after Silas ran out of gas. Don't you like butterflies?"

"Well...yes." He draws out the words.

"Good. And if they have butterflies, imagine the different plants they have to attract them."

His lips part, but he says nothing as trepidation and awe twine in his eyes.

"Sebastian." I reach over to take his hand, clasping my other one on top of his. "Let's go have a steak. Let's take a chance. I'll be right there with you, and if we don't like it, we can leave." I lock onto his nervous gaze. "Please?"

He searches me for a long moment, then his throat bobs as he swallows. "Okay." He pushes his glasses up on his nose.

I can hardly believe he agreed. "Really?"

He pulls back his shoulders, making him seem even taller. "*If* we can do the butterfly house tomorrow."

"Deal." I squeeze his hand between mine until he clears his throat.

"Where is this steak place?"

"It's called the Pink Pony." I move my top hand off his, keeping our other hands joined as I tug him in the right direction. "Come on."

I'm beyond thrilled when, even after he falls into step, he doesn't pull away.

Once we've arrived at the restaurant, we stand in line, waiting for the host to seat us. I take in the riotous shades of pink that blare from every side. The employees all wear pink shirts with the logo on them. The ceiling itself is pink. Booths, accents, even the top of the bar — pink.

When I spin around, I notice the disconcerting artwork above the bar. The three female horses are doing a can-can, only wearing garters while the male horse is fully clothed. *Hmm.* I look away to the taps behind the bar, all completely backlit in neon pink.

Maybe this is a little much. I open my mouth to change my mind, but it's our turn. Sebastian still holds my hand, as if trusting me to lead.

"Just the two of us," I say.

The host's expression never changes as he flits through his tablet. "Do you have a preference for indoor or outdoor?"

I glance at Sebastian who doesn't respond. "Whatever is open."

The host nods. "I think I have something near the bar. Let me double-check." And he winds through the tables to disappear into another room.

I squeeze Sebastian's hand, feeling the tension in his grip. His arm is rigid between us. Luckily the host returns quickly, picking up two menus and silverware before gesturing for us to follow him. We walk past the bar, turning left down a narrow walkway and duck through a door into a wholly different atmosphere.

The most immediate difference is the quiet, relaxing me in an instant. I gape at the stamped tin ceiling. It and the trim are all the purest white, absolutely pristine. We walk by yet another bar, this one small with a marbled gray top. The bartender places a white plastic cup over a shaker, and I gasp when he shakes it because the cup changes to a bright, hot pink, making the navy-blue pony stand out.

The host leads us past the dark wooden tables and high-tops to a partial booth with two chairs near the window. I look out of the window at the outdoor seating into the harbor beyond where a large passenger vessel bobs, the name *Ocean Voyager* stark on her side.

"Is this okay?" the host asks.

I glance once more at Sebastian who meekly slides into the navy-blue padded booth. He doesn't protest, so I nod and say thank you. The host disappears, and I slip into my padded chair across from Sebastian. His back is ramrod straight, making the expression "stiff as a board" hover in my mind.

I glance over the menu, but he doesn't even reach for his. "Sebastian?" I wait for him to look at me. "What are you so worried about? What makes this so difficult for you?" I just want to understand.

"Not one thing is familiar in this place." He lets out a whoosh of breath. "Eating should be comfortable, easy. But I can't relax when I'm trying to process so many new sights and smells and sounds. It's overwhelming."

My forehead crinkles as I try to comprehend. "But when you gave your talk the other day…that was new, right? New faces, new venue."

"My words were familiar. I knew many of the people in the audience, and giving speeches is familiar in that it's always unnerving. I expect to be uncomfortable…so I guess there's a comfort in actually feeling it."

I nibble on my lip. "Well, I'm familiar. You've got me." An idea pops into my head. "I could sit by you, if you want. If you think it would help." I grin, trying to put him even more at ease. "I swear it's not a seduction technique."

One corner of his mouth twitches, then stays ticked up. "Yes, please."

The quiet request sends surprised delight shooting through me. I eagerly slide in next to him, unable to contain my smile. I hesitate from sidling against him, though, unsure of how much comfort he wants, not wanting a repeat of the panic at the lecture this morning.

But the moments before crossing that line were nice, so I slowly move my knee until it brushes his. His muscles bunch at first, then relax after a few seconds.

"I don't know how much space you need, but I'm here," I say softly.

His response is to shift closer until our legs press together from knee to hip, and his shoulders sag ever so slightly. The waitress comes over to introduce herself and get our drinks. We both order water, then I open my menu again, propping it between me and Sebastian.

"They have filet mignon that comes with asparagus," I point out.

There are actually several options — surf and turf, steak by itself, steak and risotto. His shoulder brushes mine while he looks it over, and I get a whiff of coffee and mint. I inhale again.

"Are you sniffing me?"

"Yep," I say lightly. "You smell like minty coffee."

He stares for a second before he lets out a startled chuckle and relaxes even more. "I suppose that's better than body odor."

"Definitely." We share a grin. "What are you going to get?"

"The filet mignon with the asparagus," he says, then cocks his head. "You?"

"Oh, you're going to be delighted you had me come over here." I pause for effect. "I'm thinking of getting the ribs, and I'm not scared to make a mess."

Amusement dances in his eyes. "As long as the mess stays on you..."

"Didn't I tell you? It's a new seduction technique I've been toying with — secondhand sauce."

His rumbly laugh vibrates through me where our shoulders rest together, and I study the menu again. "But this Boursin chicken sounds amazing, too." A crusted chicken breast stuffed with a Boursin cheese and served with roasted red pepper sauce, Parmesan mashed potatoes, and seasonal veggies.

"Maybe that's the safer option."

I fake a glare. "Are you saying I'm saucy enough?"

He shakes his head as the waitress returns with water. She takes our orders, nodding when I order the chicken.

"Good choice." She nods, then hurries off.

"Thank you, Calliope," Sebastian breathes when she's gone. When I stiffen at my name in its entirety, he narrows his eyes, assessing me. "Why do you balk when I use your full name?"

I wrinkle my nose, staring at the table. "Dad only says my whole name when I'm in trouble. I don't like it."

Sebastian has said it plenty and I should be used to it by now, but it still catches me off guard at times, since everyone else calls me Callie. He doesn't say anything for several long moments. When I glance up, I'm startled at the tenderness in his gaze.

"Maybe if I say it enough, it'll erase those memories, and you'll finally hear how beautiful it is."

The sweet words warm me heart and soul, and my cheeks go hot.

He reaches over to take my hand in his. "I was going to say thank you for not judging me. For working so hard to put me at ease. I really appreciate it."

I squeeze his hand. "I know how it feels to be judged. Most people only see my purple hair and nose ring, or they know me because of my dad and make assumptions based on that." I shrug. "It's not hard to give someone compassion, or at least the benefit of the doubt."

His thumb glides back and forth over mine, but he doesn't say anything further on the subject. Instead, he switches over to more facts about Mackinac Island, and I listen intently until our food arrives. He removes his hand, and disappointment shoots through me at the absence of his touch, but I'm distracted by the beautiful plate slid under my nose.

My mouth waters as I take it all in. The delicately crusted chicken breast leans on top of mashed potatoes sculpted to look like a pineapple, complete with a tuft of rosemary for the stem. Thinly sliced squash and pepper make a colorful side dish, with red pepper sauce sprawling over the other half of the plate to complete the aesthetic. I can't wait to dig in.

Sebastian checks his steak, a perfect medium pink, then takes a bite and hums. "You should try this." He cuts a piece and offers me his fork, shocking me to no end. "Why are you looking at me like that?"

I lift one shoulder. "You just seem like the type that would shy away from sharing food." I pop the piece into my mouth, the steak nearly melting on my tongue. "Wow, that *is* good."

He takes his fork back. "I have three brothers. Believe me, I know how to share." He pauses, shaking his head. "Leah, on the other hand..."

I listen to more of his stories about her, prodding for more information on this woman who is so close to him. They grew up together, since their parents are good friends. She's an only child and is dating one of his other brothers, Shawn.

"Wait," I interrupt, setting down my fork as I frown. "I thought you said you'd dated her."

"I did." When I gape, he laughs again, launching into a tale about the complications of her and Shawn getting together.

"Wow, I can't imagine." I study him. "And you were okay with that?"

A smug smile tips his lips as he nods. "I helped them acknowledge their feelings. They're perfect for each other."

"Botanist, walking encyclopedia, amazing speaker..." I pretend to make a list on my hand. "And matchmaker. Got it."

I cut into my chicken, loving the way the cheesy stuffing spills out from the side. Eagerly, I take a bite, somehow managing to get some on my cheek. I wasn't lying when I said I didn't mind being messy, but I don't need to bathe in the stuff.

"You thought you were safe because I ordered chicken." I pucker my lips in Sebastian's direction, taking a chance with teasing him this way. "Kiss?"

His eyes widen slightly, his gaze dipping to my mouth, but he doesn't retreat or pull away—a win in my book. He shakes his head, smiling while I grab a napkin. The rest of our meal continues in the same lighthearted vein, and I feel absolutely effervescent from how much I enjoy our time.

Chapter Ten

Callie

After dinner, we explore the town for a while. The plastic bag with our recently purchased snacks dangles from my wrist as we walk toward the hotel, but my gaze is drawn to his strong profile. Not long ago, I was annoyed at the very sight of him.

Who knew under that awkward exterior and arrogant manner lurked a sweet, insightful guy? I linger on his lips, my joke from dinner replaying in my mind, and I imagine what a kiss from him would feel like. A thrill darts through me at the idea.

He glances over, then his eyes widen, and he grabs my hand, yanking me to his side. I nearly stumble at the sharp motion, catching myself on his firm torso. When I frown, he nods at a pile of horse manure right in the path I'd been on.

"Maybe you should stop staring at me and focus on walking." He smirks.

My cheeks go hot, but I raise my chin. "Maybe I was trying out that seduction plan." I splay my fingers over his defined chest, and to my delight, his breath hitches. "I win."

His throat bobs as he swallows. Tension ratchets up between us, and I expect him to move away, but to my surprise, he leans closer. I zero in on his lips, approaching at glacial speed as anticipation flutters within me. It's all I can do not to bounce on my tiptoes to meet him.

A horse whinnies, the sharp noise breaking the spell, and Sebastian startles, then quickly steps away. Disappointment hits me hard, but I don't let it show as we resume walking. I risk another glance at him, marveling that we even got that far.

Back in the room, I feel gross. The layers of sweat from all our hikes and being baked by the sun cling to me. My feet are sore from all the walking.

I nibble on my lip before I ask, "Would you mind if I took a bath?" I want nothing more than to soak.

Sebastian rubs the back of his neck, not meeting my eyes. "Sure. Let me use the facilities first, then it's all yours."

I smile my gratitude then get out the PJs I want to wear. A few moments later, he emerges. His phone rings as I disappear into the bathroom, and I hear him say Leah's name in a voice full of excitement.

Then he sighs. "Yes, I ate today."

I flip on the water, smiling at the exasperation in his voice—he wasn't kidding about being hovered over for his hypoglycemia. I shrug it off and strip before I get into the bathtub. A moan escapes me as I sink into the steaming water.

Just what the doctor ordered.

I get lost in my book until a knock startles me, and I call, "Come in."

The door cracks open, but Sebastian doesn't appear. "Sorry, Calliope, I need my extra medicine. It can't wait."

"You're fine, Sebastian. I said come in." I set down my book, glancing at my phone. It's been an hour already? When he still doesn't appear, I shake my head. "I've got the curtain closed. I promise you won't see anything."

The door finally moves, and he peeks in.

"Or I can get out if you want." I peer around the shower curtain, but he shakes his head.

"I can't wait." He steps in, focusing on a small black case on the bathroom counter.

Curiosity flickers through me, but I don't want to pry.

He hurries over to grab the case, then he lets out a little sigh as he reluctantly meets my gaze. "I'm also diabetic, Type 1. I thought I had enough insulin for a snack, but I didn't."

"Oh, okay." I frown, surprised he hadn't mentioned it when he told me about the hypoglycemia.

He holds up his case. "Thanks." Then he strides through the door, closing it gently behind him.

I mull over this new information as I wash and get out. It sheds light onto his reactions to a lot of things, like the thank-you chocolates I gave him. Or how he refused the cake. He could have told me, but if he'd said anything, I would have fussed about it, apologized for not making it sugar free. Caused a scene.

Not exactly the way he likes things.

When I emerge from the bathroom, he stands shirtless by the desk, zipping the case. I can't help staring at his bare torso. The smooth expanse of his chest beckons my fingers, and I remember how firm he was when I caught myself on him. The outline of his abs calls to me.

As I walk over to him, I notice the small pink mark on his abdomen. I see interest in his eyes as he takes in my damp hair and PJ-clad body, but it's quickly followed by doubt. So many times I've seen the same trepidation hovering today. I thought this man was the epitome of confidence, and while he may be a walking encyclopedia, he doesn't seem to believe anyone could accept him for who he is. I decide to be brave, to spell out exactly how I'm feeling.

So the doubts have no shadows to hide in.

"I want to tell you something. I'm not sure you're ready to hear it, but I need to say it. What you do with this information is your call, okay?" I wait for his nod, then I move closer, raking my gaze over him once more. "You are exactly my type." I meet his eyes, which widen in surprise. "Your build, your intelligence… you…it all adds up to the perfect ingredients for my favorite dish."

He shakes his head, then looks at the desk. "Once you meet my brothers—"

I touch his bare shoulder, and he freezes but doesn't move away. "I've hung out with Silas, and he's not my type. I've met Shawn, and same. Unless Steven is tall and lean and incredibly smart, you're the Wrighting brother for me."

He sucks in a sharp breath.

"I didn't like you at first, especially after that party." A wry chuckle escapes me. I slide my hand down his arm, looping my index finger through his. "But I had the wrong idea about you. You're honest, and you keep your word. You may be a little arrogant, but you're actually one of the kindest people I've ever met. And the closer I get to you, the more I want to know."

He stares at the case on the desk, then runs his free hand over it and sighs. "I was fourteen when I was diagnosed with Type 1 diabetes. I have to give myself insulin shots any time I eat, and if I don't eat regularly, I become hypoglycemic."

"Does that happen often?"

A frown creases his forehead as he nods again. "I get very…involved in my projects, and sometimes I forget to eat. It's easier at events like this because I see other people eating, so I'm reminded to do the same. When it's just me, responsible for my own schedule, I don't always remember. Even with alarms." His lips press together as he studies me. "This isn't something that will simply go away, and there isn't a cure for it."

"I understand." If he's trying to scare me off, it's not going to work.

His mouth tightens. "I have a hard time with relationships, Calliope. When I get involved in my projects, everything else ceases to exist. Time, commitments, even people. It's not easy to be with someone when you find out they're constantly forgetting you."

I let go of his hand and cup his cheek. "You don't forget people, Sebastian. Sure, you get focused on a project, but somewhere inside, you know that the people you care about exist. I get how easy it is to immerse yourself in your work. I think that's a sign you're truly doing what you're meant to. Whoever you end up with needs to know that you love your work and be willing to share."

He doesn't move for a long moment as the air between us grows heavy. "Is this another part of your seduction scheme? Understanding me at every turn? Never flinching, no matter what I throw at you?"

"There's no scheme, Sebastian. I like you, plain and simple."

One corner of his mouth ticks up. "I like you too, Calliope. More with every minute." His gaze drifts to my lips, and he swallows before whispering, "I'd like to try something."

His fingers slide over my waist in a tentative movement that has me hardly daring to breathe. Our eyes lock, then my focus drops to his bare chest. His chin dips in the barest of motions, giving me permission, and my breath catches at the unexpected reward.

I catch my lip in my teeth as I slide my hand down Sebastian's neck, grazing his collarbone and touching his firm pecs. He closes his eyes as goosebumps appear beneath my fingers, and I raise my other hand, then rest my palm on his warm skin. I let my thumb glide along the smooth muscles, entranced that I have been granted this privilege.

Then I look up, and his eyes are open. The hazel depths are nearly forest green, full of turbulent emotion as he searches my face. My lips part at the strength of the longing that surges through me.

He mouths my name, then brushes a knuckle over my cheek. Slipping his finger beneath my chin, he rests his thumb below my lip, tilting my face to meet him as he leans down, down, down. Our lips touch in the gentlest whisper, but it's enough to turn the barely controlled desire within me into a roaring flame.

I splay my fingers over his chest, using all my self-control not to fling my arms around his neck, not to barrel into him and wrap my body around his. His large hand flexes at my hip, his other still holding my chin in place.

When he pulls back, I remember I need air and suck in a stuttering breath that echoes between us. He blinks as if startled, then a slow smile tips his lips.

Still I wait, knowing he needs to lead, that this has to be at his pace. So, instead of dragging that perfect mouth back to mine, I let my hands drop when he straightens and moves away. A hint of disappointment lingers, but I let the wonder well up instead.

Sebastian kissed me. Without coercion, without manipulation, but of his own free will. And he let me touch him.

Miracles really do happen.

Sebastian

I feel as if I haven't eaten—dizzy and unsteady. But I know I did. Plus, I just gave myself insulin. I move away from Calliope, my lips still tingling from the slight brush against hers, and I know she is the reason for my malady.

It takes every effort not to toss her onto one of the beds and let my baser urges take over, but I can't allow that. My body may be ready, but my mind isn't. Her sweet handprints still burn on my chest, though we're no longer touching. I clear my throat and find my shirt, pulling it on while ignoring the flash of disappointment in her eyes.

Does she truly enjoy my body that much? I can't fathom it. I'm used to being passed over in favor of any of my brothers, not only for my appearance but due to the complicated baggage that comes along with being in a relationship with me. I have to watch what I eat, make sure I have my insulin, exercise daily.

There's a good reason people think I'm rigid. I have to be.

She still hasn't moved, as if she is waiting for me to tell her what's next. Except I don't know the answer. I can't quite move forward and backward is not an option I'll allow myself to consider.

"Do you play cards?" I blurt out.

Her eyes light up, and she nods, then a wicked smirk crosses her mouth. "Like strip poker?"

My brain short-circuits at the very idea.

She must realize I'm reacting badly because her lips form a little O before she hurries to add, "I'm just teasing, Sebastian. I'm sorry!"

I try to gather the ragged edges of my composure, sucking in a breath as I clench and unclench my fingers. "It's all right…just…maybe a little too soon?"

Her smile turns soft with understanding. "Of course. How about rummy?"

"Perfect."

We move to the little table near the balcony, and I shuffle the deck while she pops back up to find a snack. She even brings me a water before she sits down with her juice and pretzels. We play several rounds, but she seems unfocused, throwing away cards I know she needs.

When she lays down an ace I'm positive will complete a set she has, I frown. "Calliope, is something wrong?"

She blinks through her long lashes before looking at the card. Her hand still rests on it, and she gasps. "Oh! I need that! I can't throw that away."

I chuckle. "I know."

She tosses out the seven of clubs then sighs. "I'm sorry. I guess I'm not really into this. It's not the game, I just feel…restless. I want to move."

I study my hand, then draw from the deck, finding the exact card I need to go out. "So, you won't be upset with me then." And I land my hand down.

"Sebastian!" she cries, but it lacks any heat. We haven't hit our one-hundred fifty points yet, so she reaches for the cards, but I catch her wrist.

"Maybe…" The words stick in my throat.

Calliope goes still, not pushing me, waiting until I'm collected enough to continue even though it takes me a moment. I know what I want. I know what will make her happy, and the idea of touching her again has my chest nearly bursting.

But I keep getting hung up on the minutiae.

"Sebastian?"

Her voice is full of concern, and I realize I've stayed quiet for far too long. I clear my throat then force the words out. "Would you like to show me how to dance?"

Her eyes widen, and her lips part as delight floods her gorgeous face. "Really?"

I have to swallow before I can nod, but I do it and she beams, the stunning reaction burning away any vestige of lingering doubt.

Until she bounces up eagerly and reaches for my hand. I awkwardly let her pull me to my feet, aware of every big inch of me. I've never been coordinated. I'm not meant for sports, have never had enough confidence in my long limbs to not feel like I'm going to make a mess of everything. Especially now, towering a solid nine inches over her.

What if I step on her foot? What if I go the wrong way and wrench her with me? What if —?

"You're already thinking too hard," she says in a gentle tone with a smile that matches. She lets go and grabs her phone before positioning it on the table nearby. "Let's start with the movement, no music. Watch."

She walks in a square, her feet coming together with each step. Ending in front of me, she grins again. "See? Simple. And I know most people associate it with a waltz, but you can use it with all sorts of music."

She does it several more times, then adds swaying hips, arm movements and dips I could never hope to replicate. I'm already regretting this.

"Easy!"

I simply stare back, that word not coming close to defining any of the motions she just made.

She chuckles and takes my wrist, guiding me in front of her. "You look like my instructions were in German." My face must twist into an odd expression because she pauses. "What?"

"I...actually know German."

Full-blown laughter escapes her, and I can't look away from her unabashed joy. I even smile, relaxing slightly as I see the humor.

When at last she sobers, the weighted feeling of tension settles over my body once more. She takes my left hand in hers, holding it between us.

Tapping my other arm, she nods. "This one goes at my waist."

My heart pounds at the thought of being so close to her again, the memory of our kiss beckoning. But I force myself to concentrate. I step forward, sliding my fingers along her trim waistline to cup her side.

She rests her left hand on my upper arm, and we don't move for a long moment before she sucks in a breath, breaking the spell. "Okay," she says, "follow my lead."

The gentle pressure of her fingers on my arm helps direct me where to go before she moves.

"Feet together."

She steps backward, tugging me with her and brings her feet to rest next to each other as I step forward and do the same. She guides me through a square, each movement closed when we bring our feet almost touching and it becomes almost a chant.

I start to say it with her, "Step, together, step together." We make another square, and another.

Then she stops, smiling. "Ready to add music?"

I try not to balk at the idea, blowing out a quiet breath when she moves from my arms to scroll on her phone. One more layer, one more complication. I glimpse the name of some band called Lifehouse, and their song titled *You and Me* begins as she steps back in front of me, holding up her arms as we resume our positions.

My mouth goes dry when I touch her again. She doesn't move for several beats, then nods before we begin in the same cycle as before. I thought it'd be more difficult, but it isn't. With her, it feels...right.

I'm not one to get lost in song, preferring the known corners of my mind to dwell in rather than the new strains of someone else's. However, these words are perfect. I can't stop staring at her as the lyrics wrap around us. We move together, as one being, tethered by each note in an ever-strengthening cocoon of lyrics.

Longing fills me. For once in my life, I wish I was someone else. I want to be that guy who doesn't think through every aspect of my words and actions, who just takes what he wants.

Because I want Calliope. I want her in every way I can possibly have her.

But my mind isn't there yet. So many what ifs haven't been examined, so many consequences haven't been considered. I've seen dogs straining at their leashes, anxious to run after a squirrel, and I couldn't understand how they could do that to themselves.

Here I am, my heart straining against the leash of my mind, and I know exactly how they feel.

As she stares at me with those luminous eyes, I wonder if she can see straight into my soul. I feel like it's a distinct possibility as I gaze back. I've never felt closer to anyone, not even Leah. Calliope hasn't flinched at a single aspect I've shown her, taking everything in stride. I don't know if I've ever felt like I belonged so much as I do right at this moment.

With this ethereal woman.

The chorus comes on once more, and she steps even closer, her thumb gliding over my shirtsleeve. Her turbulent gaze holds a wealth of emotions that would take me days to unravel. Days I'd gladly spend with her.

She reminds me of a jewel, perfectly cut to reflect the light, and every facet a different piece I want to study until I know them as intimately as I know my roses. Her breasts graze my chest as we move, making me suck in a breath. The final strains of the song fade. I lean in, unable to resist her compelling lips and the spell she continually weaves over me.

A blaring noise that can hardly be called music blasts from her phone, making us both jump. She scrambles away, hurrying to turn it off. But it's too late. The moment has shattered, too fragile to remain intact under the strain of that racket.

I feel raw, as if my nerves have been stripped one by one, like wires from their protective casings. Calliope's eyes search mine, full of concern, and I swallow but it's not enough to stop the panic rising in my throat. The need to flee wins, so I step away, desperate for distance between us.

"I-I'm going to get ready for bed." I can't wait for a response, rushing over to grab my lounge clothes then hurry to the bathroom.

The closed door provides the shield I need to collect myself, and I lean against the cool porcelain sink, staring at my reflection in the mirror as I suck in breath after breath. Slowly, I let my head empty of thoughts. Slowly, my heart resumes its normal rhythm. Slowly, I feel like myself again.

In control.

Then the shame creeps in, that I can't even perform a normal rite of passage like dancing with a woman without running away afterward. I grip the counter harder, fury growing within me. Why can't I be like everyone else for once?

My mom's voice echoes in my mind, a remnant of a memory from of the many times I'd asked her that very question growing up. *"My sweet Sebastian."* I can almost feel her gentle touch, smoothing my hair before kissing my temple. *"You are exactly who the world needs you to be. Nothing more and nothing less. No one else can think your thoughts, no one else sees things the way you do, and that makes you special."*

It hadn't taken me long to learn that *special* meant different, but I've always prided myself on being unique. This is one of the rare cases I want to fit in. I want to be able to do normal things, like dance and hold hands and eat at new restaurants...without being overwhelmed.

But that's not who I am.

Defeat washes over me as I drop my hands from the sink and sigh in resignation. I change into my night clothes, brush my teeth, take my medicine and vitamins — all in the numb state of knowing I'm not enough. I'll never be enough.

I walk out into the main room and crawl into bed. Calliope's gaze weighs heavy on me, though I can't bring myself to look at her. I don't want to see the disappointment or pity I know will linger there. But the strain of her stare makes it impossible to give in to the pull of sleep without saying something. I close my eyes, lying with my back to her.

But over my shoulder, I tell her quietly, "Good night, and thank you for the dance."

Chapter Eleven

Sebastian

The next morning, I toy with the strap of my backpack, anxious knots forming in my stomach as I glance at Calliope who stands on the other side of the elevator. Her usual sunny smile has yet to make an appearance this morning, and there are shadows under her eyes, as if she didn't sleep well.

We're still planning to visit the butterfly house, but the air between us is tense and thick. Nothing like our casual conversations of yesterday. The welcome ding precedes the doors sliding open, but the moment we step out, I wish we could crawl back inside.

"Sebastian! Callie!" Professor Harrison booms from across the lobby.

He waves us over to a group of his colleagues, and Calliope grimaces but heads that way. I fall into step with her, watching as she transforms. Her posture becomes more rigid—shoulders back, chest out, chin up. A smile tips her lips, not meeting her eyes. Her movements are measured and careful, nothing like the carefree woman I've come to know.

It's hard not to frown, but I plaster on a smile of my own, if only to placate my boss. Another front, just like hers. I find myself frustrated, that he demands our best foot forward all the time. What is it about this man, demanding we all wear these masks? He's not a god. Doesn't our happiness matter?

"Where are you two off to?" he asks, his broad smile telling me he already knows the answer.

This is a frequent tactic of his. I know how much he loves the spotlight and, since it isn't my favorite place to be, I'm fine letting him have it. But I prefer not to be the one shining it on him.

Calliope answers first, forcing sunshine into her voice. "Sebastian and I are going to the butterfly house. We hiked some yesterday, but I know we didn't see everything."

His smile takes on an edge that I don't care for as he turns triumphantly to his colleagues. "What did I tell you? I knew they'd be perfect for each other."

The words hit me like a brick to my gut, and I instantly look at Calliope. Her gaze finds mine as the color drains from her face at the implication that her dad arranged for us to be together, and she stumbles backward, even as I shake my head in a frantic motion.

One of the other professors lets out a booming laugh, then slaps my shoulder, ignoring my flinch. "Upgrading from TA to son-in-law, are you?"

I'm absolutely frozen in my horror as Calliope's eyes brim with tears, betrayal and hurt written all over her face.

Professor Maia notices. "Callie, honey, are you all right?"

Calliope snaps her mouth closed and goes ramrod straight, shutting down all hint of emotion. "I need some fresh air." To her father — and only her father — she says, "Please excuse me. I'm going to the gardens now." And she strides away, not waiting for a response.

Professor Harrison's expression holds a hint of storminess, but he doesn't call her back. I need to go after her, to be sure she's truly okay. I must know that she doesn't believe me capable of orchestrating a twisted scheme around someone else's heart.

When her father turns to me with that pleased grin, it takes all my self-control not to punch it off his face. The fact that I'm hanging on the precipice of losing command over my emotions has them flaring even closer to the surface, coalescing into one big ball of fury at this man. For causing Calliope pain and humiliation. For complicating things between us when they've already been difficult enough. For always making everything about him.

"Sebastian, my boy, are you sure you can handle her?"

"I'm not your boy," I bite out. "Sir, that was inappropriate. Calliope and I are not in a relationship."

His eyebrows jump up. "Oh. Are you telling me you don't like my daughter?"

I curl my fingers into fists, trying to contain my anger. "Of course I like your daughter, but we have things we need to work out, and pushing us into something before we're ready isn't helpful."

He narrows his eyes as he studies me. "I see. And what is it that you have to work out?" The icy question hovers in the tension-filled air as all eyes focus on us.

I hold my ground. "While I appreciate your concern, that's between me and your daughter. Sir."

Even as he bristles, a hint of admiration flickers in his eyes.

"If you'll excuse me, I need to go find her. We have plans." I rush outside.

There's no sign of Calliope, but she mentioned the gardens and I hope she meant it. I jog across the driveway to the top of the stairs overlooking the greenery below. My heart skips a beat when a bobbing head of purple hair catches my eye, and relief fills me as I hurry down the steps to catch her.

Once I reach the lawn, I call her name. I know she hears me because she turns, but instead of slowing, she only moves faster toward the woods flanking the other side of the gardens. My stomach sinks.

But my long legs eat up the distance, her shorter strides no match for mine. I catch a glimpse of her on the path beyond the gigantic chess set, and I call for her again, but she breaks into a run. I don't give up, chasing her past the greenhouse, along the dirt path skirting the backside of the pool, down the gravel trail that leads across the road to the open beach of Lake Michigan.

Where she finally stops.

"Is it true?" She whirls around to face me.

I'm taken aback by her wet cheeks. Her violet hair is caught by the breeze, clinging to her face as the wind caresses her. But it's the desperation in her tone, in her gaze that has my stomach knotting. I can't stand seeing her in pain.

"Did you and my father plan this...this whole thing? Did he set this all up?"

I'd been expecting the words or something like them, but hearing them aloud is another stab in the heart. I don't know why she matters so much to me. All I know is the thought of her believing the worst of me is unfathomable. She may not want me after all of this, but I can't walk away with her thinking I had any part of this.

So I simply say, "No." Hope flares in those brilliant blue eyes, and I step closer. "Do you really think me capable of such a thing?"

A long moment passes as she searches me, and I remember that she's not seeing with her own view right now, but through the distorted lens of her past with her father.

Her shoulders droop and her chin falls as she whispers, "No, Sebastian, you wouldn't."

I've never wanted to hold someone as much as I want to hold her in this instant. To take her in my arms, to wipe away her tears. I settle for stepping closer, keeping my gaze locked on those still glistening eyes. "I would never conspire against anyone, especially someone I care so much about."

A sob slips through her lips and her body shakes. She shifts forward until her forehead rests on my chest. "It's just my dad twists things around so easily that I don't always know what's real and what's him." She steps back as a hint of light returns to her eyes, though the pain lingers. "I know you better than that."

My relief has me blowing out the breath until she launches herself at me. I react instinctively, catching her as she flings her arms around my neck and wrapping her body around mine.

"I'm sorry," she murmurs before hiding her face in the crook of my neck.

Sobs wrack her petite body, and I assess myself, thankful I'm okay enough to be this for her right now. I hold her tighter, stroking her back as I walk us over to a nearby bench and lower onto it. She sits astride my lap, my shirt becoming damp with her tears.

I don't know how long she cries, and I wish I knew what she is crying for. How long has she held this sadness in? It can't be easy living with the kind of pressure her father puts on her. How he distorts even the most innocent things to be a trophy for himself...

Guilt twists within me as I recall all the times I judged her and found her lacking. When her tears run dry and she sits up, my heart breaks again.

"Sorry," she repeats, sniffling, and I don't know if it's another apology for her doubt or she's embarrassed about her breakdown.

Either way, I shake my head. "It's okay. He shouldn't have implied..." I trail off when her eyes widen and her body goes rigid. "What?"

"I should—" She starts to climb off my lap, not finishing her sentence.

I clamp my hands onto her hips, holding her in place. "Calliope."

She doesn't flinch this time, only stares back with that gorgeous cerulean gaze and all the trust in the world.

"Stay."

Her throat bobs. "I didn't mean to—"

"I know." I caress her sides with my thumbs. "Don't move, not until you're ready. I'm okay."

A smile grows on her full lips. "I don't know if I ever thought I'd hear you say that. Especially after last night."

The lightness I'd begun to feel plummets at those words, and I sigh. "I'm sorry about last night. I shouldn't have run off like that. I was overwhelmed and..." I trail off, frustration welling within me again.

"It's okay, Sebastian. I know. You don't have to apologize, but...maybe, when you calm down, you could talk to me? Instead of going to bed and shutting me out?" Her chin dips as she focuses on my chest. "That hurt. I didn't know if I'd overstepped, or you'd changed your mind or what."

I gape at her. "I thought you'd changed your mind, watching me run away after a simple dance."

She looks up, the twinkle back in her eye as her lips twitch in amusement. "That's what you thought would make me change my mind? After I ate subs for how many days in a row?"

I feign indignance. "Those were high quality sub sandwiches."

"I'm not changing my mind, Sebastian. I want you. All of you."

The admission combines with the feel of her, and a kernel of desire sparks within me. My throat goes dry. "I want you, too."

Her gaze drops to my lips. "Can I kiss you?"

I'm already growing hard, and I know she can feel it. But I hesitate.

"If it's too much..."

The longing in her voice makes it impossible for me to deny her, especially when I remember the feel of her mouth touching mine. I nod. She leans forward, creating a delicious pressure on my aching erection. I can't help my groan, and it twines with her moan as she rocks her hips, just once.

Then our lips meet. She tilts her head as she cups my face with her hands. Pure pleasure shoots through me while a most delightful warmth spreads through my chest, as if my heart is not pumping blood through my veins but filling them instead with sunshine. A hum vibrates through her, and I swallow it, adding the noise to the collection I'm building in my head. I could listen to that all day.

She pulls back, removing the pressure from my hardened length, and I don't know whether to be relieved or disappointed. We stare at each other for several long moments while all I feel is awe at this amazing woman. At the depth of emotion she stirs within me.

"Should I move now? Or give you a minute? Or…um…" Pink tinges her cheeks. "I could help you take care of that, if you'd like."

Heat floods my face, and I clear my throat. "Thank you, but giving me a minute is quite acceptable." Images of her touching me spring to mind, and I have to shove them away, because they are the opposite of helpful in regaining my control.

She quickly moves off my lap, standing to one side with her back to me. I hop to my feet, adjust myself to the most comfortable position I can in my state, then walk to her side.

"Do you still want to go to the butterfly house?" she asks.

I can't think of anything else I'd rather do than spend the day with her, so I nod. Then I hold out my hand, wanting to assure her I'm all right. "Ready?"

She smiles before lacing her fingers through mine. "Ready."

And we saunter down the road to town together, hand in hand, side by side, with the waves of Lake Michigan as our background music.

Callie

Walking with Sebastian, my heart feels full. I never would have imagined a moment like this, or the one several minutes ago with me clinging to him as he comforted me. A surge of frustration darkens the horizon of my bliss when I remember how my dad tried to ruin it all with his twisted comment, and I can't help wondering how many other things he's ruined by taking credit.

The steady clip-clop of a horse-drawn carriage sounds behind us as it approaches, and I glance over my shoulder as it turns the corner. It's a larger wagon filled with bench seats, similar to the one we rode up here on. I listen as the tour guide points out several nearby sites, and it gives me a brilliant idea.

My allowance my dad gives me mostly gathers dusty interest in the bank account I have. I don't have much opportunity to spend it with the tight leash I'm kept on. This is the epitome of perfect because he should definitely foot the bill for today, and I chuckle at the way it all comes together, laughing harder at Sebastian's confused expression.

"I just had an idea," I explain, "but I want it to be a surprise. I'd like today to be my treat." He looks over warily, but I don't give up. "Please? I promise, this is right up your alley."

He insisted on paying for dinner at the Pink Pony last night, saying it was only fair since I'd pushed him out of his comfort zone. I'll mention it if I have to, but he nods, and that's that.

As we start walking again, I swing our arms in time with our steps as my mood grows lighter and lighter. Instead of heading up the hill toward the butterfly house, we make our way into the heart of town once again. We weave through the ever-present throng of people, walking several blocks until I stop in front of a small, open ticket booth.

The sign above reads Mackinac Island Carriage Tours. Sebastian tilts his head as I bound over to the window.

"Two, please. And we'd like the tour that includes the butterfly house." I glance over at Sebastian, who grins back in obvious delight.

I grab our tickets, and our carriage pulls up before we even have time to sit. The five rows of yellow benches seat four people each. I let Sebastian take the outside, though that means I'm a little squished, since the lady next to me puts her bag on the seat between us.

He notices and tugs on my shirt, letting me know I can move closer to him. I take advantage of the offer and press myself to his side. The casual way he accepts my touch sends warmth blossoming through my chest. Our tour guide introduces herself as Melanie before she snaps the reins above the two tan draft horses pulling our carriage.

Dad and I did this tour when we came here with Mom, and I soaked in all the facts and corny jokes, loving the different areas of the island we visited. Now, I eagerly watch Sebastian's face as Melanie starts talking. She rattles off information like it's a roll of toilet paper someone gave a hearty spin.

"Here's the only strip of shops that doesn't have a fudge store."

"This is the medical clinic and behind those doors is the island's biggest secret—motorized vehicles." She pauses as we laugh. "Of course, they're all for emergencies...police cars, ambulances, fire trucks."

When she stops to give the horses a break partway up a long hill, we have a nice view of the fort. She doesn't give us much information about it, saying she doesn't want to spoil the second half of our tour.

When she clicks to the horses to get them moving again, I lean over to Sebastian. "Good surprise?"

He nods, giving me a full smile that makes my stomach flip. "This is great."

As we approach the Grand Hotel, Sebastian pulls out his phone several times. Once after a tidbit about Christopher Reeve getting punched in the face for driving his car and spooking a team of horses. I soak it all in, relishing being so close to Sebastian for an extended period of time and loving his delighted reactions to each new fact or joke.

All too soon, we reach the station, and his face falls. "It's over already?"

"Nope. We pause here, stretch our legs, see the butterfly house." I point to the little building in the distance. "Then we take a second carriage with a team of three horses to go through all the out of town stuff."

His grin is huge as he offers me his hand while I climb down, and I'm so glad we did this. He doesn't let go as we walk toward the big building.

I explain our options. "There's bathrooms or food in the station. Or we can go right to the butterfly house?"

He nods eagerly, tugging on my hand to lead me down the hill. The sun shines on the quaint brown building, its bright sign standing out with the magnificent orange monarch on it. When we reach the little white porch, a young woman holds out her hand for our tickets. I pass them over, tucking them back in my purse when she's done.

She launches into the rules. "Watch where you step. Enter here, but wait until the outer door is closed before proceeding into the next section. Don't touch the butterflies' wings. Before you leave, an employee will check you over to make sure no butterflies are attached to your clothing. Enjoy." And she opens the screen door for us.

We step into a mostly white room, waiting while the outer door creaks shut. Then Sebastian eases open another lightweight door, and we tiptoe into the greenhouse.

The butterfly house is one big room lined with a walkway of brown paving stones. The air is warm and humid, amplified by the sun streaming through the glass ceiling and walls. A small stone wall winds around the outer edge of the walkway, with space behind for a beautiful array of colorful flowers in all shapes and sizes.

Informative plaques are scattered throughout the foliage. Many different household items dot the area, repurposed for butterflies to rest on—old window frames without the glass, a chandelier, a trellis, a whole fairy garden statue set.

People sit on the wall or on benches or mosey along the path. As we gingerly take a couple steps in, I can't count the number of butterflies swooping, sailing, gliding, resting. They range in size from as big as my hand to as small as a quarter and come in all the colors of the rainbow.

A dull brown one glides past, and I gasp when it lands, opening its wings to reveal a vibrant blue. I point to it, smiling at Sebastian.

He grins back, reaching again for my hand. "That's a blue morpho."

"Nice." With our fingers entwined, we stroll along, making sure our path is clear, and I say, "All right, Mr. Know-It-All. Hit me with the butterfly facts."

His grin grows wider, and his eyes crinkle at the edges. "Well, there are over twenty thousand species of butterflies."

"That's so many." I watch a black and red one drink from a feeder. Several feeding stations are positioned throughout with running water, fruit and nectar.

"Their diet is solely liquid, and they only live for a few weeks."

I jut my lip out. "Aww, that's sad."

He squeezes my hand, and my smile returns. We meander as he peppers me with interesting facts, his face lit up the entire time as he looks around in awe. I soak in every moment, loving how passionate he is about sharing information, and the fact that I had the right idea by surprising him with this outing.

Chapter Twelve

Callie

Halfway around the room, the path doubles back. I watch a black butterfly with orange patches and yellow dots swoop in to land at the edge of a bird bath.

Sebastian stands behind me, his breath warm on my cheek. "Did you know that they've found representation of butterflies in thirty-five-hundred-year-old Egyptian frescoes?"

I shake my head, unable to quit smiling. I tilt my face up, loving his nearness and seeing him in his element like this. How did I ever think of him as arrogant? I follow a delicate yellow butterfly as it glides to a feeding station. The wall is lower there, beckoning me to sit, so I lead Sebastian over.

After we make sure the wall is clear, we sit down. I relax in the peacefulness of this place. Sure, people mill around, but not too many. And even though no one asked us to, we all keep our voices down.

A lady across from us sits perfectly still. She wears a tan shirt with a bright yellow sunflower on it, and I realize she has several butterflies on her. She notices me and smiles.

"They seem to like you," I say, grinning back.

"I think it's these colors. The last time I was here, I couldn't get any to land on me."

I glance at myself, feeling a prick of disappointment that I'm not attracting any of the beautiful insects. As I turn back to Sebastian, I notice a butterfly perched on the toe of his white canvas shoe. When I point, he follows my finger, grinning at the Monarch. I quickly pull out my phone to snap a couple of pictures, then I settle beside him again.

We stay quiet for several moments, just observing, until I break the silence with my curiosity. "I saw you pulling out your phone a lot on the tour. What were you doing?" He doesn't seem like the type to be checking social media every five seconds.

His cheeks tinge with pink, and he glances at the walkway before turning back to me. "So, I told you I have a photographic memory." At my nod, he gives a sheepish shrug. "There were several new facts that I wanted to remember, so I wrote them down."

The dots connect in my head. "Oh! You only remember things perfectly if you see them. Not like Sheldon on *The Big Bang Theory*."

"I wish. No, that's called an eidetic memory."

"What you have is still pretty amazing." I nudge him with my elbow. "Aren't you afraid you're going to fill your brain too full with all those books you read?" At his eye roll, I laugh, but then I frown as I think more about it. "Wait, so is your photographic memory perfect? Like, you read a book once and can picture each word on the page?"

His nod only piques my curiosity. "Seriously?" I ask. "So, if I said what's the fourth word on page thirty-two of the Mackinac Island guidebook on your desk—"

"It's 'was'." He chuckles as I gape. "'The Grand Hotel was built...'"

"I'm checking that when we get back." I marvel at his amazing capabilities and the fact he is deigning to hang out with boring old me.

"Be my guest."

I laugh. "Technically, I already am."

He huffs out a breath, feigning annoyance, but his smirk gives him away. "Ready to go?"

Taking one more look around, I sigh because I don't want to leave. But the next part of our tour awaits. "Let's take a picture together first." I hold up my phone, freezing us in this perfect moment for all of time.

After we gently dislodge Sebastian's friend from his shoe, we saunter toward the exit where an employee makes us each spin around before leaving. I wait for Sebastian, then we walk hand in hand through the gift shop and back into the summer day.

In unspoken agreement, Sebastian and I climb the hill to the station. One of the carriages for the second part of the tour pulls away as we approach, but I'm not worried. A new one arrives every ten minutes or so, and the last one isn't until late afternoon. We've got plenty of time.

A delicious aroma wafts out of the building, and my stomach rumbles. I glance at my phone, surprised to see that it's nearly one-thirty and frown at Sebastian.

"We should probably get some food." The next part of the tour is a good hour long, if I remember right.

"Food. Right." His shoulders go rigid, and I quickly reach over to rest my hand on his arm.

"We could walk back down to town, grab a sub or stop in at the Pink Pony. We should have time."

Surprise wavers in his gaze. "You'd do that? For me?"

"Of course." We pushed his boundaries a lot yesterday, and today is supposed to be about rewarding him.

He presses his lips together as he studies the menu on the outside of the building. "It's a decent walk back to town, and I think I should eat sooner rather than later. I'm sure I can handle something here."

Admiration washes over me and my chest feels like it'll explode. "I'm proud of you, Sebastian." I squeeze his arm, then we walk ahead into the big, cement-floored, white building.

Little shops dot the perimeter, selling trinkets, fudge, snacks, ice cream, leather tooled items, clothing and more. Sebastian's expression turns annoyed as he surveys a food stand with pizza displayed in a rotating rack, as well as pretzels and popcorn.

"What's wrong?"

Shaking his head, he sighs. "As a diabetic, I don't produce insulin, so I don't do well with high sugar foods. Carbs basically turn into sugar. I allow myself one meal with carbs a day, usually if I'm going to exercise after. I would much prefer a salad or even a cheese stick and some nuts to this."

I frown, realizing I never understood how difficult food options would be on a daily basis. Another piece clicks into place. "Is that part of why you don't like to change restaurants? Once you find a good option, you stick with it because it's a guarantee?"

He nods slowly, surprise dawning over his features. "Now that you mention it, yeah. Diet and exercise are two of the most important factors in a diabetic's life."

"Which is why you like hiking," I clarify.

"I don't enjoy sports, so I had to find an activity I like that keeps me moving." He lifts a shoulder then adds, "Hiking gets me outdoors, too."

I frown at the limited food options. "I'm pretty sure they let us move around at Arch Rock, so it won't all be sitting. And we have the walk back to the hotel." They don't even have plain cheese pizza, my favorite. "Plus, you can have my pepperonis if you want more protein."

His frown is too cute. "You don't enjoy pepperoni?"

I shake my head. "Too spicy."

"Too spicy?" His eyebrows shoot up.

"Yep." I shrug. "I can't handle the heat."

An unfamiliar expression crosses his face, an intensity that has me sitting straighter as his piercing gaze bores into me. "In your food, anyway." Then he winks.

I nearly stumble backward in shock even as I resist the urge to fan myself. "Holy shit, don't do that!" I push his shoulder lightly as I laugh at my ridiculous reaction.

A smug grin tilts his lips even as he plays dumb. "Do what?"

"Flirt with me." The moment I say it, delight fills me to the brim because that's exactly what he's doing. My cheeks hurt from how wide my smile is. Sebastian was flirting with me, a phenomenon I never thought I'd witness, let alone be the subject of.

He ducks his head. "Just order your pizza."

"Why? You want some more spice in your life?" But as we walk toward the counter, my delight is overtaken by unease, and I touch his arm. "Sebastian, wait." I frown, thinking as he watches me intently. "There's a café across from the Grand, and it's right down that hill. Maybe we should go there? The carriages run all day, and it's not a far walk, but I'd bet they have better options than this."

The tenderness in his eyes makes my knees wobble as he steps closer to me. "Are you sure?"

I try to keep my wits despite his proximity and the heady wave of his minty coffee scent. "There's no cheese pizza here, anyway." I'm rewarded with a deep chuckle before he leans in to brush his lips against my cheek.

"Come on then. I'm hungry." And he holds out his hand like it's the most natural thing in the world.

* * * *

For the second leg of our tour, I take the middle once more, letting Sebastian be outside. His long legs look a little cramped since there isn't as much leg room in the front, but he doesn't complain.

Our tour guide is named Aiden, and I don't expect much of him based on his lack of reaction while the ticket-taker introduces him. His expression never changes, but when we pull away, it's as if a switch is flipped.

He smiles widely, the radio crackling to life as he introduces himself and the three broad horses pulling us—Larry, Mo, and Curly. Their names make me grin. He launches right into facts about the draft horses, telling us to ask questions whenever we want. Of course, Sebastian takes advantage of that.

"How long do they live for?"

"How much weight can they pull?"

"Are they fixed or used for breeding?"

I pat his arm after the third question, wanting to make sure others get a chance. He ducks his head, looking chagrined. But I nudge him again, smiling to let him know it's no big deal, and he relaxes once more. As we weave through the woods, someone asks about the wildlife on the island.

Aiden takes every question in stride. "Many animals cross in the winter when an ice bridge is formed from the mainland. If they don't leave before it melts, they're stuck here, which is how we ended up with a small herd of deer and several foxes."

"What about bears?" a person in the back asks.

"There isn't any record of bears," Aiden answers. "Maybe that's because the bear appeared before people kept record." He shrugs. "I wouldn't be so bold as to assume there have never been bears on the island, but currently we have no bears or wolves or moose."

He pauses the carriage to let the horses have a break, and he points to a nearby tree riddled with big holes. "We also have pileated woodpeckers. They are quite large birds, and that's what causes the holes."

Sebastian murmurs, "Pileated woodpeckers can grow up to nineteen inches tall, and both the female and male have red caps."

I lace my fingers through his to give him a squeeze. It amazes me how much he knows. The road winds between the several cemeteries, and Sebastian soaks in all the facts, asking several questions about the Native American burial ground in particular.

After the cemeteries come Skull Cave, and Aiden explains that the cave used to be much larger. When he launches into some of the facts that Sebastian shared yesterday, I lean into Sebastian's side, grinning because I already know all this. We continue to Arch Rock where we have a short ten-minute break. I'm grateful we explored yesterday at our own pace.

We both hop out to stretch our legs, and I hurry to the bathroom. When I come out, Sebastian stands near Aiden, deep in conversation. I meander over, pleased that the driver is pleasantly answering all Sebastian's questions about the draft horses. I think he might have found a new fixation.

Our break goes quickly, and the last leg is spent hearing about the War of 1812. We stop near a cleared path that Aiden says was used as a shooting range. "The interesting thing is that a variety of bullets have been found here because in that short time of the war, guns evolved from muskets to more modern-day rifles."

I sit back, enjoying the wave of facts as they wash over me. We start once more along the wooded road, and Sebastian goes rigid. As he points to the trees, I catch a flash of black and red.

Sebastian calls, "I see a pileated woodpecker."

Aiden pulls the horses to a stop, peering where Sebastian points. He grins when he spots it, announcing the find to everyone on the carriage. Before we move on, he says, "Hey, thanks for pointing that out. I never would have seen it."

And Sebastian nods, a self-satisfied smile on his face. We finish the tour without further interruption, getting dropped off near downtown. Sebastian thanks me again for the tour, then we head along main street to check out the shops.

One of my favorite stops is The Island Bookstore, where I buy him a book on draft horses — specifically their part in the history of Mackinac Island. He keeps peering into the bag, and I know how badly he wants to start reading. We walk for another hour, meandering in and out of the quaint stores while also getting in some exercise.

When Sebastian suggests subs for dinner, I don't argue, but he surprises me by getting a turkey wrap and a yogurt as a side. We sit down with our food, and I pull out my phone. "I want to check a few things if you don't mind. Maybe you want to read?"

The words barely escape my lips before his book is out and in front of his nose. His eagerness makes me grin. After dinner, we sample fudge for dessert, sugar free for Sebastian. We end up buying a slice because it's so good.

Back at the hotel room, I set down my bags, then go grab my comfy PJs, ready to be out of my cute clothes. After I've changed, I notice the guidebook on one corner of the desk, and I flip to page thirty-two, which starts exactly as Sebastian said.

"What are you doing?" he asks warily.

I lean against the edge of the desk as I thumb through several more pages. "Testing you." He scoffs, and I say, "Page thirty-six, third paragraph."

"'Two movies have been filmed on the premises of the Grand Hotel, *Somewhere in Time* and *This Time for Keeps*," he recites, not missing a beat.

I flip several chapters, almost to the end of the book. "Page ninety-three. Last word on the page."

He blinks, his jaw slightly offset as if he's holding in his exasperation. "It's 'fudge', happy?" When I start thumbing again, he stands and takes the book out of my hands. He sets it gently on the desk, then leans on the flat surface, pinning me with his intense stare.

"I remember everything I see, Calliope," he says huskily, leaning toward me. "I remember how your nostrils flared when I told you that you shouldn't be at Dean's party and how the stud in your nose moved."

Tension crackles between us, and I can't move. He frames me with his hands, one on either side of the chair. So close, but not quite touching.

"The day you brought me chocolates, I was so annoyed by the interruption, but I couldn't help watching you storm away. I didn't leave that doorway until you were out of sight."

My mouth goes dry as my lips part.

His voice gets impossibly lower. "I remember very clearly the view in the car of your lavender lacey bra. I saw two freckles near your ribs, and I was surprised you didn't have a belly button ring."

I gasp. "You said you didn't peek!"

He just smirks. "I have excellent peripheral vision for things close up, and you were right there." He puts more weight on his hands, bending his elbows to bring his face nearer to mine.

My heart pounds in my chest, anticipation coiling low in my abdomen. This is not the game I'd planned to play, but now that we've started, I can't wait to see how it ends.

Chapter Thirteen

Callie

"When you fell into my lap on the ferry, your skirt rode up. I could feel all of your thigh on mine, and that line of fabric..." Sebastian's hazel eyes drift down me, and his throat bobs when he lands on the hem of my shorts. "I didn't know if it was your skirt or your panties."

That intimate word on Sebastian's lips fills me with longing and my own panties become damp.

He leans even closer, his breath mingling with mine. "But I desperately wanted to find out."

"Why didn't you?" I whisper, scared to even move, not wanting to break the spell.

"You terrified me. All that exquisite confidence, beauty in every movement, a smile that brought me to my knees. Calliope, my brain has never failed me once in my entire life, but you are the fork that life keeps jamming into my circuits."

I let out a little laugh, but he moves his right hand, gliding so lightly along my shoulder I feel like I'm imagining it. Until he cups the back of my neck. A delicious shiver sneaks down my spine and goosebumps pebble my arms as I wait for his next move.

"Having you straddle me earlier today on the bench..." His breath hitches.

And I can't take any more. I leap from the chair, throwing my arms around him as our lips collide in all the hunger flowing between us. He spins us both and pins me to the desk. His kiss is full of desperation and desire, underlined with a raw vulnerability that steals my breath.

His lips leave my mouth, trailing across my cheek then down my neck as he pushes his hips forward and his firm length meets my apex. This is exactly what I need. I whimper, one hand clutching his shoulder, the other sliding to grip his hip as I buck against him.

My flimsy shorts are hardly a barrier, and I rock against him as he groans. I push one of his large hands down until he cups my breast through my shirt. His thumb grazes my nipple, teasing it into an eager peak.

I throw my head back as I revel in the sensations, letting Sebastian's words echo in my mind. Each one pushes me closer to the edge, and I don't know if it's the shock of him opening up, or the revision of the memories, or if it's just been a while.

Maybe...maybe it's simply because this is Sebastian. And I've never wanted anyone more.

The thought sends me tumbling over the edge as bliss floods me. I clutch his arms while I shudder against him, breathing heavily as I ride the wave coursing through me. Once the quakes subside, I realize Sebastian is still in need.

He seems frozen, so I ease my hand down to his belt. I don't want to push him too far, but he grabs my hand, guiding me to cup his hard length through his shorts. A gasp escapes him, and he thrusts against my palm as I slide over his erection. A few moments later, he grunts, going rigid beneath my fingers.

My thighs clench at the idea that I made him lose control that quickly, that easily. He straightens and steps out of my grasp, breathing hard as his hands drop to his sides. Panic flutters at the edges of his gaze, darting from me to my lap to the floor then making another circuit.

"Hey. Sebastian." I wait for him to look at me. "It's okay. You're okay." His lips press together, and he swallows frantically, so I say again, "You're okay. That was fun for me, but we don't have to do any more. I have no expectations, no agenda. We're good, all right?"

My words seem to permeate, and he takes in a slower, deeper breath before he blinks twice. "I'm going to go get cleaned up."

I watch him stride away, my high from moments ago now conflicted with his reaction. The bliss still lingers, but it's tinged with a bitter edge as I wonder if I pushed him, or if he actually enjoyed it and now regrets it. I wrap my arms around my middle, feeling hollow.

"Calliope?"

The sound of my name startles me. I didn't hear the bathroom door open, but Sebastian is right in front of me again.

"I'm sorry I panicked like that," he says, not making a move to touch me. "I want you to know I enjoyed it very much."

"Did I push you? Do you regret it?" I whisper, all my doubts welling up to make my words strained. I keep my head down as my finger rubs over my thumbnail, worrying it as my anxiety worries me.

He shakes his head emphatically. "No. Not for one second."

Some of my tension eases, and I meet his tentative gaze.

"It's been a while since I've connected to anyone on this level, where I want to know them more..." He trails off, searching me. "Intimately. I don't know if I've ever felt quite like this, and I need some time to process. To adjust to the idea."

Relief pours in. He really does want me, but it's too overwhelming at the moment. I manage a smile. "I get it, Sebastian. Thank you for explaining."

He shifts his weight then pushes his glasses up his nose. "I don't know what to do now."

"What do you want to do?"

"Read?" he asks hopefully.

Of course, he wants to escape in the comfort of his books, and I nod in understanding. "That sounds perfect."

His shoulders drop a full inch, and he lets out a breath in a whoosh. I relish how he took the next step with me, that he was honest about feeling overwhelmed and took the time to explain. Now I can fully bask in the afterglow of my surprise orgasm. He watches me settle onto my bed, but makes no move to grab his book.

"Was there something else?" I ask.

His throat bobs again. "Maybe…I could read next to you?"

I feel like someone opened the shade, letting sunlight stream into a dark room and warming it instantly. "I'd love that."

He grins, darting over to grab his book before crawling in next to me. He scoots until our shoulders are touching, and he bends his knees to rest the book on them. With one last look at me, he turns to lose himself in the pages.

But I take another minute to marvel at him, gathering all the light he brings into my life and desperately trying to hold onto it. I'll need it after we go home. The thought reminds me to text Dad, letting him know I'm in for the night.

Once I get his thumbs-up, I shove all heaviness away, not wanting to ruin the moment, so I dive into my book instead. The perfect distraction.

With him so close, I'm not even restless, as I usually am when I read. I only shift my legs occasionally, far from my usual acrobatics. The last time we'd read together, I'd been so sleepy I hadn't had to fight the urge. Tonight, the urge isn't even there.

Near eleven p.m., I yawn again, so I reluctantly put my book down to brush my teeth. Sebastian uses the bathroom after me, and I set my phone on the nightstand when he comes out. I watch him double-check the locks, then hesitate at the foot of his bed. He walks over toward me instead, with a sweet smile on his face.

"Thank you, Calliope. I had fun today."

I sit up, grinning back. "So did I."

Then he surprises me by leaning in for a kiss — a soft, tender kiss — the perfect ending to our perfect day. He pauses before me, and I hope he'll do more, but he simply says, "Good night."

Warmth encompasses my whole body from that quick encounter, bringing up memories from earlier, and I can barely whisper, "Good night, Sebastian."

I watch him climb into his bed. Each little bit of himself he offers is so much sweeter because it's his choice, a perfect gift from him. He turns out the lights, and we lie in our separate beds, where I marvel that my heart has never been fuller.

* * * *

My first thought upon waking is that tomorrow we have to go home. My second is that Sebastian is still in his bed. Sitting up and reading, but still in bed.

I grin sleepily before I stretch. "Morning."

"Good morning." He grins back. "How'd you sleep?"

"Like a log." I yawn and push the covers off me, then tug my shirt down so my stomach isn't showing. "What's on the docket for today?"

"Unfortunately, it's raining and will be for most of the day." He shuts his book. "None of the lectures interest me..." He trails off, hesitating. "I have some research I'd hoped to accomplish on this trip. I should probably work on that, but maybe we could have breakfast together before I start?"

A hint of disappointment pricks me, but I know not every day can be as perfect as yesterday. "I'd love to."

Breakfast at the Grand is as much of an event as dinner is, and I enjoy every moment. I want to have dinner here again, but savor it this time. The ambiance, the ornate décor, the drawn out meal. Hopefully with better company.

As we walk back into our room, he asks, "What are you going to do?"

The hint of concern in his tone has me smiling. "Probably read. Maybe I'll see what Jess and Lyssa are doing later, have lunch with them."

Relief lightens his expression. "I don't want to just ignore you."

Reaching over, I place my hand on his wrist. "Working isn't ignoring me. We hung out a lot over the last two days. If anyone is monopolizing time, it's me."

I make plans for lunch, alternating watching Sebastian work and reading until it's time for me to get ready. It's incomparably sexy to see him so focused. If we were in a different place in our relationship, I'd jump him right now and make him take me right on the desk, on top of his meticulous workspace.

But we're not.

I can't be too disappointed, though, because I'm already more fulfilled with him than I have been with anyone else. Somehow every crumb of his willing attention satiates me in a way no one else has. Sebastian wants to be with me, for nothing more than my company.

So, I settle for clenching my thighs as I turn back to my research. I feel like I know nothing about diabetes and hypoglycemia, but Sebastian is important to me, so I want to learn.

I never knew how important a functioning pancreas is. The more I read, the more grateful I am that my body produces what I need. I start thinking about worst case scenarios for Sebastian. Each new article or firsthand account leaves me feeling terribly unprepared. When we get home, I'll be asking him to show me where his emergency supplies are.

Just in case.

A couple of hours pass in the quiet harmony of him working and me reading. I've switched to my steamy romance, and I move through every position possible as I devour page after page. When I shift yet again, Sebastian chuckles, startling me.

"You're all over the place."

I shrug sheepishly. "Sorry. My secret's out. This is how I usually read."

We both laugh, but a glance at the clock tells me it's time to get ready for lunch. When I'm clean and dressed, I can't resist walking up behind Sebastian and sliding my arms over his shoulders. I love that he's at ease enough for me to feel comfortable giving in to my instincts like this.

"I'm going to hang out with Jess and Lyssa for a bit. You good here?" I press a quick kiss to his cheek, and he runs his hand over my arm, squeezing gently.

"Yes, have fun."

"I will."

Jess is waiting for me when I step off the elevator with Lyssa right behind her. They greet me with wide grins, then Jess says, "We thought we'd go to the little café across the street if that works for you?" At my nod, her grin turns wicked. "Good. That'll give you enough time to tell us exactly what's going on with you and Sebastian."

I let out a laugh as my cheeks warm. "Nothing like you're thinking." Jess, Lyssa and I have texted some, and they obviously know I stayed with him after my headache. They also know about my dad's request for

Sebastian to "keep an eye on me". I stare at the damp pavement, thankful the rain has stopped for now.

"We spent the past two afternoons together, and I'm falling for him. Hard. He said he likes me…that he wants me," I admit as we reach the sidewalk.

"Really?" Jess asks, skepticism coating the word.

Lyssa elbows her. "What was your response?"

I lift a nonchalant shoulder. "I kissed him."

Jess leans back in surprise while Lyssa beams and says, "Good for you."

We're seated right away. Our server hurries over with menus and waters for each of us. Once they're gone, Jess finally responds.

"Girl, you don't know what you're getting yourself into." Jess lowers her voice, leaning toward me. "It's always those quiet bookish types that are absolute freaks in bed." She straightens, giving Lyssa a coy look. "Take my girlfriend, for instance."

Lyssa's jaw drops, and she elbows Jess again.

"What? It's true," Jess says smugly.

"But you don't have to tell the world."

"Hey, I'm not ashamed. I like it like that."

I grin at their banter. "Well, we're not quite there yet." Although the idea of Sebastian unleashed has my stomach flipping.

"I've never seen him with anyone besides Leah," Jess muses, eyeing me thoughtfully. "Is he a virgin?"

I nearly spit out the mouthful of water I just took. "Jess!"

"What? It's a fair question."

Dropping my forehead to my hand, I wonder why I thought lunch with these two would be a good idea.

"Well?"

"I don't know, okay?" I say, a hint of exasperation creeping into my voice. I sigh and reluctantly explain, "We're going slow." I don't want to tell them about Sebastian's medical issues or past hang ups. Those are intimate details he's trusted me with and revealing them would be a betrayal.

But him dating Leah is common knowledge, so I settle for, "I wouldn't be his first girlfriend, but we haven't talked about more than that." My unspoken *yet* hangs in the air, and Jess exchanges a bemused look with Lyssa. I roll my eyes. "I *can* tell you that he's a good kisser."

They both lean forward, but the server reappears to take our orders. I chuckle as their faces fall. As the server starts to leave, I remember Sebastian and his tendency not to eat.

"Excuse me?" I wait for the server to turn back once more. "Could I get an order to-go? Maybe put it in when our food comes out, so it's still hot?"

"Of course. What would you like?"

I glance over the menu again, their turkey burger catching my eye. I decide on that with a side salad, of course. No fries. Hopefully, the standard condiments are all right.

Once the server is out of earshot, the girls drill me on the kiss, then we compare notes on gossip from this week. Yes, it's a bunch of professors and grad students, but there's always a new, interesting development at these conferences. We delve into the details—who ended up in whose room, who's no longer speaking.

Jess is right in the middle of a juicy story of a fight between two grad students when our food shows up. She doesn't even pause, and I soak up all the tea. One particularly hilarious anecdote involving an overeager

TA and a pot of coffee has us all doubled over in laughter.

But I stop abruptly at the familiar sound of a throat clearing behind me. I glance back to see my dad glaring. "Hey, Dad," I say uneasily.

It hadn't even crossed my mind to check in with him since I wasn't with Sebastian. I got so used to doing my own thing, and I know he's going to make a big deal out of it. I brace myself, holding out the tiniest bit of hope that he'll wait until we're in private.

"Calliope." He looks pointedly around the table. "I believe you were supposed to check in if you weren't with Sebastian."

I try to rein in my hurt. "I was with him all morning. He's researching." The waiter chooses that minute to deliver Sebastian's order, and I point to it. "I even got him lunch."

Dad sniffs derisively. "I want to be able to trust you, I do. But you make it so difficult."

My anger bubbles over, and I can't contain my frustrated words. "Because I had lunch with my friends without telling you?" When he freezes, I know I'm in serious trouble. I hold my breath for the backlash.

"You will *not* speak to me like that." Every word is an order, each syllable clipped and underlined with his low, cold tone that is absolute. "I am your father, and I deserve your respect. Especially in a place like this."

Right, how dare I question him? Let alone outside the four walls of our house. I stuff my feelings down, shoveling my self-control over them until they are buried, and I am an obedient, model daughter once more. "Yes, sir," I respond quietly, then press my lips together so I don't say more.

He flags down the server, handing him a credit card. "Their lunch is on me." To Jess and Lyssa, he says, "I apologize for my daughter."

Rage simmers within me, amplified by the uncomfortable, sympathetic looks my friends shoot my way. I shove my almost empty plate aside and stand up, snatching Sebastian's bag.

"Thanks for lunch." I direct it toward Jess and Lyssa, but glance at Dad to mollify him. "I'll just deliver this to Sebastian."

The leash around my neck chokes me as I stomp away, Dad's orders threatening to yank me obediently back to his side. I fight the constraint with every step, stewing as I storm across the street, ignoring the rain as I mutter to myself. I can't believe he berated me in public, in front of my friends.

For a harmless lunch.

My anger and hurt entwine until I can't tell where one begins and the other ends. I punch the button for the elevator, fighting the prick of tears. He doesn't deserve them. I step into the elevator, pushing the third floor. My future stretches before me, the thought of being under Dad's thumb weighing me as heavily as my rain-dampened clothes.

I walk down the hallway, each step one second closer to going home with *him*. The moments stretch into days, then months, then years, compiling into an impossible burden too heavy to bear. Their weight stamps out all hint of emotion, leaving a numbing, black emptiness in their wake.

Sebastian glances up when I shove open the door to our room, and I trudge over to plop his food next to him. "I brought you lunch. It's a turkey burger and side salad, and I did my best with the toppings." My words are dull, but I can't find the energy to put any life in them.

Sebastian frowns. "What's wrong, Calliope?"

My full name makes me wince, and I look away, unable to answer. I can't bear to mention the man who is supposed to take care of me, love me, watch out for me but instead smothers me as my jailer. My footsteps are heavy as I grab my PJs. I force myself to the bathroom, raking a towel across my damp skin after I toss my wet clothes over the shower bar.

Relatively dry and comfy, I plod back into the room and flop onto the bed. I crawl toward my pillow where I curl into a ball.

The bed dips behind me, and Sebastian rests a hand on my arm. "Callie..."

My nickname on his lips is a lifeline, and I grab his wrist, tugging him to me. "Hold me, just for a few minutes." When he doesn't move, I whisper a broken, "Please."

He lets out a heavy breath, then eases his arm beneath my head, wrapping it around my chest. I cling to his wrist as he slides his hand over my abdomen and pulls me flush to his firm torso. He curls his legs until they're touching mine, completely cocooning me. I bask in his warmth, soaking up his touch and allowing it to fill the empty places inside of me.

My mind is blank. I focus only on his touch as I stare unseeingly at the wall. The pitter-patter of rain falling is the perfect backdrop, combining with Sebastian's even breathing. My eyelids grow heavy, and soon I give in to the welcome oblivion of sleep.

* * * *

Sebastian

I held Calliope long after she fell asleep, wishing I could do more, then I forced myself to return to my work. I could only stay away for so long though, and now I'm easing back onto the bed, beside her. As soon as my weight makes the bed dip, she rolls toward me. Her fingers splay over my chest and I bring her knuckles to my lips then hold her hand.

I hated seeing her like that, and I know her dad was to blame by the way she flinched at her whole name. Her broken plea for me to hold her echoes in my ears even now.

While she was at lunch, I took a break from my research, wanting to surprise her with a special evening tonight. I made a reservation for dinner here at the hotel. Eating here is an experience I crave, and I'd like nothing more than to share it with her. Then I bought condoms.

It was quite possibly the most embarrassing experience of my life. I had to sneak out, not wanting anyone I know to see me and ask where I was going. I didn't know if I could lie, and I certainly didn't want to tell the truth.

I'm not presuming anything will happen, but I want to be prepared in case. After our heated moments yesterday where we found release, I don't know how I'm going to keep hold of my self-control. Or that I want to. I only have one more full day here with this woman, and I have no idea how I'm going to let her go back to that house. Back to our separate lives.

Sure, we'll see each other, but not to this extent. I like having her here in my space, sharing a bed and all the moments between waking and sleeping.

I trace the curve of her profile with my gaze, lingering on those full lips. The covers rise and fall as she breathes, the steady rhythm of slumber finally peaceful.

It's time for me to prepare for dinner, but I'm loath to leave her, though I know I need to. Especially if I want to give her time to get ready. With great reluctance, I force myself to pull away.

Once I've showered and shaved, I have a new dilemma. I can't decide what to wear. I don't want to go out already dressed in my suit because what if she's not up for a fancy dinner? What if the incident that upset her was bigger than the others and she needs to stay in tonight?

I mull over my options as I pull on my boxer briefs, then wrap my towel around me, deciding I want my lounge pants.

Slipping out of the bathroom, I hurry to my suitcase to awkwardly balance on one leg, then the other as I tug on my sweatpants. A quiet giggle sounds behind me, alerting me that Calliope is awake.

I pivot to face her, unable to keep from smirking. "Hoping to get a show, were you?"

She doesn't look the least bit sheepish as she grins. "Maybe." Not a hint of her earlier despair remains.

"I take it you're feeling better?"

Her smile dims slightly, but she sits on her knees, reaching her hand toward me. When I take it, her gaze turns tender as she says, "Thank you." She gestures to the bed. "For holding me, tucking me in."

"You're welcome." She shouldn't have to thank me. Those things should be the norm. "Tell me what happened?"

A moment passes as she presses her lips together and glances away before looking back at me. "I didn't let Dad know I was going to lunch without you, and he made a scene."

Shock courses through me as I frown and drop her hand, trying to make sense of what I'm hearing. "In front of Jess and Lyssa?"

"And everyone else within earshot. He even insisted on paying for our lunch as an apology to them for my behavior."

"That seems…harsh."

"Yeah." She pauses, her smile tight. "Welcome to my world."

"I'm sorry, Calliope." The words are only a drop in the bucket for what I wish I could convey, but I mean them with my entire being.

Heat flares between us. Her gaze drops to my still bare chest, her ravenous blue eyes making my mouth go dry. She gets to her feet, raising her hands to hover over my pecs, then meets my gaze. "May I?"

I can't form words, so I answer the only way I'm able, by leaning forward until her fingers sear into my skin. My breath catches in my throat at her little gasp, loving the feel of her delicate, exploring touch.

Fire blazes through my entire body when she glides those smooth fingers along my collarbone, then over my pecs. Goosebumps appear in the wake of her hands as she skates over the ridges of my abs all the way to my waistband. Her bliss-filled sigh nearly has me releasing right in my pants.

"If you don't ever wear a shirt again, I'd be okay with that."

Somehow I manage to chuckle, striving to keep my tone as light as hers. "I might get cold in the winter."

"Hmm, then you'll just have to snuggle with me." She slides her hands to rest on my shoulders as I process her words.

"Winter's a long way away."

Shock crosses her face, but I revel in the idea of being hers for that long and close the gap before she can protest. My lips touch hers as my hands lock on her waist, pulling her closer until there is no space between us. I can't hold back my want this time, allowing my desire to take over as I devour her delectable mouth. She moans into me, and I swallow it down, eating up each hungry sound while desperately wanting more.

I inch my hands down over her hips, waiting for her to stop me. But she doesn't. We both groan when I grip her perfect rear, and it fits into my hands as well as I've imagined. I give into the moment and lift her up, loving how she clings to me, wrapping her legs around my waist.

The moment my hard length nestles against her heat, she breaks the kiss to stare at me. My breaths come in shallow pants, and my fingers flex against her ass of their own accord.

"Just who is seducing who here?" she tries to tease, but her voice is husky.

"I should put you down, but I don't want to." My words come out in a growl, a sound I don't know I've ever made before.

"What do you want to do with me?" Hope gleams in her eyes.

A shudder racks me, a sure sign I'm nearing the end of my self-control. I need to reel it in or I won't be able to stop, which won't work if we want to make it to dinner. "Oh, so much."

"I'm not saying no, Sebastian." She slips her hand up to play with the hair at the nape of my neck. "Whenever you're ready."

Somehow her admission brings me back to my senses, and I take a mental step back. I'm not panicking, but I do want to give her the option of dinner. I loosen my grip, ignoring my own disappointment when she unwraps her legs and slides to the ground.

Her knees wobble though, and she sits hard on the bed. She blinks and thoughtful curiosity crosses her face before she blurts out, "Are you a virgin?"

Shock hits me, though I shouldn't be too surprised with my reactions going from one end of the spectrum to the other. I take off my glasses and swipe my hand over my face, trying to decide how much I want to say.

She quickly backpedals. "I'm sorry. That was rude. You don't have to tell me if you don't—"

"Calliope." I touch her shoulder and smile. "I'm not offended. And if anyone has a right to know my history, it's you."

A delighted smile crosses her face, growing even wider when I sit beside her. She crisscrosses her legs, her knee brushing my thigh. When I don't pull away, she relaxes, letting my leg hold her weight. It feels comfortable. Right, even. And it's nice having her to ground me as I open up.

"I'm not a virgin. For the first two summers after I started college, I interned as a clerk in my dad's law office. It was mostly pulling files and delivering them, but I interacted quite a bit with Dad's secretary. Elaine was older than me, but nice. The second summer, it became clear she was flirting with me. Being curious about gaining firsthand experience in that area, I accepted when she offered."

Calliope listens intently, without judgment. "Did you love her?"

Love is a strong word, one I've reserved for very few people in my life. My family, Leah. "We had a mutual understanding. I wanted the experience, she wanted the contact, and it worked out well." I stop, unsure if I should continue. "I...I don't know how much to tell you."

But she simply smiles and laces our fingers together. "As much or little as you want."

I swallow, feeling self-conscious as I admit, "You know how I have my research projects about animals?" At her nod, I continue, "Well, I put my photographic memory to use, researching different moves and acts."

"You...studied sex?" she asks incredulously.

"Yes."

Silence hangs between us as her mouth opens and closes then opens once more. Finally, she asks, "Did it turn out well?"

"I've had no complaints." Even I'll admit I sound arrogant, but it's not bragging if it's true, right?

Tension fills the pause that lingers between us, and she swallows hard before she speaks, her voice strained. "How did it end?"

I lift one shoulder. "I went back to college, and she had a job offer in another state that was closer to her family. She was hurt when I told her I didn't want to do a long-distance relationship. It didn't end amicably."

"I'm sorry."

But I can't bring myself to regret it. "From what I've heard, it was a lot better than most people's first time."

She chuckles, then leans against my shoulder. "Well, if you ever want to perform any more experiments, you've got a willing partner."

I glance at the clock, surprised it's already four. So much for giving her plenty of time to get ready. "Well, that will probably have to wait, as delightful as it sounds."

She tilts her head, the adorable pout to her lip making me want to kiss her all over again.

"I wanted to surprise you. When you went to lunch, I made dinner reservations for tonight. I would have told you sooner but…" We both glance at the unmade bed, the weighted afternoon making another appearance.

But she doesn't let it linger. "Dinner?" she prods.

"Here at the hotel."

"Sebastian!"

The scolding in my name tells me I went over the top, and my cheeks heat. "I thought we deserved a special night out, and I can't stay at the Grand without eating dinner here at least once. There's no one I'd rather share it with."

Her smile spreads ear to ear. "Ooh, I can't wait. When is our reservation?"

"Um, that's the thing…"

"Sebastian." She draws out my name threateningly.

"Five."

"That only gives me an hour!"

I duck my head. "I'd planned on giving you more time, but then I got distracted by —"

"Me," she finishes with a smug smile.

I roll my eyes. "Yes. You distracted me."

She dances on the bed, all triumph. "That's a win I'll take. At least the restaurant's right here so we don't have to figure in travel time." She hops up, places a hand on my chest and stretches on her tiptoes to kiss my mouth. "Thank you. This is a fun surprise."

"You're welcome." I don't look away as she gathers her things, then sashays to the bathroom.

Once the shower is on, I pull on my charcoal gray suit pants, undershirt and long-sleeved white dress shirt. I loop my tie around my neck and freeze as options race through my mind. Tie? No tie? If I don't wear a tie, do I undo my top button?

I don't think twice before dialing Shawn. He answers on the second ring and, when I tell him what's going on, he says he'll rally the crew, then call me back on video. Minutes later, my entire family hovers in the upper corner of my phone's screen as they scrutinize me. First with the tie, then without.

Leah says to keep the tie, but my brothers unanimously agree I look less like an arrogant stuffed shirt without the tie. They also vote for having the top button undone.

Before they end the call, Silas calls, "Don't forget, Seb, this is just our opinion. Be yourself and have fun!"

Shawn smiles, nodding his agreement, then we're disconnected.

I study my reflection, unsettled by the image looking back at me. I hear the bathroom door open, and I turn to ask Calliope's opinion, but I'm struck dumb at the very sight of her. She's always beautiful, but at this moment I feel as if I'm in the presence of a goddess.

The straps of the jade gown hang off her slender shoulders, accentuating every tantalizing inch of her collarbones. The fabric shimmers like the polished stone when she moves. The long hem of the dress nearly reaches the floor, but a slit splits the skirt, showing a delicious glimpse of her gorgeous leg all the way to mid-thigh.

Her violet hair is partially pulled back with a matching jeweled clip, and her cerulean eyes sparkle. She's wearing makeup, but it's subtle, emphasizing her full lips and long lashes.

"Calliope, you are more exquisite than any butterfly ever hoped to be."

She beams, walking over as she lets her gaze drift over my body. "Thank you. You look pretty exquisite yourself." She runs her hands down the lapels of my suit jacket, sending a thrill zipping through my torso. "I guess if you have to wear a shirt, I'll allow it, but only if it's with a suit."

I smirk, but my face falls when I catch a glimpse of the tie.

"What's wrong?"

My sigh escapes me before I can stifle it. I turn back toward the mirror and gesture to my reflection. "I'm not sure about my collar." I explain the whole situation as she listens intently. When I'm finished, she leans against my shoulder, and I'm struck by what a handsome couple we make.

"Would the tie make you feel more comfortable?"

The simple question makes me pause. No one else bothered to ask how it would make me feel, not even me, and I'm stunned that she cut to the heart of the matter so quickly. I study her in the mirror for a long moment. "It would. Being a formal setting, I feel like it calls for a tie."

Her sweet smile appears as she pushes off me and turns my body to face her. "Well, you're in good hands." She tugs on my sleeve, making me duck so she can loop the tie around my neck as she deftly flips up my collar, tucks the tie beneath and loops one end over the other. She pauses. "What type of knot would you like?"

My mouth goes dry. "What?"

"Windsor, Eldredge, Four in Hand, Double Windsor..." She trails off, looking embarrassed. "Did I say something wrong?"

"Quite the opposite."

She blinks, then starts laughing and shakes her head. "Sebastian, do you have any idea how many times this year I've had to listen to women complain about you never giving them the time of day?" At my frown, a wicked gleam appears in her eye. "Who knew all they had to do was bring up different ways to tie a tie?"

I know she expects me to tease her back or give her chase or flirt in some way, but she's so far from the truth that I can't. "No, Calliope. All they had to do was be you."

Chapter Fourteen

Sebastian

I can't help kissing her, those parted lips beg for it. Her hands cling to my undone tie as I cup her neck, my thumbs resting along her jaw. I catch myself before I devour her like I want to, knowing how much effort she put into getting ready. I don't want to smudge her lipstick.

I pull back, and she seems frozen, so I touch her wrists. "Can you really do an Eldredge knot?"

It does the trick, and she nods, her smile reappearing. Her nimble fingers make quick work of looping my tie this way and that until she steps back with a flourish. She turns me toward the mirror. "Ta-da!"

My smile is full and genuine as I study the flawless knot, the gray fabric laid perfectly in the intricate four layers as they crisscross each other at the base of my collar. "It's perfect. I've never been able to get that one right." I touch the indent where the rest of the tie hangs down. "You even have the dimple."

Her cheeks flush with the praise. "Dad's never been great at tying ties, so it was one more skill I picked up."

I hear what she doesn't say, that it was one more way to try to please her father. But I'm not letting Professor Harrison ruin our evening, so I push thoughts of him aside and instead lean over to kiss the top of her head. "Thank you very much. This is perfect."

"That's not even the best part."

I tilt my head and she giggles, then grabs the tie, tugging me closer until my lips hover before her.

"Ties make great handles."

It takes me a moment to find my words, to regain that hold on my fragile self-control. "Ah, well, I happen to love kissing you, so I think we both come out winners here." I kiss her gently, then offer my arm. "May I escort you to dinner?"

"First, I need my shoes." Her wicked smile tells me she knows exactly the torture she puts me through as she leans down to slip her feet into the silver heels that show off her painted toes.

I have to bite back a groan when I get an eyeful of the top of her lacy thigh-high stocking. All I want to do is drag her to me and give in to this tempest of desire storming within me.

She straightens and grins to say she's ready, so I stride to the door with my hands curled into fists to keep from acting on my longing. I open the door, allowing her to pass and careful not to touch any part of her. This dinner is important. I won't be derailed by the baser urges, especially because Calliope deserves an elegant night out.

Determined, I step into the hallway and offer her my arm. I remember my key at the same moment the door clicks behind us. *Fuck.*

The familiar lead settles in my stomach as I brace myself for her reaction to my carelessness. How many times have I heard the groan that she will surely emit when I tell her I need to go back? What if she doesn't have a key? What if we have to go to the front desk and —?

"Sebastian? Are you okay?"

I swallow, making sure to distance myself so her annoyance won't sting quite as much. "I forgot my key."

But her sunny smile never falters as she pats her clutch. "That's okay, I've got mine."

That's it. No groan, no berating, no frustration. My throat feels tight at the way she simply accepts me, and in my silence, she frowns.

"Do you want to go get your own key?"

I can only nod, too overwhelmed by the tumult of feelings inside me to speak. She lets me back in, and I walk over to the dresser where my key sits alongside my wallet and my ChapStick. After I slip them into my pocket, I force myself to go through my usual ritual of double-checking that I have everything because I don't want to come back here again. I've already wasted enough of our time.

When we step into the elevator, I reach for the button, but Calliope stops me as the doors slide closed. She asks, "Why so quiet? So you forgot your key, no biggie."

I wish I could shake the weight pressing down on me, but it's like a leech that has latched on and won't let go. "I get focused on where I'm going, and I forget things. Often. People usually get exasperated when they have to wait for me or go back." I lean against the metal wall, staring at the floor. "I hate being an inconvenience."

She runs her hand over my chest, giving a light tug on my tie so I look at her. "You're *not* an inconvenience," she says fiercely, and I wonder if she's telling herself as well. "If we didn't have a key, it'd be easy enough to stop by the front desk and get another one. It's just more time I get to spend with you."

She lifts on her tiptoes and tilts her chin up, asking silently for a kiss. I can't say no. The moment our lips meet, that familiar warmth shoots through me, piercing the lingering dread. I grow lighter each second, from her words and from *her*. The undeterred way she accepts each of my quirks and embraces them. Her unfailing optimism. The way she always lifts me up and cheers me on, buoying me.

Never once have I felt like a burden or a chore with Calliope, and I know it's because she's been made to feel like that in her own life. She knows how awful it is, so she's careful to keep from putting that upon anyone else. I've never felt so understood in my entire existence than I have in this last week.

I marvel at the beautiful woman before me, and I accept all the emotions she stirs within me. Yes, my control is compromised, but with her, I know I can let go and be safe. She will understand if I misstep or misspeak or am not perfect in my social cues. I can be myself with her.

Unhindered and undeterred.

I offer her my arm and a heartfelt smile as we exit the elevator. Though I've been in the dining room of The Grand for breakfast or peeked in throughout the week, I'm unprepared for seeing the opulence of dinner in person.

But Calliope doesn't look away from me, so I arch an eyebrow. "With all the wonderful things to look at in this room, why are you still staring at me?"

She hugs my arm tighter, leaning her head against my arm. "The last time I was here wasn't pleasant. I'm erasing that memory and letting this time with you take over."

A surge of protectiveness washes over me, the sensation quickly becoming familiar in its appearance where this woman is concerned. I rest my hand over hers. "You can always use my tie if it comes to that." And triumph has me grinning when my comment garners a giggle.

We're seated at a small table set for two, and I sink into my cushioned chair, trying not to get tangled in the pristine linen tablecloth that drapes to the floor. I study the place setting, naming each item in my mind — salad plate, cup and saucer, dinner plate, three forks, two knives, two spoons, and a perfectly folded napkin. An employee pours our water right away, then our server comes over to offer us menus.

I'd opted out of the pre-chosen chef's course when I made our reservation. With my dietary restrictions, I thought choosing our own dinner was preferable.

I set my menu down, having memorized it already, and listen instead to the soft piano music drifting through the room. A pianist tucked in the corner plays on a baby grand. Calliope doesn't stop smiling as she takes it all in, her attention lingering on the huge porch lined with vibrant baskets of hanging flowers.

"It's the world's longest porch, you know." I can't help it, the fact just slipped out, and I automatically brace myself for teasing.

"I didn't know that." She shakes her head, her smile never dimming. "Good thing you're here."

The words are a balm to me, and I fully relax as she picks up her menu. She studies it for several moments, then puts it down as the server comes back to take our orders.

After they leave, she asks, "How did you get into botany?"

"I was playing baseball in gym class in seventh grade. They positioned me way out in the field, and I grew bored. I noticed I was standing in a patch of clover, so I started looking through it, not paying attention to the ball." I chuckle. "I was never sports oriented, and gym class was my most hated period of all time."

"Gym was never my favorite either." She gives me an empathetic smile.

"I found a four-leafed clover, my first ever. I reached down to pick it, holding it in my hand as I straightened. And that's when it hit me." My lips twist into a wry smile at the memory. "The ball, that is. Right square in the face, smashing my glasses. I actually had to get stitches."

As I trace the faint line above my glasses, she leans forward, squinting at the white mark I know disappears into my eyebrow. "Aren't four-leafed clovers supposed to be lucky?"

"Well, that's the moment I decided plants are better than sports, so I count it pretty lucky for me. The very next day, I researched why some clovers have four leaves, and here I am."

"Nothing like a baseball to the face to show you your life's path." Then she pauses, tilting her head. "Why *do* some clovers have four leaves?"

Excitement rushes through me, and I lean forward, resting my elbows on the table as I lace my fingers together. "There is actually a debate about whether it is due to genetics or environment. It could be a recessive gene or several genes converging in the same plant. Which is why, if you find one four leaf clover, you're apt to find another."

"Genetics sounds plausible to me!"

I chuckle, knowing her passion for the subject. "How'd you get into genetics?"

"Punnett squares." She shrugs. "I fell in love with them the moment we were introduced in seventh grade."

"Hmm, seventh grade was a big year for both of us."

We share a chuckle, gliding through our soup and salad courses without a single lull in the conversation. I tell her more about growing up with my brothers while she reminisces with stories about her mom. This segues into how Professor Harrison was before her mom's death. The topic gets a little heavy, and Calliope seems grateful when I ask more about dancing.

I could watch her talk about dancing all day. It's clear she's as passionate about the subject as I am about my plants, and I'm glad she's found something to take joy in despite her father's pressure.

A natural pause occurs as we start our main course. The comfortable silence between us fills with the swell of the piano, and it makes me think of her dance lesson. I admit, "I had fun dancing the other night."

"You sound surprised. I told you that you would." She arches an eyebrow. "Did you doubt me?"

"Maybe." I know she's goading me. Then she raises her fork to lick off the mashed potatoes, and it's like flicking a switch, turning on the current controlling the desire that runs between us. My voice drops as I say, "Maybe I thought it was all part of your seduction technique."

"So," she replies with a saucy smirk, "if I were actually to have a seduction scheme, licking the fork and showing off lacy-topped stockings should be on my list."

Her eyes widen when I nod, as if she expected me to back down. But that's not what tonight is all about. "And if I have to wear dress shirts and ties, you are only allowed to wear skirts." My grin is wicked, and her lips part in shocked delight.

She recovers quickly, lifting her chin in the air and looking down her nose haughtily. "Well, I never. This is a *dress*, Sebastian. You, of all people, should know how important semantics are."

We both laugh, but hers dies when I study her again, letting all the intensity of my emotions into my gaze. I lean forward, stretching my hand out, and she hesitates before taking it.

I've rehearsed what I want to say, but it somehow doesn't seem like enough. "Calliope, I wanted dinner tonight to be special. I thought that we deserved to celebrate how far we've come this week."

Laughter bursts from her, garnering startled looks from nearby tables, but I can't take my eyes from her as she says, "You mean, from being at each other's throats to not being able to keep our hands off each other?"

"I was going to put it more delicately, but yes, in a certain sense." She grins, squeezing my hand, and I continue, "We started this with badly formed opinions of one another and now..." I have to pause, swallowing the emotions that threaten to overwhelm me. "Now, Calliope, I can't imagine thinking badly of you. You are one of the sweetest, most genuine people I know, and I want you in my life. I've enjoyed sharing so much with you this past week. I'd like to continue that, with you as my girlfriend." I hold my breath, forcing myself to meet her eyes.

A slow smile spreads over her lips, lighting her entire face. "Really, Sebastian? Your girlfriend?" She clings to my hand.

Hope stirs within me, brittle and fragile as I wait for her response. My chest is tight as anxiety winds around my lungs, my mind racing with all the ways she could shatter my heart.

"Yes." Her head bobs in a furious motion, her violet hair bouncing from the fervor. "A thousand times, yes."

My breath escapes me in a whoosh, and I have no idea what to do next. The server chooses that moment to interrupt, placing dessert menus in front of each of us. I let go of Calliope, thankful for a chance to collect myself.

She said yes. I can't believe it.

The server says they'll return shortly to check on us. I look across the table to meet Calliope's wondrous eyes...my girlfriend. The word makes my heart stutter, and I feel like it might burst from my chest with pride that I get to call this woman mine.

Her lips quirk into a soft smile. "As far as seduction techniques go..."

My mind races back to our talk earlier, to her offer of being a willing partner for any experimenting, and I blurt out, "I bought condoms." Those eyes widen to the size of the largest plates on our perfectly set table, making me backpedal. "I mean, just because you're my girlfriend doesn't mean we have to —"

"Sebastian!" She clamps her thumb and fingers together in a gesture indicating for me to shut up, which I do. She leans forward, keeping her voice low. "You. Bought. Condoms?"

I nod, trepidation filling me. Perhaps I overstepped.

"And we're still sitting here?" When I gape at her reaction, she glares. "I've been over here with my panties drenched, working on all the ways I can talk you out of that suit later, and you've just been...planning it all along?"

"I wasn't *planning*!" I protest, because I wasn't. "I wanted to be prepared for all possibilities."

"You..." She folds her arms, her breasts rising in a most appealing way that makes my cock sit up and take notice.

"Calliope," I try to explain. "I bought them earlier today because I'm ready. I'm not trying to push us any faster than we're already going. Believe me, I feel like we're barreling along like the European Bullet Train when I'm used to a steam locomotive. I planned to ask you to be my girlfriend, here, at this dinner. I want this to be special and memorable because you deserve that. Beyond this meal? I thought we'd see what happened."

Her stony gaze softens slightly, and I'm intrigued by the mischief lurking in her smirk. She uncrosses her arms. "You want me?"

"I think that fact has been established."

Leaning forward, she rests her elbows on the table. The bodice of her dress bows enough for me to catch a shadow of her cleavage and the way she doesn't take her eyes off me tells me she knows it. "I don't want to wait a single second more to get my hands on you."

I gulp at the hunger exuding from her, even as the same longing echoes within me. "What about dessert?"

She bends to her right, lowering one arm beneath the edge of the table. "Just how much do you want me, Sebastian? How close are you to losing control?" A second later, her stockinged foot touches my shin. I freeze, and she watches me carefully as she asks, "Shall we find out?"

I assess myself. *Am I up for this game? Can I let her push my limits like this in public, and do I want her to?* To my surprise, excitement wells within me, and my erection hardens in anticipation. I shift the leg she's not touching, clearing the path for her if she chooses to go that far. Then I smirk. "Go ahead."

Her chest heaves as she sucks in a breath while a flush spreads over her creamy skin, telling me how excited she is that I'm playing along. She glides up my leg, over my knee, to rest her heel between my legs on the padded chair.

Then she doesn't move. I wait impatiently while she takes a sip of water, and the anticipation is enough to make me burst. I want to surge forward, to press against her. The need for her touch is overwhelming, but the taunting smirk she wears makes me stay put.

After an agonizing moment, she tilts her foot to brush my inner thigh, and I force myself not to startle. Slowly, she eases closer and closer until she grazes my erection. I have to close my eyes and grit my teeth at the teasing touch. At last, she presses hard enough to elicit both torture and relief. I buck against her, needing more, needing—

"Have you two decided?" the server asks, inquiring about our dessert.

I stare up, torn between wanting to murder the server for interrupting and applauding them for stopping me before I completely lost control.

Calliope bats her eyelashes. "What do you think, dearest?" She strokes my length again. "I'll leave it up to you."

"To go," I demand. "We'll have our dessert to go."

The waiter nods, taking our orders and walking briskly away. Calliope grins in triumph as she retreats to her own space.

But two can play that game. After she's slipped on her shoe, I lean forward, keeping one hand on the table while I ease the other under the tablecloth to find her knee. My long arms make it possible for my fingers to find the slit of her skirt and touch her bare skin. She freezes at the unexpected connection.

"Shall I repay you while we wait?"

Her eyes widen.

"You can feel what it's like to be on the brink of losing control, like I constantly am around you." I circle my finger along the sensitive area above her knee on her inner thigh.

"What would you do?"

I glance each direction, pleased that no one is seated near enough to hear me if I keep my voice low. "I'd love to find out how wet you are for me. I'd slip my fingers along those beautiful thighs, reveling in how soft your skin is. Would you spread them for me, Calliope?"

She sucks in a ragged breath and nods.

"Good girl." I keep circling. "I'd play with that panty line for several moments. What kind are you wearing? Lace? Silk?" When she doesn't answer, I grin.

"Ah, you want me to find out for myself?" I inch forward slightly, nowhere near her panties, but I can see her nipples pebble beneath the silken fabric.

"Sebastian," she whispers.

"I don't think I'd plunge my fingers in quite yet. It'd be enough to brush my knuckles over your swollen bud, to caress those slick folds. I can't wait to taste your arousal, Calliope." I watch the server approach, then I move back to my side of the table, but not before I tell her, "I don't need dessert. I just need you."

Chapter Fifteen

Callie

I'm afraid if I stand there will be a dark spot on my chair where I've soaked through my dress. I don't know how Sebastian does it. The server appears with our desserts and I sit in stunned, anticipatory silence as I watch my boyfriend sign the check.

Boyfriend. Sebastian is now my boyfriend, and a part of me is still reeling.

Then he stands and holds out his hand. I can't help being disappointed that his jacket hides any evidence of his reaction to me. I ease from my chair, glancing back, relieved that there is no evidence of my own.

The little bag with our desserts dangles over his free arm, and his words echo in my mind. *"I don't need dessert. I just need you."* I lean against him, feeling small and vulnerable, eager to get to our room where we can have privacy. I quickly text my dad that I'm heading in for the night, needing my thoughts free from that avenue.

We step off the elevator, hurry down the hall, and I smile when he produces his own key to unlock the door, which he opens for me. Tension crackles between us as I glide past him and walk over to set my clutch on the dresser. I sense him behind me, meeting his hungry gaze in the mirror before his focus drops to my bare shoulders.

His long fingers brush my hair from neck, gliding over my skin to trace the low backline of the dress that dips beneath my shoulder blades. He swoops along, across the indent of my spine, all the way to the other shoulder where he plants a delicate kiss. The gentle graze of his lips sends a delicious shiver through me.

"I've wanted to do that all night," he admits. "You have a freckle, right there."

I twist to see, but all my movement does is put my face closer to Sebastian's. My hand automatically finds the edge of the dresser as my knees wobble and a needy "Please" passes between my lips.

My name is a mere breath before he brushes his lips to mine, then cups my cheek. But that's all I get before he leaves me again. His hands find my zipper, and his eyes meet mine in the mirror, asking permission. I nod.

He eases it down, exposing my bare back to the cool air. The cut of this dress is too low to wear a bra, so all he sees is skin. The straps on my shoulders keep the front in place over my breasts, and I watch delight dance in his gaze seconds before he touches a spot on the left side of my back.

"You have a butterfly tattoo."

It's a little clichéd, I know, but at this moment, it's never felt more right.

"Morpho peleides Kollar," he says, tracing it.

The big blue butterfly I just learned the common name of yesterday. I smile, meeting his eyes again in the mirror. "Blue morpho," we say together.

We are connected, he and I, by more strands than either of us can count. Both of us know what it's like to feel out of place, to feel like more of an inconvenience than anything else. All I want is somewhere I belong, and I've found that with him. He's shown me facets he hides from others, trusting me with them, and I've opened up to him more than with anyone before.

I spin to face him, running my hands over his chest as I say with all the longing I'm feeling, "Sebastian, I need you too."

It's more than a declaration of physical want, just like his admission about dessert was, and I know he understands by the way his breath catches. His hazel eyes darken as he dips to grab my thighs, lifting me as I cling to his shoulders. We lock gazes as he walks me to the bed and lays me gently on it.

He shrugs out of his jacket as I toe off my shoes, anticipation building between us. Gone is the awkwardness, burned away as want rises up. I scoot backward, and my dress slips down, baring the tops of my breasts. He sucks in a sharp breath, his gaze riveted to the newly exposed skin as a thrill rips through me. I can't wait anymore, so I reach out, grabbing his tie and pulling him closer.

He plants his large hands on either side of me as he moves nearer, nudging his leg between mine. My dress rides up, the slit pushing higher on my leg until my heat is pressed against his firm thigh. I groan at the needed friction.

His lips claim mine as I grind on him while his erection digs into my hip. When he deepens the kiss, I bump his glasses, and he pauses to set them on the end table. I stare at his handsome face, taking a moment to run my hand over his smooth cheek. I'm so in awe of this sweet, sensitive, smart man.

My gaze drifts to his tie. "As much as I like this," I say hoarsely, "maybe it could come off."

He grins, sitting back, still straddling my thigh. I rake my gaze over him, hungrily landing on the jutting front of his slacks. The tie disappears, and he arches a brow, taunting me. I glare, sitting up, and my dress slips down even more. He watches intently as I unbutton his shirt, my fingers flying until I shove it off.

But there's still an undershirt in my way. I growl at the barrier, and Sebastian laughs as I tug it over his head. Then I smile widely at the playground of his gorgeous torso. "You're right. Who needs dessert?"

Our lips collide once more, and I lean back as he follows. My hands slide over the beautiful expanse of his smooth chest, memorizing each dip and swell. His finger brushes my cheek, then he trails it along the side of my neck to dip into my cleavage.

Anticipation coils within me as he pushes the fabric of my dress down, exposing one breast completely. I arch into his fingers, needy and aching for his touch, and when he rolls my nipple, my groan is swallowed by him. Then he yanks his mouth from mine, planting kisses along the same path his finger traveled until he wraps his lips around my peaked nipple.

I grip the back of his head, holding him closer as I rock my hips again. I feel like I could explode any second, but I don't want to come alone. I hold off by sheer willpower. I want to touch my boyfriend with no barrier between him and my fingers.

Easing my hand along his torso, I toy with his belt, my movements slow and deliberate so he knows exactly what I'm thinking. He doesn't stop me as he tugs down the other side of my dress and devotes his attention to that breast. My smile fades into a desperate gasp at the sensations, making me fumble in my quest to undo his buckle.

At last, I ease down his fly. My fingers edge into his boxer briefs, and he groans as I grip his hot length. He feels as impressive as I imagined him to be, long and smooth, thick and eager. I wrap my hand around him, barely able to close my fingers around his girth.

His eyes flutter closed, and I know he's trying to control himself. He rolls my nipple once more, then eases onto his side next to me.

His hand slides over my abdomen, toying with the slit of my skirt as I freeze in excitement. He nudges my hem up and up. His fingers dance along my inner thigh, over the top of my stocking until they touch my bare skin. But he doesn't stop there. My stomach flips as he edges toward my center, and I gasp when he grazes my lace-covered pussy.

He hisses out an amazed breath. "So wet."

"Touch me," I beg, bucking my hips and gripping his cock. "Please."

His smirk irritates me, so I give him a hearty pump, ending with my thumb circling his head and flicking down that sensitive ridge. He groans, then slips a finger inside the edge of my panties, still teasing.

"Sebastian," I plead, writhing under him.

He leans down to cover my mouth with his, swallowing my noises as he glides a finger along my folds and slides it into me. I arch for him, his palm hitting my swollen clit just right. I know I won't last long with his skilled fingers. The beautiful sensations he creates overwhelm me, and I give it right back, establishing a rhythm that has him breaking away to suck in air.

Our eyes lock as we drive each other to that heady brink. I clench first as my orgasm crescendos over me. I call out his name. Then he thrusts into my fist, hot liquid spilling onto my hip, thigh and fingers as he grunts. As my aftershocks fade, he slips his fingers out of me.

He brushes his lips against mine, and I am overwhelmed by the tenderness in his gaze. He disappears, coming back with his pants zipped and a washcloth in hand. His gentle touch has warmth spreading through my chest as he thoroughly cleans my hand and leg, then lies down beside me to take me in his arms.

I snuggle into his chest, contentment and bliss enveloping me in their heady embrace. We lie like that for a good while, soaking each other in. But it's still early, and I'm nowhere near ready for sleep.

Propping my arms on his bare chest, I rest my chin on my fist. "Please tell me you're not ready for bed."

His chuckle rumbles through me. "No, not at all. Just giving us both a bit of time to recover."

I slip my leg over his, grinning widely. "I'm recovered."

He runs his hands down my bare arms, a wicked gleam in his hazel eyes. "I might be…persuaded to make a quicker recovery if I had the chance to explore a certain territory more thoroughly." His fingers dip down, caressing my breasts that are pressed between us.

I've always been a little self-conscious about my B-cups, but he makes me feel like I'm perfect. I push myself to a sitting position and raise my arms, stretching in a wide, slow motion so he gets a huge eyeful, since my dress is still pooled around my waist. "If only I had some idea what you're talking about—"

My words are cut off in laughter as he tackles me to the bed. His mouth finds mine, hungry and demanding, his chest firm against me. I moan, lacing my hands behind his neck as I try to loop my leg over his. But my skirt is in the way and I'm stuck.

I push on Sebastian, and he immediately releases me, staring down in question. I tug on my half-on dress. "How about this comes all the way off? Then I'm not all tangled in it?"

"Deal."

He smirks and whips off the offending garment, then it slips from his fingers as he stares at me as if overwhelmed with awe. He wore the same expression when I emerged from the bathroom, and I have never felt more worshiped than by this amazing man. His hands run over me, sending mini bolts of lightning through my whole being as he glides down my stomach, over my hips, my stocking-clad thighs, and back up.

"So beautiful," he murmurs.

"Your turn." I tug at his pants, and he blinks as if I pulled him out of a dream. "Please?" I bat my eyelashes, but he's not balking, only processing.

And he smiles as he gives in. Seconds later, he stands before me, a god in his own right in his boxer briefs, and he's all mine. I reach for him, sighing happily when his weight settles over me.

"So, you like to be in control?" I ask. "Does that mean being on top for sex?"

He wedges his body between my legs, resting his sufficiently recovered erection on my needy pussy with only our underwear between us. "No, Calliope, I just want to be in control of myself, but I've given up when it comes to you. I need you, and I've accepted that. I have no control when you're around." He rocks his hard length against me. "See? I need you already."

"You haven't had me yet."

"Let's fix that." He reaches over to open the drawer. "If you're ready."

"I thought that's what all this foreplay was about."

He grins and pushes down his underwear, his eager erection springing out.

"Sebastian?" He glances up, and I bite my lip before saying, "We don't have to use condoms, if you don't want to. I'm clear. I'm on birth control."

He glances at the drawer, then slowly pushes it shut. "I've never done that before, but I made sure to be tested after Elaine. Everything came back negative." His intense gaze finds mine. "I'd like to try this with you, if you're positive you're okay with it."

A thrill goes through me at being this intimate with Sebastian. "It'll be a first for me too."

He kneels on the bed and helps me take off my panties. Then he strokes me with his fingers — once, twice — making me moan. With another grin, he lies on his back. "You on top will be a dream come true."

I stare for a long moment. "I didn't mean we had to do that now."

"No time like the present."

His thick cock calls to me, and I can't resist straddling him. My pussy is wet already from round one, so I position him just so, then slide down his hard length. My moan is sinful as I take him fully, though his groan is just as loud, just as needy.

"Fuck, Sebastian, that feels amazing."

"Calliope," he growls, gripping my hips. "You are only ever allowed to say my name like that. For the rest of our lives."

I think about how I said it, then roll my hips and moan his name again, pleased when he closes his eyes, a muscle ticking in his jaw. I place my hands on his pecs. "Definitely not in control now, huh?"

His eyes pop open. "I'm in control enough."

The challenge in his gaze excites me, reminding me of the dining room and the way he didn't back down. I know I won't be left hanging here.

"A little tidbit about me being on top," I say, extra sauce in my voice. "It usually takes me longer to, you know, get there." His eyelids lower halfway, then one corner of his mouth tips up, and I know I'm in trouble.

"We'll see about that."

Gripping my hips, he tilts his own, positioning his cock at a wholly different angle that hits brand new places within me. It's like a whole other pleasure center is open for business, and I'm here for it. The first thrust has me digging my nails into that pristine chest in an effort not to cry out.

He just smirks. "Better hold on."

I don't do any of the work as he keeps me in place, lifting me so he can slam into me over and over and over again. The repeated friction against my clit, the ebb and flow within my inner walls, and that spot...G isn't a good enough name. It's at least a wow, if not a *fuck*!

Soon I'm a panting, mewling mess as I hover right at that edge with my pinnacle in sight. "Sebastian, I'm so close."

He tightens his grip in acknowledgment and somehow ups the pace, driving me home and taking himself with me. I shove my fist into my mouth to keep from screaming as I collapse on him. He pulses inside me, holding me tight as we lie there, both breathing heavily.

After a moment, he lets me go, so I take that as my cue to use the bathroom. When I emerge, he gets up and disappears into the bathroom, taking his underwear with him. I perch on the edge of my bed, uncertainty coursing through me.

I don't know what to do next, what he needs. I eye his pristine bed, imagining him crawling into it as I lie here alone again. He comes out, a soft smile on his lips as he meets my gaze.

"Do you — ?" I falter, losing my train of thought and needing to start again. "Are you...?" I can't make the words come out.

He frowns. "What, Calliope? What is it?"

I cross my arms over my bare torso, feeling small. "Where are you sleeping? I'm trying to figure out how much space to give you." I don't want to give him any. I want his arms around me, and I need that intimacy right now, but I also don't want to push.

The bed dips with his weight, and he pulls me into his warm embrace. "I don't need any space. You make me feel safe."

The sweet words fill the hollow void that threatened to overtake me, and I fling my arms around him.

"That's the nicest thing you've ever said to me." My words come out thick with the emotion he stirred.

He holds me for several more moments until something is poking my hip, and he shifts. When I let go, he clears his throat. "Remember how I said I have no control where you're concerned?"

My lips twitch at the evidence tenting his boxer briefs. "I guess I shouldn't have hugged you so exuberantly, huh?" I try to tease.

He sighs, running a hand over his hair. "We don't have —"

"Sebastian." I touch his arm. "I don't get hard every five seconds and show the world how I'm feeling, but believe me, this is new and exciting, and I am ready for more. I promise I'll tell you if it's too much."

A relieved grin lights his face. "Really? You want more?"

I bite my lip, leaning in to run my hands over his pecs, letting my breasts graze his arm. "I think I've been patient enough." His hazel eyes darken, and he reaches for me, but I roll away, grinning from the flat of my back. "This time, you're on top."

* * * *

Sebastian

I wake up warmer than usual, and it startles me to find Calliope still snuggled to my side. But it's a good thing. Like waking from the best dream, only to find you weren't dreaming at all.

My lips are curved up. I hadn't even realized I was smiling. Had I ever stopped?

This magnificent woman... I drink her in, basking in this moment until it hits me that this is it. My last morning with her. Reality settles like a boulder in my stomach, and I wish I was still asleep. At least there I could pretend that we don't have to go back to our separate lives.

I never expected to be so content sharing my space with another person, and now I can't imagine not having her here. She'll return to her dad's house, and me to mine. My bed will feel empty without her, my house too quiet without her vivacious presence.

I remember my days before the conference, the mundane, colorless existence I led before she brightened every corner of my life. Is it too soon to ask her to marry me? I've found this perfect woman, and I never want to be without her again. I contemplate it seriously for several seconds, picturing our elopement as this whirlwind week's perfect end.

But I know she's never had her freedom, and she deserves that before she is tied to someone else.

I bite back a sigh, knowing even the topic of marriage will have to wait. For now, I'll try to prolong this time we have together. Starting by texting her father about her transportation home.

I'm careful to make sure to convey that she hasn't made a decision yet and will be confirming with him one way or the other. I want her to have that choice. He's delighted at the possibility of me spending more time with his daughter.

Then I order room service with several options I know Calliope likes and ones I can live with. I take my coffee out onto the balcony, not wanting to disturb Calliope as I read. It's a beautiful day, and I continue the new book she bought me on draft horses, soon engrossed in learning about the fascinating animals.

"Hey."

Calliope's soft voice startles me, and I jerk, almost sloshing coffee on my book, but I manage to keep the pages clean.

"Oh, hi." I smile at her, but my smile dims when I take in her more subdued expression. "What's wrong?"

She crosses one arm over her body, and the soft robe she's wearing gapes slightly at the chest. "I was kind of hoping to wake up with you." She lifts a shoulder. "You know, our first morning together and all that."

It strikes me that I don't know. Elaine and I didn't do sleepovers. We cuddled some, then we'd go our separate ways.

I frown. "I haven't done this part before. I've never had a morning after."

Her expression softens. "Well, for starters, it's nice not to wake up alone. I felt a little...abandoned in there."

I reach out my hand, relieved when she takes it and allows me to pull her onto my lap. She fits so perfectly, cuddling against my chest, her head tucked beneath my chin.

Holding her tight, I say, "I'm sorry. I didn't know."

She stays quiet, and I think of what to say. I could tell her all the things I did accomplish while she slept, but I don't believe that's what she needs right now. An idea strikes me.

Kissing the top of her head, I let her go and give her a nudge. "Go back to bed."

"What?"

"I'd like a do-over. Go back to bed. Please?"

Understanding dawns in her eyes, and she scrambles off my lap as a smile spreads across her face. Then she hurries into the room. I give her a moment to get settled before I walk back in with my book and my coffee.

Chapter Sixteen

Sebastian

Calliope rests on the bed, snuggled under the covers with her eyes squeezed shut. I grin as I sit beside her, then open my book. A moment later she fakes a yawn and peeks over.

Her wide smile reappears, lighting her whole face. "Good morning."

I can't help returning it with a full smile of my own. "Good morning. How'd you sleep?"

"Best I've had all week. Finally got to scratch this itch that's been bugging me." She sits up and stretches, the covers falling to her waist to reveal that she's removed her robe. And isn't wearing anything else.

Speaking of scratching itches.

The saucy glint in her eye tells me she knows exactly what she's doing as I pointedly adjust myself so my growing erection is more comfortable. I set my book on the end table, then put my glasses on top of it. "Is this why you wanted me in bed when you woke up?" I murmur as I reach for her.

"Maybe."

I haul her right onto my lap, settling her bare opening on my hard length, still covered by my pants. She gasps, and I revel in running my hands over her smooth thighs, up her sleek hips, back to grip her tight ass. And I tug her tight to me as I rock against her. She closes her eyes and moans, holding my shoulders.

I reach between us, gliding a finger along her seam that's already soaked with arousal, and I grin, then push down my sweatpants to sheath myself in her. She gasps my name.

"What? We went slow last night." I chuckle, leaning in to nuzzle her neck. "Besides, you can't tell me you're not ready for me." I thrust inside her without any resistance.

"I just...wasn't expecting..." She hums, rocking forward, so her clit grinds on my abs.

"Someone woke up hungry." I kiss her again. "Don't worry, Calliope. I'll take care of you."

I keep still inside her while I focus on giving her pleasure in other ways. My lips trail down her neck, nibbling and nipping. I slip my hand between her legs, using her own arousal to glide to her clit, where I make languid circles as she whimpers.

But I'm not done. I use my free hand to play with her perfect breasts, toying with one nipple then the other, coaxing them into hardened peaks as I roll and flick. When she tries to bounce on my dick, I tsk and clamp my hand over her hip, keeping her still. I'm still able to reach her clit with my thumb, so I continue playing as she whimpers.

"Soon I'll let you ride me with as much abandon as you want, but first, let me take care of you."

"Sebastian," she groans, trying to writhe.

"Do you want me to let go?" I ask, hoping I know the answer as my cock grows even slicker from the evidence of her desire.

She shakes her head, so I keep going, coaxing her toward that pinnacle. I love the flush that spreads over her body, the tint of pink as her blood flow increases. It's like the physical manifestation of the fire she ignites in me.

Her ragged breaths have her bosom rising and falling in the most tantalizing way. And her gaze is hungry, wanton even, emphasized by her parted lips.

I increase my pace, creating more intense friction for the swollen bud between her creamy thighs, and she gasps before letting out a guttural moan. The noises she makes fascinate me. I want to record all of them, so I can play them back over and over until they are ingrained in my mind.

She cries my name as I feel the first flutters of her inner walls gripping my cock, and her nails dig into my bare shoulder. I hope she leaves a mark. The thought surprises me, but the more I think about it, the more I hope she does. I'd wear her marks like medals, badges of honor to show the world that she chose me.

With one more pinch of her nipple, I send her over the edge, and I can't look away as she shudders and shakes. Her pussy grips me in waves as she cries out, and I bask in the triumph of taking her there. She is beautiful, phenomenal even, and, best of all, she is mine.

She collapses against my chest. I hold her for long moments, relishing the feel of her in my arms and still being joined with her. Sure I want my turn, but I can wait. It's our last morning together, after all, for who knows how long.

Several moments later, she lifts her head, sitting up and back so my cock rests in her fully. Her gaze holds bliss and contentment, along with a depth that makes my heart soar as she rocks on my achingly hard dick. A pang shoots through my chest. I want to keep her, more than I've ever wanted to keep anything in my entire life.

"Sebastian?"

I try to snap out of the odd feeling, and I manage smile as I lean back. "Use me, Calliope. I'm all yours. You're completely in charge here."

Delight dances in her eyes. "Completely?"

I lie flat on my back, and her hands splay over my chest as she rises then sheaths my eager cock again. *Home*, my mind chants. This is what it feels like to be home. I almost come on the spot when she leans forward, sliding to my tip then sitting all the way down once again. I lace my hands behind my head to keep from taking over.

"You like that?" she asks.

"Very much."

"Good." She smirks and slows her pace to a glacial one, torturing me as she leans forward so our mouths meet.

The way she rides me, rolling her hips just right and taking me so deep, I'm seeing stars as I try to keep from losing control. But she's upping her pace, her movements increasing as she builds that need within herself as well. I love how she grinds on me with each pass.

Her breasts bounce in the most enticing way, reminding me of that unexpected fantasy that blindsided me so many weeks ago. Now I'm here, living my dream with Calliope as my girlfriend.

I can't resist touching her any longer. I reach out to rest my hands on her trim waist, but I don't hinder her movements or change her pace.

"Touch me," she begs.

"Where?"

"My clit. I need more."

I pop my thumb into her mouth, my balls tightening when she sucks, then I slip my hand between us. She grinds on me, moaning immediately, and I feel her clenching. She's close. Her pace changes, her movements are more frantic, and I grit my teeth, desperate to hold out for her.

"I'm so close," she gasps.

I grip her ass and thrust with her, taking the depth to a whole new level. It's enough to push her over, and her cry is almost a scream. She drops her face to my chest to muffle the noise as I hold her hips and drive myself home again and again. And again.

Then I let go, crying out her name as I spill into her. Neither of us move for a long minute, and when she does shift off me, I have to fight from pulling her back onto me. Somehow I refrain.

She curls in next to me, snuggling to my side as I tuck my arm around her. Then she frowns. "Oh, what time is it? I should probably check in with Dad."

"I texted him once already," I admit. "I hoped he wouldn't mind if you rode home with me. If you'd like."

She beams. "I'd love to."

"Good, I'd enjoy that. Very much."

We grin at each other, and a foreign mushy feeling bubbles within my chest. I wonder if we look similar to Shawn and Leah when they are caught up in each other, oblivious to the others around them. I always thought it was on the ridiculous side, completely over the top. But here I am.

After we're dressed and she's confirmed with Professor Harrison that she is riding with me, we eat our quick breakfast, then take a walk. I tell her some of the interesting facts I learned about draft horses this morning, as well as the updates on my roses as we meander through the gardens hand in hand.

Her smile has an odd twist to it so I ask, "What are you thinking about?"

"The last time I was here, I was running from you." She sighs, leaning into me. "I can't believe you chased me."

I laugh. "I probably looked like a madman, tearing through here. We're lucky someone didn't alert the authorities."

She squeezes my hand tighter. "Thank you for following me."

I let go of her hand and wrap my arm around her instead, sensing her need to be closer. "Of course, Calliope." We walk a few more steps then I add quietly, "If I had my way, I'd never let you go." I hope it's not too much, but she deserves to know what I'm feeling.

Silence lingers for a few steps, then she glides her hand over my stomach and tilts her face so I can see her sweet smile. "I want that, too. Maybe someday."

It's enough for now. We bask in the contented quiet lingering between us until we reach the beach. I'm used to the sandy shores of our area back home, but this one is lined with rocks. I let go of Calliope to study them as she walks toward the water's edge.

This area is known for our state stone — the Petoskey stone. The dull grayish-brown shade is nothing brilliant, but the white lace-like design peppering its surface makes it unique.

And I find one.

I pick it up, examining it closely and marveling at its smoothness as Calliope takes in the view. One of my favorite animals pops into my head — penguins. Several species of penguins find their mate then give them a perfect stone to signal they want to spend forever together. Well, I've found my mate. Finding this rare stone at this particular moment feels like fate's stamp of approval, and I slip the stone in my pocket.

Another unique stone catches my eye and I grin, picking it up before I walk over to Calliope. I offer it to her. "Make a wish."

She frowns, taking it from me to study. "What?"

I point to the white band encircling the rock. "It's a wishing rock. Legend says that if you trace your finger over the line while making a wish, then throw the stone into the water as far as you can, your wish will come true. Or if you give it to another person, your wish will come true."

She runs her thumb over the smooth surface. "What did you wish for?"

Forever, I think to myself as I brush back a strand of hair the wind has teased into her face and tuck it behind her ear. "I don't need to wish for anything else. Everything I could ever want is standing right before me."

Her fingers close over the stone as I lean in and press my lips to hers. The only thing I could wish for is more time, and that's impossible, so I'll make the most of what I have.

We pack more into those remaining hours than should be physically possible, then I savor every moment of the way home. I learn the kind of music she likes. Songs that would normally bother me take on a new light when I find out she enjoys them. I even catch myself humming along.

I let her pick the restaurant for lunch, trying a cauliflower crust pizza that turns out to be absolutely delicious. Although, I do get my usual side salad with it.

When we finally pull into her driveway, I see the first hint of sadness in her expression. We've both done our best to hide the fact that reality is knocking, but it's finally time to answer.

"Do I have to go in?" she asks, staring at her lap.

There are so many answers I want to give, but the majority of them would terrify her because they are too much too soon. Hell, if I examine them closely, they would scare me with their depths. "I wish things were different," I say, offering my most sympathetic smile. "Las Vegas is only two thousand miles away. We can always elope if it gets too bad."

She laughs, not taking me seriously, which is probably for the best, even though her dismissal stings a bit. "I'll keep that in mind." Then her smile drops, and she lets out a sigh.

I'm reminded of that night Silas ran out of gas, how she prepared herself to go inside. I imagine her putting on armor, piece by piece, and I hate that she has to protect herself. That I can't be there for her. That I can't keep her safe.

I touch her wrist, sliding my hand down until my fingers wrap around hers. "I'm only a phone call away. We can talk as much as you need, and maybe you can come work with me in the greenhouse on Tuesday." I won't be in the office tomorrow since it's Sunday, and Monday is Memorial Day. Tuesday feels like a lifetime away, but I try to keep my expression positive.

She nods, squeezing my hand. "I'd like that."

We let go, both reaching for our door handles. Heavy silence reigns as I help her with her bag. She's asked me not to go in, not wanting to deal with her father gloating over us being together. I understand. A part of me is grateful because I still haven't decided how to reconcile my new data about him with my previous image.

She touches my arm, and I bend so she can press a kiss to my cheek. Then I watch her disappear into her house while my entire body grows heavy. I have to force myself to move, my joints feeling wooden and stiff as I return to the car. I drive to my house on autopilot, and when I pull into the driveway, the usual sense of being where I belong doesn't come.

Because, for the first time, I belong to someone else, and she's not here.

* * * *

Callie

Sunday and Monday are miserable on several levels. While my dad is in a good mood from the conference and me being with Sebastian, his gloating over bringing us together is beyond annoying. Every time my phone chimes or rings, Dad gets this cocky smirk and hums to himself.

Taking credit for everything, as always.

The sour taste in my mouth appears with each comment, each look. Does he truly believe I'm not capable of choosing my own guy? Or able to secure my own relationships? It's as if I'm helpless even in this aspect of my life.

Dad keeps me home on Sunday, because I've been out enough. But Monday is even worse because he drags me to his sister's house. Compared to Aunt Deb, Dad is loose and carefree in his rules. Visiting her is always mentally exhausting because I have to watch every move, every word, and every expression.

I count each minute until I can see Sebastian again, wishing we didn't ever have to be apart.

* * * *

Tuesday morning is torture, since I have to wait to meet Sebastian until after lunch. I eat early and drive in, but I don't want to disturb my boyfriend sooner than we agreed on. It takes all my effort to walk into the office to say hi to my dad first, but he's on the phone, so all I get is a quick wave. He seems like he'll be a while, so I duck back out.

I'm still early, but screw it. I can't wait another minute to see Sebastian.

I burst into the greenhouse, a broad smile on my face as I call for him. But no one answers, and I don't see his lanky frame anywhere. I scan the area, my heart stopping when my gaze lands on the desk where Sebastian is slumped over in a heap.

I cry out his name as I race over to check if he's still breathing. He has a pulse, but it's faint. My research rushes back to me in bits and pieces as I yank open the drawers of his desk, searching for any sign of a glucagon kit. Finally, I see the oblong case and relief surges through me.

Looping my arms under Sebastian's, I drag him to the floor as carefully as I can. My hands shake as I open the orange box. Simple printed pictures line the lid, reminding me of the steps, and I read them over, trying to stay calm. I can't panic, not now.

I yank the cover off the needle, slide the point into the top of the glucagon vial, then depress the plunger. Distilled water fills the container, mixing with the powder, and I shake it until it dissolves.

My heart pounds, each beat reverberating through my chest as I tip the vial upside down and pull the plunger out slowly until all liquid is gone. I hurry to set the bottle down, grateful Sebastian is wearing shorts. The medicine needs to be injected directly into muscle, and the thigh is a perfect location.

I push up his shorts as the incessant panic flutters in me, trying to take over, trying to make me freeze. But Sebastian needs me, and I don't have time to freak out. So, I shove the feeling aside, focusing on my task at hand. Clenching my teeth, I ease the needle straight down into his skin as I suck in an anxiety-filled breath, then continue to depress the plunger.

When the syringe is completely empty, I remove the needle from his skin. I toss the syringe into the orange case before I roll Sebastian onto his left side, propping him against the desk. Then I scramble for my phone. When the nine-one-one operator picks up, I explain the situation, trying to be calm.

"Do you know the time of the injection?"

I glance at my phone. "Um, just before I called you, so within the last few minutes. But I don't know the precise time, no."

"Has your boyfriend responded to treatment?"

I crouch beside him, nudging Sebastian, but nothing changes. "No, not yet."

"Okay, ma'am, we'll send an ambulance right over."

Pacing back and forth, I never look away from Sebastian as the minutes pass. His eyes flutter open as the sirens approach. I yelp his name, bending down to clutch his hand, and he squints in my direction.

"Hey, it's me, Calliope. How are you feeling?"

But he doesn't answer, and the greenhouse door flings open. Two EMTs burst in, rushing toward us. One kneels down, relief appearing on her face when she sees he's awake.

She nods to her partner, then begins asking me questions. "When did he wake up?"

"A second ago."

"Did he say anything?"

I shake my head. "He seems really out of it."

A frown crosses her face. "Does he have a glucose monitor or an insulin pump?" Her frown deepens as I shake my head again. "What's his name?"

"Sebastian," I say, still gripping his hand. His eyelids flutter closed again, and panic clutches my chest.

"Okay, Sebastian." She speaks in a calm, quiet tone as she pulls a small orange box and bigger black device out of her kit. The machine beeps when she presses a button. "We need to test your sugar level."

She massages his finger, sanitizes the area and quickly pricks the side. Squeezing the digit, she picks up the device and presses the tip into the blood beading on his skin. I hold my breath when it beeps again and her face falls.

Sebastian grimaces then gags before tipping his head and vomiting across the floor, narrowly missing me.

When the EMTs exchange a worried look, I have to ask, "Is he okay?"

"The medicine you gave him can cause nausea as a side effect, but it can also be a sign of hypoglycemia. Since his levels aren't stable yet and he is still non-responsive, we need to take him in."

While they load him onto the stretcher, I grab his phone off the desk, swiping to his emergency contact. Shawn is listed, and I remember how Sebastian said he was closest to him. I punch his name, relieved when he answers.

"Hey, Sebastian. What's up?" a deep voice says.

"Um, Shawn?"

He pauses. "Yeah…who's this?"

"This is Callie. You were listed in Sebastian's emergency contacts—"

"Emergency? What happened? Is Sebastian okay?"

I explain, telling him we'll be going to Lakeview Medical. He assures me he'll let the rest of the family know, and they'll meet us there, then he hangs up. I haul myself into the ambulance after they've loaded Sebastian. I sit close to him, gripping his hand the entire time.

We're nearly to the hospital when Sebastian's eyes flutter open again. He squints as I gasp and clasp his hand harder. Panic floods his face, but I'm filled with relief because he's showing emotion.

"Sebastian, hey, it's okay. You're in an ambulance." I run my thumb over his knuckles. "You passed out."

His eyelids flutter closed, and he drops his head back to the pillow as his cheeks flush. Angry resignation hardens his gaze when he opens his eyes. I can practically hear him beating himself up.

One of the EMTs smiles. "It's a really good sign that he's responding to you."

Relief hits me, and I swallow at the lump in my throat, clinging with every fiber of my being to the hope that she knows what she's talking about.

Chapter Seventeen

Callie

Once we get to the hospital, I play the fiancée card to go back with Sebastian, and it feels like forever before they get him into a curtained room in the ER. It's all I can do to stay calm, using all my energy to focus my thoughts on Sebastian.

I hate waiting, unable to do anything but watch. The last time I was at a hospital was when I was drugged, and while that memory is not a pleasant one, the time prior is the one that haunts me.

The night before my mom died.

As I sit here in the uncomfortable plastic chair, the smell of disinfectant stings my nose, and it reminds me of seeing her — frail, helpless, so small and pale against the white sheets. Sebastian has the same pallor, the same fragile quality, and my memories threaten to break free of my carefully erected barrier.

His phone rings in my hand, providing a welcome distraction. I see Shawn's name and quickly move to the waiting room to answer, explaining where we are.

One of the nurses rushes by, pausing to give me an update. "He's already sitting up and talking. He's going to be okay."

As my breath whooshes out of me, I collapse onto a nearby chair. The thunder of footsteps sounds, and four people round the corner. I recognize Silas first, then Leah. One guy has his arm around her, and my dazed brain finds a hazy memory of Shawn at that party where I got drugged. Which means the last one is Steven.

The brothers are all tall, but not as tall as Sebastian. Shawn and Silas have unruly hair while Steven's is neatly styled, though they all have varying shades of brown. I can see similarities in their face structure, the slope of their nose, the curve of their mouths. And they all wear the same degree of concern as they stride toward me.

I wearily stand again to greet them.

"Callie!" Leah calls, racing over to give me a hug. "How is he?"

"What happened?" Silas asks before I can respond, his voice colliding with his brothers' as they clamor for Sebastian's progress.

I hold up my hands. "Hey!" They all quiet enough to listen, and I finally get to speak. "He's okay. A nurse told me he's awake and talking, but I haven't seen him yet."

Leah's shoulders sag, and she turns to bury her face in Shawn's chest. A moment later she lifts her head with an angry tilt to her mouth. "I'm going to kill him." And she turns a questioning gaze on me to show her which curtained room is his. When I point, she storms across the hall.

All my energy is gone, and I sink into the chair again. At least they're here. At least I'm not alone with my memories. Silas sits next to me, wiping a hand over his pale face while Steven walks away without a word.

Shawn sits on my other side, resting his elbows on his knees as he lets out a breath. "Nice to see you again, Callie," he says wryly.

I manage to lift one corner of my mouth.

He rakes a hand through his hair, then leans back against the wall. "Thank you," he whispers.

A wave of empathy crashes over me, and I pat his arm. "Of course."

A doctor hurries into Sebastian's room as Leah comes back out, pausing near the curtain to listen. Steven returns with three cups of coffee balanced precariously in his hands as well as two water bottles, one tucked under each elbow. Shawn stands to help, taking two of the cups of coffee, then they both turn to me.

Steven shrugs. "I don't know what you like to drink."

His thoughtfulness gives me enough energy to manage a small smile. "Water would be great. Thank you."

He grins and hands me a bottle, then gives the remaining coffee to Silas. We all sip as we wait until the doctor finally emerges.

"Okay, the good news is that Sebastian is responding very well. He's already had a full cup of juice and is eating cheese and crackers. If he keeps that down, he'll be free to go, as long as his blood sugar stays within a normal range." He glances from me to Leah. "Whoever gave him the shot, well done."

She looks at me gratefully.

"My biggest concern right now is getting him on a constant glucose monitor along with an insulin pump. It will decrease the likelihood of this type of event happening again. I can't believe his primary care doctor hasn't given him one already." He shakes his head.

Steven mutters, "I told Sebastian he should switch doctors. Dr. Walker is ancient."

After making sure we have no more questions, the doctor strides away.

Shawn sighs, relief then anger crossing his face. "Okay. My turn." And he stalks through Sebastian's curtains.

Leah plops beside me, almost sloshing her coffee. She opens her mouth to speak, but Sebastian's annoyed voice rings loud and clear from across the hall.

"Let me see, Calliope, dammit."

A smirk plays on Leah's mouth. "He never swears." She gives me an appraising look. "Good for you."

Unsure what to make of her words, I stand, meeting Shawn in the doorway.

"I take it you heard his highness calling for you?" His mouth twitches with amusement, and I see even more resemblance to Sebastian when he smiles.

I nod, then scoot by him, taking a deep breath before easing into the room.

Sebastian's face is full of worry and concern as he searches me. "Calliope..."

Tears threaten as all the events and panic catch up. I press my lips together as I take him in. The relief of seeing him awake and functioning nearly buckles my knees. "You scared me," I whisper.

His face falls, and his eyebrows knit together. "I know."

"Do you?" I let out a shaky breath as I twist my water bottle in my fingers. "Can you imagine if you were coming to see me at my dad's office? All excited and eager. But instead, you found me, completely unresponsive, slumped at my desk?" My words are hoarse but gaining strength. "I was terrified and felt completely unprepared."

"Hey," he says, holding out his IV-free hand. "Come here. Let me hug you."

I perch on the edge of the bed and let him pull me to his chest where I breathe him in, his minty coffee scent dulling the edges of the swirling storm inside me. He cradles me in his arms, stroking my hair.

"Thank you, Calliope." He holds me in silence for several moments. "I'm so grateful you knew what to do. And you're right—you need to be trained on how to handle an emergency..." He trails off and his pause is long enough that I lean back. His throat bobs. "*If* you still want to be with me."

I huff out an annoyed sigh and sit up. "You listen here, Sebastian Wrighting. This condition is not going to keep me away from you or make me want you any less. Stop degrading yourself just because you have diabetes. And, for all our sakes, eat!"

His mouth twitches then a full smile tilts his lips. "I don't deserve you, my little muse. But I'll keep you as long as you'll have me."

My forehead crinkles as I frown. "Muse?"

"Calliope is from Greek mythology, the muse of eloquence and epic poetry."

I snort. "No wonder my dad's always disappointed in me. I definitely didn't live up to that name."

"Maybe not for him," he says, reaching over to squeeze my hand. "But you've definitely been an inspiration to me."

Me? Inspire someone? I can't fathom that. I must look as confused as I feel because he chuckles.

"I'm serious."

Steven peeks his head in. "Sorry to interrupt, but I need to get back to work now that I know you're okay."

Sebastian frowns. "Fine." To me, he says, "Remind me to continue this later."

The rest of his family files in, and I start to move to give them space, but he doesn't let me go. They crowd us, perching on the bed and in the chairs, laughing, chatting, touching. Everyone is so at ease, so comfortable, and I'm filled with envy.

Their brother went through a terrifying situation, and yes, there were a few moments of anger, but the overwhelming emotion here is love. A far cry from when Dad came to the hospital for me after I'd been drugged.

As if my thoughts conjured him, his ringtone echoes from my pocket. I leap to my feet, knowing he's probably heard about Sebastian's episode by now and wants an update. I should have texted him. I mouth "my dad" to Sebastian, then hurry to the waiting room to answer.

"Hey, Dad."

"Calliope Harrison, is it true that Sebastian was taken away in an ambulance?"

His angry tone makes me thankful that I'm the only one in here as I reply with a wary, "Yes."

"And you didn't think to tell me? About my own assistant?" He keeps going before I can respond. "I had to hear about it from Professor Johnson. It's all over campus, and I'm the last to know."

"I was a little busy making sure my boyfriend wasn't dead," I say tightly.

"You should never be too busy for good communication. Is he awake? Coherent?"

"Yes."

"Good. And are you a nurse?"

My "No" is forced through gritted teeth.

"Then there's no reason for you to stay. You'll just be in the way, and Sebastian will need his rest. Plus there's this matter of you not keeping me apprised of the situation."

"But he just woke up. I'd like to spend —"

"Don't argue with me, young lady. Come home, now."

Frustrated almost to the point of tears, I try one last time. "Dad, I've barely been able to see —"

"Calliope."

My heart sinks as he cuts me off with my full name, and any further explanation from me is a waste of breath.

"If the next words out of your mouth aren't *'Yes, sir'*, you will be in even more trouble than you already are."

There is no room for argument in his tone, and disobeying will mean a worse outcome in the long run. Pressure chokes the air out of me as the invisible leash closes around my throat. I have to force the words out, "Yes, sir." I sound small and defeated, and I hate myself for it, but what choice do I have?

"I'll see you shortly." He ends the call.

I trudge into the hallway as I take several deep breaths.

Steven walks out of the room, nearly running into me, and he smiles, then rests a hand on my shoulder, his dark brown eyes meeting mine. "Thank you for what you did today."

Taken aback by his sincerity, I can only nod. His footsteps fade as I ease back into the room. I stand there, watching this perfect family as they support Sebastian. Leah leans in, giving him a hard time about not finishing his crackers, but they're all smiling. My throat is thick with tears. I want the wishing stone back because I know exactly what I'd wish for.

A family like this, instead of the one I've been given.

"Calliope? What's wrong?" Sebastian's concern cuts through the lighthearted chatter, and all focus shifts toward me.

I sniff and force a smile, then walk on over. "I've got to go. Dad needs me home."

Sebastian's eyes narrow. "Is everything all right?"

"A slight miscommunication. You know Dad." I try to keep it light, not wanting to burden my boyfriend further or explain the embarrassingly short leash I'm on. "He's glad you're okay, by the way." I'm sure he is on some level, even if he didn't actually say that. "I'm so sorry. I wish I could stay."

His face softens. "It's okay. I'm fine now, thanks to you."

He reaches for me and I go to him, sitting on the bed to lean into his tender embrace. I breathe in his comforting scent, soaking in his strength and warmth. The last thing I want is to leave.

They told me my mom would be fine. I went home thinking I'd see her again the next day, and that was the last time —

I cut off that train of thought and push up to kiss Sebastian. Who *will* be just fine. "Call me when you can?"

"Of course," he says softly. "And you can call me too, if you need *anything*."

The extra emphasis tells me he knows more is going on, but I simply nod. Then I leave, waving to everyone as they chorus their goodbyes and thanks. The moment I'm in the hall again I let my smile drop, and the weight of my father's expectations settles over me.

I don't understand him. I probably saved Sebastian's life today, but Dad is upset because he looked bad in front of a colleague? When did his priorities become so warped? I understand the value of a reputation, but this is a whole new level. As I walk outside, I remember I don't have my car, that it's still on campus because I rode here in the ambulance.

An image of Sebastian, pale and slumped at his desk, flashes before me, but I shove it away as I dig for my phone. I guess I'll see about getting an Uber.

"Callie!" Silas calls, rushing after me.

I turn and freeze with my heart in my throat as all my worst fears leap to the forefront of my mind. Then I realize Silas is smiling, looking completely relaxed, and the anxiety clawing at my throat begins to ebb.

"Hey, do you want a ride?"

Sebastian is fine, I assure myself, working to calm my racing heart, even as I berate myself for jumping to conclusions.

"I'm headed to soccer practice. I was going to skip, but Seb insisted I go since Shawn and Leah are staying." Silas grins. "He says they're more than capable of hovering. He doesn't need me here, too."

I manage to nod, and my pulse returns to normal. "Thanks. That'd be great." I follow him to his car, gearing myself up as best I can to face the familiar oppressive music that will be there to greet me when I get home.

* * * *

Sebastian

By Thursday evening, it takes all my effort not to drive to Calliope's house and demand to see her. I haven't spoken to her since she left the hospital Tuesday afternoon. I've called a couple of times and finally messaged Professor Harrison. He informed me that her phone isn't working, but he'd pass on the message.

They discharged me a few hours after her departure, and I had to wait for the insurance company to approve my monitors. I was warned it could be a battle with the insurance because they require months of logging sugars and injections, but I already had all that for my own records. I emailed my information and the approval came in late yesterday.

I had my follow-up appointment today, to check my glucose levels and how I'm functioning. And I walked out with a glucose monitor attached to the back of my right arm and an insulin pump connected near my left hip.

I'm still getting used to the new technology. The one on my arm isn't terrible. It's out of the way, and I usually forget about it unless I lean against it wrong. But the insulin pump is tedious. The tubing catches on things, the screen is an extra weight. It's just...*more.*

I sigh, wondering again what Calliope will think of all this. If it will impede our more intimate time together.

When I finally see her again.

"You okay?" Leah asks, coming into the living room, Shawn on her heels.

I glare at my silent phone. "Professor Harrison said Calliope's phone should be fixed tonight, but he didn't say when and I still haven't heard from her." I need to be working on compiling my data from the weekend since my experiment is right around the corner, but I tried. I can't focus on anything other than my girlfriend's absence.

Leah and Shawn exchange a look, and a pang hits me because I know they just had a whole silent conversation. I want that. I miss reading Calliope and how she reads me.

Leah sits next to me on the couch. "She'll call. I saw how worried she was about you at the hospital. And she knew how to give you that shot, which means she is invested enough to research diabetes. She wouldn't have done that if she didn't care."

"That's my Calliope." The way she shut my doubts down in the ER echo in my mind, her fierce words of reassurance. "I hope she's okay."

I try to hold off the images of Professor Harrison punishing her that pop into my head without warning. Then my phone rings and Calliope's name appears. Relief snaps the bands of tension squeezing my chest, and I stride outside as I answer.

"Sebastian!"

"Hey, little muse. I was beginning to think your dad was keeping you from me." A choked sound echoes through the phone, and I press the earpiece closer. "Calliope? Are you all right?"

"It's so good to hear your voice." The words are thick with tears.

My gut clenches, and every fiber of my being tells me she's not okay. That I need to be with her. I knew there was more to her silence, and anger fills me but I keep it out of my voice. "I'll be right over."

"No!" She sniffs and says more calmly, "No, I really am fine. It's been a long day and…"

I wait, desperate for her to finish the sentence.

"Can I see you tomorrow? First thing? I'll explain everything then."

"Yes, of course." I find myself nodding even though she can't see me. "Whatever you need." Though I wish I could see her tonight, if only for a minute.

"Okay." She sniffles again, but there's a hint of hope in her voice when she says, "I'll see you tomorrow. Good night, Sebastian."

"Good night." I hang up, feeling confused and worried.

More is going on than Professor Harrison let on. Calliope's reaction is enough to attest to that, but I'll have to wait till tomorrow to get to the bottom of it. I don't want to make things any worse for her.

Chapter Eighteen

Sebastian

My sleep is fraught with images of Calliope in trouble and me unable to get to her. I wake too early, and even after dragging my feet as I get ready, I'm left with too much time on my hands. Sitting still will be pointless, so I head to the greenhouse. I have plenty to do to keep up with my plants, and it will keep my busy while I wait.

The plant therapy calms me. My roses are beginning to open, and it won't be long before we can test the effectiveness of my experiment. Once they're fully in bloom.

I water them, checking the soil, examining the stems. I'm pleased with these specimens. They seem hardy but beautiful, and I hope they meet my expectations.

The greenhouse door swings open, and I turn to see a streak of purple barreling toward me. A rush of elation fills my chest right before Calliope collides with my torso. I let out an *oof* as she flings her arms around my waist, then I remove my gloves to hold her tight.

Her shoulders shake with heavy sobs. I guide us to my desk and sit in my chair before pulling her into my lap. She curls against me while I try to soothe her.

Her pain is so great that my own chest aches upon hearing the sobs ripping from her. The way she holds on to me as if she's afraid of letting go has me stroking her back, making sure she knows I'm here. I keep wishing I knew what happened, but I won't ask yet. Right now, she just needs to cry and be held.

When at last her tears slow and her sniffles ebb, she raises her head to give me a watery smile. "I'm sure you're wondering what that was all about."

I try to smile, but it's difficult in the wake of all that agony. I hand her a tissue as I nod. "When you're ready."

She composes herself, then explains how upset her father was about not hearing about my incident from her directly. The volume of his anger and his reaction of not only grounding her but taking away her phone and car have me nearly shaking with rage on her behalf.

"He told me your phone wasn't working."

"I mean, it wasn't, but only because he wouldn't let me have it."

I brush a damp piece of hair back from her cheek. "That seems harsh."

She lets out a short huff. "I know. I tried to explain, but all he could see was his dinged reputation." Looping her arms around my neck, she snuggles against me once more. "I'm just glad you're okay."

"They told you I'd be fine." I rub her back. "I went home a couple hours after you left, like the doctor said I would."

"Yeah, well, they said that about my mom, too." The words are hardly more than a whisper. "She died that night. I never got to see her again."

"Oh, Calliope, I'm sorry." I stiffen beneath her as a realization sweeps over me. "Wait, your father didn't tell you? I called him Wednesday night and saw him here Thursday morning. He knew I was fine."

She sits back enough to look at me. "I saw your texts. You even said in one you'd talked to him, so I confronted him last night and you know what he said?"

I wait, positive I'll hate whatever comes next.

"Maybe that will help me remember the importance of good communication."

My teeth knock together, and I have to force myself to keep from digging my hands into her hips. He knew of her trauma. He knew she'd be worried sick about me, and he couldn't even pass on a simple message? The last few days must have been hell for her.

"I'm so sorry." I wrap her in my arms and rock her back and forth as she breathes me in.

More tears leak down her cheeks, then she brokenly whispers, "Sebastian?"

"Hmm?"

"Is it too soon to tell you I love you?"

A star goes supernova in my chest as an inferno blasts through me. The words I've been afraid to say, that I've been choking back, spring up. "No, Calliope, because I love you like I've never loved anyone in my entire life. You make me feel whole."

"I love you. You see me. You understand who I am, what I need, and I can be myself with you."

We both move, fusing our lips together.

"I've missed you," I murmur before deepening the kiss to show her how much.

She runs her hands down my shoulders, and we both freeze when she touches my glucose monitor. She pulls back, her expression curious.

I brace myself for disappointment as I twist my torso and push my sleeve to reveal the slim disc not much bigger than a quarter. "This one measures my glucose levels." She nods, and I have to nudge her slightly as I lift my shirt, showing the slender tube that connects to my torso held in place by an adhesive disc. I hold up the monitor. "And this is the insulin pump. It doses me based on the monitor."

"I read about those. They talk to each other and even connect to your phone?"

I nod, a smile creeping over my face. "You were researching?"

She gives a sheepish shrug. "I didn't have much else to do with my time. Dance, clean, read…" She tilts her head. "How are you liking them so far?"

"Well, I forgot to eat lunch yesterday, and my sugars dipped. Not only did my phone go off, but it alerted my whole family so…yeah, that was fun."

Her laughter is a welcome sound after all the tears. "I can just imagine." She traces the disc outline on my abdomen, then her gaze dips lower and longing fills her eyes.

I smirk. "Ah, so you did miss me."

She bats her eyelashes, teasing right back. "Parts of you."

I rock against her hip, growing hard at our banter. "He missed you, too."

Heat flares between us, and I remember where we are, how anyone can see in through the glass panes. So I clear my throat as I shift away. A hint of disappointment flashes across her face, and I cup her cheek.

"Don't worry, I made sure to ask the doctor about, um, intimate moments." My cheeks heat, and my next words are rushed. "The monitor can be removed, or it can stay on. It's dependent on preference."

Her grin widens. "Oh darn, more experimenting."

My doubts evaporate, and I know they should never have appeared in the first place. She has accepted every facet of me without flinching so far. Why would this be any different?

She presses a quick kiss to my cheek, then hops off my lap. "What can I do? How can I help?" She glances eagerly around the greenhouse.

"I just so happen to have my next batch of roses ready for potting. I know how much you love that, so I saved them for you."

She beams as I lead her to the table in the far corner where ten plants are already a foot tall and growing steadily. I get out all the supplies for her, loving when she plunges her hands right in.

I watch her for several moments, then ask, "Why do you stay?" She pauses, those blue eyes finding mine as I add, "With your father, I mean. You're a strong, capable woman. You could be on your own, providing for yourself, making your own way." I'm careful to keep any judgment out of my voice. I'm genuinely curious.

She sighs, then resumes her work, and I grab the pot nearest me because I can't stand here unoccupied.

"A couple of reasons. My education costs nothing since Dad is tenured, and he feels that obligates me to live by his rules. I'm beyond grateful for the chance at a debt-free life, I just wish it wasn't at the cost of my other freedoms, you know?"

I nod, but stay quiet because I feel like there's more.

Silence lingers before she speaks again, her words sounding strained. "When Mom passed, she left me money in a trust fund. It's not something I talk about often," she adds quickly, glancing up with a hint of worry in her gaze. "I don't tell many people because they start looking at me differently. Silver spoon and all that."

I frown at her self-degrading comment.

"I don't have access to the money until I'm twenty-five, and believe me, I'm counting the days. I've never even had a real job. Other than taking care of me and my dad since Mom passed."

My frown deepens. "What do you mean?" I move on to the next plant, intent on her every word.

She switches pots too, ready for a new one. "I'm in charge of the meals. When Mom died, Dad didn't eat. We had friends and family bringing so much food that our fridge was full, but none of it was Mom's." A wistful smile tips her lips. "After the third day, I was really scared. I couldn't lose him too, so I pulled out her recipe book and made this ham and potato casserole we both loved. It was my first time cooking, but before I pulled it out of the oven, Dad came out of his room, asking what that smell was."

My heart cracks within my chest, imagining a young Calliope going through the weight of grieving the loss of one parent and stepping into the role of caring for another at such a tender age.

"I took over after that. I had the time since I wasn't dancing anymore, and I wanted to keep busy. Some of the recipes were harder than others, like her German chocolate cake." She gives me a saucy smile. "But it's kept us close to her."

As much as her father bullies her and twists things around, it's obvious that she does love him. Everything she does for him is out of that love, including giving up what should be the prime of her independence. All so she doesn't disappoint this man.

I wish I could see some evidence that he reciprocates. Clearing my throat, I push down the simmering anger over the hurt he's caused. "So, what are you doing this weekend?"

Her face falls and her shoulders slump. "Going to see my aunt. Dad's leaving tonight for a long weekend on his annual trip with some of his friends." She goes on to explain how her aunt is even stricter than her father.

My anger grows at the thought of being separated from her again. "Calliope, this whole thing is ridiculous. You're a grown woman. Come stay with me."

Longing fills her gaze, but she shakes her head. "I wish I could." Before I can offer to speak to her father, she says, "And please don't talk to Dad about it. About any of this. It'll just make it worse on me overall. I've had friends talk to him before, thinking they're doing me a favor. One of his professor friends even tried. She no longer works here... I'm not sure she can even teach anymore."

I knew he had pull, but that seems ridiculous.

"I don't want you jeopardizing your career for me. Especially when I'm safe. It's not like I'm starving or being tortured or something. There are plenty of people who have been in worse situations than me and survived."

My protective instincts are in high gear, and it's a struggle not to protest. I let her change the topic to my upcoming experiment, then show off my almost blooming roses. An idea occurs to me, but I keep it to myself for now.

I work hard to make the rest of the day pleasant for her, treating her to lunch and finding enough busy work to keep her immersed in plant therapy until it's time for my department meeting with her father. I walk her out, relieved he's allowing her to go home and not sticking her in that dark filing room.

At her car, I ask, "So you'll be able to talk this weekend at least?"

"As long as it's before nine p.m."

Her lips press together, and I wish I could whisk her away. Toss her over my shoulder and leave, never looking back. She reaches for the door handle, but I touch her shoulder.

"Don't I get a goodbye kiss?" I make sure my voice is low and husky, letting all my need seep into the words. I want her to know how much I'll miss her.

If my plan doesn't work.

She spins back to me, wide-eyed as that magnetic pull snaps into place between us. I couldn't move away if I wanted to. Her hands come to rest on my chest, and she lifts her chin, begging for the promised kiss. One corner of my mouth tugs up at how much she wants this. Wants me.

"I love you, Calliope Harrison."

I don't give her time to respond as I grip her waist to pull her flush against me. I hold nothing back as I devour her, uncaring that we're in the public parking lot of my campus. She seems startled at first, but quickly melts into me, returning the kiss with a ferocity of her own.

Sliding one hand along her back, I press her chest to me, wishing we could do so much more. One of her hands rests on my shoulder, the other threads through my hair. My blood roars with need as our tongues tangle together, and I groan as her nipples harden against my chest.

A throat clears next to us, and we break apart. Calliope looks ready to bolt, but I don't let her go as I calmly turn to face her father.

Professor Harrison sniffs in derision as he studies us. "PDA, Wrighting? I thought you'd be above such things."

I tighten my grip on her hip, and it takes all my effort to keep my voice even. "I got carried away, sir. I missed your daughter over the past couple of days, and it seems I won't be seeing her again for a while. I'd like to finish saying goodbye, then I'll accompany you to the office."

His gaze flicks between us before he gives a short nod and steps toward the sidewalk, calling, "Text me when you get home, Callie."

Several seconds pass before she answers, and I imagine her standing up to him, defiantly telling him no, that's she coming with me instead. But she just nods, then gives me a forced smile.

That brief moment, though, reminds me there's hope. She's not beaten yet. I lean in for one more kiss and whisper, "Keep your chin up, little muse. Don't forget who you are, and what you're capable of." I brush a piece of her hair behind her ear, then watch her get into her car.

She gives me a small wave before she drives away. My resolve strengthens as I stride over to join her father. I will not accept no for an answer.

* * * *

Callie

"I've invited Sebastian to have dinner with us before I leave" is the first thing Dad says to me when he gets home.

Luckily, I have enough food to feed my boyfriend on this short of notice. I'm making pot roast with mashed potatoes and green bean casserole, some of Dad's favorites. I'd hoped to butter him up a little, so he'll convince Aunt Deb to go easy on me for the weekend.

Dinner is in the oven, and I'm working on a no-bake sugar-free cheesecake I'd bought on a whim when Dad comes in.

"There's been a change of plans."

I turn off the beaters, uneasy hope bubbling in my chest.

"Sebastian would like you around, says you've been a big help with prepping for his experiment, and he plans to go ahead with it on Monday. Since I won't be back, he'll need the extra hands."

My jaw drops.

"He promised to be the perfect gentleman, so you'll have to keep your hands to yourself." He shoots me a pointed look, as if I was the one who initiated that kiss in the parking lot earlier.

Sebastian must have a silver tongue to convince my dad of this, although my boyfriend is Dad's golden ticket right now. The shiny new medal to pin to his chest. This paper Sebastian is working on shows a lot of promise and could be a huge breakthrough for the botany world. Dad would do anything to keep his star TA happy.

Even let his daughter off her leash.

"I won't have service, so you'll need to check in with Sebastian on a regular basis. Jess and Lyssa have agreed to stay for the weekend and have also sworn there will be no shenanigans."

I have to bite my tongue about him trusting them over me. It's a knife twisting ever deeper, the height of double standards, since they have been involved in most of the situations I got in trouble for.

"If Sebastian has another…episode, his family will alert Deb, and you will have to finish out the weekend there. Are we clear?"

Swallowing my anger, I focus on the fact that Sebastian worked a miracle by getting me out of going to my aunt's. "Yes, crystal-clear, Dad. I won't let you down, and I'll be on my best behavior. In fact, I'll be so good you won't know what to do with me."

"Good." He pauses to inhale. "Pot roast?" At my nod, he gives me a little smile. "Did Sebastian spill the beans? Is that why you made my favorite?"

"Nope." I can't even do something like cook without someone else getting the credit, but I keep my smile in place. "I wanted you to have a good send-off. I hope you have fun this weekend."

He studies me for a second, then reaches over and touches my shoulder, giving me a gentle squeeze. "You too, Callie."

I gape after him as he leaves the room, my throat thick because I can't remember the last time he showed me a hint of affection. I memorize the moment, the feel of his fingers, soaking in the words like drops of rain in the middle of a summer drought.

Blinking away the press of tears, I remind myself that Sebastian is coming, so I hurry to finish the cheesecake and rush upstairs to change. I choose a button-down, bright-blue blouse and a swingy skirt with various shades of blue in no particular pattern.

The doorbells rings, and I rush downstairs as Dad answers it. Sebastian stands in the doorway, tall, handsome, looking every bit my savior, and it takes all my restraint not to barrel over there to fling my arms around him. But I don't. Sebastian promised to be a perfect gentleman, and I don't want to risk ruining that image before our weekend even gets going.

So I settle for a little wave, my stomach flipping as he shoots me a wink when Dad can't see. I almost skip back into the kitchen, feeling lighter than air. Dad leads Sebastian to the table, and I start bringing the food out, relishing how Dad beams when he sees the pot roast.

He inhales deeply. "Ahh, that looks amazing. I haven't had pot roast in forever. It's my favorite," he tells Sebastian, who makes a non-committal noise.

Sebastian's eyes haven't moved off me, latching on whenever I appear. His gaze keeps trailing over my bare legs, and I know he appreciates my choice of skirt. Anticipation coils within me at having him all to myself.

I know exactly how I want to show my gratitude. The thought makes my thighs clench, but the timer goes off, so I rush to pull the green bean casserole out of the oven. A minute later, I sit across from Sebastian, but I slip my foot over to run down his shin, and he smiles.

"Looks good, Callie," Dad says, serving himself, then passing the roast to Sebastian.

I snap my mouth shut as I gape at my dad. First a touch, now a compliment? Maybe he's been abducted by aliens and they brought me back a more normal version.

One can only hope.

"It smells amazing." Sebastian takes a big portion. "I can't wait to have a taste." He smirks, and I know he's not just talking about the food.

Dad and Sebastian carry the conversation while I pipe in occasionally. Dad talks about his trip to his colleague's cabin near the Rocky Mountains in Colorado. It has a private lake with great fishing, plenty of hiking, and a bar that claims to hold the best fish fry ever. Sebastian lights up when Dad mentions hiking, and I have to bite back a laugh at the idea of my dad voluntarily walking a trail with any incline.

They both have seconds, but I'm already full. Especially if I want dessert. "Save room for cheesecake," I say with a grin. "It's sugar free, but I swear you can't tell the difference. I tasted it myself."

Sebastian's smile takes on a tender edge that makes me even more anxious for Dad's departure. Dad keeps checking his watch between bites. With every second that ticks by, my excitement grows, and I can't wait to be alone with my boyfriend.

Pushing away from the table, Dad stands up. "Well, I need to finish getting ready." He pats his stomach, shooting me a grin. "I won't have to worry about getting hungry on the road later."

It's as close to a thanks as I'll get, so I smile in return, relieved dinner is over. He disappears upstairs, and Sebastian stands when I do. While I grab dishes, he offers to bring the leftovers into the kitchen. Once I've set down my armload, he slides the pot roast onto the counter and pulls me to him.

"Thank you for cooking. It was simply delectable."

His praise and gratitude have a huge smile spreading over my face. The words fill an empty place within me, only amplifying my need for him. "You're welcome."

I tilt my chin up, staring into his hazel eyes with all the longing I feel. When our lips touch, my stomach flips, and I lean into him, hungry for more.

He pulls back with a chuckle. "Soon, little muse, but we should wait until your dad has actually departed."

I scrunch my nose, but step back and finish cleaning. I need to keep my hands busy or I'll be groping him in no time. Sebastian loads the dishwasher while I put away leftovers and wipe down counters. When a horn honks outside, my dad rushes in to say a quick goodbye before the door slams.

I turn to Sebastian. We're alone. I'd love to jump right into his arms, but what if Dad forgets something and comes back? "Um," I say, brushing my hair behind my ear. "Maybe you want the tour?"

"Does the tour include discovering what's under that little skirt of yours?" Sebastian steps right up to me, his gaze intense and wanting.

I keep my expression coy as I toy with the collar of his polo shirt. "Maybe. I guess you'll have to come with me and find out." I entwine my fingers with his. "Let's go."

We walk into the dining room, and I ham it up. "This is the dining room. We just left the kitchen." He rolls his eyes, but I keep going. "And here we have our illustrious living room." I sweep my arm out, gesturing to the area he had to walk through upon entry. "How am I doing so far?"

He glares, stepping right in front of me to lower his face until his lips hover near mine. His free hand slides down my hip to the hem of my skirt. I inhale sharply when his fingers brush my bare leg, and he plays with the edge of the fabric. His fingers dance toward my inner thigh where he slides one up and up, stopping where my thighs meet. Inches short of my apex.

"Perhaps this should be a quick tour," he says huskily.

I swallow, a heady thrill rushing through me. "Maybe you're right."

Chapter Nineteen

Callie

I forgo the rest of the main floor, and we tromp upstairs. He walks behind me, so I put some extra hip into my steps, smiling when he growls. He's definitely feeling impatient, and I can't help wanting to tease him, to prolong the flirting. On the landing, I dance out of his reach.

He glowers as I point out Dad's bedroom and the upstairs bathroom, taking my time and using my most carefree voice. I want to see how far I can push him before he'll lose that tenuous hold on his control. A delicious shiver of anticipation rocks me at the thought of him letting go and giving into that baser side. For me.

With my hand on another door handle, I turn to face Sebastian, pausing to bat my eyelashes and draw him in. "This is my old room." I wait until his lips are a breath away before I dart inside.

To my delight, Sebastian chases me as I race around my dollhouse and the little table with my tea set in the corner.

"Come back here," he calls.

But I don't stop running, even when his fingers brush my hip, making my stomach flip as laughter spills from me. I scurry up the ladder of my old bunk bed. On my stomach, I try to crawl away, but he grabs my ankle, hauling me back to the edge of the bed. I squeal as my skirt flies up, catching beneath me.

He gasps. "You aren't wearing underwear."

I quickly pull my skirt down then sit upright with my feet on the rung of the ladder, his hand still on my ankle. I press my thighs together, blocking his view. "Cad." I glare, pretending to be annoyed.

His hazel eyes darken to almost brown. He steps closer, running his right hand along my shin to rest on my knee. "I prefer rake. Or rogue."

When his left hand finds my other knee, my heart stops. His head is at exactly the same height as my thighs, and I suck in a breath as he shifts even closer.

I have to swallow before I can say, "But you're not promiscuous."

His intense gaze pins me to my spot. "Only with you." His gaze travels down my torso, leaving fire blazing in its wake. He lingers on my lap, his tongue darting out to lick his lips.

Desire flares within me, and I wantonly open my legs. His mouth parts in delight. He grips my knees, then slides his hands slowly toward my skirt while need coils deep within me. His thumbs graze the sensitive skin of my inner thighs, and I grip the edge of the mattress as his shoulders spread my knees even farther.

He trails heated kisses along the same path as his hands. He pauses to set his glasses aside. The anticipation is brutal, but he continues to take his time, torturing me with his languid exploration. Each fraction of an inch brings him closer to burying his face between my legs, and I can't look away from the way his lips graze my skin.

Finally, he reaches the spot where my hem brushes my thighs. He blinks as he pushes away the fabric, not stopping until he grips my ass. With a deep inhale, he grins. "Time for my next course." He pauses, his gaze drifting over my chest. "I think you'd be more comfortable without the shirt."

I smirk. "Then take it off."

He flexes his long fingers against my ass, sending a thrill straight to my core. "Sorry, my hands are full, and soon my mouth will be as well."

I'm desperate to feel his tongue on me, but I'm also happy to play. "One lick for one button."

"Deal." He eases in, licking my seam. "One."

I throw my head back at the rush of pleasure, and it takes me a second to release my grip on the mattress. But I hold Sebastian's hungry stare as I reach for my top button, slowly pushing it through the hole. He smirks and leans forward to lick me again. I close my eyes at the heady sensation, then reach for the next button. We take turns until my shirt is completely undone, and I almost am as well.

"Bra next," he demands.

The command in his voice has me clenching, but I give it right back, needing more. "Lick first."

His right hand leaves my ass, coming to spread my lower lips, and this time his tongue circles my clit while

I groan. Luckily my bra is front-clasp, and I hurry to undo it, baring my chest to him.

He sucks in a sharp breath, his eyes devouring me as I slide the shirt and bra completely off. "Pretend my hands are on your breasts. I'll continue as long as you play."

The order excites me even further. I run my hands over my aching breasts, cupping their weight as his tongue delves into me. I clamp my forefinger and thumb onto my nipples as he slides a finger into my heat. If I pause for even a second to catch my breath, he pauses too. So I keep going, the pleasure ramping up within me exponentially.

It's a torturous game as we both nudge me toward that peak. My heart swells with love for this man, and the way he knows exactly what I need. Even in this.

The first quiver of release shoots through me, and he quickens his pace, lapping up my arousal. I pinch my nipples once more, hard enough to send me cascading over that edge. I cry out his name, letting go to grip his hair and hold him tight to my core as he prolongs my release.

When I finally stop quaking, he leans back, licking his lips. "Delicious."

I push him away from the ladder, quickly climbing down to run my hand over the hard bulge at the front of his pants. "My turn." I drop to my knees.

"Calliope…"

The hesitation in Sebastian's voice has me pausing at his belt. "What's wrong?"

"I've…I've never…" He gestures between us.

A wide grin spreads over my face as his words sink in. "Oh, Sebastian, I think you're going to like this." When he still hesitates, I stand, running my hands over his abdomen to his shoulders, avoiding his monitors. "Let me make you feel as good as you make me feel. Please?"

His mouth is tight, but an eagerness lights his eyes, and he nods.

I smile again, then raise on tiptoe to press my lips to his. "If I have to be shirtless, I think it's only fair if yours comes off."

"Are you going to make me play with my nipples?"

I burst out laughing, shaking my head. "If that's what you're into."

He yanks his polo over his head, and I kiss my way to the waist of his pants. This time, I get to unbuckle the belt then undo his fly. His heat scorches my fingers through the thin fabric of his boxer briefs, and I eagerly tug his hard cock through the opening of his underwear while he clips the insulin pump to the waistband.

I glide my hand down his shaft, humming in delight, then I run my tongue over his ruddy head. Sebastian's breath whistles as he sucks air through his teeth, his hand clamping around a rung of the ladder. I grin before I take him wholly in my mouth. He's not small, and I have to suppress my gag reflex to fit his entire length, but I manage.

Sebastian grunts a quiet, "Holy shit." His fingers thread into my hair, like he needs to ground himself.

Sliding back, I swirl my tongue over his tip, then repeat the process. His grip grows tighter, and soon his hips buck in time with my motions. I taste that first salty drop as he hardens even more.

"Calliope, I'm going to—"

I dig my fingers into his hips, not wanting him to pull out. I earned every last drop of him, and I swallow it down as he shudders into me, grunting my name.

I sit back on my heels, a satisfied smile on my face. "Now you know just how amazing it feels when you do that to me."

His heavy gasps gradually slow, and amazement dances in his eyes as he caresses my cheek. "If that's how I make you feel, I count myself a lucky man."

We spend the rest of the evening together. I don't think of my dad at all until I'm crawling into bed and check my phone to see a missed text from Jess in our group chat. *Right, she's supposed to be staying here.*

I snuggle into the curve of Sebastian's side after I set my phone down. "So this brilliant plan of yours, how'd you come up with it? And how'd you get Jess and Lyssa to agree?"

"Well, I obviously need you with me on Monday. I'm not going through the biggest day of my career without you at my side."

I wonder if it's possible for one's insides to liquefy. I think my heart might be a puddle now.

"And your friends were easy. The moment I said you needed help, they were in. I didn't think your dad would approve of me sleeping over, so I found a compromise that works for all of us. If your dad asks why you didn't check in with him, I'll just explain how much time we spent together."

A shadow crosses over me, and I roll onto my back as I mutter, "You've thought of everything."

He sits up, propping himself on his elbow as he frowns. "I tried to. Why does that upset you?"

"Because me spending a weekend with my boyfriend shouldn't require this level of subterfuge."

Quiet lingers between us until he says, reaching for my hand. "I agree. So move out."

"Sebastian!" I sit up, annoyance flaring within me. "We've been over this."

He lifts a shoulder. "You have to decide if it's worth it, Calliope. You could still go to school and pay your way like the majority of people do. Or you could look into exactly how much pull your father has, see whether he truly could revoke your free education." He frowns. "I'm assuming that you took him at his word and haven't researched that already."

Chagrin creeps through me, and I shake my head because it never occurred to me to distrust him. He's my dad.

"I know it's frightening to think of embarking on your own. I know you love your father, but I want you to consider your needs as well, and what's best for you."

I'm frozen, paralyzed at the thought that I have options that I've never considered before because...why? Have I been too scared? Too complacent? As much as I complain and feel choked, do I secretly want to be here?

I turn to Sebastian, my frustration quickly morphing into something more, my emotions out of control as I spiral. My breathing turns ragged as panic grips me.

His eyes widen. "Hey, Calliope, it's okay. You're okay. Breathe with me."

I follow his breaths and concentrate on his touch on my back. One minute bleeds into another, but I finally start to calm and he pulls me to his chest.

"I'm sorry," he murmurs.

"No, I think I needed to hear that. I just...wasn't expecting it." I pull back to give him a tremulous smile. "You've given me a lot to think about."

Trepidation weighs in his gaze. "Should I leave?"

I don't hesitate to answer. "No, please stay." I snuggle into his embrace once more, sighing happily when holds me tight. Though his suggestions keep flitting through my mind, I sleep soundly in Sebastian's arms, safe and happy in his embrace.

* * * *

After I have brunch and go shopping with Jess and Lyssa the next day, Sebastian is taking me to dinner. I adjust my hem of my floral print dress where it's ridden up on my thigh, then stare out of the window again. We turn onto a side road ten minutes out of town, past the crowded suburbs where the houses have more space between them.

I frown, wondering where we could possibly be going, but he only smirks. When we pull into the driveway of a two-story house with a long driveway, my heart starts beating faster. "Sebastian, where are we?"

"For the record, this wasn't my idea. They wanted to surprise you." He nods as the garage door opens, and his family rushes out.

I freeze in shock as his brothers race toward the car with wide grins. Silas opens my door, and Leah steps out from behind him, laughing at my shock as she pulls me out of the car.

"Surprise!" she shouts.

"What...?" I look from brother to brother then at Sebastian, needing an explanation.

"This is my parents' place. Mom and Dad wanted to thank you and have a welcome to the family party, so when they heard your dad was out of town—"

"We decided to make Sebastian kidnap you." Leah grins, linking her arm with mine and dragging me toward the house. "Don't worry, Trey and Judy are amazing."

I look helplessly over my shoulder, but my boyfriend is already engrossed in conversation. I'm at Leah's mercy. She leads me into the house where amazing smells greet me. I make out mac and cheese as well as baked beans, but the others all blend together only serving to make me hungry.

In the kitchen stands a taller woman, older than all of us and obviously related to the guys. Her face shape is so similar and her sandy brown hair is the same shade as Shawn's. The original owner of that devastating Wrighting smile stands before me, and her eyes are hazel like Sebastian's.

"Callie! Welcome!" She hurries over, wiping her hands on a towel draped over her shoulder. She wears a cute flowy shirt that reminds me of a forest in dark greens and browns, with tan shorts and perfectly pedicured toes peeking out of her athletic sandals.

"Callie, Judy," Leah says. "Judy, this is the infamous Callie you've heard so much about."

Judy doesn't give me a choice before sweeping me into her arms for a tight hug. "Oh, sweet girl, thank you."

I stand there, shocked and overcome by her fierce tone.

"All right, Mom," Sebastian's welcome voice sounds behind me. "She needs to breathe."

Judy laughs, pats my shoulder and steps back. I scurry to Sebastian's side, unused to all the commotion and overwhelmed with the exuberance being shoved in my face. He wraps a comforting arm around me, and I lean in, welcoming the grounding hint of minty coffee I get.

Silence has me glancing back at his mom and Leah, who both look shocked. I take in my position, pressed against Sebastian. How'd I'd run to him and he'd embraced me easily. I guess they hadn't realized how comfortable we are with each other.

His mom recovers first. "Well, Callie, I hope you're hungry. Trey's outside grilling burgers — don't worry, Sebastian. He's got a turkey burger for you."

I grin at my boyfriend who squeezes me tighter, then I glance at Leah, who still seems shocked. Shawn, Silas and Steven pile into the kitchen as Judy takes a pan of mac and cheese out of the oven. Hopefully they also have a veggie or something lower carb for Sebastian.

"Oh, that smells amazing." Steven leans over his mom's shoulder to snatch a piping hot noodle into his mouth.

She swats his hand. "Steven, how many times do I have to tell you — ?"

But Silas swoops in from the other side and does the same thing. "That's delicious, Mom. Your mac and cheese bake is the best."

She turns to shove Silas away, and Shawn moves in, but she grabs a nearby wooden spoon and whirls around, brandishing it like a sword. "Outside, boys. Now. Go bother your father."

"Love you, Mom." Steven kisses her cheek, then Silas follows suit.

Shawn snatches a noodle while she's occupied and licks his fingers when she glares. He just shrugs. "It's only fair."

She steps toward him with the spoon, so he trots away with his hands in the air, but his laughter echoes back to us. She sags against the counter. "I'm getting too old for this."

"Dammit, Silas!" A booming voice echoes to us from the open slider where the guys disappeared. "The burgers aren't ready yet."

Leah tilts her head back and laughs. "Okay, I'll go wrangle them, but I get an extra helping of dessert for this."

"Lee-bug, you are a life saver." Judy gives her a warm smile as Leah disappears.

Her voice drifts as she calls, "Silas, want to go show Steven and Shawn how to play volleyball?"

"Anything we can do, Mom?" Sebastian asks.

They fall into a quiet rhythm of her handing him things to go put on the patio, and I stay out of the way, just watching. I get the feeling this is his usual role, hanging back to help. It makes sense. Leah and the others off in their chaotic world of perpetual motion while Sebastian is here, behind the scenes.

When Judy says the mac and cheese has sat long enough, Sebastian carries it out to the table. I follow, holding an extra pot holder to set the dish on. Once the sacred mac and cheese is safely on the table, Sebastian introduces me to his dad, who mans the grill.

"Dad, this is Calliope."

"Callie," I quickly correct and stick out my hand.

"Trey." He shakes my hand, giving me an easy smile. "It's nice to meet you." He's tall too, over six feet. His hair is darker like Silas', but straight like Steven's, and his eyes are brown, a shade between theirs. He has a casual, friendly air that immediately puts me at ease. Just like the rest of the family.

"Help yourself to a drink." He points to the cooler near the railing.

I feel Sebastian watching me, and by the weight of his gaze I know there's alcohol in the cooler. But he doesn't say anything one way or the other, leaving it up to me. I want to make a good first impression, so, I grab a Sprite and lean against the railing to watch the heated volleyball game in the corner of the yard as I open the can.

Judy comes out, sliding her arm around Trey's waist as she leans in for a kiss. "How much longer until the burgers are done?"

"Ready any time."

A flash of my parents blazes to life in my mind — Mom in the kitchen, Dad sidling up behind her as he nuzzled her neck. They had that once, the easy air between them, the obvious affection. Love, stability, warmth...

The pang that hits me at my loss takes my breath away, and I drop my gaze to the pool below.

"You okay?" Sebastian asks quietly, leaning next to me.

I nod, my throat still thick.

"You had a weird look just now."

I manage a teasing glare. "You're saying I look weird?"

His assessing gaze doesn't ease. "I know they can be a lot..."

"They're fine, Sebastian."

A triumphant shout draws our attention as Silas punches his fist in the air, then does a complicated high-five with Leah, and I can't help smiling.

"She's really a big part of your family, isn't she?"

He nods. "She takes care of all of us."

"And you take care of her."

It's not a question, so I don't expect him to answer. I need to learn more about this woman, though. I envy her closeness with all of them, and the easy way Sebastian talks about her, but I don't think she's a threat. She's in his life, and I'll have to find out how she fits into mine.

Trey lets out an ear-splitting whistle that has me and Sebastian flinching. Then he booms, "Dinner's ready."

Sebastian guides me to the table, pulling out my chair before taking the one next to me. Judy bustles out with a few more things as Trey brings burgers and toppings to the table. He sets a plain burger, no bun on Sebastian's plate with a wink. The others tromp up the stairs and into the house to wash their hands then come back, grabbing drinks and sitting.

I notice the empty chair at the same time Silas does, and he groans as he looks at Leah. "Don't tell me you invited Meg."

Behind me, an unfamiliar voice answers, "Sorry, wish not granted."

I turn to see a curvy woman not much taller than me with long black hair and perfect skin. Her disdainful glare only makes Silas snort, but her expression turns warm when she looks at me, and she hurries over.

"We haven't been officially introduced. I'm Meg."

"Hi," I smile back, instantly at ease with her friendliness. "I'm Callie."

Trey smiles from his spot next to me at the head of the table as Meg scurries to her seat. "To our guest of honor." He lifts his beer, and everyone lifts their various beverages. "Callie, we're so thankful you came into our lives. Sebastian is still with us because of you."

"And he's a lot less grumpy," Silas adds, making everyone laugh.

"To Callie," calls Leah.

My cheeks are hot as drinks are raised and clinks sound all around. I take a sip of my Sprite, unsure what to do with the accolades. I'm not used to being praised. Warmth spreads through me all the same, the acknowledgment settling in as I feel welcomed and seen.

Sebastian squeezes my leg beneath the table, and I cover his hand with mine, grateful for something to anchor me. Then the mad dash for food begins.

Chapter Twenty

Callie

After that delicious dinner, we're all groaning about how we can't possibly eat another bite, even as we keep picking at more food.

Leah turns to me. "Wanna go for a walk?"

I know we need to do this, to see where we stand with each other. I've seen how protective she is of the brothers — she is the test I have to pass. Unease sits in my stomach, but I say, "Okay."

As I stand, Sebastian catches my hand then tugs me in for a kiss. Silence reigns when I let go, and I look around at genuine shock on everyone's faces. I knew he had an aversion to touch, but I thought it'd be different around his family. Has he never been this casual with anyone? The idea leaves my head spinning, and I'm feeling off balance as I follow Leah down the steps.

Once we're out of earshot of the others, she says, "Okay, I know Sebastian told you we dated. Ask me anything."

I'm taken aback by the direct approach but I'm also grateful for it. We walk along the edge of the landscaped house, beautifully done with dark mulch and various bushes. Not a weed in sight. "So you guys dated for quite a while, and...what? You just weren't compatible?"

She frowns. "Sebastian didn't tell you about my history?" When I shake my head, she sighs. "My boyfriend before Sebastian was..." She trails off with a grimace. "Well, it was Vance, so you can see how that would turn out."

The name settles like lead in my stomach. The guy who drugged me. I swallow and start walking again, needing to move.

She hurries to catch up to me. "Do I need to stop talking?"

"No, but I want to keep moving while we do. Please."

We walk in silence for several steps, then she tells me how awful Vance was. That Shawn saved her and she stayed with Sebastian while Shawn went after the asshole.

I hate that I wasn't the only one who was hurt by that jerk. Hate that anyone else suffered at his hands.

"Sebastian was safe, and I needed that to dip my toe back into the dating pool. I needed to know that there were good guys out there." She glances at me with a half-smile. "It was never about romance between us. He's always been my best friend, and he helped me navigate some heavy stuff."

My heart warms at the new image of their relationship. I can see him helping her, stepping up to be whatever she needed in the moment.

"Actually, he's the one who brought me and Shawn together."

He'd mentioned that, but I listen to her side of the story, convinced by the end that she isn't a threat to me at all. "Thank you for telling me," I say when she finishes, marveling at how head over heels she is for Shawn. I wonder if I come off that way when I talk about Sebastian. Then a determined look crosses her face, and I know it's my turn to be grilled.

"He's different with you, Callie. I've never seen him like this."

I try to smile, though my chest is tight because she's so serious. "Is this the part where you tell me if I hurt him, you'll kill me?"

"Something like that." She sighs. "More than that...if you're not ready to be in this for the long haul, if you're not serious about being with him, you need to tell him now. Because he is. Has he told you about the penguins? The ones that give each other rocks when they find their mate?"

I shake my head, smiling because it sounds like something Sebastian would know.

Her lips curve up, her smile soft. "If you two were penguins, he would be biding his time before he gave you a rock."

My breath hitches at the idea, but what shocks me most is the lack of alarm that accompanies it. I want to reassure Leah, let her know I'm not planning to turn tail and run. "I'm in this for as long as he'll have me. He sees me like no one else ever has and makes me feel whole. We're good for each other."

She frowns, but I take a deep breath and keep going. "I love him, Leah. I've told him that, and he loves me too. I know I'm young. I know most people would say I've barely lived, but I don't want anything else. Any*one* else."

"Well then, Callie, I have only one thing to say to you."

I wait with bated breath as wispy tendrils of tension curl in my gut.

"Welcome to the family."

She wraps me in a hug, and I take the moment to cover my shock, even as I soak in the words. Leah is the gatekeeper to the brothers, and I have passed her test. It seems I'm truly in. I'm no longer lingering on the outskirts, I'm one of them.

And I couldn't think of a better place to belong.

Back at the house, Sebastian looks relieved when I appear in one piece and smiling. To my surprise, everyone gathers around the table, taking their previous seats.

"What's going on?" I ask him.

"Cards."

Trey starts shuffling a regular deck. "Ever play horse thief, Callie?"

I shake my head. My family isn't much for games. Awkward silence or uncomfortable conversation is more our forte.

It takes me a couple of rounds to get the hang of it. Meg deals and only needs two points when she turns over the ace of spades, a guaranteed point.

Silas tosses his cards into the middle. "There goes any chance of stopping her."

She rolls her eyes. "That's just like you, quitting without seeing things through. I'm not guaranteed to win."

I've seen them pick at each other all night, but this feels different. There's a truth underlying her words, a dig that makes Silas bolt upright and glare. He snatches his cards back, muttering to himself.

I lean toward Sebastian to whisper, "What happened there?"

He shrugs. "No one knows."

Now I'm even more curious, but I push it aside to concentrate on the game. When she's held to one point by Steven, Meg sticks out her tongue, and Silas' expression darkens further. It doesn't help when Steven pulls ahead and wins, proving Meg's point. Silas storms inside, and I shift uncomfortably in my chair.

Sebastian's phone rings, breaking the silence. He frowns. "It's Professor Maia. I'd better take this." He gets to his feet and strides away.

My Sprite is long empty, so I go over to the cooler to help myself to a water. When I settle back into my seat, Judy startles me by reaching over to touch my wrist.

"Callie, I want to say thank you again." She gives me a squeeze, then returns to her own space. "Not only did you save his life, you've changed him. I've never seen him so at ease before. He's completely relaxed around you."

A hint of annoyance bubbles in me, but I keep my smile in place as I nod. They make it sound like I worked some miracle.

"Yeah, Callie," Shawn pipes in, leaning forward. "What gives? You a witch or something? Cast a spell on him?"

"What do you mean?"

"I mean" — his words hold a hint of a challenge — "I've never seen him like this before, and I'm wondering what you did to my brother."

I hold his gaze for a moment, then calmly take a sip of my water. The tension builds between us. "You want to know the truth?"

He nods, the rest of his family following suit. They're not going to like the answer, though, and fear creeps in, telling me to bite my tongue, to keep my head down. But this is my chance to help them see Sebastian in a new light, to help him have a safer space where he doesn't have to mask. So I suck in a bolstering breath and force the words out.

For him.

"You guys are amazing. It's obvious how much you love and support one another, and I wish I had one iota of that in my life." Their cautious smiles fall when I add, "But as much as you claim to accept Sebastian, he still has to watch himself around you."

Steven's brow furrows, and Trey glances at the table.

I continue before anyone can comment. "When we started actually hanging out, he would catch himself anytime he shared an animal fact or talked about his work. I'd see glimpses of him as he lit up with this joy, this passion, then he'd shut himself down. He eventually opened up, explaining how he watched people glaze over when he spoke of those things."

Judy's expression is full of chagrin, and she won't look at me. When Shawn begins to shift and fidget, I know I'm hitting a nerve.

"I know it's mostly society in general, but it's not just there. Like when he called you guys for advice when he took me to dinner at the Grand Hotel, none of you asked what *he* was comfortable with." I pause. "I'm not some magician. I'm a safe space where Sebastian can truly be himself, and I accept him, every part. I love him just the way he is."

As hard as that is, it's not all I have to say, and I turn to Judy. "You said that you've never seen him this relaxed or comfortable. Have you ever considered he may be neuro atypical? One of my college genetics courses was about the genetic predisposition to some of these conditions, and we spent some time on them. It made me curious, so I took a corresponding psych course the following semester."

She swallows, and her lips press together before she answers tightly. "It occurred to us, but we didn't want him labeled."

Frustration bubbles within me. "For you or for him?" I ask quietly.

Her face loses color, but I press on. "Sebastian thrives on labels and knowledge. He hates the unknown. The more he knows, the more he can research, and the better he does. If he has a condition, having a name for it and a starting place to look into could help him in so many ways. Not only to understand himself but to make him feel not so out of place."

Judy has tears shining in her eyes, and no one else says a word. The silence grows louder as the weight of their stares grows heavier, but I can only look at the table.

I've ruined a perfectly good family dinner, one in my honor no less. I shove away from the table. "Excuse me."

* * * *

Sebastian

I return from my phone call to find Calliope missing, and no one will look at me.

Except Silas, who appears with a beer in his hand and frowns. "What's going on? I leave for two seconds, and it looks like someone kicked a puppy."

Leah speaks first. "I'm so sorry, Sebastian."

"Yeah, Seb," Shawn agrees, clearing his throat. "We didn't think about it that way."

Silas' frown deepens, and I mimic him, beyond confused. He finally tosses his free hand. "Seriously! Will someone explain what happened?"

Mom stands and walks over to take my hand. Her eyes shine suspiciously, as if she's on the verge of crying, and her smile is tremulous. I recognize the expression.

I've seen it many times over the years — when the teacher called her in about kids picking on me and Mom came to talk to me afterward. When she got done defending Shawn to the administrators for standing up for me. When I feigned a stomachache so I wouldn't have to go to school.

Each time, she'd take my hand and tell me she loved me. Just like now.

"Sebastian, sweetie, you know we love you."

"Yes, of course." My only conclusion makes me ask, "Did Calliope say something?"

"Nothing that we didn't ask her to." Mom draws me in for a hug, and I stand here, bewildered.

When she lets go, I straighten and step back, wanting space. Again, I'm the focal point, and without a full explanation, I'm uncomfortable. Even more so because Calliope isn't here, and I'm worried. "I'm going to go check on her."

I stride into the house, unsure of where to go. Luckily, she's emerging from the bathroom, and the pinched look on her face tells me she's upset. Her eyes widen when she sees me. Her gaze drops, and she shoves her hair behind her ear, making me contemplate what's going through her mind.

Does she think I'm going to yell at her? I'd like to know what happened, but Mom already said they asked for whatever Calliope told them.

I keep my tone gentle, trying to be the opposite of her father as much as possible. "Hey, little muse. How about I show you my room?"

Hope lights her eyes. A small smile tips her lips before she nods, and it grows when I offer her my hand. I feel better the second her fingers slide across mine. She relaxes too, her shoulders not so rigid, her expression no longer pinched.

I lead her downstairs to the finished basement. The laundry room is located here along with a utility room, and not much else besides my old bedroom. But I prefer it that way — quiet.

Nudging open the door, I grin to see it exactly the same as I left it. My same green and tan striped comforter lies on my bed, which is framed by two matching bookcases. Several shelves are empty now since I brought many of my books with me, but others... I step up, trailing my hand over some of my very first non-fiction books.

I pull one out, grinning at the surprised look on Calliope's face. "I was obsessed with dinosaurs for a long time."

"I can just picture you, walking around telling everyone the differences between the dinosaurs and flawlessly pronouncing those ridiculous names they have." Amusement dances in her eyes as she smirks. "And getting annoyed when someone said one wrong."

My cheeks warm. "You see me so well."

She grows serious as she studies my face. "Is your family mad?" I shake my head, and she drops my hand to wander around the room. "Did they tell you what happened?"

"Not really." I sink onto the bed, waiting.

"I guess I didn't realize it bothered me so much, but all day I've been getting these looks and comments. Every time you touch me, it's like I performed some magic trick." She stops to study the map of the world on my wall. "When you went inside, the subject came up, and Shawn asked me how I did it, how I got you to relax like that. When I asked if they really wanted to know, they said yes, so I told them."

I frown, still not quite understanding.

She spins around. "I told them that I accepted every part of you. I didn't shut you down when you wanted to talk about animals or your work. When you find something fascinating, I love that for you and enjoy hearing about it."

My chest grows tight because my family loves me, and I know that, but she's right. She is my safe space, and I'm more comfortable with her than any of them because I don't have to watch myself.

"You don't have to mask around me." She sits on the bed, then reaches out to rest her hand over mine. "I also mentioned a course I took on being neuro atypical."

At the phrase, my gaze flies to hers, and my muscles go rigid.

"You know me and my genetics. The predisposition fascinated me, and I studied several types in depth. Including autism. Some of your tendencies could indicate being on the spectrum." She squeezes my hand, pressing her lips together, then adds, "Your mom said she considered getting you tested but decided against it, and I kind of got upset."

As she recounts the rest of the conversation, I feel like my head is spinning. I've never had anyone stand up for me like she did, especially to my family. And I have a confession to make, one I haven't even told them. "I...I am autistic. I'm on the spectrum, like you said."

That had been a whole process in itself — the testing and diagnosis. But it had been a relief to have a reason for my idiosyncrasies, as well as a solid lead to research.

She gapes. "Why didn't you say anything?"

I lift a shoulder, withdrawing my hand because I need my space. "It's a lot. Everyone already worries because of my diabetes and my hypoglycemia." I push my glasses up on my nose, the action calling attention to yet another complication. "I wear glasses, I don't play sports, I'm always reading. This is just one more thing to separate me from everyone else."

The admission hurts, but it also feels good to say it out loud. I do feel apart from my family, as if they get to be in one room all happy and together. Maybe I'm in that room too, but a pane of glass separates me from them. I can hear them, see them, but I'm not fully with them.

"Sebastian..." Calliope stands and walks around, stopping in front of me. "May I?"

She glances at my lap, and I appreciate that she asked first, especially when I drew away moments ago. I'm ready for her touch, though, so I nod. She straddles me, wraps her arms around my shoulders, and holds me tight. I don't move for a long second, but then I slowly ease my hands up to hug her back.

"The only reason I mentioned it," she says quietly, "was because I thought it would give you power. You do better when you can name things, when you can learn details and research all those questions that pop up. I thought a diagnosis would give you that, and maybe it'd make you feel less alone, to know that there are others out there dealing with the same things you are."

"I'm not too...much?" I need the reassurance even though I feel pitiful for having to ask. My stomach still churns with the idea that one of these things will be too much for her, and she'll leave.

"Not at all." She sits back, rubbing my shoulders as she searches my face. "I love you, Sebastian. I'll tell you as many times as it takes to sink in, but I love *every* part of you. A label doesn't change anything for me."

Relief floods me, the knots in my gut loosening as I pull her back to my chest, clinging tightly to her. "Thank you." The words are strangled by unshed tears rising in me. This beautiful woman makes me feel whole in ways I never knew I was missing, but now that she's here, now that I'm complete, I never want to let her go again.

Our return upstairs is slightly awkward, and I force myself to announce the diagnosis I've kept hidden. Everyone is accepting, encouraging even, and it feels good to have the truth in the open. Each of my family members takes a turn to apologize privately to me as the night wears on, and it's more emotional than I can usually handle, but Calliope makes it bearable.

After several more rounds of horse thief, I need to decompress, and I glance at Calliope. "Ready to go?"

She nods, and we make our round of goodbyes, but Steven surprises me, saying he'll walk us out. Near the car, he pulls out his phone and fiddles with the screen, then my message notification sounds. I stare in confusion.

"I made you something." He waits for me to pull my phone from my pocket. "It's an app, and it should integrate with your other monitoring apps. I made it to be more of an umbrella type, getting the info from the others so you only have one to go to. It's geared for hypoglycemia specifically, with set meal times and reminders that only go away when you upload photos of food. But it works with diabetes, too."

I'm speechless. As I flip through the different menus and options on the app, the knowledge that my brother created this for me is overwhelming. In the best possible way.

"If your blood sugar dips too low, there's even a setting for it to call nine-one-one. It gives you a certain amount of time to respond first, but if there's no response..." He swallows, and I know we're all remembering when Calliope found me.

"Oh good," she says. "I don't have to walk into that again."

But I can't joke about this. It's too personal a gift, and I reach out to hug my brother. "Thank you, Steven. This means a lot."

He smacks my back twice, then steps away, clearing his throat. "And let me know if you find any bugs or have any suggestions on improving it. You're my guinea pig."

"I will." As he walks away, I nearly sag against the car. I'm more drained than I have been in a long time.

"Hey," Calliope says, touching my arm. "How about I drive home?"

I hand her the keys, grateful that she understands and doesn't push me to talk. I look out of the window, replaying moments from today. When we get back to her house, I want nothing more than to lose myself in a book. I go upstairs and change into comfier clothes.

Calliope comes in and changes too. "I thought I'd dance for a while." She goes over to her dresser and pulls out a small box then hands it to me. "I got you these, if you want to come watch."

I stare at the noise-filtering earbuds and smile. They're absolutely perfect because I'd love to be around her, but I don't want the chaos of her music as I try to read. I hug her again. "Thank you."

Chapter Twenty-One

Sebastian

We head downstairs to her dance studio, and the earbuds work perfectly. I'm able to read my book in peace, but still look up to see Calliope. Watching her is entrancing. She moves so gracefully and gets lost in her rhythm the way I get lost in my books. I love sharing this with her, me in my quiet bubble, her doing what she loves. I never imagined a relationship could be like this.

I keep thinking about those penguins giving the perfect rock to show they've chosen their lifelong mate. Do they feel like this? As if a part of them was missing until they meet that other penguin.

The rock I found on the beach at Mackinac sits in my pocket, like it does every day. Its weight is comforting because I know it's too soon, but I also see Calliope in my future. I see days like this spent together in quiet harmony. I see challenges and achievements, all conquered side by side.

Still, she's so young, and she's lived under her dad's oppressive hold for so long. I don't want to feel her pressured in any way, so I'll keep these feelings to myself for now. We have plenty of time, and I know how to be patient.

She's worth waiting for, no matter how long it takes.

* * * *

We spend all of Sunday being lazy together. It's a rainy day, perfect for snuggling, exploring one another and playing with Steven's app. It's unique in its persistence. I silence the alarms for meals, but they sound again until I actually take a picture of food. I even try taking a picture of my book, but the app comes back with a message saying, *Nice try, but you can't eat that.*

I chuckle at his thoroughness and, despite the annoyance of it, I appreciate the tenacity because when I'm hyper-focused on a project, only something on this level will get through.

A thread of tension winds through me. My experiment is tomorrow, and my career hinges on it going well. The anxiety amplifies as evening draws near. We'll set up everything tonight, after Jess' bees are tucked into their hive for the evening. Excitement overrides all other emotions when it's finally time to leave the house to go to campus.

We meet Jess at the botany department to relocate my roses into her control room. What a fascinating setup she has. A long window spans one wall looking into the garden where the bees are housed, and part of the roof is retractable.

Two tables sit beneath the viewing window, and we position my roses on the rightmost one. To the left are the normal roses, a perfect control group.

For the first part of tomorrow, Jess will keep the rest of the garden area closed off, so the hive only has access to these plants. It won't be enough to sustain the bees all day, and eventually she'll open the full room, but it'll give us a great idea initially of how my plants perform.

Once we're all set up, I ensure everything is perfect with one more lap around the room before following Jess outside. "Thanks again," I tell her and Lyssa.

"No problem," Lyssa says with a cheery smile.

"Happy to help." Jess eyes me, and I wonder if she can sense the endless energy thrumming through me. She glances at Calliope, then hands her a little bag. "Here. You might need these if he's going to get any sleep tonight."

I frown at the exchange, but Calliope simply tucks the bag into her pocket before hugging her friend. We exchange goodbyes and depart.

In the car, I ask, "What did Jess give you?"

"Just some marijuana gummies. She uses them for anxiety, and they really help you relax, take the edge off."

Despite feeling as if caffeine has been infused directly into my veins, I can't imagine wanting to change my chemistry like that. And on the night prior to a life-changing experiment? I shake my head. "I won't be taking them."

"I know."

"Then..." I struggle to understand. "Why did you accept them?"

She waves her hand. "It's easier than fighting with her. I learned that the hard way."

And she changes the subject back to the experiment. I let it go, chatting easily the rest of the ride. Once we get inside, I lock up, deliberating if I'm going to be able to sleep. But Calliope crooks her finger, and I follow her upstairs.

Her ministrations are the perfect distraction, and after several rounds of pleasure, I feel comfortable and sated. I drift off easily, and my sleep is sound. But when I wake at five a.m., full of excitement and energy, I know there's no use trying to doze off again.

I ease out of bed, careful not to disturb Calliope. I grab a handful of nuts when I get downstairs, then try to figure out what I should do with my time. I itch to review my notes once more, to ensure I have perfected every detail, but I won't be able to sit still long enough for that. Which means reading is also out of the question.

A smudge on the slider catches my attention. Surely I can find some glass cleaner and fix that. I search the cupboards in the kitchen and tackle the slider, then another spot on the other pane catches my eye. I already have the stuff out, so I move to the next window and the next.

Calliope comes downstairs sometime later, and I'm in the living room, cleaning the panes of her door. I freeze as if she caught me doing something heinous.

She grins. "Couldn't sleep?"

I finish the section and sigh. "No. And I'm too anxious to read."

My phone starts beeping, a high, obnoxious alert that I don't recognize. I pull it out of my pocket, and an alert from Steven's app fills the screen. My sugar levels are low. I silence the alert as Calliope watches with a frown.

"It's okay. I woke up earlier than usual and have been doing plenty of activity. I just didn't eat enough first. I'll grab a juice, then get a real breakfast."

As we head toward the kitchen, she says, "Maybe the app needs a wake-up feature. Some place to input when you get up for the day, especially if it's outside of your normal routine."

"That's a great idea." I hurry to text Steven as she offers to make eggs and sausages.

* * * *

We arrive at the office just before eight. Jess isn't there yet. Calliope has to stop me from calling her and shoots me a triumphant grin when her friend arrives at eight-oh-three, with Lyssa on her heels.

"Okay, come on in." Jess ushers us into the viewing room, and I hurry to press my face to the glass.

I study my bushes on my table, noting the movement of the bees, then glance over at the normal roses and find almost no activity. Elation bubbles within me. "They like my roses." I turn to Calliope, who gazes at me with so much pride and adoration that I feel like I might burst. "They like my roses!"

She flings her arms around my neck, and I laugh, unable to contain my joy. All the hard work, all the studying, all the formulas—it paid off. I swing her around, then lean down to kiss her soundly. She sways when I step away, so I keep one hand on her waist.

"Well done, Sebastian," Jess says, patting my shoulder.

Lyssa nudges me and says, "Yeah, good job."

Their contact is brief enough that I don't feel discomfort, especially on the heels of my elation. We all stand there watching for several more moments before Calliope's friends decide to leave. We coordinate a pick-up time for my roses, say our goodbyes, then it's just me and Calliope.

I slip my arm around her waist, tugging her to my side. A wave of contentment washes over me, and I sigh happily. "Okay. Ready to go?"

She looks up, bewilderment etched into every inch of her face. "That's it? All that hype and we're here for half an hour?" She shakes her head. "I thought this would take all day while you examine the pattern of each bee's flight or whatever."

I laugh, holding her closer. "That's what the cameras are for. I'll watch all that later, but right now? I want to celebrate with my little muse."

Delight sparkles in her eyes. "What did you have in mind?"

"It's supposed to be a beautiful day. How about we spend it at the beach? I can show you my favorite hiking trails, maybe we can bring a picnic."

"That sounds lovely."

After a quick stop for our supplies and to change clothes, we head out. It's a perfect day for the beach. I make sure to fuel my body as we drive, eating a granola bar and drinking some juice. Hiking is a more strenuous activity and I don't want to risk becoming lightheaded. I also have to set my insulin pump to exercise mode, so it's not giving me insulin to counteract the carbs I just ate.

There isn't a cloud in the sky when we arrive, and I'm thankful for the shade of the trails. A light breeze keeps the bugs away. We walk for a couple of hours, exploring the dunes and the woods of the state park. When my phone starts beeping, I know my levels have dipped, and it's time for lunch. We return to where I left the cooler, then we have a picnic in the shade of a sprawling oak tree. It's my favorite spot to sit because we can see everything.

"This is perfect," Calliope says, finishing her last bite and surveying the beach below. She lets out a contented sigh, then settles against the tree trunk. "I can watch people or gulls or listen to the waves. Maybe I'll just stay here forever."

I chuckle as I finish packing up the leftovers. When everything is tucked away, I sit beside her for several long moments before I grow antsy. People watching is not my thing. I want to move or read or be occupied in some way, and the need becomes like a physical itch I have to scratch.

I try to fight it by adjusting my position, but Calliope starts laughing. "I wondered how long you'd be able to sit still without a book."

A self-deprecating snort escapes me. "Not long, obviously."

"Well, go on then."

I freeze. I'd tried to be covert about packing my current read, not wanting her to think I planned to ignore her.

"You *do* have one, don't you?"

"Of course, it's just...are you sure?"

She nods. "I'm perfectly content to sit here with you."

Happiness wells in me as I study her, not finding a hint of untruth. I eagerly grab my book, then settle back beside her, but she touches my shoulder.

"You could lay on me, if you like. Use my legs as a pillow."

I don't hesitate to take her up on her offer. I rest my head on her thighs and smile as she lays a hand on my chest. "This brings back memories. We had frequent movie nights with Leah growing up, and my brothers would always fight for the spot next to her. She gave the best head pets."

"Head pets?"

"Not quite a head massage, but not just stroking your hair either." I frown, trying to think of a more accurate description.

"You said your brothers would fight over that spot. Not you?"

"I tried several times, but it made me uncomfortable." A wistful longing fills my chest, creating an ache. "Even with Leah, I've had a distance. You're the first person I feel truly comfortable with, Calliope, on every level. Thank you for that. I don't know if I can express how much that means to me."

She blinks several times and gives me a soft smile. "I feel the same way about you." Then she offers, "I could try the head pet thing, if you wanted."

A surge of delight courses through me, that she's offering, that I don't have to miss out. I nod eagerly. "Yes, please."

Her fingers wind through my hair, brushing firmly along my scalp. I wait for the discomfort to set in, but it doesn't, and she continues stroking as I revel in her touch. My little muse has done it again, stealing my breath and my very soul just by being her amazing self.

Love feels like too tame a word for what I feel as I gaze at her, but it's the only one I have so I whisper, "I love you, Calliope." And I will never grow tired of her answer.

"I love you, too, Sebastian."

* * * *

Callie

I miss my boyfriend. It's been four days since the beach, since we came home and made love. Dad returned the next morning, and my life is back to its normal monotony. He hasn't been bad, though, just tiresome. I spend my days cooking and cleaning, but rarely get any acknowledgment. I guess it's better than being yelled at.

Being around Sebastian has me used to being praised and complimented, though. His gratitude is natural, and I never realized how much I need that in my life. It makes me miss him even more.

It doesn't help that his words about me having choices replay in my mind. I don't like the thought of leaving Dad. I remember after Mom died, how he didn't eat...what would my choosing to leave do to him?

But I can't help wondering if he'll eventually push me too far. If I'll reach twenty-five before that happens. And if he does cross that line, what will I do then? Maybe a miracle will happen, and he'll actually listen. Maybe he'll finally see what he's doing, how he's pushing me away.

And maybe pigs will fly.

Feeling restless, I decide to dance. Dad came home early today since it's Friday, and I give him a quick wave on my way by. Then I lose myself in my music and movements.

Little moments keep popping into my mind from my weekend with Sebastian. I let them play out as I dance, allowing my emotions to flow through me, entwining with the music.

The initial shock at his arrival. The feral look in his eyes when he'd caught me on the bed. Spending the night in his arms. Climbing into his lap when we spoke about autism and how tightly he'd held me. The unbridled giddiness when his experiment was a success. How he practically purred as I stroked his hair on the beach.

I feel like I've found my other half. I love how unhindered he is with me, that we can be completely ourselves with each other.

My song ends, and I check my phone, trying to decide if I want to start another or not. Then Dad bellows my name — my full name. I trot upstairs to find him standing in the living room, arms crossed with a scowl on his face. I'm on high alert, racking my brain for what I've done.

Nothing comes to mind, so I cautiously say, "Hi, Dad. What's up?"

"You tell me." His nostrils flare as he holds out the bag of gummies from Jess.

"How...?" I trail off. I'd stashed them in a drawer and promptly forgotten about them, which means he went through my room. Hurt and indignation swirl within me. "Why are you searching my things like I'm a common criminal?"

"Someone has to save you from yourself." He stalks over to throw the bag in the trash.

"I didn't even eat any of the gummies. My friend gave them to me, but — "

He cuts me off with a fierce glare. "You obviously haven't learned anything this past year. Sebastian has been singing your praises, talking about how much of a help you were in coordinating his experiment. I thought maybe, just maybe, you had grown up, but obviously, I was wrong." Then he launches into a familiar diatribe about how many college careers were ruined by drugs and alcohol.

As I watch him berating and belittling me, Sebastian and his family keep appearing in my mind. How they talk and interact. How I don't have to hold in my thoughts around them. I realize that being with Sebastian has given me another piece I didn't even know I was missing.

Somewhere along the line, I forgot that I matter too. My thoughts and my feelings matter. And I'm allowed to express them.

"Dad." When he doesn't even pause in his rant, I raise my voice. "Dad!" I never yell, especially at him. He stops, blinking in surprise, and I take advantage of his shock. "That's enough! I'm twenty years old, I get good grades, and I don't let the occasional party interfere with my work. I have a steady boyfriend who I care very much about, and I have good friends. You can't keep pinning the mistakes of other students you've seen fail on me."

My phone rings in my pocket, but I ignore it. We need to settle this.

I need to settle this.

His face turns a mottled shade of red. "Listen here, young lady, if you want to continue your education and retain your privileges, you will obey my rules."

"Dad, I obey every rule you put down. I toe the line. I spend every minute trying to live up to your ridiculous expectations." Frustration saturates my tone. "But you're impossible to please. My best is never enough, and even when I'm perfect, you find some imagined slight to lord over my head." I shake my head. "It's exhausting."

My phone chimes with a text, but my dad explodes.

"How dare you question my authority like that? Give me your phone and your car keys, then go to your room."

As if he didn't hear a single word I said.

I stand there for a long moment, nearly vibrating with frustration. It's like talking to a boulder and expecting it to move. I yank my phone out of my pocket and the screen flares to life with a text from Leah. Two words stand out before Dad snatches it from my hand.

Sebastian. Hospital.

Panic flutters in me as I reach for my phone. "Wait, Dad—"

"Not another word." He holds it out of reach. "Keys."

I don't care about anything else but my boyfriend. "Sebastian's in the hospital—"

"I'll be sure to check on him, then. But right now, we have bigger issues to take care of. Keys."

He pointedly holds out his hand, and I stare at him. He'll never understand. The realization washes over me, and my stomach roils. He doesn't care that the love of my life is in the hospital, not when I dinged his pride.

My thoughts pause as I rewind my mind. Sebastian. The thought of him settles on me like a cozy blanket right from the dryer. He is the only thing that matters to me, the only thing I want for myself.

Which leaves me two choices—obey like I usually do and worry myself sick, or...

Leave.

The word hangs in my mind. The door is only four steps behind me and beyond that is the entire world. I won't have my car, I won't have my phone, but I would have my freedom.

All the things I've been afraid of suddenly seem so minuscule. I'll figure it out because I'm a strong, capable woman, and I know I have support if I need it. The leash my dad keeps me on snaps. A lightness washes over me, so profound the room spins.

"Well, young lady?" Dad's voice pulls me back to the present.

I decide to try once more, because what do I have to lose? "Dad, I'm worried about Sebastian. If you would let me call and see — "

"I said, that's enough. Keys."

My heart sinks even as my resolve strengthens. I walk over to grab my purse from the counter and remove the car keys from the clip I keep them on. I drop them into Dad's hand.

A smug smile tips his lips. "Now, go to your room."

But I'm done playing his games, so I straighten my shoulders, leveling my chin as I tighten my grip on my purse. "No." Ignoring his gaping mouth, I turn on my heel and stride over to fling open the door. I stalk down the steps to the sidewalk.

"Calliope Jean Harrison, you come back here this instant! If you don't, I will cut off every single one of your accounts. You'll have nothing." He doesn't stop shouting, but he doesn't come after me either.

I just walked away from all my worldly possessions. I literally have no safety net, but it doesn't matter because I'm free. Every step I take has me feeling lighter and happier. I hadn't realized how oppressive that house was, how heavy the mantle my Dad laid on me was. But now it's gone.

The partial text rears up in my mind once more, tamping down my glee with the heaviness of worry for my boyfriend. I hurry my steps. It'll be a decent walk, but hopefully someone will be at his house and can give me a ride. If not... The thought sobers me, threatening to derail me because I have no phone, no cash.

Then I square my shoulders again. I'll figure it out.

My feet ache by the time I reach his house, and I'm beyond sweaty. I must look a mess, still in my loose tank top and stretchy shorts from dancing. My hasty bun has tendrils escaping every direction, but I knock anyway. Relief pours through me when I hear footsteps.

Chapter Twenty-Two

Callie

Silas flings open the door, his eyes going wide when he sees my disheveled state. "Callie?"

"Is Sebastian okay?"

He frowns. "Yeah, didn't you get the texts?"

It takes all my resolve not to crumple right there in the overwhelming wash of emotions. I shake my head.

"He has food poisoning, couldn't keep anything down. Steven's app called the ambulance before any of us even knew what was happening. They've got him on an IV and some meds to help with the nausea, but he's stable now."

Tears blur my vision.

"Do you want me to take you there?"

"Yes, please," I croak.

"Okay, give me a minute to change. Come in, grab a bottle of water or whatever you need." He swings the door wide open, then disappears upstairs.

I grab a bottle of water like he suggested then visit the bathroom, making an attempt to freshen up. I splash my face, then dry off as I try to calm my racing heart. My hair is truly a mess, so I redo the bun, smoothing the tendrils as best I can. Eventually, though, I decide I'm as good as I'm going to get.

Back in the living room, I feel out of place so I decide to step outside again. Perching on the front stoop, I allow my relief to swell within me. Sebastian's okay. I drink my water and try to find peace in Silas' words, but I know I won't be truly okay until I lay eyes on my boyfriend.

On either side of the steps, landscaping rocks coat the ground between bushes, and I study them. One catches my eye, so I pick it up, marveling at how smooth it is. And it has a perfect band all the way around. I slip it into my pocket for Sebastian, wondering what he'll wish for.

Silas pokes his head out, and seeing me, steps out completely. We hurry to the SUV. "You going to tell me why you don't have your car? Why you walked instead of taking an Uber?"

I explain everything, and his eyes grow wider with each word. I finish with, "So, I left and had no choice but to walk here."

"Wow. I didn't realize things were that bad with you and your father. Sebastian mentioned some stuff, but that's…" He glances over. "I'm sorry, Callie."

"Thanks."

"You know there's room with us, right? I mean, I'm sure you want to talk to Sebastian, but in case he doesn't come home tonight or whatever, you have a place."

The sweet offer makes my throat thick, even as the realization that I'm homeless hits me hard. "Thanks, Silas. I appreciate it."

We pull into the parking lot and rush into ER. We find Leah and Shawn emerging from a room, and I jog over to them. "How is he?"

Her eyebrows shoot up in disbelief. "You didn't seem so concerned when you couldn't even bother to answer —"

"Her dad took her phone," Silas interrupts, giving her an admonishing look. "She was so worried that she walked to our house from her place." He rests a hand on my shoulder. "Trust me, she did everything in her power to get here."

Leah frowns, and I know she's going to ask more questions, but I have a burning one I need to have answered first. "Please, is he okay?"

"Yes." Her words are skeptical. "He's sleeping now, finally."

Her words bring me some relief, but I'm disappointed not to be able to talk to him.

"So, what happened with your dad?"

Her short tone still holds judgment, so I restrain myself from running into Sebastian's room. We need to settle this. I explain the situation to Leah and Shawn, trying to make it quick. Sympathy wells in her eyes as my story unfolds.

"Oh, you poor thing." Leah hugs me before I even know what's happening. "I'm sorry I was pissed. I was just so worried about Sebastian, but you've been through so much, too."

Pesky tears prick my eyes, but I swallow them down and wave her off.

Shawn wraps an arm around her. "We were about to go grab lunch. Want to come?"

I glance at the closed door. "I know he's asleep, but I just need to see him. I'll stay here in case he wakes up."

"Can we bring you back something?" Silas asks.

I accept the offer, then they're on their way, and I slip into Sebastian's room. My chest constricts the moment I see my boyfriend — pale, eyes closed, an IV hooked to his left wrist. Memories of my mom in the same position superimpose on my vision, and I squeeze my eyes shut. He's only sleeping, I remind myself.

I force my eyes open and watch his chest. The tension seeps out of me when the covers rise and fall in a steady rhythm.

The man I love.

The reminder echoes through me as I sit in the chair next to his bed and slip my hand under his. I automatically reach for my phone, and the reality of what I've done crashes into me again. But for the first time, I'm also completely free. Because of Sebastian.

This love for him has untangled the knotted strands of my life, making them feel silky smooth for once. I may not have much in the way of possessions, but I have this man. I know he'll help me however he can, and now I have a true chance to prove myself capable.

My excitement builds as the expanse of my freedom stretches before me. I can do anything, be anyone. I can find out what it truly means to be myself.

Once Sebastian is on his feet again.

Forty-five minutes later, he stirs. His eyes flutter open, his gaze landing on me, and he mouths my name.

"Hey, you." I smile broadly, gripping his hand, and he squeezes back. "What happened?"

One corner of his mouth tips up. "It's all your fault," he croaks, then clears his throat. "I decided to try something new for breakfast, a food truck. Look where it got me."

I let out a startled laugh. "Oh, Sebastian, only you." I shake my head. "Do you need anything?"

He clears his throat again. "Maybe some water."

A tray sits off to one side with a white Styrofoam cup resting on it, and I hand the cup to him. He quickly drinks then sighs.

"Better." He tilts his head, staring as his brow crinkles. "You look different, somehow."

"Well, a lot happened while you were napping." I launch into the story for a third time, hoping this will be the last.

"You left?"

I nod, unable to keep the smile off my face. "It feels amazing."

"I'm so proud of you." He brushes my cheek lightly.

"It's your fault," I tease, mimicking him and grinning wider when he raises his eyebrows. "I couldn't imagine leaving my dad alone and facing the world on my own. Then Leah's text came in, and you were the only thing that mattered to me at that moment. You've bolstered me and sharpened me, and I'm here because you helped me find my strength. I love you."

"Love you, too."

"Oh, and I have something for you." I hurry to dig in my pocket, pulling out the rock I found on the walk. "Make a wish."

"You're giving me a stone?"

My cheeks are warm. "Not exactly a Rolex, but it made me think of our time on Mackinac."

He spins the rock in his hand, studying it in silence for a long moment. "Have I ever told you what my favorite animal is?"

I shake my head.

"Penguins. They fascinate me in so many ways, from the varied climates they live in to their size difference. But one of my favorite things about them is their courtship." His gaze turns tender, stealing my breath as he reaches for my hand. "They give one another rocks, similar to how we give out engagement rings."

"That's so sweet."

His lips tip up as he spins the rock end over end in his long fingers. "Could you do me a favor?"

"Of course."

"The clothes I was wearing are in that cupboard. Bring me my shorts?"

Puzzled, I do as he asks, and he reaches into the pocket, then extends his fist. I hold my hand out, smiling when he drops a rock into my palm. I gasp as I study the gorgeous oval stone. It's smooth and covered with an etched white pattern. Almost like lace.

"It's a Petoskey stone," he explains, then his gaze drops before meeting mine once more. He quietly admits, "I found it that day we walked the beach on Mackinac Island, and I've been wanting to give it to you ever since."

"Really?" The implication hits me with the depth of his feelings.

"I fell hard for you, Calliope, and I haven't stopped." He looks at the rock in my hand. "I know we're young, and it's so soon, but I can't fathom giving a rock to anyone else. You're my person."

Surprised delight washes over me. "And you're mine, Sebastian." I'm not looking to get married tomorrow, but I roll the idea in my mind, and I have to say, I like the way the future looks with him by my side.

* * * *

Sebastian

I'm discharged Friday night, and I use the weekend to help Calliope settle in. We share my room, though

Shawn offered his. I'm surprised to find I don't mind not having my own space. It was easy enough at the conference, but I thought it might be different giving up my area. It's not. We belong together.

Before they left the hospital, I'd given Leah some money to take Calliope shopping for some clothes and essentials. Leah and Meg lent her several items to fill in the gaps.

We get Calliope set up with an old phone of Meg's, which is still in decent condition. Then Calliope reaches out to her dad to arrange a time to collect her clothes, but his only response is that she needs to come home.

I'm thankful I have the weekend to prepare for seeing Professor Harrison, so I have a chance at keeping my temper in check. Luckily the department has staff training this week, so he'll be occupied most of the time. I won't be running into him much.

By Sunday evening, I'm able to eat like normal. Calliope and I are curled up on the couch reading when Shawn and Leah come in. She is holding a familiar brown paper bag that has my mouth immediately watering.

"Hey," she says, grinning. "I heard you were feeling up to eating real food."

"I am." I crane my neck, trying to get a peek at the logo. "Is that what I think it is?"

"Your favorite lasagna? Why yes, yes it is."

Calliope pops off the couch. "Can I help get things ready?"

"Yes, please," Shawn says, giving Leah an exasperated look. "I'm dying for a run, and Lee keeps trying to rope me into making a salad."

The three of them disappear into the kitchen, and I go back to my reading. It takes ninety minutes for the frozen lasagna to cook, so Calliope wanders in and out between helping Leah. Shawn leaves for his run, returning in plenty of time.

When the timer rings, a text comes through saying it's time. I meander into the kitchen where Calliope stares wide-eyed at the ceiling as my brothers thunder to the stairs.

"You should see what happens when I sauté garlic," Leah says, grinning.

Shawn races in, and Silas grabs the wall, swinging into the room behind Shawn. Steven ambles in after, shaking his head at their antics. Meg rushes to the table, and they all scramble for seats. Leah sets the lasagna in the middle of the table with a satisfied smile.

When she straightens, I put a hand on her shoulder, then pull her in for a hug. "Thanks, Lee-bug." I want to show how much I truly appreciate this.

She freezes for a second, startled at the use of her nickname, then squeezes me tight. "You're welcome. Just glad you're feeling better."

I take the open seat beside Calliope, loving how she leans against me for a second. This feels right, having her here as part of our family.

We dive right in, taking turns talking about our weekend or plans for the week. I listen intently as everyone hands their plates to Shawn, who dishes out the lasagna. A bowl of salad is passed around, and I smile as Meg digs out the red onion, then Silas slides over his bowl while offering her his cucumbers.

"I thought they hated each other," Calliope whispers.

"Meg hates onions more," I whisper back, making Calliope grin. Then I get to discuss my week. "Well, I should be able to submit my paper soon. The rough draft is finished, and my colleagues are scheduled to read it over next weekend."

Everyone cheers, encouraging me with their bolstering words. When the noise dies down, we all look at Calliope. Her eyes widen when she realizes she gets a turn, and she glances over anxiously. I dip my chin as I rest my leg against hers, wanting her to be comfortable.

"I-I'm not sure what's next for me. I guess I'll start looking for a job within walking distance." A weight settles over her, and she sighs. "I wish I had access to that trust Mom left me. Just to get started."

Silas cocks his head. "What sort of trust?" She tells him as many details as she can, and he offers to look it over. "Many trusts have stipends for the guardian of the benefactor, to help offset the cost of living. Often that stipend is turned over to the benefactor once they become eighteen. I take it that didn't happen?"

She slowly shakes her head. "This is the first I've heard of it."

"Well, I'd have to see the document to know for sure."

This time when she glances at me, determination ignites in her gaze. "I'll see what I can do."

Her predicament has been needling me. I know everyone has to start somewhere, but most people have someone to help with the initial liftoff.

The next day, I arrive at work, intent on working on my paper, but I'm immediately interrupted. Professor Harrison storms into my office, shutting the door behind him. His face is a mottled purplish red as he slams his hands on my desk.

I'm really not prepared for a confrontation, but the sight of him has me tensing.

"Where is Callie?"

Her name in his mouth has the anger that's been simmering for days turn to a raging roil. How could he treat someone as precious as my girlfriend the way he has? I grip the arms of my chair to keep from lunging across the space between us. I've never been a violent person, but I can't stop thinking about how satisfying it would be to smash my fist into his nose.

I keep my temper and tightly say, "I thought you had training today."

"This is more important. Tell me where she is!"

That's the first time I've heard him sound like he actually cares. "She's staying with me."

He lets out a long breath as he glares. "I trusted you. I brought you into this position, helped you start your career, set you up with my daughter. This is how you repay me?" His voice grows louder with each word, and he's practically shouting by the end.

"She's an adult, Professor. Maybe if you treated her as such, you wouldn't be in this predicament."

His lips pinch together. "Mark my words, Wrighting. I have pull here, I have connections. If you don't convince my daughter to come home, I'll make sure you lose all credibility in the academic circles. Your name will be mud." He stands and adjusts his tie, which is tied in the poorest Windsor knot I've ever seen. "You have until the end of the week." Then he turns on his heel and storms out.

I stare after him for a long moment as I try to process his threat. Maybe I should be more afraid, but I don't see how he could possibly hurt me enough to affect my career. Professor Harrison may have clout here, but he's a big fish in a small pond.

If my pond gets too muddy, I'll move elsewhere.

I've had offers from other universities wanting me to join their team, and once I publish this paper, I'm sure my standings in the academic circle will be even more solidified. My resolve strengthens at the thought.

I'll get this paper out there, the sooner the better.

My phone chimes, and I glance over to see a text from Calliope. My stomach sinks. How am I going to tell her about her father? It would break her heart and she's already in enough pain. I waffle for a long moment, trying to discern the best course of action.

I'll wait. I'll tell her after she gets her trust straightened out. Maybe there will be good news, and it'll soften the blow.

Tuesday, I finish my paper and schedule a celebratory dinner with Calliope at seven at Maria's. Her father's threat hangs over me, dampening my sense of accomplishment.

I don't like keeping information from her, but every time I think about mentioning her father's threat, I see the weight she's already carrying. Professor Harrison hasn't backed down. He even sent me a reminder text this morning, reiterating his terms.

If he keeps this up, I'll take it up with the Dean. For now, though, I just want to celebrate with my girlfriend.

Calliope is getting ready in the bathroom when I arrive home. She taps on the open door of our room as I'm sorting out my bag, and my breath catches the moment I lay eyes on her. Her white sundress has a fitted bodice with a whimsical skirt that flares to right above her knees. Her purple hair is pulled back from her face with intricate braids and her pink lips shine, begging to be kissed.

So I give in. "You look amazing."

She runs her hands down my chest. "Thank you."

"Maybe we should stay home."

Her lower lip juts out. "But I'm hungry."

My voice drops as I reply. "So am I."

A satisfied smile tips her lips, but she nudges me aside. "Sorry, we're going out. Case closed."

I hurry to get ready, not the least bit disappointed. Now that she's living with me, I have all night with her, every night. I can resist losing control for that short amount of time, though it may be difficult.

We decide to walk to the restaurant, which is only a few blocks away. Once we're seated, Calliope looks over the menu. "What are you getting?" she asks when I don't even pick mine up.

"Prime rib, mashed potatoes and green beans."

"That sounds amazing. I was waffling between that and the salmon." She nibbles on her lower lip as she thinks.

"We could share," I offer, loving how her face lights up at the suggestion.

"You don't mind?"

"Not at all." Especially when she looks like I gave her the moon.

We put our orders in. After the server leaves, I draw a stapled packet from my inner pocket. "Thought you might like to see this."

"Sebastian! Is that your paper?" She takes it from me, bouncing in her seat as she looks it over. Then she goes still. "Why is my name on this?"

Beneath my name as author is a special acknowledgment for her. "I thought about giving you a byline, but knew you'd think it was too much. I wanted to acknowledge you, though, and all your help, so I came up with that."

Her hand lifts to rest on her chest as her eyes glisten. I know she is rarely thanked for her actions, that she has been taken for granted much of her life. I refuse to do that. I give credit where credit is due, and she deserves the accolades.

She reads through the entire paper, then reaches out to grasp my hand. "It's really well done, Sebastian. And thank you."

"You're welcome." I bring her hand up, touching my lips to her knuckles. "So, how's the job hunt going?"

She found a few places nearby that are hiring, but she hasn't heard anything yet. She's still optimistic, though. Our food comes and every bite is delicious.

"Now that my paper is done," I say, "and my workload is a little bit lighter. Maybe you could come have lunch with me tomorrow?"

She stares at the table. "I don't want to risk running into my dad."

"Then I'll pick you up."

She still doesn't look at me, and she rubs her thumb over her nail, letting me know she's anxious. I stretch out my arm, resting my hand palm up on the table, not relaxing until she slides her fingers into my grip.

"What's wrong?"

"Won't you get sick of me? Spending all this time together?"

"No, little muse." I almost laugh at the ridiculousness of the idea. "I want you with me whenever I can. Telling me every thought that jumps into your gorgeous mind. Touching me however you want to."

She finally raises her head, but uncertainty lingers in her gaze.

"Calliope, you're a blessing, not a burden, and I'll spend my whole life showing you that if you'll let me."

Her cheeks flush and a soft smile tips her lips. I start to say more, but her attention shifts to a commotion at the side of the room. One corner is set up with a piano and two microphones. The restaurant falls silent as two men and a woman take their places. The woman holds a guitar, settling on a stool before she gives it a strum.

"I didn't know they did live music," Calliope says, watching the band with interest.

"I've heard that they occasionally do this, but I didn't know it was tonight."

"Can we stay?" she asks hopefully.

Our plates are empty, and I'm sure the server will be around to ask about dessert any time, so I lift a shoulder. "Depends on what they sound like."

She laughs, nodding her agreement, then she adjusts our grip, allowing her to sit back in her chair and watch.

Chapter Twenty-Three

Sebastian

The music is a nice fit for the cozy atmosphere. The songs are more melodic than I expected, and the man's voice is smooth. Several couples get up to dance, swaying back and forth in the small clearing between the tables.

I have never volunteered to dance in my entire life, but I know Calliope would love it. When the song ends and another one starts up, I squeeze her hand. "Would you like to dance?"

Her eyes brighten as she nods. I stand, then help her to her feet before guiding her to the floor. The other couples move with their hands on their partners' shoulders or hips, but I hold up my hand while wrapping the other around her waist. She slides her fingers across my palm, the movement sensual, awakening a deep longing in me.

I let my desire for her show in my steady gaze as I hold her tight, and her lips part as she rests her hand on my chest. "Will you start us off?" I ask.

She nods, and I read her lips counting, then she presses gently right before we need to move. Once I find the rhythm, I don't have to concentrate as intently. I can focus on the beautiful woman in my arms, staring at me with all the adoration I feel for her.

We glide around our space on the floor, ignoring everyone else. When the song ends, she raises on her tiptoes for a kiss, and I brush my lips against hers, feeling like the luckiest man in the world.

"Thank you," she whispers, then links hands with me before we head back to our table.

We haven't been seated long when an elegant woman saunters over. "Pardon me," she says to Calliope. "I couldn't help noticing how well you did out there. How long have you been dancing?"

Calliope glances first at me but then she answers, explaining her history.

"You wouldn't happen to be looking for some extra work, would you?" The lady sighs. "Our ballroom dancing instructor broke her ankle last week, and we have a full class of beginners all signed up."

"I'd love to." Excitement shows in her eager smile, and I can tell how hard she's fighting to keep from squealing.

"Here's my card. Why don't you drop by tomorrow, and we can discuss it further?" When Calliope nods, the lady smiles. "I'll let you get back to your dinner."

As soon as she's out of earshot, Calliope leans over and beams. "Did you hear that?" I nod, smiling back, and she studies the card. "And look, it's only a few blocks away from our house. Totally walkable!"

This is exactly the win she needed. I feel bad for the person who broke their ankle, but the way Calliope is walking on air, I can almost believe in fate.

* * * *

Callie

Wednesday morning, Sebastian wakes me from a delicious dream involving him and a desk to tell me he's leaving me the car. He doesn't want me to be a sweaty mess for my interview. But that means I have to pick him up or meet him for lunch, and he wants to make sure I'm okay with that.

He's the best.

Getting ready for my interview is difficult because I keep getting pulled back to the heated flashes of my interrupted dream. The steamy scene teases me. Who knew I'd get so bothered by Sebastian and a desk? So much for not being a sweaty mess for the interview.

I pull myself together and nail the job application. Esther hires me on the spot. I can't wait to tell Sebastian. I check in with him, and once he assures me my dad isn't on the premises, I offer to bring him lunch.

As I put together a cooler, I can't help recalling our dance last night. A dull ache throbs low in my midsection at the memory. The interrupted dream won't let me go, and I decide to say the hell with it. Why not see about making that fantasy come true? And if I'm going to get the TA to bend me over his desk, I might as well look the part.

I find a white dress shirt in Sebastian's closet. After rolling up the sleeves and tying off the hem, I think I can pull it off. I pair it with one of the skirts I'd found thrift shopping with Leah, a cute pleated one. Wishing

I had knee-high socks, I'm thankful I at least have one pair of dress shoes that will go with this outfit. I step back, taking one last look in the mirror, and grin.

The house seemed fairly quiet when I came through, so my chances of being seen are slim. I grab the cooler, then head to the car.

I pull into the parking lot and glance in the rearview mirror. Anticipation twines with a hint of worry that Sebastian will refuse. We are at his place of employment after all, and he doesn't like to lose control. But maybe this will be good for both of us.

Smoothing my hair, I step out of my car and shut the door. Campus is dead between summertime and training, so hopefully no one will see me. And he'd better be in the office, because fulfilling my fantasy in a crystal-clear greenhouse is out of even my comfort zone.

When I peek into his office, I find Sebastian hunched over his desk. He's so engrossed, he doesn't even look up. I love the way his brow furrows when he concentrates, how his attention is absolute.

As I walk in, I spy the sign from the greenhouse the other day, warning others that an experiment is in progress and not to enter. Smiling, I quickly hang it on the handle before I lock the door and prop a chair against it for good measure. Then I saunter over to the edge of his desk. The corner is clear enough for me to perch on, and I rest my bare thigh near his elbow.

He freezes, noticing me at last. It's almost comical how slowly his gaze slides along my body, taking in the short plaid skirt then the partially unbuttoned white shirt. I put all my hunger into my smile.

His throat bobs as he swallows. "Calliope, hi." He glances at his phone. "A little early, I see." But there's no scolding in the words, only curiosity.

"I missed you." I run a finger down my chest, toying with the open edge of my shirt.

He sucks in a breath. "That's quite the outfit you're wearing."

I twirl a strand of hair around my finger, leaning forward so my cleavage is on full display. "Well, I am dating the TA. Thought I might as well look the part."

He scans my length once more. "Do you only…look the part?"

"Depends." My grin turns feral. "What do I have to do to get an A?"

He glances at the door, and I know he's weighing his options.

"All the other offices I passed are empty. Plus I put the sign outside and locked it," I say huskily.

Any hold he has on his self-control snaps as my words tip the scale. He leaps to his feet, his chair toppling backward and, with one sweep of his arm, he clears his desk. Papers and books go flying, but I barely have time to be shocked before he drags me in front of him.

His lips cover mine, swallowing my startled gasp as he thrusts his still-covered erection against my apex. Then he eases me back on the now-clear desk. He breaks the kiss, diving for the buttons on my blouse and freeing my breasts within seconds. His frantic movements only stoke the flames burning in me, and desire churns between us.

Sebastian unleashed is beyond my wildest dreams.

He lavishes one breast then the other with passionate attention as he sucks and tweaks. He lets go of my taut nipple with a quiet pop. I squirm as he slides his hands down my torso. Need drenches me, and I want all of him. Now.

"The biggest question is whether you wore underwear or not." His breath hitches when he glides under my skirt against my bare, wet pussy. "You definitely get an A," he whispers.

I sit up, pulling on his belt desperately. "I need you, Sebastian. Please."

"You'd deny me the pleasure of tasting you?" He *tsks*. "That'll cost you."

I flop back onto the desk as he kneels before me. His skilled tongue slides along my seam, then delves into my center, and I fly up on my elbows before I stuff my fist against my mouth to muffle my scream. He thrusts his tongue into me relentlessly, only letting up to swirl around my clit before returning to his tongue fucking.

The pent-up desire combined with all the fantasizing that dream inspired is a dangerous concoction. The first flutters of my orgasm blindside me in no time, and I buck against his mouth, helpless to stop the pleasure. It hits me full force, leaving me shuddering as he laps up every bit.

"See," he says with a wicked grin. "Now we're both happy."

I push upright again and fumble to undo his buckle. "I won't be happy until you're inside me."

"Hmm, I think that can be arranged."

The smirk on his face is too much as I push down his pants, but I pause for him to reposition his monitor. He shoves it into the pocket of his shirt, then drops his pants and underwear the rest of the way. I grab his hips, tugging him toward me until his blunt tip nudges my entrance. He eases into me, and I purposefully clench around him, making the smirk fall off his face as he lets out a tortured groan.

"Who's laughing now, Mr. TA?"

He narrows his eyes, pulling out only to slam back into me. I collapse onto the desk, reaching one hand behind me to grip the edge so I don't shatter on the spot. He has no cute retort, but his body speaks louder than any words. He pounds into me over and over until the stars of bliss fill my vision.

But he doesn't stop there. He just straightens up, lifts my legs so my heels dig into his chest and grips my shins before he starts all over again.

The depth to this angle awakens a whole new set of nerves, and the tension is overwhelming. I dive right into another orgasm, the pleasure nearly drowning me. I can't take another second, but he thrusts twice more, then goes rigid as he finds his own release. I am in awe of this man and his many facets. His reaction to me, to my seduction, caught me off guard in the best possible way.

He eases out of me, gently lowering my legs, then leans down to kiss my lips. Slowly, tenderly. The way he always does when we're done making love.

"So, do I pass?"

His grin resurfaces. "Pass? You're my top student."

I frown.

"What?"

"Then why was I on the bottom?"

He chuckles at my quip, then we clean up — ourselves and the desk. Now that one appetite is sated, we can move on to actual food. We have a wonderful lunch, I tell him all about my new job, and I leave feeling content on so many levels.

Back at his house, Silas is trotting up the steps with a soccer ball under his arm. "Hey," he greets me.

"Hey." We walk inside where I pause to ask him, "Were you serious about looking over the trust?"

"Of course. I wouldn't offer to help if I didn't mean it."

I explain how Dad is in training this week, so it's the perfect opportunity to find a copy. "He keeps everything important in his study." I rub my thumb over my nail at the thought of returning to the house. "His computer is in there, too. I don't know if he'll have the trust on paper or electronic or what."

I've been toying with the idea of trying to get my clothes and things while I'm there, but just the thought of crossing that threshold is anxiety-inducing enough. The place had been my cage for so long. We'll have to see how it goes.

Silas snaps his fingers, a wicked glint accompanying the grin on his face. "We need Steven." A few minutes later, he's talked his brother into taking an extended lunch tomorrow while we break into my dad's place.

The butterflies are already swarming. When Sebastian gets home, I wait for him upstairs, wondering how he'll take the news. But he's got news of his own.

"Guess what?" he says, beaming as he walks into our room.

I force a smile, trying to ignore the worry pulling me down. "What?"

"I'm getting interviewed tomorrow!" His words flow at an incredible pace as he speaks about how great his paper is doing, the amazing attention it's getting in all the right circles.

I hurry over to wrap my arms around his torso, giving him a gentle squeeze. "That's so great! I'm so proud of you, Sebastian."

"Thank you." He holds me tighter. "I couldn't have done it without you."

We stand like that for another moment, then I sigh and step back. "Um, I've got a big day tomorrow too."

I fill him in on my plans, my stomach in knots just talking about it.

He pulls me back in for another hug and kisses the top of my head. "I'm sorry I won't be able to come, but you're in capable hands. There's no one else I'd rather have with you."

Steven, Silas and I finalize details of our break-in over dinner with the whole gang. I mention getting my clothes, but that I'm not positive I'm up for it. Despite having a plan, I'm still anxious about all that can go wrong. I sleep badly, waking at the slightest noise. When the sun peeks in through the edges of the curtain, I get up. I go downstairs, eat a muffin, read, drink some coffee and return only when it's time for Sebastian's alarm to go off.

He's as nervous about his interview as I am about my task. I pace the length of his room as he undoes his tie for the third time.

"Want me to do that for you?"

He sighs in relief, dropping the ends. "Yes, please."

"And just what sort of knot would you like?"

I tie an immaculate Double Windsor on the first try, thankful for the distraction. I can't wait to have this mission over with. My mind keeps running through the worst possible scenarios, and I have this deep fear that today will end with one or all of us in jail. Although Sebastian assured me that is most unlikely.

He didn't say impossible.

"Perfect." Sebastian grins in the mirror, then picks up his jacket.

"Your tie may be perfect, but I think you're missing something." I glance at his bare legs, chuckling as he frowns.

He looks down and sighs before stomping over to grab his slacks from the back of the chair. "I wouldn't have walked out of here without them."

Suspicion wafts over as my lips twitch. "Have you, though? Have you left the house without pants?"

His cheeks go pink, and he won't meet my gaze as he mumbles, "No, someone always stops me before I get that far."

Laughter bubbles out of me, a welcome release from the tension holding me in its grip. I let the warmth take over as I picture his brothers or Leah crying out for him to wait as he puts his hand on the doorknob.

I shake my head, then place my hands on his chest, tilting my chin up. "I love you."

He pouts for a moment before he relents. "I love you, too." He gathers me to him in a perfect kiss that has me forgetting all of my problems. Until he steps away with a sigh. "I've got to go."

And all my worries come flooding back. I nibble on my lip.

Sebastian reaches over to brush his thumb against my mouth. "You can do this, Calliope. Everything will work out, and it'll all be over soon."

I let the words bolster me, soaking in his confidence and pretending it's my own. I straighten my shoulders before giving a firm nod. "Good luck with your interview."

The car ride is excruciating. My fear that Dad will be waiting for us fills me, and my anxiety takes the reins, imagining the block will be crowded with police cars. An empty street greets us and some of my nerves loosen as we survey the house in terse silence, making sure Dad is indeed gone.

Silas' phone blares, making us all jump. Steven and I glare as he fumbles to turn down the volume.

His shoulders lift sheepishly. "Sorry."

Steven parks nearby, wanting the car close in case we have to make a quick getaway. We hurry to the front door, and I use my house key, relief flowing through me when it unlocks the deadbolt. I don't breathe again until the door clicks shut behind us.

Resting against the wall, I inhale through my nose and demand my thundering heart calm down.

"Your dad doesn't have cameras, does he?" Steven whispers.

I shake my head. Not that now is the best time for that question. "He doesn't like the idea of being recorded."

As much as he loves the spotlight and keeping tabs on me, his disdain for cameras has always been consistent. It works to our advantage right now.

I lead the way to the study, thankful to find it unlocked. His computer sits in the middle of his desk, so I plop into the seat and turn it on. I drum my fingers, waiting for it to boot while Steven and Silas fidget behind me. Anxiety thrums in a constant current through my body as I try the last password I remember. It fails.

Steven leans over, grabs a stack of sticky notes and slides them to me. "Write down your mom's full name and any dates that are important to your dad." Once I'm done, I shove away from the desk, relinquishing the chair, and Steven gets to work.

Silas tries the filing cabinet. "It's locked."

Hopefully, Dad didn't re-hide the key. I nudge Steven to one side, reaching under the slender main drawer. A triumphant smile crosses my face as I emerge with a magnetic box in hand. I quickly open it, offering Silas the key, then notice a slip of paper resting in the container.

No, it can't be that easy.

It reads *Tenure2016!*. I hand it to Steven, who shrugs, then types it in. *Success!* He holds his fist up for me to tap my knuckles to his.

Silas pulls open the top drawer of the cabinet and hands the key back to me. The only thing I have to do is wait.

And listen.

Silence reigns, but I can't quiet my mind from playing out every awful scenario I can think of. Each passing second increases our chances of getting caught. Despite my best efforts to quit chewing, soon I only have a jagged nub left of my nail.

"Got it!" Silas exclaims after rifling through the second drawer.

The document in his hand is thicker than I expected, and I huff at the weight as he hands it to me. "Is this the only copy?"

Silas nods. "Afraid so."

Well, shit. We can't just take it. I heave the trust over to the copier where I remove the binder clip and shove a chunk of pages into the feeder at the top. Then I push the button. I hand sections to Silas as they come out, warm and fresh. The words swim in front of me, all written in unfamiliar legalese, but Silas dives right in.

We're going to get caught copying the files, I know it. Every noise has me jumping, especially when the copier beeps because it's out of paper. Grumbling to myself, I hurry to refill the tray and shove it back in. I start nibbling on my other nail. Ten minutes and three fingernails later, the original is back in the re-locked cabinet.

Steven smacks the desk, and I spin on my heel, worried we've been caught. My heartbeat slows when I find him grinning and pointing at the screen.

"I got into his Quickbooks. If there is a stipend, it'll be listed there. Let me copy the file, and we'll be set." He stuffs a USB drive into the port and clicks *Save As*.

Silas secures our copy with a binder clip. Steven pops out his USB drive and shuts down the computer. I quickly replace the paper and the key in exactly the same position before tucking the magnetic box back under the desk.

I triple-check that everything is exactly as Dad left it, then we ease out of the study. My heart leaps into my throat when a floorboard creaks beneath Silas' weight. I feel like my head might explode if I don't get out of here. *Now.*

Steven touches my arm, and I nearly jump out of my skin. "What?" I whisper, trying not to glare.

He glances at the stairs. "Do you want to get your things while we're here?"

The idea of staying one minute more than I have to has panic clawing at my lungs. I shake my head furiously. "I need to leave."

Understanding crosses his face and he nods, then places his hand on my shoulder, giving it a gentle squeeze. "Let's go," he tells Silas, who had paused while we spoke.

Silas hurries to the door, peeking out before throwing it open when the coast is clear. I race outside, the guys on my heels. They hurry to the car while I lock up. I dive into the back seat, then Steven drives away. My heart is pounding, and I can't seem to find any saliva for my mouth.

But here we are, mission accomplished, driving away unscathed. I can't quit grinning.

We did it.

Chapter Twenty-Four

Sebastian

My interview is via Zoom, and I set up in the greenhouse with my roses behind me. The interviewer engages me immediately as I answer question after question. When he finally signs off, I sag back in my chair, drained.

I check my phone, wondering how Calliope is coming along with her mission. Glancing around the greenhouse, I note that all my work is done, so I decide to go home. I've only been there a few moments when the front door opens, and Calliope comes in, laughing with Silas and Steven on her heels.

Her eyes widen when she sees me, then she rushes over to fling her arms around me. "Sebastian! You're home!"

I hug her back, grinning. "I take it things went well."

Silas slings his free arm around Steven and says, "Yep, total success!"

Steven extricates himself from Silas' grasp. "I'll have to look at the files later, though. I need to get to work."

"Thanks, Steven." Calliope smiles, and he returns it. "Anytime."

Silas waves a thick bundle of papers. "I'm also gonna get to work." He pivots and heads for the kitchen table as I turn to Calliope.

"I'd like to change my clothes."

She falls into step with me as we walk toward the stairs. "How'd the interview go?"

I tell her all about it, shutting the door when we get into my room.

"And you're done working?"

"Yes. I'm all caught up, and the whole process was pretty draining. Plus, I wanted to be here, to see how you fared." I hang up my shirt and tie, then turn to find Calliope right there for another hug.

She rests her cheek against my torso and sighs. "It was stressful, and I'm glad it's done. I just knew Dad would be home any second."

I rub her back. "At least that's over with."

"Now we have to wait to see what Silas finds."

I don't let go until she does, then I change into some jersey shorts and a T-shirt. "Go downstairs?"

She nods and takes my hand, entwining our fingers. Her presence is soothing, and I hope the reverse is true as well. We make our way to the kitchen where Silas is hunched over the table, scanning each page. He doesn't say anything, so we each grab a water, then head to the couch to wait.

It feels good to settle together. She curls against me, and we open our books without saying a word. When Silas emerges sometime later, we both sit up.

He plops onto the other couch with a sigh. "So, there is a stipend." He rattles off a decent amount. "It's supposed to be available to the beneficiary after they reach eighteen."

Calliope goes rigid beside me, her lips pressed together in a thin line.

"We don't know the full story," I say gently, rubbing her arm. "Maybe your dad has been setting the money aside or using it for something to benefit you."

She gives the barest of nods.

"There's more. As of right now, your dad is the only trustee. It's highly unusual to only have one because life is unpredictable, but it does happen. Changing the trustee is a strenuous process." Silas leans forward to rest his elbows on his knees. "We can help, since our dad is friends with Judge Paulson, but without having any other close family, it may take time to find someone suitable to replace him. Unless you want to hire a lawyer to fulfill that role for you."

Calliope sags further with every word, and I wish I could do more for her. I tug her against my side, resting my chin on top of her head.

"Steven will go over the Quickbooks file when he gets home, then we'll know for sure."

"Thanks, Silas," she says, but there isn't any feeling behind the words.

I stand, tugging on her wrist. "Let's go."

"Where?"

"To our room. You need to decompress."

This time when I pull, she lets me haul her to her feet. Her expression doesn't change, until I scoop her into my arms. She gasps, her gaze so vulnerable an ache forms in my chest.

I press a kiss to her forehead, then carry her upstairs. Nudging the door shut behind us, I lay her on the bed and hold her tight, her back to my stomach. I know she's engulfed in overwhelming thoughts, so I simply ask, "Tell me?"

"The stipend...that's why my dad wanted me there. That's why he didn't let me work." Her voice cracks, and my gut wrenches.

It crossed my mind too, but I can't imagine anyone doing that to their child.

She sounds broken as she continues in a small voice. "He wasn't worried about me. He just wanted the money."

I can't bear the pain in her words, can't fathom the hurt she must be feeling. Professor Harrison could be callous and obstinate, but to be this cruel? To only want her around for the money? How could someone be that greedy, that selfish? "I know it seems like that's the most obvious explanation," I say, running my hand over her arm. "But I think we should give him the benefit of the doubt until we have proof."

She nods, then nuzzles her cheek on my arm that rests beneath her head.

"I'm with you, Calliope, every step of the way. You know my family is, too. We'll help you, however we can."

She squeezes my arm and says tightly, "I know." Then she tips her head back, a light smile on her lips. "Which is why I'm able to face this."

My phone buzzes, and I pull it out, wincing when Calliope sees the screen.

She shoots upright. "Is that him?" I reluctantly nod, and she frowns. "What'd he say?"

I don't want to tell her, don't want to reveal another ugly side of her father, but I also won't lie. Especially to her. My hesitation has her putting the pieces together.

"It's about me, isn't it?"

I reluctantly nod. "He wants you home by tomorrow or…" I let out a big sigh. "He's threatening my career."

Her eyes widen, and I know not all the hurt blooming there is because of him.

"I didn't know how to tell you. You've had enough to deal with between leaving your home and this trust business." I reach over to take her hand. "I'm sorry."

She shakes her head, then pops to her feet to pace the room. "You can't be involved in this. You can't risk everything you've worked for because of me. I was afraid this would happen." She frowns, her small hands curled into fists. "I should just go back."

I stand, determination searing through me as I grip her biceps, needing her to meet my gaze. "You have the wrong idea about me if you think for one second that I would fail to back you up in this."

Hope flashes in those cerulean eyes, outweighing the pain and fear for a split second.

"I have plenty of options, and my reputation is stellar, even more so since my paper has taken off. If your dad chooses to do something as underhanded as attempting to ruin my career, he'll have a hell of a lot of explaining to do. I already have a meeting scheduled with the Dean for Monday."

The hope flares even more, and I think she's going to give in, to agree, but instead she deflates. "It's too much, Sebastian. I…" Her head drops. "I don't deserve it."

"Yes. You do." I glide my thumbs along her arms, desperate for her to hear me. Needing her to see herself as I do. "Calliope, you deserve all that your heart desires, especially love and safety and the ability to trust those you care about. I will give everything in my power to make sure you have that."

A small gasp escapes her, then tears well in her eyes before spilling down her cheeks. I kiss them gently away, one after the other. I know what she needs in this moment, and I don't care who hears. I scoop her up again, depositing her on the bed to reassure her of my love in every way possible.

* * * *

After dinner, Calliope and I sit at the table while Steven reviews the Quickbooks data. I know he's found something when his mouth tightens. He meets my gaze first, and a wave of protectiveness washes over me. I want to whisk her away from all of this, but she needs to know, so I stay and hold her hand instead.

"A monthly deposit matching the stipend amount goes right into your father's main checking account. I don't see any other main accounts, so if he's stashing it somewhere, it's not recorded here." He rakes his hand over his hair, then adds, "I'm sorry."

I wait for Calliope to crumple, but she just leans back against her chair and lets out a long breath. "I guess it's time to accept that my dad isn't the man I thought he was."

The resignation in her voice guts me, and I wrap my arm around her, relieved when she snuggles into my side. Leah and Shawn walk in, hand in hand, their faces falling when they see us.

"Bad news?" Leah asks. Steven fills them in, and she walks over to lay a hand on Calliope's shoulder. "I'm sorry, Callie. Let us know if there's anything we can do."

Shawn murmurs his agreement as gratitude swells within me. I have the best family, and I love how they've rallied behind my girlfriend. We'll take care of her now.

"Thanks, guys," Calliope says. "I think I need to let this all sink in. I'm gonna go upstairs."

When she stands, her gaze is raw and vulnerable. I raise my eyebrows, unsure if she wants me to come with her or if she'd rather be alone. She extends her hand, and I take it, following her upstairs.

"What do you need, little muse?" I ask once we're in our room.

"Can we just curl up and read? I want to get lost in one of my books, be somewhere else for a while."

I squeeze her hand. "Of course."

We spend a quiet night together, and I'm careful not to push her into talking, content to be by her side if that's what she wants. She's still not her usual bubbly self the next morning, and I hate that I have to leave her to go to work. I even offer to skip again, but she won't let me.

At least she has a dance class this afternoon. Hopefully that will help take her mind off the situation.

I come home that evening, arriving before her, and Leah rushes over to me with a big smile. "Do you guys have plans for tonight?" she asks, grinning wider when I shake my head. "I want to do a girls' night with Meg and Callie. It's been forever, and maybe it'll help her."

"That sounds perfect, if she's up for it. She should be home any minute."

",Meg had a rough day too." She wraps an arm around herself. "Chad broke up with her."

The front door opens before I can reply, and Calliope strides in. She looks happier, her ponytail swinging behind her and a smile tipping her lips. Her eyes brighten when she sees me, and she rushes over for a kiss.

"Nice to see you too," I murmur when we break apart.

"You guys are too cute," Leah says, and Calliope grins. "So, how would you feel about having a sleepover tonight? You, me and Meg, in our little suite."

"I..." My girlfriend glances at me, and I nod encouragingly as she continues, "I've never been to a sleepover before. I'd love that."

"Never?"

"My mom had weak lungs, so I rarely had friends over and wasn't allowed to do much outside of school." She lifts a shoulder.

"Well, then we definitely have to do this." Leah jerks her chin toward the mini suite. "Wanna help set up? We're gonna take over the sitting room."

They chat eagerly as I watch them walk away, my heart so full it feels like it might explode. Leah has always been amazing at including people and taking care of them, and I'm thrilled my best friend is doing that for Calliope. I take the time to send Leah a quick text, telling her thank you.

The front door opens and in walks Shawn, who grins. "Hey, Seb. I hear we're baching it tonight."

I nod, though it hadn't yet occurred to me. I hadn't thought that far ahead, focused instead on how excited Calliope would be.

"Maybe us guys should hang out? It's been a while since the four of us did anything."

"I'd like that."

He nods. "Okay, I'll see about rounding up Silas and Steven, then we can make a plan." He pulls out his phone, sending a message.

Moments later, Steven comes inside, home from work. "Just saw your text. I'm in."

Silas trots down the stairs, groaning. "No fair, guys. I've got a date."

"You've got a date every night of the week." Steven rolls his eyes. "When's the last time all of us hung out?"

"Fine." Silas pouts for a moment, but he grabs his phone and sends a text. "Hopefully, she can reschedule."

Leah and Calliope reappear as we discuss what to do, everyone tossing out options. I could handle bowling, but axe throwing sounds like a little much.

"Maybe you guys should go see Sebastian's roses," Calliope suggests, stopping to give me a hug. "Have you ever been to his greenhouse?"

I freeze with my arm partially around her. No, they've never been to the greenhouse. Leah stops by once in a while, but I've never thought to offer a tour to the others. It's not something they'd be interested in.

Shawn is the first to respond. "Hey, that's a great idea. You okay showing off your plants, Seb?"

I blink, unable to believe he said yes. "Um, sure. If you really want to see them."

Steven and Silas exchange a look, then they both smile, saying they want to come.

"We can do that first," Silas says. "Then we've gotta get some food because I'm starving."

Shawn laughs. "You're always starving."

I still haven't moved, and Calliope rubs her hand over my chest. I glance down at her, overwhelmed by what she just did for me. Her soft smile tells me she knows, and I can't help leaning in for a kiss. "Thank you," I whisper.

"Anytime."

I give her one more squeeze. "Have fun." I look over to find Leah watching us by her door, her eyes overly bright. I nod to her, and she rests her hand on her chest, letting me know she understands how big this is for me.

"C'mon, Seb," Shawn calls, startling me. "Let's get this show on the road."

I clear my throat. "Okay, I'm coming."

He races over to kiss Leah, pulling her in tight against him. "Love you, Lee." Then he winks and jogs back over to the door.

I wave one last time at the girls before I slip on my shoes and follow my brothers.

Chapter Twenty-Five

Callie

My heart is full as I watch Sebastian leave with his brothers. Leah rests her hand on my shoulder, and I turn to see her eyes glistening.

"That was great, Callie." Her voice is thick. "The guys never would have thought of going to Sebastian's greenhouse on their own."

"And Sebastian wouldn't have asked," Meg says, poking her head out from their suite. She grins, but it lacks its usual spunk. "Yes, I was eavesdropping."

Leah and I chuckle, then she catches my hand in hers, squeezing tightly. "I'm so glad he found you."

Meg walks over, nodding. "Yeah, you two are really perfect for each other."

I have no words, choking up at their support. Even if I did, I wouldn't be able to speak over the lump in my throat, so I settle for a wobbly smile of my own.

Dropping my hand, Leah dances between us. "All right, let's get this party started."

Meg claps, some of her normal energy appearing as she bounces on her toes. "I'm so ready for this. Girls' night!"

My own enthusiasm flares to life, but its spark dims as I mentally go through my limited wardrobe. Both Leah and Meg look so comfy in their worn lounge pants and soft tank tops. My favorite comfies are still at Dad's.

"Hey, what gives?" Meg says, nudging me.

My shoulders droop. "I'm sick of not having my stuff." Annoyance flares in me as I think of all of the texts Dad has brushed off, only telling me to come home. I hadn't been brave enough to grab them while I was there earlier, but now… "Those are my clothes, my shoes, my jewelry. I deserve to have them, no matter what Dad thinks."

A cunning grin spreads over Leah's face. "So, let's go get them."

* * * *

Meg pulls to the curb, taking the same spot that Silas, Steven and I parked in when we broke in. But this time, I'm not sneaking around like some criminal. I'm going to march up those steps and demand to get my things.

Best of all, I don't have to do it alone.

As Meg and Leah flank me on the sidewalk, I glance between them, feeling an overwhelming wave of gratitude. "Hey," I say softly, waiting until they look at me. "You guys are the best."

They both grin back, then Leah nods. "Let's do this."

The three of us stride to the front door as I marvel at the difference in me. I was just here two days ago. Then I was a trembling mess, but now, I have no room for fear. This man does not own me. He lied to me, stole from me, and kept me caged when all I wanted to do was fly.

I knock firmly on the door. Lights are on in the living room, and Dad's car is in the driveway, so I know he's home. Shuffling footsteps sound from within, then the door is flung open.

"Callie!" Dad leans on the door jamb, a delighted smile on his face even as I wrinkle my nose in the wake of his whiskey-laden breath.

Dad doesn't drink alone. Ever. I frown as I actually look at him, taking in his scruffy chin, greasy hair, and stained T-shirt. "Dad?"

"You're home." His words are slurred as he pushes upright and smooths his hair back. Or tries to. "I told Sebastian you'd come home."

Leah shoots me a sympathetic look as I try to steel myself against the prick of guilt. "I'm just here for my clothes, Dad. I'm not staying."

His whole body sags and he stumbles backward to land heavily in his chair. I nudge the door open all the way, fighting a gasp as I see inside the house. How did it get so bad in just two days?

Several plates are scattered about—on the coffee table, on the end table, one on the floor. A half-empty bottle of whiskey sits next to his chair, no glass in sight and the cap is off. He reaches down, grabbing the neck of the bottle and lifting it to his lips as he drinks right from it.

My stomach churns. I wonder when he last ate.

"C'mon, Callie," Leah says, touching my arm. "Let's get your things."

Meg squeezes my shoulder, and I suck in a bolstering breath then lead them upstairs to my room. I pull out my luggage, and we hurry to pack as much as we can. When I put the picture of my family on top, my mom smiles back.

The guilt pours in. I'm supposed to be taking care of Dad, now that she's gone. He doesn't have anyone else. He needs me.

I turn the photo over, zipping the bag closed, then sink to the bed. "I can't do this."

Meg and Leah exchange a worried look, flanking me in an instant. They both wrap an arm around me, waiting for an explanation.

"That's not my dad. He can't function without me, and maybe he doesn't know how to show it but it's obvious I'm needed here. How am I supposed to leave him?"

Leah frowns, rubbing my shoulders. "You were suffocating here, Callie. Just because your dad needs you, doesn't mean it's the best thing. For either of you."

Meg nods. "You've been the one holding your family together, and I know just how heavy a weight that is. But you deserve to have a life, too. Your happiness is important, and you're allowed to follow your dreams. His actions and the consequences are on him. You can't control that."

"Your dad is an adult and perfectly capable of learning to take care of himself. It's time to cut those strings."

I let out a resigned breath, soaking in their words. I know they're right, but I needed to hear it. If I'd come alone, I don't think I'd have the strength to walk out of the door right now. I'd stay, but then what? I'd wake up tomorrow, back in this gilded cage that would be even more stifling now that I've tasted freedom.

With a determined nod, I stand. "Thanks, guys."

"You're one of us now, Callie," Leah says. "We've got you."

Leah pulls me into a hug, then Meg wraps us both in her arms. I stand there, sandwiched between them, and bolstered by their support. My throat is thick and my eyes burn as I'm overtaken by gratitude for the chain of events that brought them into my life. My new friends.

It takes us a few trips to get all my things to the car, and I trudge back upstairs to get my one last little case holding my makeup and toiletries. Back downstairs, I risk a last look at my dad, and my heart nearly breaks.

His eyes are closed and his head is tipped back, but a trail of moisture runs down his cheek. He's been crying? I poke my head out of the door, holding a finger up to the girls to let them know I'll be a moment.

Setting down my case, I walk back to my dad. My heart aches at the life we could have had, if only he could have just let me go the way a parent should. Instead he held on so tight, and now, I don't know if things will ever be okay between us again. But right now, for one last time, I'm going to take care of him.

The way I always have. I shake his shoulder, calling to him until he rouses. "Hey, Dad, let's get you to bed."

He blearily obeys, stumbling to his feet, and I help him up the stairs. He sinks onto his bed, flopping onto his pillow. I pull the covers up, tucking him in, then I walk back downstairs for a bottle of water and the bottle of aspirin. I put both on the nightstand where he'll be sure to see them.

His eyes stay closed the whole time, his breathing even.

I bend down, resting a hand on his shoulder, then kiss his scruffy cheek. "Goodbye, Dad. I love you." I can barely get the whispered words out around the thickness in my throat.

As I straighten, he hums and shifts in his sleep, then murmurs, "Love you too, Callie-girl."

My heart shatters, and I'm unable to breathe, unable to move. It's been so long since I heard those words. A few tears slip down my cheeks, but I blink the rest away.

It may not change everything, but it's an unexpected gift that I tuck in a safe nook of my mind to pull out and treasure when I look back at all of this. Turning off the light, I gently close the door, then make my way out of the house.

For good.

* * * *

Late the next morning, Lee, Meg, and I stumble out of the mini suite in search of coffee and breakfast. Despite how tired I am, I can't help smiling as I remember how much fun we ended up having last night.

My first sleepover was an undeniable success. Once my belongings were tucked away upstairs, we went into full party mode, all of us needing to let off steam after that tense outing. We did all the things. Painted nails, played truth or dare, asked ridiculous questions, talked about boys, and had chick flicks on in the background.

Sebastian sits at the table in the kitchen, a steaming mug in front of him and a book hiding the lower half of his face. My chest feels like it will burst at the sight of him. I hurry over to touch his shoulder.

"Hi," I say, unable to stop my smile.

His lips part and undeniable joy lights his whole face. "Calliope," he breathes, pulling me right onto his lap.

I let out a surprised laugh, but don't hesitate to cuddle up to him. "Missed me, hmm?"

"Yes, little muse. I did," he whispers.

Lee watches us with a tender smile, and I grin back, beyond content on my perch. Meg stands at the counter, watching the coffee drip into the pot as she drums her nails. I've been warned she's not a morning person — not to expect much out of her until she gets coffee in her.

I'm happy to wait for my cup. Maybe I'll never move again.

Silas strides in, stopping when he sees Meg near the pot. His lips press together, but I catch a flash of longing in his amber eyes, and I frown. He quickly schools his face back to neutral, then walks over and takes a mug from the cupboard.

Meg snorts. "You know there's a line, right?"

He moves to stand on the other side of the pot, giving her a smirk. "I work at a coffee shop, Meg. I think I understand the concept."

The tension between them has me sitting up as I observe, and Sebastian glances over to see what I'm so curious about. I lean in to whisper to him, "Do you think if they slept together, all their problems would just go away?"

His hazel eyes widen. I watch as he looks at the ceiling, his gaze shifting back and forth like he's assembling a puzzle in his mind. I know when the last piece clicks because he blinks three times and one corner of his mouth tips up as awe crosses his face.

He looks back at them. "You slept together, didn't you?"

Meg freezes for a moment then shoots an alarmed look at Silas. "What?"

Silas' jaw is set, and he glances around the room at each of us, panic in his gaze.

Sebastian repeats himself, "You two slept together. That's what changed between you, isn't it?"

Leah looks at Silas, then Meg before asking, "Is that true?"

Meg's cheeks are pink as she bites her lip and glances sidelong at Silas, then she nods. A shocked gasp escapes me, and the color drains from Lee's face. She turns on her heel to rush from the room.

Silence hangs in the air, then Meg shakes her head. "Dammit." She glares at Sebastian. "That's not how I wanted her to find out. We were trying not to hurt her." She hurries after her friend.

Silas lets out a sigh, then swipes a hand over his face. "Sebastian, for such a smart guy, you can be pretty dumb sometimes."

After he leaves, I peek at Sebastian, my heart aching at the dejection in his eyes. I slide my hand along his shoulder, resting at the back of his neck. "Hey," I say softly, offering a little smile when he glances down. "I guess I don't get what the big deal is. Care to explain?"

"I wasn't thinking." Pain pinches his face. "Leah is quite protective of all of us, but honesty is very important to her. She's very close to both of them, and for neither of them to tell her..." He glances down. "I'm sure that had to hurt."

Understanding settles on me. We'd even touched on the tension between Meg and Silas at our sleepover last night, but Meg had waved us off, not giving an explanation. For her to keep something like that from her best friend, well, I could see why Leah would be upset.

But I'm more concerned with my boyfriend who is still wallowing. "Sebastian, you didn't mean to hurt anyone, and it was bound to come out eventually."

He sighs. "I know my tact is lacking—"

"But," I interrupt, easing my hand down to his chest, "your heart is in the right place. And that's what counts."

Some of his pain eases, and he leans forward to rest his forehead against mine. "Thank you, Calliope."

I kiss his cheek, then pop off his lap. "C'mon, let's go upstairs. I want to know what you guys did last night, and I need to tell you about what we did."

He stands, taking my hand. "I can't wait to hear all about it."

Safely in his room, I go through every detail of returning to my dad's house. He holds me through it all, rubbing my back, stroking my hair, listening intently.

I let out a big sigh when I'm finished. "It was really hard, but I'm glad I did it. I didn't know if I was strong enough to leave."

He embraces me firmly. "I'm glad Leah and Meg were with you."

"Me too." I smile at the thought of them, though it diminishes as I remember Meg storming after Lee. "I hope they'll be okay."

Sebastian nods. "Me, too. But they've always worked things out before, so I'm sure they'll get through this as well."

"Tell me about your night," I say, changing the subject as I move away to prop my bent knee between us on the bed.

I love watching his expressions as he goes through his night with his brothers. They all told him how proud they are of him and his roses, paying him compliments through the whole tour. Then they went bowling, and he had a decent time with that too, to my surprise. I'm so glad they had a guys' night.

He pushes his glasses up his nose, shifting his weight, and I know he has something important to say. "So, while we were at the bowling alley, we were brainstorming about this issue with your trust, and Silas had a suggestion."

Hope wells within me.

Sebastian looks at the table, then says softly, "We could get married."

I gape, stunned not only by the idea itself but by the fact that he's actually considering it.

"I know how young we are," he says, the words coming out in a rush. "And if you don't want to, it won't hurt my feelings. This is really fast. You're just coming out of a traumatic situation. But I wanted you to know that option is on the table."

"How —?" My voice cracks and I have to start again. "How would that help?"

"Well, it's an older precedent, the spouse taking over for legal things like trusts and guardianships. It was much more popular before women had equal rights, so the man controlled the assets."

I try not to flinch.

"I would never do that to you, Calliope. This would simply be a means of getting the trust away from your father and into your hands. We could even divorce afterward, if that's what you wanted." He swallows. "I don't plan on ever being with anyone else, but I will give you your space if that's what you need."

My throat is thick at the lengths this wonderful man is willing to go through for me. I lean forward and take both his hands. "Sebastian, I love you. Thank you for offering, but it's a big step and I need to think it over."

"Of course." He smiles. "I love you, too."

As I sit back to finish my chicken wrap, thoughts keep popping into my head. "If we did this, I'd want to be your partner. I'd want to pay for half of whatever living expenses we have — housing, groceries, utilities, the works."

He nods, and I go on, "I know I need a real job, but the dance studio is talking about expanding. They received a grant for offering free dance classes to lower income families, and they want me to be a part of that."

"That's great, Calliope. I'm so proud of you."

I beam. As we finish eating, I keep circling back to his offer. *Mrs. Calliope Wrighting.* I could legally be one of the family.

I try to imagine my future with him, and it pops into play effortlessly. Us on the holidays, opening presents, celebrating with his brothers and Leah and Meg. Taking hikes along his favorite trails and exploring new places. Supporting him in his career as he cheers me on in mine.

Just because I'm young doesn't mean I don't know what I want, and I want my future to include Sebastian. That's one thing I'm absolutely sure of.

* * * *

Sebastian speaks to Dean McArthur first thing Monday morning. The meeting is interrupted by my dad storming into the office. A heated discussion turns into a raging argument, ending with both of them banned from the grounds for a week.

When I ask my boyfriend what he's going to do, he just smiles. "Would you mind calling Jess to see if she could tend my roses?"

He refuses to give me a different answer, so I finally stop trying and call Jess. She wants me to have lunch, so I put my hand over the mouthpiece and explain, asking, "Does that work with whatever you've got up your sleeve?"

He makes a shooing motion and returns to scribbling in his notebook. I sigh at the lack of information, but immediately perk up at the thought of lunch with my friend. We agree to meet at the little fifties diner down the road, where I fill her in about my dad.

It dampens things, but she rallies with the news that she and Lyssa are moving in with each other. I give her my heartfelt congratulations and before we leave, I ask her about looking after Sebastian's roses. Her hearty yes has me feeling excited as I return home.

Until I see Sebastian.

He looks over from his desk in his room, and my face falls at the reminder of all he's lost. His eyebrows knit together as he stands to meet me. He shakes his head, gently touching my protruding lower lip. "Not allowed."

I sigh, then lean into him. "You got kicked out because of me."

"Nope, this one is solely your dad's responsibility." He grins. "It actually works in my favor. We're leaving." He hands me a piece of paper. "Make sure you pack these things and enough clothes for three days." To my frustration, he doesn't answer a single other question of mine as he starts packing a bag for himself.

When I'm done, I walk up behind him and wrap my arms around his waist. "Sebastian?"

He quickly turns to give me his full attention.

I stare at him for a long moment, trying to find the right words. "If that offer's still good, I'd like to, um, look more into the marriage option."

A huge smile spreads over his face, and he bends down to touch his lips to mine. "Whatever you say, little muse. How about we discuss it more after our trip?"

I nod, and we depart shortly after. Our several hour drive has my spirits lifting with each mile. Then I see the sign for Mackinaw City, and I ask if we're headed to the island. Sebastian remains irritatingly silent, but when we pull into the ferry parking lot, I know I'm right.

"We're going to Mackinac Island!" I bounce in my seat before flinging my arms around my amazing boyfriend.

It's the perfect day for a ferry ride, the sun shining bright with a few puffy white clouds in the sky. Sebastian wraps an arm around my shoulders, pulling me into his side. I nestle against him, my spirits buoyed more with every rock of the boat.

"Wanna tell me what this is all about?" I ask, tipping my head back.

He gives me an infuriating smirk. "I thought we'd take advantage of my suspension."

"And you thought the best place to go was Mackinac Island?"

Lifting one hand casually, he says, "Where else would we go?"

I can think of so many places I haven't been, so many new destinations I want to explore. But the island is special to us, and I can't fault him for his pick. So I stay silent and snuggle into his embrace once more.

When we arrive, he glances at the taxis then back to me. "Do you mind walking?"

"Yes. Please!" After sitting for half the day, I am definitely ready for a walk. The only luggage I have is my backpack, which I'm perfectly capable of carrying.

We link hands and wind our way through the town. My excitement grows as we turn on to the street that leads to the Grand. I nearly burst when he leads me to the front doors, but I know how exorbitant the price of staying here is, and I tug him to a stop. "Are you sure? This is a lot."

He chuckles, adjusting his backpack strap. "Calliope, my grandparents give us a ridiculous amount of money any chance they get—birthdays, Christmas, even Easter. My parents pay for my education and my rent, as long as I'm going to school. I worked different jobs every summer since high school, and the only thing I've spent money on is books. I've got this."

Of course, he does...although he also has a lot of books.

Our room has a king bed this time, but the décor is as opulent and unique as before. I sigh happily when I step in. Sebastian shuts the door as I drop my backpack to the floor.

"So, I have an idea…"

His heated stare meets mine as I begin unbuttoning my shirt. This place is already flooding me with memories of exploring him, and my thighs clench in anticipation. His throat bobs as his gaze follows my fingers.

"Is my seduction scheme working?"

"Hell yes, it is." The words are guttural, erupting from the rawest part of him.

He strides over to shove the edges of my shirt apart until his hands grip my waist. His hungry lips find mine, and I groan as he yanks me flush against him. My fingers thread through his hair before I graze my hands down to his shoulders to his abdomen where I tug his polo out of his khaki shorts.

"Lose the shirt, mister."

His expression is smug. "Yes, ma'am."

The shirt comes off as does my bra, and he backs me up to the bedpost where I hold on as he bends to suck on my peaked nipple. I fumble at his pants, finally freeing him, then he slips mine off as well. I take a minute to soak it in, this man touching me so casually and allowing me to touch him in return.

A far cry from our rough beginning.

"What's that smile for?" he asks, tracing a finger over my lips.

"Just remembering the last time we were here." I can't help teasing him as I add, "I would've brought some lingerie if you'd told me where we were going."

His eyes slowly ease down my naked body, lingering on every curve and dip. When he's done, my temperature has shot up a thousand degrees. It's hard to keep from fanning myself in the face of his feral grin.

"I like this better."

"Prove it," I breathe.

Delight tips his mouth further, then he pushes me backward onto the bed. I'm too far from the edge, so he hauls my ass toward him. He kneels before me, draping my legs over his shoulders. One of his hands finds my nipple while the other drags along my already damp seam, followed by his skilled tongue. He doesn't ease into me this time, plunging his finger right into my welcoming pussy as he teases and swirls my aching clit.

He knows exactly what I want, and I reach my peak in no time. Crying out his name, I dig my fingers into his hair as pleasure crashes over me. He licks his lips when he pulls away to stand up. A thrill shoots through me, that this delicious man is mine. All mine.

I sit up, running my hands over his chest. "I want to be on top."

In answer, he tosses me back on the bed, covering my body with his. He grinds his erection against my soaked pussy and smirks when I throw my head back. But I won't be distracted. I shove at his chest as he does it again, and this time he rolls over, taking me with him so I land astride his hard length.

It's my turn to grind against him, both of us groaning. When I take him fully in, I sigh. This is what I need—him, all of him, all of the time. And staring down into his love-filled, ravenous eyes, I know I can have him any time, any way.

I rock my hips as he thrusts up to meet me, never looking away from his tumultuous gaze. I try to pour my heart into my stare, hoping he can feel even a tenth of my emotions—ones I can't put into words. His hands come to grip my waist, holding me steady as he sets our pace, and I lean forward, gasping at the change in position that increases the friction between us.

His lips part as I cup his face, tenderly stroking his cheek. "I love you," I gasp out as the first waves of delight wash over me.

He tightens his grip, pounding into me until I'm clenching around him, crying his name. He doesn't stop there, reaching between us to brush my clit and suspend me in a sea of pleasure. Finally, he moves his hand, then shudders into me. His words are barely audible when he whispers, "I love you too."

And there's not a doubt in my mind or my body that he means every syllable with his entire being.

Chapter Twenty-Six

Sebastian

The next day, we spend the morning lounging in bed and even order room service. Calliope appears more relaxed by the minute, thank goodness. I have a plan for this evening, and anxious tension coils in my stomach as a restless energy fills me. As much as I'd like to lounge in the room for the day, I physically can't.

Or else I might spoil the surprise.

It takes some prodding to get her out of bed, and it's hard to resist her pout. But I finally coax her into getting dressed. As we leave the hotel, I slip my hand into hers, loving that she is mine to hold. We fall into our easy rhythm of conversation, and I end up talking about my latest animal — rabbits.

My stomach clenches as I reach my free hand into my pocket, making sure I have everything I need. Relief courses through me when my fingers brush the small box. Hopefully, this all goes as planned.

We meander down main street, popping in and out of shops. We have a late lunch at the Pink Pony, and it's just as good as last time. Although I'm different from last time. It feels like ages ago, but also like it was just yesterday, the two of us sitting here, my anxiety through the roof. But she put me at ease, like she always does.

That hasn't changed.

Eating takes longer than I expected, and I keep peeking at my phone to check we're not running late. We have just enough time when we pay the check, then we walk back up the hill, out of town.

When I steer her toward the butterfly house, she frowns. "Don't they close at six?"

I wave her off, hardly able to contain my excitement. We're right on schedule. "Wait here."

I talk to the attendant, who can't stop smiling, then I tug Calliope inside. We have the place to ourselves. The only sounds are the occasional hiss of the watering system and a fan to keep the air circulating. Butterflies glide around us, and she follows a blue morpho as it flies to the center of the room where it lands on a gorgeous pink hibiscus.

This is the moment. I take a deep breath and kneel behind her, pulling the ring box out of my pocket. I clear my throat, and she turns, gasping as her hand flies to her mouth.

"Calliope." I swallow hard, overwhelmed by this beautiful woman. "My little muse, you are everything I want in this life, more than I could possibly have dreamed. I love you. I'm more certain of that than anything in the world, and I would love the chance to be with you forever."

"Sebastian…" My name is a tender breath on her lips as her eyes glisten.

"I want you to know that this isn't only about your trust. I've known since I picked up that rock on the beach that you're the one I want to spend my life with. I'm just offering this to you sooner than planned."

She tugs on my arm, and I rise, watching her intently as she removes the ring. The silver band holds two heart-shaped jewels in the center, flanked by two butterflies. The stones are purple and blue.

"It reminded me of you," I say softly. "Purple hair, blue eyes."

She looks at me then, not a hint of hesitation in sight. "Yes." She nods and joy fills her gaze. "I will most definitely marry you, Sebastian Wrighting."

My cheeks hurt from how widely my grin stretches across my face as I take the ring from her and slip it on her finger. A perfect fit. I cradle her face in my hands. "How did I ever get so lucky?"

Our lips touch as I seal the deal by kissing my fiancée. I never have to let her go again.

Epilogue

Calliope
Three weeks later
Mid-July

Sebastian gives me a soft smile as he unboxes our new set of pans. I grin back before moving on to the next box of dishes. With Jess and Lyssa deciding to take the next step and live together, they offered to let us sublet Lyssa's apartment when I told them about Sebastian's proposal. And we leaped at the chance.

I take another glance around the room, marveling at how everything just fell into place. We received so many nice gifts at our wedding, despite how little notice we gave everyone. And before we left on the honeymoon his brothers, Leah and Meg had pitched in to get us, Leah had asked for the apartment key.

When we'd returned home, all our things had been moved here for us. Sebastian had been somewhat overwhelmed with the idea that someone else had packed his stuff, especially his books, but Leah had been meticulous in her efforts to keep his shelves and desk in the exact same order he'd left them. She'd taken pictures and everything. To be honest, I think having his desk and books in place has grounded him and made the transition that much easier overall.

Someone pounds on our apartment door, startling me. Sebastian stops unboxing as he frowns, then he runs a hand over my shoulders before heading toward the door.

I hurry after Sebastian, peering around him to see who's here. My jaw drops, and a tendril of fear threads through me when I find my dad on our threshold. But as I look closer, the fear dissipates. Something is wrong.

"Dad?"

"Callie." My name is full of anguish, and his throat bobs as he swallows. His gaze drops to my hand, taking in the wedding band I now wear and the matching one on Sebastian's hand. "I'd heard—" His voice cracks, and tears glisten in his eyes. "I really did miss the wedding."

I exchange a glance with Sebastian, then open the door wider. "Do you want to come in?"

He sniffs, then nods before stepping into our new apartment. He takes his time looking around. We're still decorating, and boxes litter the room, but it already feels like home.

"I'm sorry," he chokes out, grabbing my hand. "I'm so sorry. I was so scared to lose you that I held on too tight, and I lost you anyway."

I pull away, not ready to forgive him so quickly. "I know about the stipend."

His face pales.

"Is that why you wanted me to stay so badly? For the money?"

"I..." His chin droops nearly to his chest. "I made some bad decisions while you were in high school. I took out a second mortgage on the house to cover my debts, and it made me realize the path I was on. I needed the stipend to cover the payment. I'm sorry, Calliope. I didn't want to lose the house and uproot you on top of everything else."

"So you stole from me instead? Kept me locked up like a prisoner?" I sigh, pinching the bridge of my nose. "Dad, all I ever wanted was for us to be a happy family. You're all I had." I lean into Sebastian's warm touch, grounding myself. "The Wrightings have shown me what it's like to be loved, how good communication really works and what it's like to be supported."

Guilt saturates his expression, and he glances at my husband. "Sebastian, thank you for taking care of her and showing her what I was supposed to." Turning back to me, he says, "Callie, I know I don't deserve it, but I would love another chance."

I can't bring myself to hope, not after everything he's put me through, but talking like this hasn't been bad, and maybe that's a glimpse of what our future could be. "I'll think about it."

He nods and takes one last look around the apartment. "You'll be just fine, Callie. You've got a good head on your shoulders. Take care now."

And he walks out, leaving me gaping after him.

"Are you okay, Mrs. Wrighting?" Sebastian asks, wrapping his arms around me.

"That was a compliment. He gave me a compliment."

"One you very much deserve."

He wraps me in a comforting hug, and we stay like that for several moments before I clear my throat, then step away. A quick glance at the clock shows I have a solid hour before I have to leave for lunch with Leah and Meg.

So, I get back to work.

The next box is full of pictures and memorabilia from Sebastian. I smile as I pull things out. He notices, coming to stand next to me. He has a story for each award, several science fair trophies, and a baseball. I frown, holding it up in confusion.

He just laughs. "This is the ball that made me realize I wanted to study plants." He turns it over and an actual slice runs through the fabric. "My glasses didn't just cut me."

I shake my head with a grin, then pull the next item out of the box, a framed picture of him, his brothers, Leah, and Meg. I study it in longing silence as the juxtaposition between my family and his hits me hard. My throat gets thick, but Sebastian puts his arm around me.

"You're one of us now, Calliope." His soft smile warms me to the core, but then he adds, "We should probably get a new family photo, since we've expanded."

The idea is as delightful as a warm chocolate chip cookie fresh from the oven. "I'd love that."

I glance once more at the picture and frown as Silas catches my eye. Him and Meg, to be precise. I hold up the photo. "Look." I point to their hands, the way their knuckles are touching in a sweet, intimate way. "When was this taken?"

"Just before Leah's incident." Sebastian hums smugly, like he knows something I don't.

"What?" I look at him. "Did Silas say something?"

He smirks. "Brother confidentiality."

"Fine," I say, just as smugly, "then I won't tell you what Meg told us."

"I'll wear you down eventually." His grin widens, and he tugs me to him. "I have a whole lifetime to get it out of you."

The future beckons, arrayed in all its glorious wonder now that my own dreams have come true. "I'm looking forward to it."

I tug him to me, moaning contentedly the moment our lips meet. This may have started with us having the wrong idea about one another, but our future is beginning after one right idea. Because of it, I get to spend the rest of my days with Sebastian, and that's a happy ending no one can take from me.

Sign up for our newsletter and find out about all our romance book releases, eBook sales and promotions, sneak peeks and FREE romance books!

Want to see more from this author? Here's a taster for you to enjoy!

Wrighting the Wrongs: The Wrong Move
Maren Jenner

Excerpt

Meg

A break-up is never easy, but having amazing friends helps. My best friend, Leah, threw together a last-minute sleepover when she heard Chad dumped me. Not that I'd been heartbroken. Although I'd seen it coming, we'd had a good run of four months and I'd gotten used to having that constant, the other half of my couple.

Now it's back to the drawing board.

Our sitting room is littered with pillows and sleeping bags. The newest addition to our clan, Callie, curls up in one corner, looking at her phone. A small crate of nail polish, cotton balls, and remover sits to one side, evidence of our self-given mani-pedis from last night. The remnants of snacks are scattered between sleeping spaces, and we're still in our PJs, our bedheads wild.

A perfect way to start a Saturday.

It's only missing one thing—coffee. I hit the bathroom then nudge Leah, who's lying on her back with her phone in front of her face. "Need caffeine." I could just go get some by myself, but she swore she was getting up. Plus I'm not ready for our girl time to end.

"Oh, Meg." She rolls her eyes. "You and your coffee." But she sighs and sits up, then gives me a fond smile.

Her brown hair is falling out of her ponytail on every side, with parts of it sticking straight up. Mine wasn't much better, but I'd tamed my sleek black hair into a quick braid without much trouble.

Leah and I have always been close, but when my dad left, Mom started dropping me off at her house on a more frequent basis. Leah's not just my best friend, she's my cousin, so Mom saw it as built-in babysitting. More often than not, Leah and I would end up at the Wrightings's.

The six of us grew up together, and while I'm not as close to them as Leah is, they're still my people. Now we share a house with them. Leah and I each have a bedroom in a mini suite, our own little sanctuary. The guys have the upstairs, and the rest is fair game.

Though Shawn Wrighting is down here more often than not, since he and Leah are dating. We had to kick him out for girls' night, but he was a good sport about it.

Callie sits up and stretches, her purple hair looking rumpled but not bad. I adore Callie and her spunk. She's got an infectious laugh and a zest for life that I envy.

Impatient, I stick my arms straight out in front of me and tilt my head like a zombie. "Coffeeeee," I moan.

"Okay, we're coming." Leah rolls her eyes, but she and Callie get to their feet. "I'd say your first sleepover was a success," she says to Callie, who grins and nods.

I can't imagine being twenty and never attending a traditional sleepover. I wasn't the only one who needed this. She's had a rough time these last few weeks. She just moved out of her dad's house after discovering he'd been taking money that was rightfully hers.

Leah ducks into the bathroom, coming back with a re-done ponytail that won't scare anybody. She links arms with Callie, and we head out into the shared living room toward the kitchen.

Sebastian sits at the table, a steaming cup of coffee next to him and a book in front of his nose. A completely normal position for him. If he's not researching in his botany field, he's reading books about different animals. And telling us all the "interesting" facts. He's a nice enough guy, but he and I have never been on the same level.

Callie lights up and runs to him. Of all the brothers, I'd never have pictured her with Sebastian. Straight-laced, rule-following, need-for-order Sebastian. I shake my head, not understanding how it works, but definitely not judging.

I've seen for myself how well they get along and how grounded he is with her. To each their own.

When she touches his shoulder, he lights up just as much, and my breath catches as a surprisingly painful jolt of longing hits me. Chad never looked at me like that. I don't know that anyone has ever stared at me with that depth of unhindered joy and love.

But I want that in my life.

The uncomfortable feeling doesn't go away and I have to stop watching as Sebastian pulls Callie onto his lap. I walk over to the coffee, annoyed to find the pot mostly empty. The steady drip-drip tells me it won't be long. I stifle a groan at the idea of waiting, especially with those two being so lovey-dovey. I grab a mug, then set it on the counter as movement catches my eye.

Silas Wrighting strides up, his usual cocky grin on his face. He doesn't even say excuse me as he reaches in front of my face to grab his own mug out of the cupboard.

I snort my annoyance. "You know there's a line, right?"

His grin changes to a smirk, annoying me even more. "I work at a coffee shop, Meg. I think I understand the concept."

It's all I can do to bite my tongue. I don't need to get into it with him, don't need to start my day with a fight. But I just might without my coffee.

Sebastian and Callie are talking quietly amongst themselves as I try to keep from staring at Silas. At the way his sleeveless shirt highlights his toned arms and tanned skin. Just because he's arrogant and we have a messy history doesn't mean I can't appreciate his looks.

Silas has always been my particular brand of eye candy. On top of being at his house all the time growing up, we were in the same grade at school. He was my instant friend, always ready with a smile and a bolstering touch. He soon became the one I looked to when I had a bad day or needed cheering up.

And my feelings grew steadily into a childhood crush.

I risk another glance at his unruly curls, standing every which way. His amber eyes meet mine, and I duck my head, hating that he caught me. There was a time I thought he felt the same way, but that was before. That flame has long since died, buried in the rubble of secrets and resentment that has piled up ever since.

Sebastian's voice carries to me. "You two slept together, didn't you?"

Every muscle in my body freezes, and I know he's talking to us. I risk a glance at Silas, trying to keep my panic at bay as I say, "What?"

Silas' jaw is set, the same panic dancing in his gaze. We've kept this secret for two years. We've been able to avoid his scrutiny this long. Why would Sebastian figure it out now? I notice Callie staring at us, and a flash of guilt darts over her face.

"You two slept together," Sebastian repeats. "That's what changed between you, isn't it?"

Callie must've said something that connected the dots, showing Sebastian how my friendship with Silas changed to the prickly relationship it is now. Honestly, I'm surprised Sebastian hadn't pieced it together before, but did he have to blurt it out like that? He sounded so triumphant, as he'd just figured out the final answer to Clue.

Leah looks at Silas, then me before quietly asking, "Is that true?"

Heat rushes to my cheeks as I glance at Silas once more and bite my lip. This is not how I wanted her to find out. Lee values honesty above just about everything else, plus she's always been the most protective of the brothers. For us to keep this from her will be a punch in the gut.

I wanted to find the right time to explain, to be able to tell her the whole story, but it never came. Now, here we are, caught red-handed in our lie. Silas looks resigned, and I can't hide any longer.

So I dip my chin in a nod, admitting our secret.

The color drains from Leah's face, then she turns on her heel and rushes from the room. Bile churns within me as I feel sick for causing my best friend pain. Frustration and anger follow on its heels. Why couldn't Sebastian keep his mouth shut?

"Dammit," I mutter, turning to Sebastian with a glare. "That's not how we wanted her to find out. We were trying not to hurt her."

Then I hurry after my friend.

* * * *

Silas

Reeling from the bomb that Sebastian just dropped, I swipe a hand over my face. A tangled mix of emotions storms within me as I look at my brother. "Sebastian, for such a smart guy, you can be pretty dumb sometimes."

I stride out of the room, not waiting for a response. In the living room, I anxiously look at the closed door of the mini suite. I hear lowered voices, but no yelling or fighting, and relief trickles through me. Not that I can see Leah actually yelling at either of us about this, but I know she has to be hurting.

Lee is like a sister to me. She's one of us, and we protect our own. Even from our dumb mistakes.

When Meg and I caved to that endless magnetic pull tugging at us, our timing couldn't have been worse. We'd just begun to explore the tension that had built between us for years. And our fledging relationship couldn't handle the severity of the storm life threw our way.

I clench my fists at the memories, shoving them aside, then stomp upstairs to my room. A few carefully placed punches to my pillow give me an outlet for the leftover rage at my helplessness in this situation. We'd done so well for two whole years, no one the wiser. For Sebastian to just blow our cover like that...

My pillow gets another punch.

The alarm on my phone goes off, reminding me to get ready for work. This weekend starts my new schedule before I begin my new internship on Monday.

I'll be at Dad's law office, working the rest of the summer, and if all goes well, some during the next semester as well. So I'm limiting my coffee shop shifts to weekends.

A shower helps calm me down and I climb out, toweling off. I wrap the towel around my waist, more conscious about my state of dress with Callie staying in Sebastian's room. The other girls rarely came up, but now we're trying to adjust to putting the toilet seat down when we're done. Among other things.

I dart to my room, nudging the door mostly closed. It takes me a second to find a clean pair of underwear, and I drop my towel then pull them on.

Just before the door swings open.

Startled, I stare back at a wide-eyed Meg holding a basket of clothes.

"It wasn't closed," she says. "I thought—"

Quickly I paste a smirk on my face, not wanting to appear anything but confident. "Nothing you haven't seen before." At my smirk, she glares, so I add a hasty, "What's up?"

She drops the basket of clothes onto the messy floor. "Forget something?"

"Shit." I'd started a load...yesterday? The day before? And got side-tracked when Steven, my oldest brother, asked me to play soccer with him. "How'd you know they're mine?"

She wrinkles her nose and picks a pair of black briefs off the top, holding them gingerly between her index finger and thumb. "I recognized your signature undies."

I cock my jaw to one side at the word undies, but then I catch her sneaking a peek at my torso. And lower. I cross my arms, knowing it makes my biceps stand out. "See something you like?"

Anger flashes in her dark brown eyes, and her hands fly to her hips. "Just because you have a nice package, doesn't mean I want to open it."

I blink at the word package.

Her cheeks flush and she stammers, "I-I mean..." She drops her head with a quiet, "Fuck."

I'd much rather see her riled and ready to fight than embarrassed, so I shrug. "Just take off your shirt and we'll call it even."

Her head snaps up, that feisty glare back in her gaze, and my cock twitches. I fight the urge to cover my front with my hands, hoping she'll leave before I have a real situation. The heat between us flares.

Just because we've tried this and failed, doesn't mean there's nothing here. Meg's the very definition of my type and when she looks at me like that, all spunk and hotness, I'm going to react.

Because I know just how spunky and hot she can be.

I can't handle the tension, and I reach for my jeans, tugging them on. "I've got to get ready for work."

"Fine. I've got my own laundry to tend to." But she lingers in the doorway.

The shirt I wanted to wear is in that basket, damp and probably smelly. *Double shit.* Maybe I can persuade Meg...

Straightening, I put on my most charming smile and walk over to lean on the wall next to her. Satisfaction courses through me when her gaze slides over my torso, roaming back up to the arm I rest above my head. "You wanna do me a favor?"

Her eyes narrow.

"Maybe you could pop those clothes back into the wash?" I bob my eyebrows. "I'm sure I can find some way to repay you."

"Fuck off, Silas." She tosses her hair and starts to walk down the hall.

I'm disappointed in her refusal. I expected nothing less, but there is one more thing. "Hey, Meg?" I call, stepping out after her. When she pauses, I ask, "How's Lee?"

Meg's shoulders droop and she turns to face me. "She says we're fine. We didn't get to talk much because she's going out with Shawn, but she hugged me and told me she loved me." A wry smile tips her lips. "I suppose that probably goes for you too."

Relief makes me breathe easier. "Good." And I mean it.

We stare at each other for a long moment before a real smile appears on her full lips. "You're still gonna have to do your own stinky laundry. You're lucky I even brought it up here. I could have left it in a heap on the floor and not even told you about it."

I mutter a reluctant "thank you" then walk back into my room to finish getting ready for work.

* * * *

About halfway through my shift, I see Meg coming up the sidewalk. It's not unusual for her to stop in for a pick-me-up. She's here often enough for me to have memorized her standard order—a grande mochaccino with extra whip.

I grin as she comes in and makes her way to the counter, but a middle-aged woman steps in front of her.

"Excuse me, young man," she says in an entitled tone that sets my teeth on edge.

Meg blinks, and I lift a shoulder then focus on the woman in front of me. "What can I help you with?" I ask as nicely as I'm able.

"I asked for a white mocha with four shots — two on the bottom and two on top. With almond milk, extra hot. And caramel drizzled inside the cup." She lifts the lid, a triumphant gleam in her eye. "This caramel is *on top* of the whip cream."

My smile falls as I stare at the woman. "And?"

"I said inside the cup, not on the whip cream."

I turn to Sasha, who made the drink while I was taking orders, and she's scowling out of sight of the customer. "Did you put caramel inside the cup?" When she nods, I face the customer once more. "Our staff followed your instructions to put the caramel inside the cup as well, so it seems you just have a little bit of extra caramel."

It's the wrong thing to say. The lady's eyes narrow and she pins me with a glare so menacing that if looks could kill, I'd keel over. "I did not ask for extra caramel —"

Meg steps up next to her, not saying anything as she pulls out her wallet.

The lady side-eyes her, then continues, "I specifically asked for caramel inside the cup. It's not that difficult of an instruction."

Meg slips a dollar bill into the tip jar and smiles sweetly at the woman. I can see the feral edge to that smile, recognize it from all the times I've coaxed it out of her. And I know the customer is in for it.

The woman freezes, but her wrath will not be deterred as she plops the drink onto the counter with enough force that it sloshes over the side. "The customer is always right, and I demand you remake my drink correctly. Unless that's too difficult for you."

Another dollar goes into the jar. Meg's expression doesn't change as the lady glares at her.

"Ma'am, I'll have to get a manager because we didn't technically do anything wrong."

"I am a paying customer," she screeches, and Meg slips another bill into the jar. "Just what do you think you are doing?" the woman demands of Meg, turning that furious gaze on her.

"Oh," Meg says, all innocence. "I believe in treating people like human beings, so I'm making sure this man is well-compensated for dealing with an entitled customer like you."

"Excuse me?" she says, her eyes widening.

Meg waves a stack of dollar bills. "I've got plenty, and I know there's an ATM right around the corner. We could do this all day." She grins at me. "I'm sure he won't mind."

The woman sputters and stammers but no full words come out. Finally she glares at me then the cup and mess of coffee on the counter. "Well? Aren't you going to fix this?"

"As I said, I'd have to get my manager since—"

Meg drops another bill into the jar and the woman growls then huffs, "Never mind. I'll just get my coffee elsewhere. Don't expect to see me in here again!" And she storms out.

A scattered round of applause follows her out from the customers who had been watching the scene unfold. I quickly toss out the coffee in question then wipe the counter while Meg watches.

"Now," I say with a big smile. "That was something to see."

She grins. "I thought she was going to explode there for a second."

A pang of longing hits me at the easiness of this moment. I miss my friend, I miss how things used to be before life screwed us over. The usual resentment and bitterness are gone, replaced by nostalgia, and it takes me a second to recover. "So, um, your usual?"

"Yes, please."

I nod. "Coming right up." I make it myself, exactly as she likes it, then wave her off when she offers her card. I get two free drinks per shift, so I'll take it out of that. "Nah, you deserve this. Thank you."

She lifts the lid to blow on the hot liquid, pursing her lips in a way that has me unable to look away. "Mmm," she hums, smiling before licking a bit of whipped cream off her upper lip. "Don't worry, Silas. I've got your back. It's one thing for *me* to pick a fight with you, because I earned it." With a sassy wink, she saunters away.

I shake my head, trying to clear my mind from the wisps of desire clouding it. But my gaze is pulled back to her retreating form and I watch her until she's out of sight.

About the Author

Maren Jenner lives in Michigan with her supportive husband and spunky daughter. She loves writing, and when she's not working on her next book, she's got her nose in a different one. Her summers are spent on any lake she can visit, but the beaches of Lake Michigan are her favorite.

She's been writing for as long as she can remember, and it's always been her dream to become a full time author. None of this would be possible without the love and support of her family and friends, and of course, her amazing readers!

Maren loves to hear from readers. You can find her contact information, website details and author profile page at https://www.firstforromance.com

ENTWINED PUBLISHING

www.ingramcontent.com/pod-product-compliance
Lightning Source LLC
Chambersburg PA
CBHW022141010726
47493CB00002B/287